THE FOREIGN CORRESPONDENT

THE FOREIGN CORRESPONDENT

ALAN FURST

LARGE PRINT PRESS

An imprint of Thomson Gale, a part of The Thomson Corporation

THOMSON

GALE

Detroit • New York • San Francisco • New Haven, Conn. • Waterville, Maine • London

Copyright © 2006 by Alan Furst.

Map copyright © 2006 by Anita Karl and Jim Kemp.

Thomson Gale is a part of The Thomson Corporation.

Thomson and Star Logo and Large Print Press are trademarks and Gale is a registered trademark used herein under license.

The text of this Large Print edition is unabridged.

Other aspects of the book may vary from the original edition.

Set in 16 pt. Plantin.

LIBRARY OF CONGRESS CATALOGING-IN-PUBLICATION DATA

Furst, Alan.
   The foreign correspondent / by Alan Furst.
     p. cm.
   ISBN 0-7862-8908-2 (hardcover : alk. paper)
   1. Journalists — France — Paris — Fiction. 2. Underground newspapers
— France — Paris — Fiction. 3. Europe — History — 1918–1945 — Fiction.
4. Ovra (Organization : Italy) — Fiction. 5. Germany. Geheime Staatspolizei
— Fiction. 6. Large type books. I. Title.
   PS3556.U76F67 2006b
   813'.54—dc22   2006018607

ISBN 13: 978-1-59413-191-2 (lg. print : sc : alk. paper)

Published in 2007 by arrangement with Random House, Inc.

Printed in the United States of America on permanent paper
10 9 8 7 6 5 4 3 2 1

By the late winter of 1938, hundreds of Italian intellectuals had fled Mussolini's fascist government and found uncertain refuge in Paris. There, amid the struggles of émigré life, they founded an Italian resistance, with a clandestine press that smuggled news and encouragement back to Italy. Fighting fascism with typewriters, they produced over five hundred journals and newspapers.

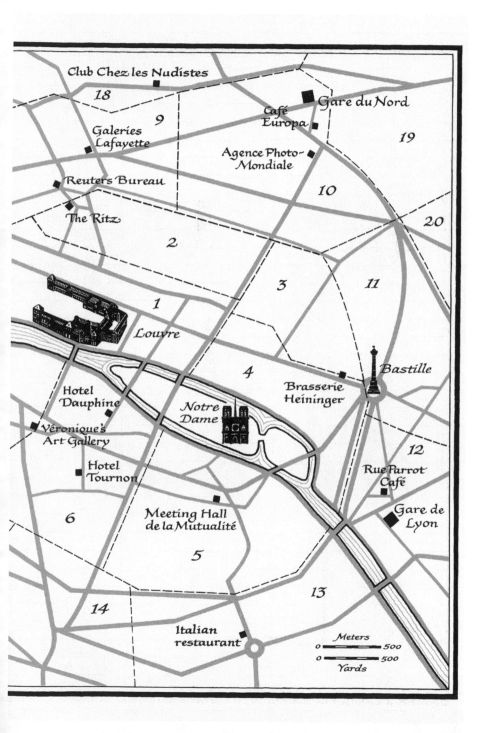

Club Chez les Nudistes

18

9

Galeries
Lafayette

Reuters Bureau

The Ritz

2

Café
Europa

Gare du Nord

Agence Photo-
Mondiale

19

10

20

1

Louvre

3

11

Hotel
Dauphine

Véronique's
Art Gallery

Hotel
Tournon

4

Notre
Dame

Brasserie
Heininger

Bastille

12

Rue Parrot
Café

Gare de
Lyon

6

Meeting Hall
de la Mutualité

5

13

14

Italian
restaurant

Meters

0 _____ 500

0 _____ 500

Yards

■ ■ ■ ■

IN THE RESISTENZA

■ ■ ■ ■

In Paris, the last days of autumn; a gray, troubled sky at daybreak, the fall of twilight at noon, followed, at seven-thirty, by slanting rains and black umbrellas as the people of the city hurried home past the bare trees. On the third of December, 1938, in the heart of the Seventh Arrondissement, a champagne-colored Lancia sedan turned the corner of the rue Saint-Dominique and rolled to a stop in the rue Augereau. Then the man in the backseat leaned forward for a moment and the chauffeur drove a few feet further and stopped again, this time in the shadow between two streetlamps.

The man in the back of the Lancia was called Ettore, *il conte* Amandola — the nineteenth Ettore, Hector, in the Amandola line, and *count* only the grandest of his titles. Closer to sixty than fifty, he had dark, slightly bulging eyes, as though life had surprised him, though it had never dared to do that, and a pink flush along his cheekbones, which suggested a bottle of wine with lunch, or excitement in the anticipation of an event planned for the evening. In fact, it was both. For the rest of his colors, he was a very silvery sort of man: his silver hair, gleaming with brilliantine, was brushed back to a smooth surface, and a thin silver mustache, trimmed daily with a scissors, traced his upper lip. Beneath a white wool overcoat, on the lapel of a gray silk suit, he wore a ribbon holding a silver Maltese cross on a blue enamel field, which meant he held the rank of *cavaliere* in the Order of the Crown of Italy. On the other lapel, the silver medal of the Italian Fascist party; a tipped square with diagonal fasces — a bundle of birch rods tied, with a red cord, to an axe. This symbolized the power of the consuls of the Roman Empire, who had the real rods and axe carried before them, and had the authority to beat with the birch rods, or behead with the axe.

Count Amandola looked at his watch, then rolled down the rear window and peered through the rain at a short street, the rue du Gros Caillou, that intersected the rue Augereau. From this point of observation — and he had twice made sure of it earlier that week — he could see the entry

12

of the Hotel Colbert; a rather subtle entry, only the name in gold letters on the glass door, and a spill of light from the lobby that shone on the wet pavement. A rather subtle hotel, the Colbert, quiet, discreet, that catered to *les affaires cinq-à-sept;* amours conducted between five and seven, those flexible hours of the early evening. *But,* Amandola thought, *a little taste of fame for you tomorrow.* The hotel commissionaire, holding a large umbrella, left the entry and headed briskly down the street, toward the rue Saint-Dominique. Once more, Amandola looked at his watch. 7:32, it said. *No,* he thought, *it is 1932 hours.*

For this occasion, twenty-four-hour time, *military* time, was obviously the proper form. He was, after all, a major, had taken a commission in 1915, served in the Great War, and had the medals, and seven lavishly tailored uniforms, to prove it. Served with distinction — officially recognized — in the purchasing office of the Ministry of War, in Rome, where he had given orders, maintained discipline, read and signed forms and letters, and made and answered calls on the telephone, his military decorum scrupulous in every way.

And so it had remained, since 1927, in his tenure as a senior official in the *Pubblica Si-*

13

curezza, the department of Public Security of the Ministry of the Interior, set up by Mussolini's chief of national police a year earlier. The work was not so different from his job during the war; the forms, the letters, the telephone, and the maintenance of discipline — his staff sat at attention at their desks, and formality was the rule in all discourse.

1944 hours. Rain drummed steadily on the roof of the Lancia and Amandola pulled his overcoat tighter, against the chill. Outside on the sidewalk, a maid — under her open raincoat a gray-and-white uniform — was pulled along by a dachshund wearing a sweater. As the dog sniffed at the pavement and began to circle, the maid squinted through the window at Amandola. *Rude, the Parisians.* He did not bother to turn away, simply looked through her, she did not exist. A few minutes later, a black square-bodied taxi pulled up to the entry of the Colbert. The commissionaire hopped out, leaving the door open, as a couple emerged from the lobby; he white-haired, tall and stooped, she younger, wearing a hat with a veil. They stood together under the commissionaire's umbrella, she raised her veil and they kissed passionately — *until next Tuesday, my beloved.* Then the woman climbed into the taxi, the man tipped the commissionaire, raised his own umbrella, and strode around the corner.

1950 hours. *Ecco, Bottini!*

The chauffeur was watching his side-view mirror. *"Il galletto,"* he said. Yes, the cockerel, so they called him, for he did indeed strut. Heading along the rue Augereau toward the Colbert, he was the classical short man who refused to be short: posture erect, back stiff, chin high, chest out. Bottini was a Turinese lawyer who had emigrated to Paris in 1935, dissatisfied with the fascist policies of his native country. A dissatisfaction no doubt sharpened by a good public beating and a half a bottle of castor oil, administered by a Blackshirt action squad as a crowd gathered and gawked in silence. Always a liberal, probably a socialist, possibly a secret Communist, Amandola suspected — slippery as eels, these types — Bottini was a friend to the oppressed, and prominent in the friends-to-the-oppressed community.

But the problem with *il galletto* wasn't that he strutted, the problem was that he crowed. Arriving in Paris, he had naturally joined the *Giustizia e Libertà* — justice and liberty — organization, the largest and most determined group of the antifascist opposition, and then become editor of one of their

15

clandestine newspapers, *Liberazione,* written in Paris, smuggled into Italy, then printed and covertly distributed. *Infamità!* This paper kicked like a mule; barbed, witty, knowing, and savage, with not a wisp of respect for Italy's glorious *fascismo* or *Il Duce* or any of his achievements. But now, Amandola thought, this *galletto* was done crowing.

As Bottini turned the corner of the rue Augereau, he took off his steel-framed eyeglasses, wiped the rain from the lenses with a large white handkerchief, and put the glasses in a case. Then he entered the hotel. He was precisely on schedule, according to the surveillance reports. On Tuesday evenings, from eight to ten, always in Room 44, he would entertain his mistress, the wife of the French socialist politician LaCroix. LaCroix, who had headed one ministry, then another, in the Popular Front government. LaCroix, who stood beside the Prime Minister, Daladier, in the newspaper photographs. LaCroix, who dined at his club every Tuesday and played bridge until midnight.

It was 2015 before a taxi pulled up to the Colbert and Madame LaCroix emerged, and ran with tiny steps into the hotel. Amandola got only a glimpse of her — brick red hair, pointy white nose, a Rubenesque woman, fleshy and abundant. And greatly appetitious, according to the operatives who'd rented Room 46 and eavesdropped on the other side of the wall. Subjects are vocal, and noisy, said one report. Describing, Amandola supposed, every sort of moan and squeal as the two went at their coupling like excited swine. Oh, he knew her sort; she liked her food and she liked her wine and she liked her naked pleasures — any and all of them no doubt, the full deck of naughty playing cards. Libertines. A full-length mirror faced the foot of the large bed in Room 44 and surely they took advantage of it, thrilled to watch themselves thrashing about, thrilled to watch — everything.

Now, Amandola thought, *one must wait.*

They had learned it was the lovers' custom to spend a few minutes in conversation before they got busy. So, give them a little time. Amandola's OVRA operatives — OVRA was the name of the secret police, the political police, established by Mussolini in the 1920s — were already inside the hotel, had taken rooms that afternoon, accompanied by prostitutes. Who might well, in time, be found by the police and interrogated, but what could they say? *He was bald, he wore a beard, he said his name was Mario.* But bald Mario and bearded Mario would be, at that point, long gone across the border, back in Italy. At most, the girls would get their pictures in the newspaper.

Madame LaCroix, when the OVRA men burst into the room, would no doubt be indignant, this was, she would assume, some vile trick perpetrated by her serpent of a husband. But she would not assume it for long, and when the revolver appeared, with its long snout of a silencer, it would be too late to scream. Would Bottini? Or would he plead for his life? No, Amandola thought, he would do neither. He would curse them, a vain *galletto* to the end, and take his medicine. In the temple. Then, the silencer unscrewed, the revolver placed in Bottini's hand. So sad, so dreary, a doomed love affair, a lover's despair.

And would the world believe it? The tryst that ended in tragedy? Most would, but some wouldn't, and it was for them that this event had been staged, the ones who would know immediately that this was politics, not passion. Because this was not a quiet disappearance, this was public, and flamboyant, so meant to serve as a warning: *We will do anything we want to do, you cannot stop us.* The French would be outraged, but then,

18

the French were habitually outraged. Well, let them sputter.

It was 2042 when the leader of the OVRA squad left the hotel and crossed to Amandola's side of the rue Augereau. Hands in pockets, head down, he wore a rubber raincoat and a black felt hat, rain dripping off the brim. As he passed the Lancia, he raised his head, revealing a dark, heavy face, a southern face, and made eye contact with Amandola. A brief glance, but sufficient. *It's done.*

4 December, 1938. The Café Europa, in a narrow street near the Gare du Nord, was owned by a Frenchman of Italian descent. A man of fervent and heated opinions, an idealist, he made his back room available to a group of Parisian *giellisti,* so-called for their membership in the *Giustizia e Libertà* — known informally by the initials *GL,* thus *giellisti.* There were eight of them that morning, called to an emergency meeting. They all wore dark overcoats, sitting around a table in the unlit room, and, except for the one woman, they wore their hats. Because the room was cold and damp, and also, though nobody ever said it out loud, because it was somehow in keeping with the conspiratorial nature of their politics: the

antifascist resistance, the *Resistenza*.

They were all more or less in midlife, émigrés from Italy, and members of a certain class — a lawyer from Rome, a medical school professor from Venice, an art historian from Siena, a man who had owned a pharmacy in the same city, the woman formerly an industrial chemist in Milan. And so on — several with eyeglasses, most of them smoking cigarettes, except for the Sienese professor of art history, lately employed as a meter reader for the gas company, who smoked a powerful little cigar.

Three of them had brought along a certain morning newspaper, the very vilest and most outrageous of the Parisian tabloids, and a copy lay on the table, folded open to a grainy photograph beneath the headline MURDER/SUICIDE AT LOVERS HOTEL. Bottini, bare-chested, sat propped against a headboard, a sheet pulled up to his waist, eyes open and unseeing, blood on his face. By his side, a shape beneath the sheet, its arms flung wide.

The leader of the group, Arturo Salamone, let the newspaper lie open for a time, a silent eulogy. Then, with a sigh, he flipped it closed, folded it in half, and put it by the side of his chair. Salamone was a great bear of a man, with heavy jowls, and thick eyebrows that met at the bridge of his nose. He had been a shipping agent in Genoa, now worked as a bookkeeper at an insurance company. "So then," he said. "Do we accept this?"

"I do not," said the lawyer. "Staged."

"Do we agree?"

The pharmacist cleared his throat and said, "Are we completely sure? That this was, assassination?"

"I am," Salamone said. "Bottini had no such brutality in him. They killed him, and his lover — the OVRA, or someone like them. This was ordered by Rome; it was planned, prepared, and executed. And not only did they murder Bottini, they defamed him: 'this is the sort of man, unstable, vicious, who speaks against our noble fascism.' And, of course, there are people who will believe it."

"Some will, always, anything," the woman chemist said. "But we shall see what the Italian papers say about it."

"They will have to follow the government line," the Venetian professor said.

The woman shrugged. "As usual. Still, we have a few friends there, and a simple word or two, *alleged* or *supposedly,* can cast a shadow. Nobody just *reads* the news these days, they decipher it, like a code."

"Then how do we counter?" the lawyer said. "Not an eye for an eye."

"No," Salamone said. "We are not them. Not yet."

"We must expose it," the woman said. "The true story, in *Liberazione*. And hope the clandestine press, here and in Italy, will follow us. We can't let these people get away with what they've done, we can't let them *think* they got away with it. And we should say where this monstrosity came from."

"Where is that?" the lawyer said.

She pointed upward. "The top."

The lawyer nodded. "Yes, you're right. Perhaps it could be done as an obituary, in a box outlined in black, a *political* obituary. It should be strong, very strong — here is a man, a hero, who died for what he believed in, a man who told truths the government could not bear to have revealed."

"Will you write it?" Salamone said.

"I will do a draft," the lawyer said. "Then we'll see."

The professor from Siena said, "Maybe you could end by writing that when Mussolini and his friends are swept away, we will pull down his fucking statue on a horse and raise one to honor Bottini."

The lawyer took pen and pad from his

pocket and made a note.

"What about the family?" the pharmacist said. "Bottini's family."

"I will talk to his wife," Salamone said. "And we have a fund, we must help as best we can." After a moment, he added, "And also, we must choose a new editor. Suggestions?"

"Weisz," the woman said. "He's the journalist."

Around the table, affirmation, the obvious choice. Carlo Weisz was a foreign correspondent, had been with the Milanese *Corriere della Sera,* then emigrated to Paris in 1935 and somehow found work with the Reuters bureau.

"Where is he, this morning?" the lawyer said.

"Somewhere in Spain," Salamone said. "He's been sent down there to write about Franco's new offensive. Perhaps the final offensive — the Spanish war is dying."

"It is Europe that's dying, my friends."

This from a wealthy businessman, by far their most openhanded contributor, who rarely spoke at meetings. He had fled Milan and settled in Paris a few months earlier, following the imposition of anti-Jewish laws in September. His words, spoken with gentle regret, brought a moment of silence, because he was not wrong and they knew it. That autumn had been an evil season on the Continent — the Czechs sold out at Munich at the end of September, then, the second week of November, a newly emboldened Hitler had launched *Kristallnacht,* the smashing of Jewish shop windows all across Germany, arrest of prominent Jews, terrible humiliations in the streets.

Finally, Salamone, his voice soft, said, "That's true, Alberto, it cannot be denied. And, yesterday, it was our turn, we were attacked, told to shut up or else. But, even so, there will be copies of *Liberazione* in Italy later this month, it will be passed from hand to hand, and it will say what it has always said: don't give up. Really, what else?"

In Spain, an hour after dawn on the twenty-third of December, the Nationalist field guns fired their first barrage. Carlo Weisz, only half-asleep, heard it, and felt it. *Maybe,* he thought, *a few miles south.* At the market town of Mequinenza, where the river Segre met the river Ebro. He stood up, unwound himself from the rubber poncho he'd slept in, and went out the doorway — the door was long vanished — into the courtyard of the monastery.

An El Greco dawn. Towering billows of

gray cloud piled high on the southern horizon, struck red by the first shafts of sunlight. As he watched, muzzle flares flickered on the cloud and, a moment later, the reports, like muttering thunder, came rolling up the Segre. *Yes, Mequinenza.* They had been told to expect a new offensive, "the Catalonian campaign," just before Christmas. Well, here it was.

To warn the others, he walked back into the room where they'd spent the night. At one time, before war came here, the room had been a chapel. Now, the tall, narrow windows were edged by shards of colored glass, while the rest of it glittered on the floor, there were holes in the roof, and an exterior corner had been blown open. At some point, it had held prisoners — that was evident from the graffiti scratched into the plaster walls: names, crosses topped by three dots, dates, pleas to be remembered, an address without a city. And it had been used as a field hospital, a mound of used bandages piled up in a corner, bloodstains on the burlap sacking that covered the ancient straw mattresses.

His two companions were already awake; Mary McGrath of the *Chicago Tribune,* and a lieutenant from the Republican forces, Sandoval, who was their minder, driver, and bodyguard. McGrath tilted her canteen, poured a little water into her cupped palm, and rubbed it over her face. "Sounds like it's started," she said.

"Yes," he said. "Down at Mequinenza."

"We had better be on our way," Sandoval said. That in Spanish. Reuters had sent Weisz to Spain before, eight or nine assignments since 1936, and this was one of the phrases he'd picked up early on.

Weisz knelt by his knapsack, found a small bag of tobacco and a packet of papers — he'd run out of Gitanes a week ago — and began to roll a cigarette. Age forty for another few months, he was of medium height, lean and compact, with long dark hair, not quite black, that he combed back with his fingers when it fell down on his forehead. He came from Trieste, and, like the city, was half-Italian, on his mother's side, and half-Slovenian — long ago Austrian, thus the name — on his father's. From his mother, a Florentine face, slightly hawkish, strongly made, with inquisitive eyes, a soft, striking gray — a face descended from nobility, perhaps, a face found in Renaissance portraits. But not quite. Spoiled by curiosity, and sympathy, it was not a face lit by a prince's greed or a cardinal's power. Weisz twisted the ends of the cigarette, held it between his lips, and flicked a military lighter, a steel cylinder that worked in the wind, until it produced a flame.

Sandoval, holding a distributor cap with dangling wires — the time-honored way to make sure one's vehicle was still there in the morning — went off to start the car.

"Where is he taking us?" Weisz asked McGrath.

"North of here, he said, a few miles. He thinks the Italians are holding the road on the east side of the river. Maybe."

They were in search of a company of Italian volunteers, remnants of the Garibaldi Battalion, now attached to the Republican Fifth Army Corps. Formerly, the Garibaldi Battalion, with the Thaelmann Battalion and the André Marty Battalion, German and French, had made up the Twelfth International Brigade, most of them sent home in November as part of a Republican political initiative. But one Italian company had elected to fight on, and Weisz and Mary McGrath were after their story.

Courage in the face of almost certain defeat. Because the Republican government, after two and a half years of civil war, held only Madrid, under siege since 1936, and the northeast corner of the country, Catalonia, with the administration now situated in Barcelona, some eighty-five miles from the foothills above the river.

McGrath screwed the top back on her canteen and lit an Old Gold. "Then," she said, "if we find them, we'll head up to Castelldans to file." A market town to the north, and headquarters of the Fifth Army Corps, Castelldans had wireless/telegraph service and a military censor.

"Certainly today," Weisz said. The artillery exchanges to the south had intensified, the Catalonian campaign had begun, they had to wire stories as soon as they could.

McGrath, a veteran correspondent in her forties, responded with a complicit smile, and looked at her watch. "It's one-twenty A.M. in Chicago. So, afternoon edition."

Parked by a wall in the courtyard, a military car. As Weisz and McGrath watched, Sandoval unhinged the raised hood and stepped back as it banged shut, then slid into the driver's seat and, presently, produced a string of explosions — sharp and loud, the engine had no muffler — and a stuttering plume of black exhaust, the rhythm of the explosions slowing as he played with the choke. Then he turned, with a triumphant smile, and waved them over.

It was a French command car, khaki-colored but long bleached out by sun and rain, that had served in the Great War and, twenty years later, been sent to Spain despite European neutrality treaties — *non-intervention élastique,* the French called it. Not *élastique* enough — Germany and Italy had armed Franco's Nationalists, while the Republican government received grudging help from the USSR and bought whatever it could on the black market. Still, a car was a car. When it arrived in Spain, someone with a brush and a can of red paint, someone in a hurry, had tried to paint a hammer and sickle on the driver's door. Someone else had lettered *J-28* in white on the hood, someone else had fired two bullets through the rear seat, and someone else had knocked out the passenger window with a hammer. Or maybe it had all been done by the same person — in the Spanish war, an actual possibility.

As they drove off, a man in a monk's robe appeared in the courtyard of the chapel, staring at them as they left. They'd had no idea there was anyone in the monastery, but apparently he'd been hiding somewhere. Weisz waved, but the man just stood there, making sure they were gone.

Sandoval drove slowly on the rutted dirt

track that ran by the river. Weisz smoked his cigarettes, put his feet up on the backseat and watched the countryside, scrub oak and juniper, sometimes a village of a few houses, a tall pine tree with crows ranged along its branches. They stopped once for sheep; the rams had bells around their necks that sounded a heavy clank or two as they walked, driven along by a scruffy little Pyrenees sheepdog who ran ceaselessly at the edges of the flock. The shepherd came to the driver's window, touched his beret in salute, and said good morning. "They will cross the river today," he said. "Franco's Moors." Weisz and the others stared at the opposite bank, but saw only reeds and poplars. "They are there," the shepherd said. "But you cannot see them." He spat, wished them good luck, and followed his sheep up the hill.

Ten minutes later, a pair of soldiers waved them down. They were breathing hard, sweating in the chill air, their rifles slung over their shoulders. Sandoval slowed but didn't stop. "Take us with you!" one of them called out. Weisz looked out the back window, wondering if they would fire at the car, but they just stood there.

"Shouldn't we take them?" McGrath said.

"They are running away. I should've shot them."

"Why didn't you?"

"I don't have the heart for it," Sandoval said.

After a few minutes, they were stopped again, an officer walking down the hill from the forest. "Where are *you* going?" he asked Sandoval.

"These are from the foreign newspapers, they are looking for the Italian company."

"Which?"

"Italians. From the Garibaldi."

"With red scarves?"

"Is that correct?" Sandoval asked Weisz.

Weisz told him it was. The Garibaldi Brigade had included both Communist and non-Communist volunteers. Most of the latter were officers.

"Then they are ahead of you, I believe. But you had better stay up on the ridge."

A few miles further on, the track divided, and the car crawled up the steep slope, the hammering of its lowest gear echoing off the trees. On the top of the ridge, a dirt road ran north. From here, they had a better view of the Segre, a slow river, and shallow, gliding past gravel islands in midstream. Sandoval drove on, past a battery firing at the opposite bank. The artillerymen were working hard, carrying shells to the loaders, who put their fingers in their ears as the cannon fired, wheels rolling back with each recoil. Halfway up the hill, a shell burst above the trees, a sudden puff of black smoke that floated off on the wind. McGrath asked Sandoval to stop for a moment, then she got out of the car and took a pair of binoculars from her knapsack.

"You will be careful of the sun," Sandoval said. Snipers were drawn to the reflective flash of sunlight off binoculars, could put a round through a lens from a great distance. McGrath used her hand as a shield, then gave the binoculars to Weisz. In pale, drifting smoke, he caught a glimpse of green uniform, perhaps a quarter mile from the western shore.

When they were back in the car, McGrath said, "They can see us, up on this ridge."

"Certainly they can," Sandoval said.

The line of the Fifth Army Corps strengthened as they drove north and, at the paved road that ran to the town of Serós, on the other side of the river, they found the Italian company, well dug in below the ridge. Weisz counted three Hotchkiss 6.5-mm machine guns, mounted on bipods — manufactured in Greece, he'd heard, and smuggled into Spain by Greek antiroyalists. There were, as well, three mortars. The Italian company had been ordered to hold an important position, covering the paved road, and a wooden bridge across the river. The bridge had been blown apart, leaving charred pilings standing in the riverbed, and a few blackened boards, washed up on the bank by the current. When Sandoval parked the car, a sergeant came over to see what they wanted. As Weisz and McGrath got out of the car, he said, "This will be in Italian, but I'll translate for you later." She thanked him, and they both produced pads and pencils. That was all the sergeant needed to see. "A moment, please, I'll get the officer."

Weisz laughed. "Well, your name, at least."

The sergeant grinned back at him. "That would be Sergeant Bianchi, right?" *Don't use my name,* he meant. Signor Bianchi and Signor Rossi — Mr. White and Mr. Red — were the Italian equivalent of Smith and Jones, generic names for a joke or a comic alias. "Write whatever you want," the sergeant said, "but I have family back there." He strolled off and, a few minutes later, the officer arrived.

Weisz caught McGrath's eye, but she didn't see what he did. The officer was dark, his face not handsome, but memorable, with

33

sharp cheekbones, beaked nose, inquisitive, hooded eyes, and a scar that curved from the corner of his right eye down to the middle of his cheek. On his head, the soft green cap of a Spanish infantryman, its high top, with long black tassel, flopped over. He wore a heavy black sweater beneath the khaki tunic, without insignia, of some army, and the trousers of another. Looped over one shoulder, a pistol belt with a holstered automatic. On his hands, black leather gloves.

In Italian, Weisz said good morning and added, "We are correspondents. My name is Weisz, this is Signora McGrath."

"From Italy?" the officer said, incredulous. "You're on the wrong side of this river."

"The signora is from the *Chicago Tribune,*" Weisz said. "And I work for the British wire service, Reuters."

The officer, wary, studied them for a moment. "Well, we're honored. But please, no photographs."

"No, of course not. Why do you say 'the wrong side of the river'?"

"That's the Littorio Division, over there. The Black Arrows, and the Green Arrows. Italian officers, enlisted men both Italian and Spanish. So, today, we will kill the *fascisti,* and they'll kill us." From the officer, a grim smile — so life went, but sad that it did. "Where are you from, Signor Weisz? Your Italian is native, I would say."

"From Trieste," Weisz said. "And you?"

The officer hesitated. To lie, or tell the truth? Finally, he said, "I am from Ferrara, known as Colonel Ferrara."

His look was almost rueful, but it confirmed Weisz's hunch, born the instant he'd seen the officer, because photographs of this face, with its curving scar, had been in the newspapers — lauded or defamed, depending on the politics.

"Colonel Ferrara" was a *nom de guerre*, use of an alias common among volunteers on the Republican side, particularly among Stalin's Eastern European operatives. But this *nom de guerre* predated the civil war. In 1935, the colonel, taking the name of his city, had left the Italian forces fighting in Ethiopia — raining mustard gas from airplanes onto villages and native militia — and surfaced in Marseilles. Interviewed by the French press, he'd said that no man of conscience could take part in Mussolini's war of conquest, a war for empire.

In Italy, the fascists had tried to destroy his reputation any way they could, because the man who called himself Colonel Ferrara was a legitimate, highly decorated, hero. At the age of nineteen, he'd been a junior officer fighting the Austro-Hungarian and German armies on Italy's northern, alpine, border, an officer in the *arditi*. These were shock troops, their name taken from the verb *ardire,* which meant "to dare," and they were Italy's most honored soldiers, known for wearing black sweaters, known for storming enemy trenches at night, knives held in their teeth, a hand grenade in each hand, never using a weapon effective beyond thirty yards. When Mussolini launched the Fascist party, in 1919, his first recruits were forty veterans of the *arditi,* angry at the broken promises of French and British diplomats, promises used to draw Italy into the war in 1915. But this *ardito* was an enemy, a public enemy, of fascism, not the least of his credentials his wounded face, and one hand so badly burned that he wore gloves.

"So I may describe you as Colonel Ferrara," Weisz said.

"Yes. My real name doesn't matter."

"Formerly with the Garibaldi Battalion, Twelfth International."

"That's right."

"Which has been disbanded, sent home."

"Sent into exile," Ferrara said. "They could hardly go back to Italy. So they, with

36

the Germans and Poles and Hungarians, all of us stray dogs who won't run with the pack, have gone looking for a new home. Mostly in France, the way the wind blows lately, though we aren't much welcome there."

"But you've stayed."

"We've stayed," he said. "A hundred and twenty-two of us, this morning. Not ready to give up this fight, ah, this cause, so here we are."

"Which cause, Colonel? How would you describe it?"

"There are too many words, Signor Weisz, in this war of words. It's easy for the Bolsheviks, they have their formulas — Marx says this, Lenin says that. But, for the rest of us, it's not so cut-and-dried. We are fighting for the freedom of Europe, certainly, for liberty, if you like, for justice, perhaps, and surely against all the *cazzi fasulli* who want to run the world their way. Franco, Hitler, Mussolini, take your pick, and all the sly little men who do their work."

"I can't say '*cazzi fasulli.*'" It meant "phony pricks." "Want to change it?"

Ferrara shrugged. "Leave it out. I can't say it any better."

"How long will you stay?"

37

"To the end, whatever that turns out to mean."

"Some people say the Republic is finished."

"Some people could be right, but you never know. If you're doing the sort of job we do here, you like to think that one bullet, fired by one rifleman, could turn defeat to victory. Or, maybe, someone like you writes about our little company, and the Americans jump up and say, *By God that's true, let's go get 'em, boys!*" Ferrara's face was lit by a sudden smile — the idea so far beyond hope it was funny.

"This will be seen mostly in Great Britain and Canada, and in South America, where the newspapers run our dispatches."

"Fine, then let the British do the jumping up, though we both know they won't, not until it's their turn to eat Adolf's *wiener schnitzel.* Or let everything go to hell in Spain, then just see if it stops here."

"And the Littorio Division, across the river, what do you think about them?"

"Oh, we know them, the Littorio, and the Blackshirt militia. We fought them in Madrid, and when they occupied the Ibarra Castle, we stormed it and sent them running. And we'll do it again today."

Weisz turned to McGrath. "Anything you

38

want to ask?"

"How is it so far? What does he think about the war, about defeat?"

"We've done that — it's good."

From across the river, a voice shouted *"Eià, eià, alalà."* This was the fascist battle cry, first used by the Blackshirt squads in their early street battles. Other voices repeated the phrase.

The answer came from a machine-gun position below the road. *"Va f'an culo, alalà!"* Go fuck yourself in the ass. Somebody else laughed, and two or three voices picked up the cry. A machine gunner fired a short burst, cutting down a line of reeds on the opposite bank.

"I'd get my head down if I were you," Ferrara said. Bent low, he went trotting off across the hillside.

Weisz and McGrath lay flat, McGrath produced her binoculars. "I can see him!"

Weisz took a turn with the binoculars. A soldier was lying in a patch of reeds, his hands cupped around his mouth as he repeated the battle cry. When the machine gun fired again, he slithered backward and vanished.

Sandoval, revolver in hand, came running from the car and flopped down beside them.

"It's starting," Weisz said.

"They won't try to cross the river," Sandoval said. "That comes tonight."

From the opposite bank, a muted *thunk,* followed by an explosion that shattered a juniper bush and sent a flock of small birds flying from the trees, Weisz could hear the beating of their wings as they flew over the crest of the hill. "Mortar," Sandoval said. "Not good. Maybe I should get you out of here."

"I think we should stay for a while," McGrath said.

Weisz agreed. When McGrath told Sandoval they would stay, he pointed at a cluster of pines. "Better over there," he said. On the count of three, they ran, and reached the trees just as a bullet snapped overhead.

The mortaring went on for ten minutes. Ferrara's company did not fire back, their mortars were ranged in on the river, and they had to save what shells they had for the coming night. When the Nationalist fire stopped, the smoke drifted away and silence returned to the hillside.

After a time, Weisz realized he was hungry. The Republican units barely had enough food for themselves, so the two correspondents and their lieutenant had been living off stale bread and a cloth sack of lentils —

known, after the Republican finance minister's description, as "Dr. Negrín's victory pills." They couldn't build a fire here, so Weisz dug around in his knapsack and produced his last tin of sardines — not opened earlier because the key needed to roll back the metal top was missing. Sandoval solved that problem, using a clasp knife to cut the top open, and the three of them speared sardines and ate them on chunks of bread, pouring a little of the oil over the top. As they ate, the sound of fighting somewhere to the north, the rattle of machine guns and rifle fire, rose to a steady beat. Weisz and McGrath decided to go have a look, then head northeast to Castelldans and file their stories.

They found Ferrara at one of the machine-gun positions, said goodby, and wished him luck. "Where will you go, when this ends?" Weisz asked him. "Perhaps we can talk again." He wanted to write a second story about Ferrara, the story of a volunteer in exile, a postwar story.

"If I'm still in one piece, France, somewhere. But please don't say that."

"I won't."

"My family is in Italy. Maybe, in the street, or at the market, somebody says something, or makes a gesture, but mostly they are left alone. For me it's different, they might do something, if they knew where I was."

"They know you're here," Weisz said.

"Oh I believe they do know that. Across the river, they know. So all they have to do is come up here, and we'll pass the time of day." He lifted an eyebrow. Whatever else happened, he was good at what he did.

"Signora McGrath will send her story to Chicago."

"Chicago, yes, I know, white socks, young bears, wonderful."

"Goodby," Weisz said.

They shook hands. A strong hand, Weisz thought, inside the glove.

Somebody on the other side of the river shot at the car as it rode along the ridge line, and a bullet came through the back door and out the roof. Weisz could see a ragged piece of sky through the hole. Sandoval swore and stomped on the gas pedal, the car accelerated and, as it hit the holes and ridges in the road, bounced high in the air and slammed down hard, crushing its old springs and landing steel on steel with a horrible bang. Weisz had to keep his jaw clamped shut so he wouldn't break a tooth. Under his breath, Sandoval asked God to spare the tires, then, after a few minutes, slowed down. McGrath turned around in the passenger seat and poked a finger into the bullet hole. Calculating the distance between Weisz and the bullet's path, she said, "Carlo? Are you okay?" The sound of the fighting ahead of them grew louder, but they never saw it. In the sky to the north, two airplanes appeared, German HE-111 Heinkels, according to Sandoval. They dropped bombs on the Spanish positions above the Segre, then swooped down and machine-gunned the east side of the river.

Sandoval pulled off the road and stopped the car beneath a tree, as much cover as he could find. "They will finish us," he said. "There's no point to it, unless you wish to see what has happened to the men by the river." Weisz and McGrath did not need to see this, they had seen it many times before.

So then, Castelldans.

Sandoval turned the car around, drove back to the paved road, and headed east, toward the town of Mayals. For a time, the road was deserted, as it climbed a long, upward slope through oak forest, then emerged on a high plain and met a dirt road that passed through the villages to the south and north.

Up here, the sky had closed in; gray cloud above empty scrubland and a ribbon of road that wound across it. On the road, a slow gray column that stretched to the far horizon, an army in retreat, miles of it, broken only by the occasional truck, pulled by mules, which carried the ones who could not walk. Here and there, among the plodding soldiers, were refugees, some with carts drawn by oxen, loaded down with chests and mattresses, the family dog on top, next to the old people, or women with infants.

Sandoval turned off the engine, Weisz and McGrath got out and stood by the car. In the hard wind that blew down from the mountains, there was not a sound to be heard. McGrath took off her glasses and rubbed the lenses with her shirttail, squinting as she watched the column. "Dear God," she said.

"You've seen it before," Weisz said.

"Yes, I've seen it."

Sandoval spread a map across the hood. "If we go back a few miles," he said, "we can go around it."

"Where does this road go?" McGrath said.

"To Barcelona," Sandoval said. "To the coast."

Weisz reached for a pad and pencil. *By late morning, the sky had closed in, with low*

44

gray cloud above the high plain, and a ribbon of road that wound across it, wound east, toward Barcelona.

The censor, in Castelldans, didn't like it. He was an army major, tall and thin, with the face of an ascetic. He sat at a table in the back of what had been the post office, not far from the wireless/telegraph equipment and the clerk who operated it. "Why do you do this?" he said. His English was precise, he had once been a teacher. "Can you not say, 'moving to reposition'?"

"An army in retreat," Weisz said, "is what I saw."

"It does not help us."

"I know," Weisz said. "But it is so."

The major read back through the story, a few pages covered in penciled block print. "Your English is very good," he said.

"Thank you, sir."

"Tell me, Señor Weisz, can you not simply write about our Italian volunteers, and the colonel? The column you describe has been replaced, the line is still being held at the Segre."

"The column is part of the story, Major. It must be reported."

The major handed it back, and nodded toward the waiting clerk. "You may send it

45

as it is," he said to Weisz. "And then you may deal with your conscience in whatever way suits you."

26 December. Weisz sat back against the faded plush seat in a first-class compartment as the train chugged slowly past the outskirts of Barcelona. They would be at the border crossing in Port Bou in a few hours, then France. Weisz had the window seat, across from him a pensive child, next to his mother and father, a fastidious little man in a dark suit, with a gold watch chain looped across his vest. Next to Weisz, an older daughter, wearing a wedding ring, though no husband was to be seen, and a heavy woman with gray hair, perhaps an aunt. A silent family, pale, shaken, leaving home, likely forever.

This little man had apparently followed his principles, was either an ally of the Republican government or one of its minor officials. He had the look of a minor official. But now he had to get out while he could, the flight had begun, and what awaited him in France was, if he was unlucky, a refugee camp — barracks, barbed wire — or, if his luck held, penury. To avoid train sickness, the mother reached into a crumpled paper bag and, from time to time, dispensed a lemon drop to each member of the family; the small economies had begun.

Glancing at the compartment across the aisle, Weisz could see Boutillon, of the Communist daily *L'Humanité,* and Chisholm, of the *Christian Science Monitor,* sharing sandwiches and a bottle of red wine. Weisz turned to the window and stared out at the gray-green brush that grew at the edge of the track.

The Spanish major had been right about his English: it was good. After finishing secondary school at a private academy in Trieste, he'd gone off to the *Scuola Normale* — founded by Napoleon, in imitation of the *Ecole Normale* in Paris, and very much the cradle of prime ministers and philosophers — at the University of Pisa, probably the most prestigious university in Italy. Where he'd studied political economics. The *Scuola Normale* was not particularly his choice, but, rather, had been ordained at birth. By Herr Doktor Professor Helmut Weisz, the eminent ethnologist, and Weisz's father, in that order. And then, according to plan, he'd entered Oxford University, again for economics, where he'd managed to stay for two years. At which time his tutor, an incredibly kind and gentle man, had suggested that his intellectual destiny lay elsewhere. It wasn't that Weisz couldn't do it — become a professor — it was that he didn't want to do it, not really. At Oxford, *not really* was a variant spelling of *doom.* So, after one last night of drinking and singing, he left. But he left with very good English.

And this turned out, in the strange and wondrous way the world worked, to be his salvation. Back in Trieste, which in 1919 had passed from Austro-Hungarian to Italian nationality, he spent his days in the cafés with his hometown pals. Not a professorial crowd: scruffy, smart, rebellious — a would-be novelist, a would-be actor, two or three don't know/don't care/don't bother-mes, a would-be prospector for gold in the Amazon, one Communist, one gigolo, and Weisz.

"You should be a journalist," they told him. "See the world."

He got a job with the newspaper in Trieste. Wrote obituaries, reported on an occasional crime, now and then interviewed a local official. At which point, his father, always cold, positively glittered with frost, pulled a string, and Weisz returned to Milan, to write for Italy's leading newspaper, *Corriere della Sera.* More obituaries, at first, then an assignment in France, another in Germany. At these, now age twenty-five, he worked — worked harder than he ever had, for he had at last discovered life's great motivation: fear of failure. Presto, the magic potion!

Too bad, really, because Mussolini's reign had begun, with the March on Rome — Mussolini had gone by train — in 1922. Restrictive press laws soon followed and, by 1925, the ownership of the paper had passed to fascist sympathizers, and the editor had to resign. Senior editors went with him, a determined Weisz hung on for three months, then followed them out the door. He thought about emigrating, then returned to Trieste, conspired with his friends, tore a poster or two off a wall, but generally kept his head down. He'd seen people beaten up, he'd seen people with blood on their faces, sitting in the street. Not for Weisz.

Anyhow, Mussolini and his crowd would soon be gone, it was simply a question of waiting it out, the world had always righted itself, it would again. He took tepid assignments from the Trieste newspapers — a soccer match, a fire on a cargo ship in the port — tutored a few students in English, fell in and out of love, spent eighteen months writing for a commercial journal in Basel, another year at a shipping newspaper in Trieste, survived. Survived and survived.

Forced by politics to the margins of professional existence, he watched as his life drifted away like sand.

Then, in 1935, with Mussolini's ghastly war in Ethiopia, he could bear it no longer. Three years earlier, he'd joined the *giellisti* in Trieste — the would-be novelist was now locked up on the prison island of Lipari, the Communist had become a fascist, the gigolo had married a countess and both had boyfriends, and the would-be prospector had found gold and died rich; there was more than treasure to be found in the Amazon.

So Weisz went to Paris and took a room in a tiny hotel in the Belleville district and commenced to live on the diet imagined by every dreamer who went to Paris; bread and cheese and wine. But very good bread — its price controlled by the brutally sagacious French government — pretty good cheese, supplemented with olives and onions, and wretched Algerian wine. But it did the job. Women were a classic, and effective, addition to the diet: if you were thinking about women, you weren't thinking about food. Politics was a tiresome addition to the diet, but it helped. It was easier, much easier, to suffer in company, and the company sometimes included dinner, and women. Then, after seven months of reading newspapers on café rollers, and looking for work, God sent him Delahanty. The Great Autodidact, Delahanty. Who had taught himself to read in French, to read in Spanish, to read — Lord have mercy!— in *Greek,* and to read, providentially, in Italian. Delahanty, the bureau chief of the Reuters wire service in Paris. *Ecco,* a job!

Delahanty, white-haired and blue-eyed, had many years earlier left school in Glasgow and, as he put it, "worked for the papers." Selling them, at first, then moving from copyboy to cub reporter, his progress powered by grit and insolence and genteel opportunism. Until he reached the top; chief of the Paris bureau, who, as trusted specialist, saw copies of dispatches from the important — Berlin, Rome — European offices. Which made him very much the spider at the center of the web, in the wire-service neighborhood near the place de l'Opéra, where, one chilly spring day, Carlo Weisz showed up. "So, Mr. Weisz — you say *Weiss,* not *Veisch,* correct?— you wrote for the *Corriere.* Not much of it left now. A sad fate, for a fine newspaper like that. Now tell me, would you happen to have any clippings of what you wrote?" The snipped-out articles, carried around in a cheap briefcase, were not in the best condition, but they could be read, and Delahanty read them. "No, sir," he said, "you needn't bother to translate, I can get along in Italian."

Delahanty put on his glasses and read with a forefinger. "Hmm," he said. "Hmm. It ain't so bad. I've seen worse. What do you mean by this, right here? Oh, that makes sense. I believe you can do this sort of work, Mr. Weisz. Do you like to do it? And do you care what you do, Mr. Weisz? The new sewers of Antwerp? The beauty contest in Düsseldorf? You don't mind, that sort of thing? How's your German? Spoke it at home? A little Serbo-Croatian? Can't hurt. Oh I see, Trieste, yes, they speak everything there, don't they. How's your French? Yes, me too, I get along, and they look at you funny, but you manage. Any Spanish? No, don't worry, you'll pick it up. Now let me be frank, here we do things the Reuters way, you'll learn the rules, all you have to do is follow 'em. And I have to tell you that you won't be *the* Reuters man in Paris. But you'll be *a* Reuters man, and that ain't so bad. It's what I was, and I wrote about every damn thing under the sun. So tell me, how does that sit with you, sir? Can you do it? Ride on trains and mule carts and whatnot and get us the story? With emotion? With a feel for the human side, for the prime minister at his grand desk and the peasant on his little patch of earth? You believe you can? I know you can! And you'll do just fine. So, why not get down to it straight away? Say, tomorrow? The previous incumbent, well, a week ago he went up to Holland and passed out in the queen's lap. It's the curse of this profession, Mr. Weisz, I'm sure you know that. Very well, do you have any questions? None? Allright, then, that will bring us to the gloomy subject of money."

Weisz drifted off to sleep, then woke as the train pulled in to Port Bou. The Spanish family stared at the platform across the tracks, at a few *Guardia Civil* lounging against the wall of the ticket office. At a small crowd of refugees standing amid trunks and bundles and suitcases tied with rope, waiting for the southbound train. Not everybody, it seemed, was allowed to cross the border. After a few minutes, Spanish officers came through the car, asking for papers. When they reached the adjoining compartment, the older daughter, next to Weisz, closed her eyes and pressed her hands together. She was, he realized, praying. But the officers were polite — this was, after all, first class — took only a cursory glance at the documents and then went on to the next compartment. Then the train blew its whistle and rolled a few hundred feet down the track, where the French officers were waiting.

Report of Agent 207, delivered by hand on the fifth of December, to a clandestine OVRA station in the Tenth Arrondissement:

> The *Liberazione* group met on the morning of 4 December at the Café Europa, the same subjects attending as in previous reports, with the engineer AMATO and the journalist WEISZ absent. It was decided to publish a "political obituary" of the lawyer BOTTINI, and to state that his death was not a suicide. It was further decided that the journalist WEISZ will now assume the editorship of the *Liberazione* newspaper.

28 December. With prosperity, or at least its distant cousin, Weisz had found himself a new place to live, the Hotel Dauphine, on the rue Dauphine in the Sixth Arrondissement. The proprietor, Madame Rigaud, was a widow of the 1914 war and, like women to be seen everywhere in France, still, after

twenty years, wore the black of mourning. She liked Weisz, and did not much overcharge him for his two rooms, linked by a door, up four endless flights of stairs, on the top floor. From time to time she fed him, poor boy, in the hotel kitchen, a pleasant break from his little haunts, *Mère* this and *Chez* that, sprinkled through the narrow streets of the Sixth.

Worn out, he slept late on the morning of the twenty-eighth, and when the sun slanted through the slats on the closed shutters, forced himself awake, to find, on getting to his feet, that pretty much everything hurt. Even a visit to a war, for a few weeks, took its toll. So he would eat the three-course lunch, stop briefly at the office, see if any of the regulars at his café were around, and maybe call Véronique, once she got home from the gallery. A pleasant day, at least in the anticipation of it. But the dusty sun shafts revealed a slip of paper, slid under his door at some point while he was away. A message, brought up by the clerk at the hotel desk. Now what could that be? Véronique? *My darling, you must come and see me, how I yearn for you!* Pure fantasy, and he knew it. Véronique would never even consider doing such a thing, theirs was a very pallid love affair, off and on, now and then. Still, one never knew, anything was possible. On the slim chance, he read the note. "Please telephone as soon as you return. Arturo."

He met Salamone in a deserted bar near the insurance company. They sat in back and ordered coffee. "And how does it go in Spain?" Salamone said.

"Badly. It's almost finished. What remains is the nobility of a lost cause, but that's thin stuff in a war. We're beaten, Arturo, for which we can thank the French and the British and the nonintervention pact. Outgunned, not outfought, end of story. So now it's up to Hitler, what happens next."

"Well, my news is no better. I must tell you that Enrico Bottini is dead."

Weisz looked up sharply, and Salamone handed him a page cut from a newspaper. Weisz flinched when he saw the photograph, read quickly through the tabloid prose, then shook his head and gave it back. "Something happened, poor Bottini, but not this."

"No, we believe this was done by the OVRA. Staged to look like a murder/suicide."

Weisz felt it, the sharp little bite that sickened the heart; it wasn't like being shot at, it was like seeing a snake. "Are you sure?"

"Yes."

Weisz took a deep breath, and let it out. "Let them burn in hell for doing this," he said. Only anger cured the fear that had reached him.

Salamone nodded. "In time, they will." He paused, then said, "But for today, Carlo, the committee wants you to replace him."

From Weisz, a nod of casual assent, as though he'd been asked the time. "Mmm," he said. *Of course they do.*

Salamone laughed, a bass rumble inside a bear. "We knew you'd be eager to do it."

"Oh yes, *eager* barely says it. And I can't wait to tell my girlfriend."

Salamone almost believed him. "Ahh, I don't think . . ."

"And the next time we go to bed, I must remember to shave. For the photograph."

Salamone nodded, closed his eyes. *Yes, I know, forgive me.*

"All that aside," Weisz said, "I wonder how I can do this and run around Europe for the Reuters."

"It's your instinct we need, Carlo. Ideas, insights. We know we'll have to stand in for you, day to day."

"But not when it comes to the great moment, Arturo. That's all mine."

"That's all yours," Salamone said. "But,

kidding aside, it's yes?"

Weisz smiled. "Do you suppose they have a Strega here?"

"Let's ask," Salamone said.

What they had was cognac, and they settled for that.

Weisz tried for the pleasant day, proving to himself that the change in his life didn't affect him all that much. The three-course lunch, *céleri rémoulade,* veal *à la Normande, tarte Tatin,* was consumed — some of it, anyhow — and the waiter's silent query ignored, but for a generous tip inspired by guilt. Brooding, he passed up his regular café and had coffee elsewhere, sitting next to a table of German tourists with cameras and guidebooks. Rather quiet and sober German tourists, it seemed to him. And he did, that evening, see Véronique, at her art-laden apartment in the Seventh. Here he did better; the ritual preliminaries pursued with greater urgency, and at greater length, than usual — he knew what she liked, she knew what he liked, so they had a good time. Afterward, he smoked a Gitane and watched her as she sat at her dressing table, her small breasts rising and falling as she brushed her hair. "Your life goes well?" she said, catching his eye in the mirror. "Right now it does." This she acknowledged with a warm smile, affectionate and reassured, her Frenchwoman's soul demanding that he find consolation in making love to her.

Leaving at midnight, he did not go directly home — a fifteen-minute walk — but found a taxi at the Métro rank, went to Salamone's apartment, in Montparnasse, and had the driver wait. The transfer of the editorial office of *Liberazione* — boxes of five-by-eight index cards, stacks of file folders — required two trips up and down the stairs at Salamone's, and two more at the Dauphine. Weisz took it all to the office he'd made for himself in his second room; a small desk in front of the window, a 1931 Olivetti typewriter, a handsome oak filing cabinet that had once served in the office of a grain brokerage. When the moving was done, the boxes and folders covered the top of the desk, with one stack on the floor. So, there it was, paper.

Paging through a few back copies, he found the last article he'd written, a piece about Spain, for the first of the two November issues. The story was based on an editorial in the International Brigade's weekly paper, *Our Fight*. With so many Communists and anarchists in the ranks of the brigade, the conventions of military discipline were often viewed as contrary to egalitarian ideals. For instance, saluting. Weisz's story had a nice ironic flair to it — we must find a way, he told his readers in Italy, to cooperate, to work together against *fascismo*. But this was not always so easy, just have a look at what goes on in the Spanish war, even amidst the ferocious combat. The writer in *Our Fight* justified saluting as "the military way of saying hello." Pointed out that the salute was not undemocratic, that, after all, two officers of equal rank would salute each other, that "a salute is a sign that a comrade who was an egocentric individualist in private life has adjusted himself to the collective way of getting things done." Weisz's article was also a gentle dig at one of *Liberazione*'s competitors, the *Communist L'Unità*, printed in Lugano and widely distributed. Our crowd, he implied, we democratic liberals, social democrats, humanist centrists, is not, thank heaven, afflicted with all that doctrinal agony over symbols.

His article had been, he hoped, entertaining, and that was crucial. It was meant to offer a respite from daily fascist life — a much-needed respite. For instance, the Mussolini government issued a daily communiqué on the radio, and anyone within hearing had to stand up during the broadcast. That was the law. So, if you were in a café, or at work, or even in your own home, you stood, and woe betide those who didn't.

Now, what did he have for January. The lawyer from Rome was writing the obituary for Bottini. That had to be, *who would murder an honorable man?* Weisz anticipated that Salamone would do a revision, and so would he. There was always a digest of world news — news which was withheld or slanted in Italy, where journalism had been defined, by law, as a supportive adjunct to national policy. The digest, taken from French and British papers, and particularly from the BBC, was the preserve of the chemist from Milan, and was always factual and precise. They had also, always tried to have, a cartoon, usually drawn by an émigré employed by the Parisian *Le Journal.* For January, here was baby Mussolini, in a particularly frilly baby hat, seated on Hitler's knee, and being fed a heaping spoonful of swastikas. "More, more!" cries baby Mussolini.

The *giellisti* wanted, more than anything, to drive a wedge between Hitler and Mussolini, because Hitler meant to bring Italy into the coming war, on his side, despite the fact that Mussolini himself had declared that Italy would not be prepared to go to war until 1943.

Fine, what else?

Salamone had told him that the professor from Siena was working on a piece, based on a smuggled letter, that described the behavior of a police chief and a fascist gang in a town in the Abruzzi. The point of the article was to name the police chief, who would quickly hear of his new fame once the paper reached Italy. *We know who you are, and we know what you're doing, and you will be held accountable when the time comes.* Also, when you're out in the street, watch your back. This exposure would make him angry, but might serve to make him think twice about what he was doing.

So then: Bottini, digest, cartoon, police chief, a few odds and ends, maybe a political-theory piece — Weisz would make sure it was brief — and an editorial, always passionate and operatic, which pretty much always said the same thing: resist in small ways, this can't go on, the tables will turn. The great Italian liberal heroes, Mazzini, Garibaldi, Cavour, to be quoted. And always, in boldface across the top of the front page: "Please don't destroy this newspaper, give it to a trusted friend, or leave it where others may read it."

62

Weisz had four pages to fill, the paper printed on a single folded sheet. Too bad, he thought, they couldn't run advertisements. *After a long, hard day of political dissent, discriminating giellisti like to dine at Lorenzo's.* No, that was not to be, the remaining space was his, and the subject was obvious, Colonel Ferrara, but . . . But what? He wasn't sure. Somewhere in this idea he sensed a ticking bomb. Where? He couldn't find it. The Colonel Ferrara story was not new, he'd been written about, in Italian and French newspapers, in 1935, and the story had no doubt been picked up by the wire services. He would appear in the Reuters story, which would likely be rewritten as human interest — the wire services, and the British press in general, did not take sides in the Spanish war.

His story in *Liberazione* would be nothing like that. Written under his pseudonym, Palestrina — they all used composers as pen names — it would be heroic, inspiring, emotional. The infantryman's hat, the pistol on a belt, the shouting across the river. Mussolini had sent seventy-five thousand Italian troops to Spain, a hundred Caproni bombers, Whippet tanks, field guns, ammunition, ships — everything. A national shame; they'd said it before, they would say it again.

But here was one officer, and a hundred and twenty-two men, who had the courage to fight for their ideals. And the distributors would make sure to leave copies in the towns by the military bases.

So this had to be written, and Ferrara himself had asked only that his future destination not be named. Easy enough to do that. *Better* — the reader might well imagine that he was off to fight somewhere else, wherever brave men and women were standing up against tyranny. Otherwise, Weisz asked himself, what could go wrong? The Italian secret services surely knew that Ferrara was in Spain, knew his real name, knew everything about him. And Weisz would make sure that this article would say nothing that could help them. And, in fact, these days, what *wasn't* a ticking bomb? Very well then, he had his assignment and, that settled, he returned to the file folders.

Carlo Weisz sat at his desk, his jacket hung over the back of the chair; he wore a pale gray shirt with a thin red stripe, sleeves rolled up, top button undone, tie pulled down. A pack of Gitanes sat next to an ashtray from the San Marco, the artists' and conspirators' café in Trieste. His radio was on, its dial glowing amber, tuned to a Duke Ellington performance recorded at a Harlem nightclub, and the room was dark, lit only by a small desk lamp with a green glass shade. He leaned back in the chair for a moment, rubbed his eyes, then ran his fingers back through his hair to get it off his forehead. And if, by chance, he was watched from an apartment across the street — the shutters were open — it would never occur to the watcher that this was a scene for a newsreel, or a page in some *Warriors of the Twentieth Century* picture book.

From Weisz, a quiet sigh as he went back to work. He was, he realized, for the first time since the meeting with Salamone, at peace. Very odd, really, wasn't it. Because all he was doing was reading.

10 January, 1939. Since midnight, a slow, steady snow had fallen over Paris. At three-thirty in the morning, Weisz stood at the corner of the rue Dauphine and the quay that ran along the left bank of the Seine. He peered into the darkness, took off his gloves, and tried to rub a little warmth into his hands. A windless night; the snow floated down over the white street and the black river. Weisz squinted, looking up the quay, but he couldn't see a thing, then looked at his watch. 3:34. *Late, not like Salamone, maybe . . .* But before he could concentrate

on the possible catastrophes, he saw a pair of dim headlights, wobbling as the car skidded over the slippery cobbles.

Salamone's cranky old Renault slid sideways and stopped as Weisz waved. He had to pull hard to open the door as Salamone leaned over and pushed from the other side. "Ohh, fuck this," Salamone said. The car was cold, its heater had not worked for a long time, and the efforts of its single windshield wiper did little to clear the window. On the backseat, a parcel wrapped in brown paper and tied with twine.

The car bumped and skidded along the quay, past the great dark bulk of Notre Dame, traveling east by the river to the Pont d'Austerlitz, the bridge that crossed to the right bank of the Seine. As the window fogged up, Salamone bent forward over the wheel. "I can see nothing," he said.

Weisz reached over and cleared a small circle with his glove. "Better?"

"Mannaggia!" Salamone said, meaning damn the snow and the car and everything else. "Here, try this." He fumbled in his overcoat pocket and produced a large white handkerchief. The Renault had waited patiently for this moment, when the driver had one hand on its wheel, and spun slowly in a circle as Salamone swore and stomped

on the brake. The Renault ignored this, completed a second pirouette, then came to rest with its back wheels in a mound of snow that had drifted up against the streetlamp at the end of the bridge.

Salamone put his handkerchief away, started the stalled car, and shifted into first gear. The wheels spun as the engine whined; once, twice, again. "Wait, stop, I'll push it," Weisz said. He used his shoulder to open the door, took one step outside, then his feet flew up and he landed hard.

"Carlo?"

Weisz fought his way upright, and, taking baby steps, circled the car and put both hands on the trunk. "Try it now."

The engine raced as the wheels spun themselves deeper into the grooves they'd built. "Not so much gas!"

The window squeaked as Salamone cranked it down. "What?"

"Gently, gently."

"Allright."

Weisz pushed again. There would be no *Liberazione* this week.

From a *boulangerie* on the corner, a baker appeared, in white undershirt, white apron, and a white cloth knotted at the corners that covered his head. The wood-burning ovens of the bakeries had to be fired up at three in the morning, Weisz could smell the bread.

The baker stood next to Weisz and said, "Now we do it." After three or four tries, the Renault shot forward, into the path of a taxi, the only other car on the streets of Paris that morning. The driver swerved away, blew his horn, shouted, "What the hell's the matter with you?" and circled his index finger beside his temple. The taxi slid on the snow, then drove across the bridge as Weisz thanked the baker.

Salamone crossed the river, going five miles an hour, then turned left and right on the side streets until he found the rue Parrot, close by the Gare de Lyon railroad station. Here, for travelers and railroad workers, was an all-night café. Salamone left the car and walked to the glassed-in terrace. Seated alone at a table by the door, a short man in the uniform and hat of a conductor on the Italian railways was reading a newspaper and drinking an apéritif. Salamone tapped on the glass, the man looked up, finished his drink, left money on the table, and followed Salamone to the car. Maybe an inch or two over five feet tall, he wore a thick, trainman's mustache, and his belly was big enough to spread the uniform jacket between the buttons. He climbed into the backseat and shook hands with Weisz. "Nice weather, eh?" he said, brushing the snow off his shoulders.

Weisz said it was.

"All the way up from Dijon, it's doing this."

Salamone got into the front seat. "Our friend here works on the seven-fifteen to Genoa," he said to Weisz. Then to the conductor: "That's for you." He nodded toward the parcel.

The conductor lifted it up. "What's in here?"

"Galley trays, for the Linotype. Also money, for Matteo. And the newspaper, with a makeup sheet."

"Christ, must be a lot of money, you can look for me in Mexico."

"It's the trays, they're zinc."

"Can't he get trays?"

"He says not."

The conductor shrugged.

"How's life at home?" Salamone said.

"It doesn't get any better. *Confidenti* everywhere, you have to watch what you say."

"You stay at the café until seven?" Weisz said.

"Not me. I go to the first-class *wagon-lit* and have a snooze."

"Well, we better be going," Salamone said.

The conductor got out, carrying the parcel with both hands. "Please be careful," Salamone said. "Watch your step."

"I watch it all," the conductor said. He grinned at the idea and shuffled off through the snow.

Salamone put the car into gear. "He's good at it. And you can't ever tell, about that. The one before him lasted a month."

"What happened to him?"

"Prison," Salamone said. "In Genoa. We try and send a little something to the family."

"Costly, this business we're in," Weisz said.

Salamone knew he meant more than money, and shook his head in sorrow. "Most of it I keep to myself, I don't tell the committee more than they need to know. Of course, I'll fill you in as we go along, just in case, if you see what I mean."

20 January. It stayed cold and gray, the snow mostly gone, except for soot-blackened mounds that clogged the gutters. Weisz went to the Reuters bureau at ten, up near the Opéra Métro station, close by the Associated Press, the French Havas bureau, and the American Express office. He stopped there first. "Mail for Monsieur

70

Johnson?" There was one letter — only a few of the Paris *giellisti* were allowed to use the system, which was anonymous, and, they believed, not yet known to the OVRA spies in Paris. Weisz showed the Johnson *carte d'identité,* collected the letter — return address in Bari — then went up to the bureau.

Delahanty had the corner office, its tall windows opaque with grime, his desk stacked high with papers. He was drinking milky tea with a spoon in the cup and, as Weisz paused at the doorway, gave him a tart smile and pushed his glasses up on his forehead. "Come in, come in, said the spider to the fly."

Weisz said good morning and slid into the chair on the other side of the desk.

"Your lucky day, today," Delahanty said, riffling through his out box and handing Weisz a press release. The International Association of Writers was, shockingly, holding a conference. At 1:00 P.M. on 20 January, at the Palais de la Mutualité, by place Maubert in the Fifth. The public cordially invited. Listed speakers included Theodore Dreiser, Langston Hughes, Stephen Spender, C. Day-Lewis, and Louis Aragon. Aragon, who had started as a Surrealist, became a Stalinist, and wound up as both, would make sure the Moscow line was maintained. On the agenda: Spain falling to Franco, China attacked by Japan, Czechoslovakia dominated by Hitler — none of it good news. The indignation engines, Weisz knew, would be running at full steam, but, no matter the red politics, it was better than silence.

"You've earned a little boredom, Carlo, and it's your turn for one of these chores," Delahanty said, sipping at his cold tea. "We'll want something from Dreiser — dig around in the Marxism and get me an honorable quote — and La Pasionaria is always worth a graph." The affectionate nickname for Dolores Ibarurri, the orator for the Republican cause, described always as "fiery." "Just a wee dispatch, laddie, you won't hear anything new but we have to have somebody there, and Spain is important for the South American papers. So, be off with you, and don't sign anything."

Dutifully, Weisz arrived on time. The hall was full, crowds milling about in a haze of cigarette smoke — *engagés* of every description, the Latin Quarter in full throb, a few red banners visible above the throng, and everybody seemed to know everyone else. Reports from Spain that morning said that the line on the east bank of the Segre had been abandoned, which meant that the taking of Barcelona wasn't far off. So, as they'd always known, Madrid, with its stubborn pride, would be the last to give in.

Eventually, the thing got itself started, and the speakers spoke, and spoke, and spoke. The situation was *dire.* Their efforts had to be *redoubled.* A survey of the League of American Writers showed that 410 of the 418 members favored the Republican side. There was a notable absence of Russian writers at the conference, as they were busy mining gold in Siberia or being shot in the Lubyanka. Weisz, of course, could not write anything like that — it would have to be entered in the great book of *stories that I never wrote* kept by every correspondent.

"Carlo? Carlo Weisz!"

Now who was this — this man in the aisle peering down at him? It took a moment for memory to work; somebody he'd known, distantly, at Oxford. "Geoffrey Sparrow," the man said. "You do remember, don't you?"

"Of course, Geoffrey, how are you?"

They were talking in whispers, while a bearded man pounded his fist on the lectern. "Let's go outside," Sparrow said.

He was tall and fair and smiling and, now it came back to Weisz, rich and smart. As he went up the aisle, all long legs and flannel, Weisz saw that he wasn't alone, had with him *a smashing girl.* Naturally, inevitably.

When they reached the lobby, Sparrow said, "This is my friend Olivia."

"Hullo there, Carlo."

"So, you're here for Reuters?" Sparrow said, his eyes on the pad and pencil in Weisz's hand.

"Yes, I'm based in Paris now."

"Are you. Well, that can't be *too* bad."

"Did you come over for the conference?" Weisz said, a journalist's version of *what the hell are you doing here?*

"Oh, actually not. We sneaked away for a long weekend, but, this morning, we just couldn't face the Louvre, so . . . just for a lark, you know, we thought we'd have a look." His smile turned rueful, it hadn't really been all that much fun. "But damned if I thought I'd see someone I knew!" He turned to Olivia and said, "Carlo and I were at university together. Uh, what was it, Harold Dowling's course, I think, right?"

"Yes, that's right. Very long lectures, I recall."

From Sparrow, a merry laugh. They'd had such fun together, hadn't they, Dowling, all that. "So, you've left Italy?"

"I did, about three years ago. I couldn't

stay there any longer."

"Yes, I know, Mussolini and his little men, damn shame, really. I do see your name on a Reuters dispatch, now and again, and I knew there couldn't be two of you."

Weisz smiled, graciously enough. "No, it's me."

"*Well,* a foreign correspondent," Olivia said.

"He is, the rogue, while I sit in a bank," Sparrow said. "Actually, now that I think about it, I have a friend in Paris who's rather a fan of yours. Damn, what was it he mentioned? Some story from Warsaw? No, Danzig! About *Volksdeutsche* militia training in the forest. Was that yours?"

"It was — I'm surprised you remember it."

"I'm surprised I remember anything, but my friend went on about it — fat men in short pants with old rifles. Singing around the campfire."

Weisz was, despite himself, flattered. "Frightening, in its way. They mean to fight the Poles."

"Yes, and here comes Adolf, to help them out. Say, Carlo, have you got plans for this afternoon? We're booked for dinner, damn it all, but what say you to drinks? At six? Maybe I'll call my friend, I'm sure he'd want to meet you."

"Well, I do have to write this story." He nodded toward the hall, where a woman's voice was building to a crescendo.

"Oh *that* won't take long," Olivia said, her eyes meeting his.

"I'll try," Weisz said. "Where are you staying?"

"At the Bristol," Sparrow said. "But we won't drink there, maybe the Deux Magots, or watchamacallit next door. Drinks with old Sartre!"

"It's the Flore," Weisz said.

"Please, darling," Olivia said. "No more filthy beards — can't we go to Le Petit Bar? We're not here every day." Le Petit Bar was the much-more-chic of the two bars at the Ritz. Turning to Weisz, she said, "Ritz cocktails, Carlo!" *And when I'm tiddly I just don't care what goes on under the table.*

"Done!" Sparrow said. "The Ritz at six. Can't be *too* bad."

"I'll call if I can't make it," Weisz said.

"Oh do try, Carlo," Olivia said. "Please?"

Weisz, clacketting steadily away at the Olivetti, was done by four-thirty. Plenty of time to call the Bristol and cancel the drinks. He stood up, ready to go downstairs and use the telephone, then didn't. The

76

prospect of an hour with Sparrow and Olivia and friend appealed to him as, at least, a change. Not another evening of gloomy politics with fellow émigrés. He knew perfectly well that Sparrow's girlfriend was only flirting, but flirting wasn't so bad, and Sparrow was bright, and could be amusing. *Don't be such a hermit,* he told himself. And if the friend thought he was good at what he did, well, why not? He heard few enough compliments, absent Delahanty's backhanded ironies, a few kind words from a reader wouldn't be the end of the world. So he put on his cleanest shirt and his best tie, his silk red-and-gray stripe, combed his hair with water, left his glasses on the desk, went downstairs at five-forty-five, and had the not inconsiderable pleasure of telling a taxi driver, *"Le Ritz, s'il vous plaît."*

No floral print tonight for Olivia, a cocktail dress for cocktails, her smart little breasts swelling just above the neckline, and a tight, stylish hat on her golden hair. She took a Players from a box in her evening bag and handed Weisz a gold lighter. "Thanks, Carlo." Meanwhile, a splendid Sparrow in high London tailoring talked cleverly about nothing, but no guest, not yet. They chattered while they waited, in the dark wood-paneled bar with its drawing room furnishings — Sparrow and Olivia on a divan, Weisz in an upholstered chair by the draped French door that led to the terrace. Oh it felt very good to Weisz, all this, after abandoned monasteries and smoky meeting halls. Very good indeed, better and better as the Ritz 75 went down. Basically a French 75, gin and champagne, named after the French 75-mm cannon of the Great War, and later a staple at the bar of the Stork Club. Bertin, the famous barman of the Ritz, added lemon juice and sugar and, *voilà,* the Ritz 75. *Voilà* indeed. Weisz loved all humankind, and his wit knew no bounds — delighted smiles from Olivia, toothy *har-hars* from Sparrow.

Twenty minutes later, the friend. Weisz had expected a Sparrow friend to be cast from the same mold, but this was not the case. The friend's aura said *trade,* loud and clear, as he looked around the room, spotted their table, and ambled toward them. He was older than Sparrow by at least a decade, fattish and benign, a pipe clenched in his teeth, a slipover sweater worn beneath the jacket of a comfortable suit. "Sorry to be late," he said as he arrived. "Damnedest gall I've ever seen, that cabman, drove me all around Paris."

"Edwin Brown, this is Carlo Weisz," Sparrow said proudly as they rose to greet the friend.

Brown was clearly pleased to meet him, his pleasure indicated by an emphatic "Hmmm!" spoken around the stem of his pipe as they shook hands. After he'd settled in his chair, he said, "I think you are a hell of a fine writer, Mr. Weisz. Did Sparrow tell you?"

"He did, and you're kind to say it."

"I'm right, is what I am, you can forget 'kind.' I always look for your byline, when they let you have one."

"Thank you," Weisz said.

They had to order a third round of cocktails, now that Mr. Brown had arrived. And, in Weisz, the spring of life burbled ever more happily. Olivia had a rosy blush on her cheeks and was somewhere well east of *tiddly,* laughed easily, met Weisz's eyes, now and again. Excited, he sensed, more by the elegance of Le Petit Bar, the evening, Paris, than whatever she might see in him. When she laughed, she tilted her head back, and the soft light caught her pearl necklace.

Conversation wandered to the afternoon conference, Sparrow's Tory sneer not so very far from Weisz's amiable liberalism, and for Olivia it all began and ended with beards. Mr. Brown was rather more opaque, his political views apparently held in secrecy, though he was emphatically a Churchill man. Even quoted Winston, addressing Chamberlain and his colleagues on the occasion of the cowardly cave-in at Munich. " 'You were given a choice between shame and war. You have chosen shame, and you shall have war,' " adding, "And I'm sure you agree with that, Mr. Weisz."

"It certainly looks that way," Weisz said. In the small silence that followed, he said, "Forgive a journalist's question, Mr. Brown, but may one ask what sort of business you're in?"

"Certainly you may, though, as they say, not for publication." Here the pipe emitted a large puff of sweetish smoke, as though to underline the prohibition.

"You're safe for tonight," Weisz said. "Off the record." His tone was playful, Brown couldn't possibly think he was being interviewed.

"I own a small company that controls a few warehouses on the Istanbul waterfront," he said. "Just plain old commerce, I fear, and I'm only there some of the time." He produced a card and handed it to Weisz.

"And you can only hope that the Turks

don't sign on with Germany."

"That's it," Brown said. "But I think they'll stay neutral — they had all the war they wanted, by 1918."

"So did we all," Sparrow said. "Let's not do that again, shall we?"

"Can't stop it, once it starts," Brown said. "Look at Spain."

"I think we should've helped them," Olivia said.

"I suppose we should've," Brown said. "But we were thinking about 1914 ourselves, y'know." To Weisz he said, "Haven't you written something about Spain, Mr. Weisz?"

"Now and then, I have."

Brown looked at him for a moment. "What did I read, was it recently? I was up in Birmingham, something in the paper there, the Catalonian campaign?"

"Perhaps you did. I filed down there a few weeks ago, end of December."

Brown finished his drink. "Very nice, shall we try one more? Have you time, Geoffrey? On me, this round."

Sparrow waved at the waiter.

"Oh Lord," Olivia said. "And wine with dinner."

"Got it," Brown said. "About some Italian

fellow, fighting the Mussolini Italians? Was that you?"

"Likely it was. They subscribe to Reuters, in Birmingham."

"A colonel, he was. Colonel something."

"Colonel Ferrara." *Tick.*

"With a hat, of some sort."

"You have quite a memory, Mr. Brown."

"Well, sad to say I don't, not really, but that stuck, somehow."

"A brave man," Weisz said. Then, to Sparrow and Olivia: "He fought with the International Brigades, and stayed on when they left."

"Much good it will do him now," Sparrow said.

"What will become of him?" Brown said. "When the Republicans surrender."

Slowly, Weisz shook his head.

"It must be odd," Brown said. "To interview people, to hear their *story,* and then, they're gone. Do you ever keep track, Mr. Weisz?"

"That's hard to do, with the way the world is now. People disappear, or think they might have to, tomorrow, next month . . ."

"Yes, I can see that. Still, he must've made an impression on you. He's quite unusual, in his way, a military officer, fighting for another nation's cause."

"I think he saw it as one cause, Mr. Brown. Do you know the line from Rosselli? He and his brother founded an émigré organization in the twenties, and he was murdered in Paris in '37."

"I know the Rosselli story, I don't know the line."

" 'Today in Spain, tomorrow in Italy.' "

"Which means?"

"The battle is for freedom in Europe; democracy versus fascism."

"Not communism versus fascism?"

"Not for Rosselli."

"But for Colonel Ferrara, perhaps?"

"No, no. Not for him either. He is an idealist."

"That's very romantic," Olivia said. "Like a movie."

"Indeed," Brown said.

It was almost eight when Weisz left the hotel, passed up the line of taxis at the curb, and headed toward the river. Let the weather, cold and damp, clear his head, he'd find a taxi later. He often told himself this, then didn't bother, choosing his streets for the pleasure of walking them. He circled place Vendôme, its jewelers' windows lying in wait for the Ritz clientele, then took rue Saint-Honoré, past fancy shops, now closed, and the occasional restaurant, its sign gold on green, a secret refuge, the scent of rich food drifting through the night air.

Mr. Brown had offered him dinner, but he'd declined — he'd been questioned enough for one evening. *Continental Trading, Ltd.* said the card, with telephone numbers in Istanbul and London, but Weisz had a pretty good idea of Mr. Brown's real business, which was the espionage business, he believed, likely the British Secret Intelligence Service. Nothing new or surprising here, not really, spies and journalists were fated to go through life together, and it was sometimes hard to tell one from the other. Their jobs weren't all that different: they talked to politicians, developed sources in government bureaux, and dug around for secrets. Sometimes they talked to, and traded with, one another. And, now and again, a journalist worked directly for the secret services.

Weisz smiled as he recalled the afternoon — they'd done a pretty fair job on him. It's your old college chum! And his sexy girlfriend who thinks you're sweet! Have a drink! Have six! Oh look, here's our friend Mr. Brown! Mr. Green! Mr. Jones! Sparrow and Olivia were probably civilians, he guessed — the lives of nations were lately perilous, so one helped out if one were asked — but Mr. Brown was the real thing. And so, Weisz said to himself, what was it about this particular pee on this particular lamppost that so excited this particular hound? Was Ferrara suspected of something — had he gotten himself on a list? Weisz hoped not. But, if not, what? Because Brown wanted to know who he was and wanted to find him and had gone to some trouble over it. Damn, he'd *felt* this coming, as he contemplated writing about Ferrara, why hadn't he listened to himself?

Calm down. The spies were always after something. If you were a journalist, here all of a sudden came the warmest Russian, most cultured German, most sophisticated Frenchwoman you ever met. Weisz's personal favorite in Paris was the magnificent Count Polanyi, at the Hungarian legation — lovely old European manners, dire honesty, and a sense of humor: very appealing, very dangerous. A mistake to be anywhere near these people, but sometimes one erred. Weisz certainly had. With, for example, the British spy Lady Angela Hope — she made no secret of it — and the memory of her produced a drunken snort of laughter. He had twice, in her Passy apartment, erred with Lady Angela, who made a loud, elaborate opera of it all, surely he was at least Casanova to produce such shrieks — Christ, there were *maids* in the apartment. Never mind the maids, the neighbors! *Oh my dear, Lady Angela's been murdered. Again.* This performance had been followed by a pillow interrogation of considerable length, all for the unreported tidbits from his interview with Gafencu, the Roumanian foreign minister. Which she'd not had, any more than Brown had found out where Colonel Ferrara had gone to ground.

By nine, Weisz was back in his room. He'd wanted dinner, by the time he reached the Sixth, but dinner at *Chez* this or *Mère* that, with a newspaper for company, had not appealed to him, so he'd stopped at his café and had a ham sandwich, coffee, and an apple. Once home, he thought about writing, writing from the heart, for himself, and would've worked on the novel in his desk drawer, but for the fact that there was no novel in the drawer. So he stretched out on the bed, listened to a symphony, smoked cigarettes, and read Malraux's *Man's Fate* — *La Condition Humaine,* in French — for the second time. Shanghai in 1927, the Communist uprising, peasant terrorists, Soviet political operatives working against

Chiang Kai-shek's Nationalist forces, secret police, spies, European aristocrats. Overlain with the French taste for philosophy. No refuge here from Weisz's vocational life, but he did not, would not, seek refuge.

Still, there was at least, thankfully, one exception to the rule. He put the book down from time to time and thought about Olivia, about what it might have been like to make love to her, about Véronique, about his chaotic love life, this one and that one, wherever they were that night. Thought particularly about the, well, not the love of his life perhaps, but the woman he never stopped thinking about, because their hours together had been, always, exciting and passionate. "It's just that we were made for each other," she would say, a melancholy sigh in her voice. "Sometimes I think, why can't we just, continue?" Continue meant, he supposed, a life of afternoons in hotel beds, occasional dinners in out-of-the-way restaurants. His desire for her never ended, and she told him it was that way for her. *But.* It would not translate to marriage, children, domestic life, it was a love affair, and they both knew it. She'd married, three years earlier, in Germany, a marriage of money, and social standing, a marriage, he thought, brought on by turning forty and fatigue with love affairs, even theirs. Still, when he was lonely, he thought about her. And he was very lonely.

He'd never imagined it would turn out that way, but the political maelstrom of his twenties and thirties, the world gone wrong, the pulse of evil and the unending flight from it, had turned life on its wrong side. Anyhow he blamed it, for leaving him alone in a hotel room in a foreign city. Where he fell asleep twice, by eleven-thirty, before giving up on the day, crawling under the blanket, and turning out the light.

28 January, Barcelona.
S. Kolb.

So he was called, on his present passport, a workname they gave him when it suited their inclinations. His real name had disappeared, long ago, and he had become Mr. Nobody, from the nation of Nowhere, and he looked it: bald, with a fringe of dark hair, eyeglasses, a sparse mustache — a short, inconsequential man in a tired suit, at that moment chained to two anarchists and a water pipe in the WC of a café on the bombed-out waterfront of an abandoned city. Sentenced to be shot. Eventually. There was a queue, one had to wait one's turn, and the executioners might not go back to work until they'd had lunch.

Terribly unfair, it seemed to S. Kolb.

His papers said he was the representative of a Swiss engineering firm in Zurich, and a letter in his briefcase, on Republican government stationery, dated two weeks earlier, confirmed his appointment at the office of military procurement. Fiction, all of it. The letter was a forgery, the office of military procurement was now an empty room, its floor littered with important papers, the name was an alias, and Kolb was no salesman.

But even so, unfair. Because the people who were going to shoot him didn't know about any of that. He'd tried to enter a riding stable, the temporary encampment of a few companies of the Fifth Army Corps, where a guard had arrested him and taken him to the office of the *Checa* — secret police — at that moment stationed in a waterfront café. The officer in charge, seated at a table by the bar, was a bull of a man, with a fat moon face covered in dark blue beard shadow. He'd listened impatiently to the guard's story, raised up on one haunch, scowled, then said, "He's a spy, shoot him."

He wasn't wrong. Kolb was an operative of the British Secret Intelligence Service, a secret agent, yes, a spy. Nevertheless, this was terribly unfair. For he was, at that moment, not spying — not stealing documents, suborning officials, or taking photographs. Mostly that was his work, with the occasional murder thrown in when London demanded it, but not this week. This week, at the direction of his boss, an icy man known as *Mr. Brown,* S. Kolb had checked out of a comfortable whores' hotel in Marseilles — an operation to do with the French Merchant Marine — and come running down to Spain in search of an Italian called Colonel Ferrara, thought to have retreated to Barcelona with elements of the Fifth Army Corps.

But Barcelona was a nightmare, not that Mr. Brown cared. The government had packed up its files and fled north to Gerona, thousands of refugees followed, headed to France, and the city was left to await the advancing Nationalist columns. Anarchy ruled, the municipal street cleaners had abandoned their brooms and gone home, great heaps of garbage, attended by clouds of flies, were piled on the sidewalks, refugees broke into empty grocery stores, the city now governed by armed drunks riding through the streets on the roofs of taxicabs.

Yet, even in the midst of chaos, Kolb had

tried to do his job. "To the world," Brown had once told him, "you may seem a meager little fellow, but you have, if I may say so, the balls of a gorilla." Was that a compliment? God had made him meager, fate had ruined his life when he was accused, as a young man, of embezzlement while working in a bank in Austria, and the British SIS had done the rest. Not a very nice compliment, if that's what it was. Still, he did persevere, had in this case found what remained of the Fifth Army Corps, and what was his reward?

Chained to anarchists, black scarves around their necks, and a pipe. Outside, in the adjacent alley, several shots were fired. Well, at least the queue was moving — when was lunch? *"Hora de . . . ?"* he asked the nearest anarchist, making a spooning motion with his free hand. From the anarchist, a look of some admiration. Here was a man at death's door, and he wanted lunch.

Suddenly, the door swung open and two militiamen, pistols in hand, came strolling into the WC. As one of them unbuttoned his fly and used the tiled hole in the floor, the other began to unlock the chain on the pipe. "Officer," Kolb said. No response from the militiaman. *"Comandante,"* he tried. The man looked at him. *"Por favor,"*

Kolb said politely. *"Importante!"*

The militiaman said something to his companion, who shrugged and began to button his fly. Then he grabbed Kolb by the shoulder and hauled the three chained men out the door and into the café. The *Checa* officer had a well-dressed man, head down, standing before him, and was making a point by tapping his finger on the table. *"Señor!"* Kolb called out as they headed for the door. *"Señor Comandante!"*

The officer looked up. Kolb had one chance. *"Oro,"* he said. *"Oro para vida."* Kolb had worked this out while standing in the WC, trying desperately to assemble odd scraps and snips of Spanish. What was gold? What was life? The result — "gold for life" — was terse, but effective. The officer beckoned, Kolb and the anarchists were dragged up to the table. Now sign language took over. Kolb pointed urgently to the seam of his trouser leg and said *"Oro."*

The officer followed the pantomime with interest, then extended his hand. When Kolb just stood there, the officer snapped his fingers twice and opened his hand again. A universal gesture: *give me the gold.* Hurriedly, Kolb unbuckled his belt and undid the buttons and managed, with one hand, to take his pants off and hand them to the officer, who ran a thumb down the seam. A very good tailor had been at work here, and the officer had to press hard to find the coins sewn into the material. When his thumb found a hard circle, he stared at Kolb with interest. *Who are you, to arrange these matters with such care?* But Kolb just stood there, now in baggy cotton under-drawers, gray with age, attire that made him, if possible, even less imposing than usual. The officer took a flick knife from his pocket and produced, with a snap of the wrist, a bright steel blade. He cut the seam open, to reveal twenty gold coins, Dutch guilders. A small fortune, his eyes widened as he stared at them, then narrowed. *Clever little fellow, what else do you have?*

He sliced open the other seam, the fly, the waistband, the cuffs, and the flaps on the back pockets, leaving the trousers in shreds. He tossed them into a corner, then asked Kolb a question he didn't understand. Rather, almost didn't, because he recognized the expression that meant "for all." Did Kolb mean to ransom himself, or the two anarchists as well?

Kolb sensed danger, and his mind sped over the possibilities. What to do? What to say? As Kolb hesitated, the officer grew impatient, dismissed the whole business with a cavalier wave of the hand, and said something to the militiaman, who began to unchain Kolb and the anarchists, who looked at each other, then headed for the door. On the table, Kolb saw his passport — his briefcase, money, and watch had disappeared, but he needed the passport to get out of this accursed country. Meekly, with the greatest diffidence he could manage, Kolb stepped forward and took the passport, nodding humbly to the officer as he backed away. The officer, gathering up the coins from the table, glanced at him but said nothing. Heart pounding, Kolb walked out of the café.

Outside, the waterfront. Burned-out warehouses, bomb craters in the cobbled street, a half-sunk tender tied to a pier. The street was crowded: soldiers, refugees — sitting amid their baggage, waiting for a ship that would never arrive, local citizens, with nothing to do, and nowhere to go. One of Barcelona's horse-drawn fiacres for hire, with two elegantly dressed men in the open carriage, moved slowly through the crowd. One of the men looked at Kolb for a moment, then turned away.

Well he might. A little clerk of a man in his underpants, otherwise dressed for a day at the office. Some people stared, others didn't — Kolb was not the strangest thing they'd seen that day in Barcelona, not by a great deal. Meanwhile, S. Kolb's legs were cold in the wind off the bay, should he tie his jacket around his waist? Maybe he would, in a minute, but for the moment, he wanted only to get as far away from the café as he could. *Money,* he thought, *then a train ticket.* He walked quickly, heading for the corner. Should he try to return to the riding stable? Hurrying along the waterfront, he considered it.

3 February, Paris.

The weather broke, to a false, cloudy spring, the city returning to its normal *grisaille* — gray stone, gray sky. Carlo Weisz left the Hotel Dauphine at eleven in the morning, for a meeting of the *Liberazione* committee at the Café Europa. He was surely followed once, perhaps twice.

He walked over to the Saint-Germain-des-Prés Métro, on his way to the Gare du Nord, stopped to look at a shop window he liked, old maps and nautical charts, and, out of the corner of his eye, noticed that a man at mid-block had also stopped, to look, apparently, in the window of a *tabac.* Nothing unusual about this man, in his thirties, who wore a gray peaked cap and had his hands in the pockets of a tweed jacket. Weisz, done with looking at *Madagascar, 1856,* continued on, entered the Métro, and descended the stairs that led to the *Direction Porte de Clignancourt* side of the tracks. On his way down, he heard hurrying footsteps above him, and glanced back over his shoulder. At that moment, the footsteps stopped. Now Weisz turned around, and caught a glimpse of a tweed jacket, as whoever it was reversed direction and disappeared around the corner of the stairway. Was it the same jacket? The same man? Who in the world went down Métro stairs, then up? A man who had forgotten something. A man who realized he was on the wrong Métro line.

Weisz heard the train coming, and walked quickly down to the platform. He entered the car — only a few passengers this time of the morning. As he went to take a seat, he saw the man in the tweed jacket again, running for the car closest to the foot of the stairway. That was that. Weisz found a seat and opened a copy of *Le Journal.*

But that was not quite that. Because, when the train stopped at Château d'Eau, someone said "Signor," and, when Weisz looked up, handed him an envelope, then went quickly out the door, just before the train started to move. Weisz had only a brief look at him: fifty or so, poorly dressed, dark shirt buttoned at the throat, a deeply lined face, worried eyes. As the train picked up speed, Weisz went to the door and saw the man hurrying away down the platform. He returned to his seat, had a look at the envelope — brown, blank, sealed — and opened it.

Inside, a single folded sheet of yellow drafting paper with the carefully drawn schematic of a long, tapered shape, its nose shaded dark, a propeller and fins at the other end. A torpedo. Extraordinary! Look at all the apparatus the thing contained, lettered descriptions, in Italian, ranged along its length — valves, cables, a turbine, an air flask, rudders, fuse, drive shaft, and plenty more. All of it fated, alas, to blow up. On the side of the page, a list of specifications. Weight: 3,748 pounds. Length: 23 feet, 7 inches. Charge: 595 pounds. Range/speed: 4,400 yards at 50 knots, 13,000 yards at 30 knots. Power: wet heater. Which meant, after he thought about it for a moment, that the torpedo was driven through the water by steam.

Why was he given this?

The train slowed for the next station, Gare du Nord, blue tile set in the curve of the white tunnel wall. Weisz refolded the drawing and put it back in the envelope. On the short walk to the Café Europa, he tried every way he knew to see if somebody was following him. There was a woman with a shopping basket, a man walking a spaniel. How was one to know?

At the Café Europa, Weisz had a quiet word with Salamone, saying that a stranger on the Métro had handed him an envelope — a copy of a mechanical blueprint. The expression on Salamone's face was eloquent: *this is the last thing I needed today.* "We'll look at it after the meeting," he said. "If it's a . . . blueprint? I better ask Elena to join us." Elena, the Milanese chemist, was the committee's adviser on anything technical, the rest of them could barely change a lightbulb. Weisz agreed. He liked Elena. Her sharp face, long, graying hair worn back in a clip, her severe dark suits, did not especially reveal who she was. Her smile did; one corner of her mouth upturned, the reluctant half smile of the ironist, witness to the absurdities of existence, half amused, half not. Weisz found her appealing and, more important, he trusted her.

It was not a good meeting.

They'd all had time to brood about Bottini's murder, about what it might mean to *them,* to be targets of OVRA — not as *giellisti,* but as individuals, trying to live their daily lives. In the first flash of anger, they had thought only of counterattack, but now, after a discussion of articles for the next issue of *Liberazione,* they wanted to talk about changing the location of the meeting, about security. They believed themselves to be skilled amateurs, at newspaper production, but security was not a discipline for skilled amateurs, they knew that, and it frightened them.

When everyone else had left, Salamone said, "Allright, Carlo, I guess we'd better take a look at your drawing."

Weisz laid it out on the table. "A torpedo," he said.

Elena studied it for a time, then shrugged. "Someone copied this, from an engineering blueprint, so someone thought it was important. Why? Because it's different, improved, perhaps experimental, but God only knows how, I don't. This is meant for an ordnance expert."

"There are two possibilities," Salamone said. "It's an Italian blueprint, so it can only have come from Pola, on the Adriatic, from what used to be the Whitehead Torpedo Company — founded by the British, taken

99

over by Austria-Hungary, then Italian after the war. You're right, Elena, it must be significant, surely secret, so, by having it, we're involved in espionage. Which means that the man in the Métro could have been an *agent provocateur,* and this paper is planted evidence. On that basis, we burn it."

"And the other possibility," Weisz said, "is that it's a gesture. Of resistance."

"What if it is?" Elena said. "This is of interest only to a navy, likely it's meant for the British navy, or the French. So, if that idiot in Rome gets us into a *war,* with France, or Great Britain, God forbid, it would lead to the loss of Italian ships, Italian lives. How? I can't work out the details, but secret knowledge of a weapon's capabilities is always an advantage."

"That's true," Salamone said. "And, on that basis, we don't want anything to do with it. We are a resistance organization, and this is spying, this is treason, not resistance, though there are those on the other side who think it's the same thing. So, once again, we burn it."

"There's more," Weisz said. "I think I might have been followed, earlier this morning, when I walked to the Métro." Briefly, he described the behavior of the man in the tweed jacket.

"Were the two of them somehow working together?" Elena said.

"I don't know," Weisz said. "Maybe I'm seeing monsters under the bed."

"Ah yes," Elena said. "*Those* monsters."

"Under all our beds," Salamone said tartly. "The way the meeting went today."

"Is there anything we can do?" Weisz said.

"Not that I know about, short of ceasing publication. We try to be as secretive as we can, but, in the émigré community, people talk, and the OVRA spies are everywhere."

"On the committee?" Elena said.

"Maybe."

"What a world," Weisz said.

"Our very own," Salamone said. "But the clandestine press has been a fact of life since 1924. In Italy, in Paris, in Belgium, everywhere we ran to. And OVRA can't stop it. They can slow it down. They arrest a socialist group in Turin, but the *giellisti* in Florence start a new publication. And the major newspapers have survived for a long time — the socialist *Avanti,* the Communist *Unità.* Our older brother, the *Giustizia e Libertà* paper published in Paris. The émigrés who issue *Non Mollare!,* as the name of their journal states, *don't give in,* and the Catholic Action people publish *Il Corriere degli Ital-*

iani. The OVRA can't kill us all. They might want to, but Mussolini still craves legitimacy in the eyes of the world. And, when they do assassinate — Matteotti in 1924, the Rosselli brothers, in France, in '37 — they create martyrs; martyrs for the Italian opposition, and martyrs in the world's newspapers. This is a war, and, in a war, sometimes you lose, sometimes you win, and, sometimes, when you think you've lost, you've won."

Elena liked that idea. "Maybe this needs to be said to the committee."

Weisz agreed. The fascists didn't always have things their way. When Matteotti, the leader of the Italian Socialist party, disappeared, after making a passionate antifascist speech, the reaction in Italy, even among members of the Fascist party, had been so intense that Mussolini was forced to support an investigation. A month later, Matteotti's body had been discovered in a shallow grave outside Rome, a carpenter's file driven into his chest. The following year, a man named Dumini was arrested, tried, and found guilty, more or less. He was guilty, said the court, of "nonpremeditated homicide extenuated by the subnormal physical resistance of Matteotti and by other circumstances." So, yes, murdered, but not very murdered.

"And *Liberazione?*" Weisz said. "Do we, as you say of the major newspapers, survive?"

"Maybe," Salamone said. "Now, before the cops come rushing in here . . ." He crumpled the yellow drafting paper into a ball and dropped it in the ashtray. "Who'll do the honors? Carlo?"

Weisz took out his steel lighter and lit a corner of the paper.

It was a brisk little fire, flaring and smoking, tended by Weisz with the point of a pencil. As the ashes were stirred about, a tap at the door was followed by the appearance of the barman. "Everything allright in here?"

Salamone said it was.

"If you're going to burn the place down, let me know first, eh?"

4 February. Weisz sat back in his chair for a moment and watched people in the street below his office window, then forced himself back to work.

ìMONSIEUR DE PARISî DEAD AT 76
Anatole Deibler, the Grand High Executioner of France, died of a heart attack yesterday in the Ch,telet station of the Paris MÈtro. Known by the traditional honori c ìMonsieur de Paris,î Deibler was

on his way to his 401st execution, having attended France's guillotine for forty years. Deibler was the last male heir to the position held by his family, executioners since 1829, and it is said that he is to be replaced by his assistant, known as "the valet." Thus André Obrecht, Monsieur Deibler's nephew, will be the new "Monsieur de Paris."

Would this take a second paragraph? Deibler had been, according to his wife, a passionate *bicycliste,* and had raced for his bicycle club. He had married into another family of executioners, and his father, Louis, had been the last to wear the traditional top hat as he lopped off heads. Any of that? No, he thought not. What about *the invention of Dr. Joseph Guillotin in revolutionary France?* You always saw that when the contraption was mentioned, but did they care in Manchester or Montevideo? He doubted they did. And the rewrite man would likely strike it out anyhow. Still, it was sometimes useful to give him something he could strike out. No, leave it alone. And, with any luck at all, Delahanty would spare him an afternoon at a February funeral.

FRANCE SUPPORTS CVETKOVICH APPOINTMENT

The Quai d'Orsay today announced its support of the new premier of Yugoslavia, Dr. Dragisha Cvetkovich, designated by the Yugoslav ruler, Prince Paul, to replace Dr. Milan Stoyadinovich.

That much they had from the press release — a few colorless diplomatic paragraphs marching after. But of sufficient weight to send Weisz off to see his contact at the Foreign Ministry. Off to the regal headquarters on the quai d'Orsay, next to the Palais Bourbon, back in time to the eighteenth century: vast chandeliers, miles of Aubusson carpet, endless marble stairways, the hush of state.

Devoisin, a permanent undersecretary in the ministry, had a magnificent smile, and a magnificent office, his windows looking down on a wintry, slate-colored Seine. He offered Weisz a cigarette from a fruitwood box on his desk and said, "Off the record, we're glad to see the back of that bastard Stoyadinovich. A Nazi, Weisz, to his very marrow, which is no news to you."

"Yes, the *Vodja*," Weisz said dryly.

"Dreadful. The *leader,* just like his pals; the *Fuehrer,* the *Duce,* and the *Caudillo,* as

Franco likes to call himself. And old *Vodja* had the rest of it as well, Greenshirt militia, stiff-arm salute, the whole nasty business. Anyhow, *adieu,* at least for the moment."

"This *adieu,*" Weisz said. "Were your people involved?"

Devoisin smiled. "Wouldn't you like to know."

"There are ways to say it. Not quite so, direct."

"Not in this office, my friend. I suspect the British might have helped out, Prince Paul is their great chum."

"So then, I'll just say that the Franco-Yugoslav alliance is expected to strengthen."

"It surely will — our love deepens with time."

Weisz pretended to write. "I rather like that."

"Actually, it's the Serbs we love, you can't do business with the Croats, they're headed directly for Mussolini's kennel."

"They don't like each other, down there, it's in their blood."

"Isn't it. And, incidentally, if you should hear something about that, Croatian state-hood, a word from you would be very much appreciated."

"You'll be the first to know. In any event, would you like to elaborate on the official statement? Not for attribution, of course. 'A senior official says . . .' "

"Weisz, please, my hands are tied. France supports the change, and every word in the statement was hammered out of steel. Would you care for a coffee? I'll have it brought up."

"Thanks, no. I'll use the Nazi background, without using the word."

"It doesn't come from me."

"Of course not," Weisz said.

Devoisin shifted the conversation — he was soon off to Saint-Moritz for a week of skiing, had Weisz seen the new Picasso show at Rosenberg's, what did he think about it. Weisz's internal clock was efficient: fifteen minutes, then he had "to get back to the office."

"Don't be such a stranger," Devoisin said. "It's always good to see you." He had, Weisz thought, a truly magnificent smile.

12 February. The request — it was an order, of course — arrived as a telephone message in his mailbox at the office. The secretary who'd taken the message gave him a certain look when he came in that morning. *So what's all this?* Not that he would tell her, not that she had any business asking, and it was only a momentary look, but a longish,

107

concentrated sort of a moment. And she watched him as he read it — his presence required at Room 10, at the *Sûreté Nationale,* at eight the following morning. What did she think, that he would tremble? Break out in a cold sweat?

He did neither, but he felt it, in the pit of the stomach. The *Sûreté* was the national security police — what did they want? He put the slip of paper in his pocket, and, one foot in front of the other, got through his day. Later that morning, he made up a reason to stop by Delahanty's office. Had the secretary told him? But Delahanty said nothing, and acted as he always did. Did he? Or was there, something? Leaving early for lunch, he called Salamone from a pay phone in a café, but Salamone was at work, and, beyond "Well, be careful," couldn't say much. That night, he took Véronique to the ballet — balcony seats, but they could see — and for supper afterward. Véronique was attentive, bright and talkative, and one didn't ask men what was wrong. They hadn't talked to *her,* had they? He considered asking, but the right moment never came. Walking home, it wouldn't leave him alone; he made up questions, tried to answer them, then tried again.

At ten of eight the next morning, he

walked up the avenue de Marigny to the Interior Ministry on the rue des Saussaies. Massive and gray, the building stretched to the horizon and rose above him; here lived the little gods in little rooms, the gods of émigré fate, who could have you put on a train, back to wherever it was, back to whatever awaited you.

A clerk led him to Room 10 — a long table, a few chairs, a hissing steam radiator, a high window behind a grille. A powerful presence, in Room 10: the smell of cooked paint and stale cigarette smoke, but mostly the smell of sweat, like a gymnasium. They made him wait, of course, it was 9:20 before they showed up, dossiers in hand. There was something about the young one, in his twenties, Weisz thought, that suggested the word *probationary.* The older one was a cop, grizzled and slumped, with eyes that had seen everything.

Formal and correct, they introduced themselves and spread their dossiers out. Inspector Pompon, the younger one, his boiled white shirt gleaming like the sun, led the interrogation, and wrote out Weisz's answers on a printed form. After sifting through the particulars, date of birth, address, employment, arrival in France — all of that from the dossier — he asked Weisz if he'd known Enrico Bottini.

"Yes, we were acquainted."

"Good friends?"

"Friends, I would say."

"Did you ever meet his paramour, Madame LaCroix?"

"No."

"Perhaps he spoke of her."

"Not to me."

"Do you know, Monsieur Weisz, why you are here today?"

"In fact, I don't know."

"This investigation would normally be conducted by the local *Préfecture,* but we have interested ourselves in it because it involves the family of an individual who serves in the national government. So, we are concerned with the, ah, political implications. Of the murder/suicide. Is that clear?"

Weisz said it was. And it was, though French was not his native language, and answering questions at the *Sûreté* was not the same as chatting with Devoisin or telling Véronique he liked her perfume. Fortunately, Pompon took considerable pleasure in the sound of his own voice, mellow and precise, and that slowed him down to a point where Weisz, working hard, could pretty much understand every word.

Pompon put Weisz's dossier aside, opened

another, and hunted around for what he wanted. Weisz could see the impression of an official stamp, made with a red ink pad, at the upper corner of each page. "Was your friend Bottini left-handed, Monsieur Weisz?"

Weisz thought it over. "I don't know," he said. "I never noticed that he was."

"And how would you describe his political affiliation?"

"He was a political émigré, from Italy, so I would describe his politics as antifascist."

Pompon wrote down the answer, his careful hand the product of a school system that spent endless hours on penmanship. "Of the left, would you say?"

"Of the center."

"You discussed politics?"

"In a general way, when it came up."

"Have you heard of a newspaper, a clandestine publication, that is called *Liberazione?*"

"Yes. An opposition newspaper distributed in Italy."

"Have you read it?"

"No, I've seen others, the ones published in Paris."

"But not *Liberazione.*"

"No."

"And Bottini's relationship to this newspaper?"

"I wouldn't know. He never mentioned it."

"Would you describe Bottini? What sort of man he was?"

"Very proud, sure of himself. Sensitive to slights, I would say, and conscious of his — do you say 'standing'? His place in the scheme of things. He had been a prominent lawyer, in Turin, and was always a lawyer, even as a friend."

"Meaning what, precisely?"

Weisz thought for a moment. "If there was an argument, even a friendly argument, he still liked to win it."

"Was he, would you say, capable of violence?"

"No, I think that violence, to him, meant failure, a loss, a loss of . . ."

"Self-control?"

"He believed in words, discourse, rationality. Violence, to him, was a, how to say, descent, a descent to the level of, well, beasts."

"But he murdered his paramour. Was it, do you think, romantic passion that drove him to do such a thing?"

"I don't believe that."

"What then?"

"I suspect this crime was a double murder, not a murder/suicide."

"Committed by whom, Monsieur Weisz?"

"By operatives of the Italian government."

"An assassination, then."

"Yes."

"With no concern that one of the victims was the wife of an important French politician."

"No, I don't think they cared."

"Was Bottini, then, to your way of thinking, the primary victim?"

"I believe he was, yes."

"Why do you believe that?"

"I think it had to do with his involvement in the antifascist opposition."

"Why him, Monsieur Weisz? There are others in Paris. Quite a number."

"I don't know why," Weisz said. It was very hot in the room, Weisz felt a bead of sweat run from beneath his arm down to the edge of his undershirt.

"As an émigré, Monsieur Weisz, what is your opinion of France?"

"I have always liked it here, and that was true long before I emigrated."

"What exactly is it that you like?"

"I would say," he paused, then said, "the tradition of individual freedom has always been strong here, and I enjoy the culture, and Paris is, is everything that's said of it. One is privileged to live here."

"You are aware that there are disputes between us — Italy claims Corsica, Tunisia, and Nice — so if, regrettably, your native country and your adopted country were to go to war, what would you do then?"

"Well, I wouldn't leave."

"Would you serve a foreign country, against your native land?"

"Today," Weisz said, "I don't know how to answer that. My hope is for change in the government of Italy, and peace between both nations. Really, if ever there were two countries who ought not to go to war, that would be Italy and France."

"And would you be willing to put such ideals to work? To work for what you believe should be harmony between these two nations?"

Oh fuck you. "Truly, I cannot imagine what I could do, to help. It all takes place high up, these difficulties. Between our countries."

Pompon almost smiled, started to speak, to attack, but his colleague, very quietly, cleared his throat. "We appreciate your candor, Monsieur Weisz. Not so easy, these politics. Perhaps you're one of those who in his heart thinks that wars should be settled by diplomats in their underwear, fighting with brooms."

Weisz smiled, intensely grateful. "I'd pay to watch it, yes."

"Unfortunately, it doesn't work like that. Too bad, eh? By the way, speaking of diplomats, I wonder if you've heard, as a journalist, that an Italian official, from the embassy here, has been sent home. *Persona non grata,* I believe that's the phrase."

"I hadn't heard."

"No? You're sure? Well, maybe a communiqué wasn't issued — that's not up to us, down here in the trenches, but I'm told it did happen."

"I didn't know," Weisz said. "Nothing came to Reuters."

The cop shrugged. "Then better keep it under your hat, eh?"

"I will," Weisz said.

"Much obliged," the cop said.

Pompon closed his file. "I think that's all, for today," he said. "Of course we'll be speaking with you again."

Weisz left the ministry, a lone figure amid a stream of men with briefcases, circled the building — this took a long time — at last left its shadow, and headed toward the Reuters office. Going back over the interview, his mind spun, but in time settled on the official sent back to Italy. Why had they told him that? What did they want from him? Because he sensed they knew he'd become the new editor of *Liberazione,* had expected the *pro forma* lie, then tempted him with an interesting story. Officially, the clandestine press did not exist, but it was, potentially, useful. How? Because the French government might wish to make known, to both allies and enemies in Italy, that they had taken action in the Bottini affair. They had not issued a communiqué, did not want to force the Mussolini government to send home a French official, the traditional pawn sacrifice in diplomatic chess. On the other hand, they could not simply do nothing, they had to avenge the wrong done to La-Croix, an important politician.

Was this true? If it wasn't, and the story appeared in *Liberazione,* they would be very annoyed with him. *Keep it under your hat, eh?* Best to do that, if you valued the head that wore it. No, he thought, leave it alone, let them find some other newspaper, don't take the bait. The French allowed *Liberazione* and the others to exist because France publicly opposed the fascist government. Today. Tomorrow, that could change. Everywhere in Europe, the possibility of another

116

war forced alliances governed by *realpolitik:* England and France needed Italy as a partner against Germany, they couldn't have Russia, and they wouldn't have America, so they had to fight Mussolini with one hand, and stroke him with the other. The waltz of diplomacy, and Weisz now invited to join the dance.

But he would decline, with silence. He'd been summoned to this meeting, he decided, as the editor of *Liberazione* — an assignment for Inspector Pompon, the new man on the job: Would he spy for them? Would he be discreet on the subject of French politics? And *we'll be speaking with you again* meant *we're watching you.* So then, watch. But the answers, *no,* and *yes,* would not change.

Now Weisz felt better. Not such a bad day, he thought, the sun in and out, big, fancy clouds coming in from the Channel and flying east over the city. Weisz, on his way to the Opéra quarter, had left the ministry neighborhood and returned to the streets of Paris: two shop girls in gray smocks, riding bicycles, an old man in a café, reading *Le Figaro,* his terrier curled up beneath the table, a musician on the corner, playing the clarinet, his upturned hat holding a few centimes. All of them, he thought, adding a one-franc coin to the hat, with dossiers. It had shaken him a little to see his very own, but so life went. Still, *triste* in its way. But no different than Italy, the dossiers there called *schedatura* — someone presumed to have a police file termed *schedata* — where they had been compiled by the national police for more than a decade, recording political views, the habits of daily life, sins great and small, everything. It was all written down.

By ten-fifteen, Weisz was back in the office. To, once again, a certain look from the secretary: *What, not in chains?* And she had, as he'd feared, told Delahanty about the message, because he said, "Everything allright, laddie?" when Weisz visited his office. Weisz looked at the ceiling and spread his hands, Delahanty grinned. Police and émigrés, nothing new there. The way Delahanty saw it, you could be a bit of an axe murderer, as long as the foreign minister's quote was accurate.

With the interview behind him, Weisz treated himself to a gentle day at the office. He put off a call to Salamone, drank coffee at his desk, and, a *cruciverbiste,* as the French called it, fiddled with the crossword puzzle in *Paris-Soir.* Making little headway there, he found three of the five animals in the picture puzzle, then turned to the entertainment pages, consulted the cinema schedules, and discovered, in the distant reaches of the Eleventh Arrondissement, *L'Albergo del Bosco,* made in 1932. What was *that* doing out there? The Eleventh was barely in France, a poor district, home to refugees, one heard more Yiddish, Polish, and Russian than French in those dark streets. And Italian? Perhaps. There were thousands of Italians in Paris, working at whatever they could find, living wherever rent was low and food cheap. Weisz wrote down the address of the theatre, maybe he'd go.

He looked up, to see Delahanty strolling toward his desk, hands in pockets. At work, the bureau chief looked like a workman — a consummately rumpled workman: jacket off, sleeves rolled up, collar points bent, trousers baggy and worn low beneath a big belly. He half-sat on the edge of Weisz's desk and said, "Carlo, my oldest and dearest friend . . ."

"Yes?"

"You'll be pleased to hear that Eric Wolf is getting married."

"Oh? That's nice."

"Very nice indeed. Going back to London, he is, to wed his sweetie and carry her off for a honeymoon in Cornwall."

"A long honeymoon?"

"Two weeks. Which leaves Berlin uncovered, of course."

"When do you want me there?"

"The third of March."

Weisz nodded. "I'll be there," he said.

Delahanty stood. "We're grateful, laddie. With Eric gone, you're my best German speaker. You know the drill: they'll take you out to eat, feed you propaganda, you'll file, we won't publish, but, if I don't cover, that little weasel will start a war on me, just for spite, and we wouldn't want that, would we."

The Cinéma Desargues was not on the rue Desargues, not quite. It was down at the end of an alley, in what had once been a garage — twenty wooden folding chairs, a bedsheetlike screen hung from the ceiling. The owner, a sour-faced gnome wearing a yarmulke, took the money, then ran the film from a chair tilted back against the wall. He watched the movie in a kind of trance, the smoke from his cigarette drifting through the blue light beamed at the screen, while the dialogue crackled above the hiss of the sound track and the rhythmic whir of the projector.

In 1932, Italy is still in the grip of the Depression, so nobody comes to stay at *l'albergo del bosco* — the inn of the forest, near a village outside of Naples. The innkeeper, with five daughters, is beset by debt collectors and so gives the last of his savings to the local *marchese* for safekeeping. But, through a misunderstanding, the *marchese*, very decayed nobility and no richer than the innkeeper, donates the money to charity. Accidentally learning of his error — the innkeeper is a proud fellow and pretends he wanted to give the money away — the *marchese* sells his last two family portraits, then pays the innkeeper to hold a grand feast for the poor people of the village.

Not so bad, it kept Weisz's interest. The cameraman was good, very good, even in black and white, so the hills and meadows, tall grass swaying in the wind, the little white road bordered by poplars, the lovely Neapolitan sky, looked very real to Weisz. He knew this place, or places like it. He knew the village — its dry fountain with a crumbling rim, its tenements shadowing the narrow street, and its people — the postman, the women in kerchiefs. He knew the *marchese*'s villa, tiles fallen from the roof stacked hopefully by the door, the old servant, not paid for years. Sentimental

Italy, Weisz thought, every frame of it. And the music was also very good — vaguely operatic, lyrical, sweet. Really very sentimental, Weisz thought, the Italy of dreams, or poems. Still, it broke his heart. As he walked up the aisle toward the door, the owner stared at him for a moment, this man in a good dark overcoat, glasses in one hand, the index finger of the other touching the corners of his eyes.

CITIZEN OF THE NIGHT

3 March, 1939.

Weisz had taken a compartment in a *wagon-lit* on the night train to Berlin, leaving at seven from the Gare du Nord, arriving Berlin at midday. A restless sleeper at best, he had spent the hours waking and dozing, staring out the window when the train stopped at the stations — Dortmund, Bielefeld — along the way. After midnight, the floodlit platforms were silent and deserted, only the occasional passenger or railway porter, now and then a policeman with a leashed Alsatian shepherd, their breaths steaming in the icy German air.

On the night he'd had drinks with Mr. Brown, he'd thought about Christa Zameny, his former lover, for a long time. Married three years earlier, in Germany, she was now beyond his reach, their elaborate afternoons together destined to remain a remembered love affair. Still, when Delahanty had ordered him to Berlin, he'd looked her up in his address book, and considered writing her a note. She'd sent him the address in a farewell letter, telling him of her marriage to von Schirren, telling him that it was, at this point in her life, the best thing for her. *We will never see each other again,* she'd meant. Followed, in the final paragraph, by her new address, where he would never see her again. Some love affairs die, he thought, others stop.

Now, at the Adlon, he would sleep for an hour or two, preparing for rest by unpacking his valise, stripping down to his underwear, hanging his suit and shirt in the closet, turning down the bedspread, and opening the Adlon's stationery folder on the mahogany desk. A fine hotel, the Adlon, Berlin's best, with such fine paper and envelopes, the hotel's name and address in elegant gold script. Life was made easy for a guest here, one could write a note to an acquaintance, seal it in a thick creamy envelope, and summon the hall porter, who would provide a stamp and mail it off. So very easy, really. And Berlin's postal system was fast, and efficient. Before ten o'clock on the following day, a delicate and very reserved little jingle from the telephone.

Weisz sprang like a cat — there would be no second ring.

At four-thirty in the afternoon, the bar at the Adlon was almost empty. Dark and plush, it was not so very different from the Ritz — upholstered chairs, low drink tables. A fat man with a Nazi party pin in his lapel played Cole Porter on a white piano. Weisz ordered a cognac, then another. Perhaps she wouldn't come, perhaps, at the last minute, she couldn't. Her voice had been cool and courteous on the phone — it crossed his mind that she was not alone when she made the call. How thoughtful of him to write. Was he well? Oh, a drink? At the hotel? Well, she didn't know, at four-thirty perhaps, she was not really sure, a terribly busy day, but she would try, so thoughtful of him to write.

This was the voice, and the manner, of an aristocrat. The sheltered child of an adoring father, a Hungarian noble, and a distant mother, the daughter of a German banker, she'd been raised by governesses in the Charlottenburg district of Berlin, attended boarding schools in England and Switzerland, then university in Jena. She wrote imagist poetry, often in French, privately published. And found ways, after graduating, to live beyond wealth — for a time managed a string quartet, served on the board of a school for deaf children.

They'd met in Trieste, in the summer of 1933, at a loud and drunken party, she with friends on a yacht, cruising the Adriatic. Thirty-seven when the love affair began, she maintained a style conceived in Berlin's, and her own, twenties: very erotic woman costumed as very severe man. Black chalk-stripe suit, white shirt, sober tie, chestnut hair worn short, except in front, where it was cut on a sharp bias and pointed down at one eye. Sometimes, at the extreme of the style, she pomaded her hair and combed it back behind her ears. She had smooth, fair skin, a high forehead, wore no makeup — only a faint touch of seemingly colorless lipstick. A face more striking than pretty, with all its character in the eyes: green and pensive, concentrated, fearless, and penetrating.

The entry to the Adlon bar was up three marble steps, through a pair of leather-sheathed doors with portholes, and, when they parted, and Weisz turned to see who it was, his heart soared. Not so long after that, maybe fifteen minutes, a waiter approached the table, collected a large tip, half a cognac, and half a champagne cocktail.

It wasn't only the heart that absence made grow fonder.

Outside the window, Berlin in the half-tones of its winter twilight, inside the room, amid the snarled and tumbled wreckage of the bed linen, Weisz and Christa lay flopped back on the pillows, catching their breath. He raised up on one elbow, put three fingers on the hollow at the base of her throat, then traced her center down to the end. For a moment, she closed her eyes, a very faint smile on her lips. "You have," he said, "red knees."

She had a look. "So I do. You're surprised?"

"Well, no."

He moved his hand a little, then let it rest. She laid a hand on top of his.

He looked at her for a long time.

"So, what do you see?"

"The best thing I ever saw."

From Christa, a dubious smile.

"No, it's true."

"It's your eyes, love. But I love to be what you see."

He lay back, hands clasped beneath his head. She turned on her side and stretched an arm and a leg over him, her face pressed against his chest. They drifted in silence for a time, then he realized that his skin, where her face rested, was wet, and it burned. He started to speak, to ask, but she put a gentle finger on his lips.

Standing at the desk, with her back to him, she waited for the hotel operator to answer the phone, then gave her a number. She was, without clothing, slighter than he remembered — this always struck him — and enigmatically desirable. What was it, about her, that reached him so deeply? Mystery, lover's mystery, a magnetic field beyond words. She waited as the phone rang, shifting her weight from one foot to the other, one hand unconsciously smoothing her hair. It stirred him to watch her; the nape of her neck — hair cut short and high, her long, taut back, pale curve of hip, deep cleft, nicely shaped legs, scuffed heels.

"Helma?" she said. "It's me. Would you please tell Herr von Schirren that I am delayed? Oh, he isn't. Well, when he gets home then, you'll tell him. Yes, that's it. Goodby."

She placed the phone back on its high cradle, then turned, read his eyes, rose on the toes of one foot, hands raised, fingers in the castanet position, and did a Spanish dancer's twirl on the Adlon's carpet.

"*Olé*," he said.

She came back to the bed, found an edge of quilt, and pulled it over them. Weisz reached across her and turned off the bedside lamp, leaving the room in darkness. For an hour, they would pretend to spend the night together.

Later, she dressed by the light of the streetlamp that shone in the window, then went into the bathroom to comb her hair. Weisz followed and stood in the doorway. "How long will you stay?" she said.

"Two weeks."

"I will call you," she said.

"Tomorrow?"

"Yes, tomorrow." Looking in the mirror, she turned her head to one side, then the other. "At lunchtime, I can call."

"You have an office?"

"We all must work, here in the thousand-year Reich. I'm a sort of executive, at the *Bund Deutscher Maedchen,* the League for German Girls — part of the Hitler Youth organization. A friend of von Schirren's got me the job."

Weisz nodded. "In Italy, they go down to the six-year-olds, make fascists of children, get them while they're young. It's awful."

"It is. But *must* is what I meant. One must take part, otherwise, they come after you."

"What do you do?"

"Organize things, make plans — for parades, or mass gymnastic exhibitions, or whatever it is that week. Sometimes I have to take them out to the countryside, thirty teenagers, for the harvest, or just to breathe the air of the German forest. We have a fire, and we sing, then some of them go off hand in hand into the woods. It's all very Aryan."

"Aryan?"

She laughed. "That's how they think of it. Health and strength and *Freiheit,* freedom of the body. We're supposed to encourage that, because the Nazis want them to breed. If they don't wish to marry, they should go and find a lonely soldier and get pregnant. To make more soldiers. Herr Hitler will need all he can get, once we go to war."

"And when is that?"

"Oh, that they don't tell us. Soon, I would think. If a man is looking for a fight, sooner or later he'll find it. We thought it would be the Czechs, but Hitler was handed what he wanted, so now, maybe, the Poles. Lately he screams at them, on the radio, and the Propaganda Ministry puts stories in the newspapers: those poor Germans in Dan-

132

zig, beaten up by Polish gangs. It isn't subtle."

"If he goes for them, the British and the French will declare war."

"Yes, I expect they will."

"They'll close the border, Christa."

She turned and, for a moment, met his eyes. Finally, she said, "Yes, I know." A last look at herself in the mirror, then she returned the comb to her purse, hunted around for a moment, and brought out a piece of jewelry, holding it up for Weisz to see. "My *Hakenkreuz,* all the ladies wear one, out where I live." On a silver chain, a swastika made of old silver, with a diamond on each of the four bars.

"How beautiful," Weisz said.

"Von Schirren gave it to me."

"Is he in the party?"

"Heavens no! He's old, rich Prussia, they hate Hitler."

"But he stays."

"Of course he stays, Carlo. Maybe he could've left three years ago, but there was still hope, then, that somebody would see the light and get rid of the Nazis. From the beginning, in 'thirty-three, nobody here could believe what they were doing, that they could get away with it. But now, to cross the border would be to lose everything. Every house, every bank account, every horse, the servants. My *dogs*. Everything. Mother, father, family. To do what? Press pants in London? Meanwhile, life here goes on, and in the next minute, Hitler will reach too far, and the army will step in. Tomorrow, maybe. Or the next day. This is what von Schirren says, and he *knows* things."

"Do you love him, Christa?"

"I am very fond of him, he's a good man, a gentleman of old Europe, and he's given me a place in life. I couldn't go on any longer, living the way I did."

"Everything else aside, I fear for you."

She shook her head, put the *Hakenkreuz* back in her purse, closed the flap, and snapped the button shut. "No, no, Carlo, don't do that. This nightmare will end, this government will fall, and then, well, one will be free to do what one wants."

"I'm not so sure it will fall."

"Oh, it will." She lowered her voice and leaned toward him. "And, I guess I can say this, there are a few of us in this city who might even give it a little push."

Weisz was at the Reuters office, at the end of the Wilhelmstrasse, by eight-thirty the next morning. The other two reporters hadn't come in yet, but he was greeted by the two secretaries, both in their twenties, who, according to Delahanty, spoke perfect English and French and could get along in other languages if they had to. "We are so happy for Herr Wolf, will he return with his bride?" Weisz didn't know — he doubted Wolf would do that, but he couldn't say it. He sat in Wolf's chair and read the morning news, in the thinking man's newspapers, the Berlin *Deutsche Allgemeine Zeitung* and Goebbels's *Das Reich.* Not much there, Dr. Goebbels writing of the potential replacement of Chamberlain by Churchill, that "swapping horses in midstream is bad enough, but swapping an ass for a bull would be fatal." For the rest, it was whatever the Propaganda Ministry wanted to say that day. So, government-controlled newspapers, nothing new there.

But control of the press could have unexpected consequences — Weisz recalled the classic example, the end of the Great War. The surrender of 1918 had sent waves of shock and anger through the German public. After all, they had read every day that their armies were victorious in the field, then, suddenly, the government capitulated. How could this happen? The infamous *Dolchstoss,* the stab in the back, *that* was the reason — political manipulation at home had undermined their brave soldiers and dishonored their sacrifice. So it was the Jews and the Communists, those crafty political guttersnipe, who were responsible for the defeat. This the German public believed. And the table was set for Hitler.

Done with the newspapers, Weisz started on the press releases, stacked in Wolf's in box. He tried to make himself concentrate, but he couldn't. What was Christa *doing?* Her lowered voice would not leave him — *give them a little push.* That meant clandestine business, conspiracy, resistance. Under the rule of the Nazis and their secret police, Germany had become a counterintelligence state, eager informers, and *agents provocateurs,* everywhere, did she know what could *happen* to her? Yes, she knew, damn her aristocratic eyes, but *these people* were not going to tell Christa Zameny von Schirren what she could and couldn't do. Blood told, he thought, and told hard. But was it so different from what he was doing? *It is,* he thought. But it wasn't, and he knew it.

The office door was open, but one of the secretaries stood at the threshold and knocked politely on the frame. "Herr Weisz?"

"Yes, uh . . ."

"I'm Gerda, Herr Weisz. You are to have a meeting, at the Propaganda Ministry press club, at eleven this morning, with Herr Doktor Martz."

"Thank you, Gerda."

Leaving time for a leisurely walk, Weisz headed down the Leipzigerstrasse toward the new press club. Passing Wertheim's, the vast block-long department store, he stopped for a moment to watch a window dresser taking down a display of anti-Soviet books and posters — book titles outlined in flames, posters showing garish Bolshevik thugs with big hooked noses — and stacking them neatly on a handcart. When the window dresser stared back at him, Weisz went on his way.

Three years since he'd been in Berlin — was it different? The people on the street seemed prosperous, well fed, well dressed, but there was something in the air, not exactly fear, that reached him. It was as though they all had a secret, the same secret, but it was somehow unwise to let others know you had it. Berlin had always looked official — various kinds of police, tram conductors, zookeepers — but now it was a city dressed for war. Uniforms everywhere: the SS in black with lightning-flash insignia, *Wehrmacht, Kriegsmarine, Luftwaffe,* others he didn't recognize. When a pair of SA storm troopers, in brown tunics and trousers, and caps with chin straps, came toward him, nobody seemed to change direction, but a path opened for them, almost magically, on the crowded sidewalk.

He stopped at a newspaper stand, where rows of magazines displayed on the kiosk caught his attention. *Faith and Beauty, The Dance, Modern Photography,* all their covers showing nude women engaged in wholesome activities of one sort or another. The Nazi administration, on assuming power in 1933, had immediately banned pornography, but here was their version of it, meant to stimulate the male population, as Christa had suggested, to hop on the nearest *Fräulein* and produce a soldier.

At the press club — the former Foreigners' Club on Leipzigerplatz — Dr. Martz was the merriest man alive, fat and sparkling, dark, with a toothbrush mustache and active, chubby hands. "Come, let me show you around!" he sang. Here was a journalist's heaven, with a sumptuous restaurant, loudspeakers to page reporters, reading rooms with newspapers from every major city, workrooms with long rows of desks bearing typewriters and telephones. "For you, we have everything!"

They settled in red leather easy chairs in a lounge by the restaurant, and were immediately served coffee and a huge platter of Viennese coffee buns, *babka,* moist, buttery cake rolled around crushed walnuts flavored with cinnamon and sugar, or a ribbon of thick almond paste. *Surprising, Weisz, that you became a Nazi. Oh, it's a long story.* "Have another, oh go ahead, who's to know." Well, maybe one more.

And that was just for starters. Martz gave him his own red identification card. "If you have a problem with a policeman, God forbid, just show him this." Did he want tickets to the opera, or a film, or anything? "You need only ask." Also, filing dispatches here was gloriously easy, there was a counter at the Propaganda Ministry, leave your story there and it would be cabled, uncensored, back to your office. "Of course," Martz said, "we will read what you write in the newspapers, and we expect you to be fair. Two sides to every story, right?"

Right.

Clearly, Martz was a man happy in his work. He'd been, he told Weisz, an actor, had spent five years in Hollywood, playing Germans, Frenchmen, any role requiring a Continental accent. Then, on returning to

Germany, his idiomatic English had landed him his present employment. "Mostly for the Americans, Herr Weisz, I must admit it, we want to make life pleasant for them." Eventually, he got down to business, producing from his briefcase a thick dossier of stapled reports. "I've taken the liberty of having this compiled for you," he said. "Facts and figures on Poland. Maybe you'll take a look at it, when you have a moment."

After wiping his fingers on a white linen napkin, Weisz paged through the dossier.

"It's about the corridor we require, through Poland, from Germany to East Prussia. Also the situation in Danzig, getting worse every day, the treatment of the German population there, which is appalling. The Poles are being stubborn, they refuse to compromise, and our side of the story isn't being told. Our concerns are legitimate, nobody can say they aren't, we must be allowed to protect our national interest, no?"

Yes, of course.

"That's all we ask, Herr Weisz, fair play. And we want to help you — any story you want to write, just say the word and we'll supply the data, the appropriate periodicals, a list of sources, and we'll arrange the interviews, excursions, anything you like.

Go out into Germany, go see for yourself what we've accomplished here, with hard work and ingenuity."

The waiter appeared, offering more coffee, a silver pitcher of thick cream, sugar from a silver bowl. From his briefcase, Martz produced one last sheet of paper: a schedule of press conferences, two every day, one at the Propaganda Ministry, the other at the Foreign Ministry. "Now," he said, "let me tell you about the cocktail parties."

Weisz trudged through the daytime hours, hungry for twilight.

Christa managed to come to the hotel almost every afternoon, sometimes at four, when she could, or at least by six. Very long days for Weisz, waiting, daydreaming, thinking of this, or maybe that, some neglected appetizer on the Great Menu, then making plans, detailed plans, for later.

She did the same thing. She didn't say it, but he could tell. Two taps at the door, then Christa, cool and polite, no melodrama at all, only a brief kiss. She would settle in a chair, as though she just happened to be in the neighborhood and had stopped by, and, perhaps, this time, they would merely converse. Then, later, he would find himself led by her imagination to something new, a variation. The gentility of her bearing never changed, but doing what she liked excited her, charged her voice, quickened her hands, and this made his heart pound. Then it was his turn. Nothing new under the sun, of course, but for them it was a very broad sun. One night, von Schirren went away, to a family property up on the Baltic, and Christa spent the night. With leisure, they sat together in the bathtub, her breasts shining wet in the light, and talked about nothing in particular. Then he reached below the water until she closed her eyes, held her lower lip, delicately, between her teeth, and lay back against the porcelain curve.

Work grew harder every day. Weisz was infinitely dutiful, filing away, as Delahanty had suggested, asking press-conference questions of colonels or civil servants. How they hammered away at it: Germany wished only economic progress — just see what's happened at our Pomeranian dairies! — and simple justice, and security, in Europe. Please take note, ladies and gentlemen — it's in our communiqué — of the case of one Hermann Zimmer, a bookkeeper in the city of Danzig, beaten up by Polish thugs in the street before his house while his wife, looking out the window, cried for help. And then they killed his little dog.

Meanwhile, at small restaurants in Berlin neighborhoods, open the menu and find a slip of red paper with black printing: *Juden Unerwünscht.* Jews not welcome here. Weisz saw it in shop windows, taped to barbers' mirrors, tacked to doors. He never got used to it. Great numbers of Jews had joined the Italian Fascist party in the 1920s. Then, in 1938, German pressure on Mussolini had finally prevailed, articles appeared in the papers suggesting that Italians were in reality a Nordic race, and Jews were anathematized. This was new, for Italy, and generally disliked — they weren't like that. Weisz stopped going to the restaurants.

12 March. On Tuesday morning, at eleven-twenty, a telephone call at the Reuters office. "Herr Weisz?" Gerda called from the reception area. "It is for you, a Fräulein Schmidt."

"Hello?"

"Hello, it's me. I need to see you, my love."

"Is something wrong?"

"Oh, a domestic stupidity, but we must talk."

A pause. "I'm sorry," he said.

"It isn't your fault, don't be sorry."

"Where are you? Is there, a bar? A café?"

"I'm up at Eberswalde, something for work."

"Yes . . ."

"There's a park, in the center of the town. Maybe you can take the train, it's, oh, forty-five minutes."

"I can take a taxi."

"*No.* Forgive me, better to take the train. Easier, really, they run all the time, from the Nordbahnhof station."

"Allright. I can leave immediately."

"There's a carnival here, in the park. I'll find you."

"I'll be there."

"I must talk to you, to, to deal with this. Together, maybe it's for the best, I don't know, we'll see."

What was this? It sounded like a lovers' crisis but it was, he sensed, some form of theatre. "Whatever it is, together . . ." he said, playing his part.

"Yes, I know. I feel the same."

"I'm on my way."

"Hurry, my love, I can't wait to see you."

He was in Eberswalde by one-thirty. In the park, several carnival rides had been set up and calliope music played from a staticky

144

loudspeaker. He wandered over to the merry-go-round and stood there, hands in pockets, until, five minutes later, she appeared, having been watching, apparently, from some vantage point. The day was icy, with a sharp wind, and she wore a beret and a trim gray ankle-length coat with a high collar buttoned at the throat. On a long lead she held two whippets, with wide leather collars on their slim necks.

She kissed him on the cheek. "Sorry to do this to you."

"What is it? Von Schirren?"

"No, nothing like that. The phones aren't safe, so this had to be a, a rendezvous."

"Oh." He was relieved, then not.

"There's somebody I want you to meet. Just for a moment. You don't need to know a name."

"Allright." His eyes wandered, looking for surveillance.

"Don't be furtive," she said. "We're just star-crossed lovers."

She took his arm and they walked, the dogs straining at their lead.

"They're beautiful," he said. They were: fawn-colored, lean and smooth, with tucked bellies and strong chests, built for speed.

"Hortense and Magda," she said fondly. "I'm coming from home," she explained. "I threw them in the car and said I was taking them out for a run." One of the dogs looked over her shoulder when she heard the word *run.*

They walked past the merry-go-round to a ride with a brightly painted sign above the ticket booth: THE LANDT STUNTER. LEARN TO DIVE-BOMB! Attached to a heavy steel centerpiece was a pole bearing a miniature airplane, a black Maltese cross on its fuselage, which flew in a circle, sweeping close to the grass, rising twenty feet into the air, then plunging back toward the ground. A young boy, maybe ten years old, was flying the plane. He sat in the open cockpit, his face intense with concentration, his hands white as he clutched the pilot's controls. When the plane dove, toy guns on the wings rattled and the mouths of the barrels sparkled like Roman candles. A long line of boys, eyes rapt with envy, some in *Hitlerjugend* uniforms, some holding their mothers' hands, waited for their turn to fly, watching the plane as it fired its machine guns, then came around for another attack.

A middle-aged man in a brown overcoat and hat moved slowly through the crowd. "He's here," Christa said. He had the face, Weisz thought, of an intellectual — deeply lined, with deep-set eyes; a face that had read too much, and brooded about what it

146

read. He nodded to Christa, who said, "This is my friend. From Paris."

"Good afternoon."

Weisz returned the greeting.

"You are the journalist?"

"Yes, that's right."

"Christa suggests you might help us."

"If I can."

"I have an envelope in my pocket. In a minute, the three of us will walk away from the crowd, and, as we approach the trees, I'm going to hand it to you."

They watched the ride, then began to walk, Christa leaning back against the pull of the dogs.

"Christa tells me you're Italian," he said.

"I am, yes."

"This information concerns Italy, Germany and Italy. We cannot mail it, because our mail is read by the security forces, but we believe it should be made known to the public. Perhaps by a French newspaper, though we doubt they will publish it, or by a newspaper of the Italian resistance. Do you know such people?"

"Yes, I know them."

"And will you take it?"

"How do you come to have it?"

"One of our friends copied it, from documents in the finance office of the Interior

Ministry. It is a list of German agents, operating in Italy with Italian consent. There are people, in Berlin, who support our work, and they would want to see it, but this information does not directly concern them, so it should be in the hands of people who understand that it must be revealed, not just filed."

"In Paris, these newspapers are issued by people of various factions, do you have a preference?"

"No, we don't care about that, though centrist parties are more likely to be believed."

"That's true," Weisz said. "The extreme left is known to improvise."

Christa let the dogs take her around in a circle, so that she faced the other way. "It's good now," she said.

The man reached in his pocket and handed Weisz an envelope.

Weisz waited until he was back at the office, then made sure he was not observed as he opened the envelope. Inside, he found six pages, single-spaced, a list of names, typed on thin paper, like airmail stationery, on a machine that used a German font. The names were principally, though not entirely, German, numbered from R100 to V718, thus six hundred and nineteen entries, preceded by various letters, *R, M, T,* and *N* predominant, with a scattering of several others. Each name was followed by a location, offices or associations, in a specific city — *R* for Rome, *M* for Milan, *T* for Turin, *N* for Naples, and so on — and a payment in Italian lire. The heading said, "Disbursements — January, 1939." The copying had been done hastily, he thought, mistakes x-ed over, the correct letter or number handwritten above the entry.

Agents, the man in the park had called them. That covered a lot of ground. Were they spies? Weisz thought not; the names might be aliases, but they weren't code names — CURATE, LEOPARD — and, studying the locations, he found no armament factories, no naval or army bases, no laboratories or engineering firms. What he did find was a surveillance organization, built into the Italian Ministry of the Interior, its *Direzione della Pubblica Sicurezza,* Department of Public Security, and, in turn, its branches of national police, called *Questura,* situated in every Italian town and city. In addition, these agents were attached to the offices of the *Auslandsorganisation* and *Arbeitsfront* in various cities, the former for German professionals and businessmen, the latter for salaried employees working in Italy.

What were they doing? Watching Germans abroad, from an official perspective, at the *Pubblica Sicurezza* in Rome and the *Questura,* and from a clandestine perspective, at the associations — in other words, managing dossiers or going to dinner parties. And a German security force, stationed in Italy, with Italian consent, would gain real command of the language, and a thorough understanding of the structures of national administration. This had begun — and the *giellisti* in Paris knew it — in 1936, with the installation of a German racial commission at the Italian Ministry of the Interior, sent down by Nazi officials to "help" Italy organize anti-Jewish operations. Now it had grown, from a dozen to six hundred, a force in place if, someday, Germany found it necessary to occupy its former ally. It occurred to Weisz that this organization, watching for disloyalty among Germans abroad, could also watch anti-Nazi Italians, as well as any other — British, American — foreign nationals resident in Italy.

Reading the list, his thumb running down the margin, he wondered who these people were. G455, A. M. Kruger, at the *Auslandsorganisation* in Genoa. An avid party member? Ambitious? His job to make friends and report on them? *Do I,* Weisz thought, *know anyone who might do something like that?* Or J. H. Horst, R140, at the *Pubblica Sicurezza* headquarters in Rome. A Gestapo official? Following orders? Why, Weisz asked himself, was it hard for him to believe in the existence of such people? How did they turn into . . .

"Herr Weisz? It is Herr Doktor Martz, sir. An urgent call for you."

Weisz jumped, Gerda was standing in the doorway, had apparently called out to him and received no response. Had she seen the list? Certainly she had, and it was all Weisz could do not to clap his hand over it like a kid in school.

Amateur! Angry with himself, he thanked Gerda and picked up the receiver. The afternoon press conference at the Foreign Ministry had been moved to four o'clock. Significant developments, important news, Herr Weisz was urged to attend.

The press conference was addressed by the mighty von Ribbentrop himself. A former champagne salesman, he had, as foreign minister, inflated himself to an astonishing stature, his face beaming with pomposity and *amour propre.* He was, however, on 12

March, visibly annoyed, his face faintly red, the sheaf of papers in his hand tapped forcefully against the top of the lectern. Units of the Czech army had marched into Bratislava, deposed the fascist priest, Father Tiso, as premier of Slovakia, and dismissed the cabinet. Martial law had been declared. Von Ribbentrop's demeanor said what his words didn't: *How dare they?*

Weisz made furious notes, and rushed to cable as the conference ended. REUTERS PARIS MARCH TWELVE DATE BERLIN WEISZ VON RIBBENTROP THREATENS REPRISAL AGAINST CZECHS FOR DEPOSING FATHER TISO AS PREMIER SLOVAKIA AND DECLARING MARTIAL LAW END. He then hurried to the office and wrote the dispatch, while Gerda obtained a line from the international operator and held it open, chatting with her counterpart in Paris.

By the time he was done dictating, it was after six. He returned to the Adlon, stripped off his sweaty clothes, and had a quick bath. Christa arrived at seven-twenty. "I was here earlier," she said, "but they told me at the desk that you were away."

"Sorry, I was. The Czechs have thrown the Nazis out of Slovakia."

"Yes, I heard it on the radio. What will happen now?"

"Germany sends troops, France and En-

152

gland declare war. I am interned, to spend the next ten years reading Tolstoy and playing bridge."

"You, play bridge?"

"I'll learn."

"I thought you were angry."

He sighed. "No, I'm not angry."

Her mouth was set hard, her look determined, close to defiant. "I would hope not." Clearly, she'd spent some time, wherever she'd gone earlier, preparing to answer his anger with her own, and she wasn't quite ready to give that up. "Would you prefer that I go away?"

"Christa."

"Would you?"

"*No.* I want you to stay. Please."

She sat on the edge of a chaise longue angled into a corner. "I asked you to help us because you were here. And because I thought you would. Would want to."

"That's true. I've looked at the papers, they're important."

"And I suspect, my sweet, that you, in Paris, are no angel."

He laughed. "Well, maybe a fallen angel, but Paris isn't Berlin, not yet it isn't, and I don't talk about it because it's better not to. No? Makes sense?"

"Yes, I suppose it does."

"It does, believe me."

She relaxed, made a sour face, and shook her head. *I can scarcely believe this world we live in.*

He knew what she meant. "For me it's the same, love." The sentence in German, except for the last word, *carissima.*

"What did you think of my friend?"

He paused, then said, "An idealist, certainly."

"A saint."

"Close to it. Doing what he believes in."

"It's only the very best, now, who will do anything. Here, in this, monstrosity."

"I only worry, well, it's that the lives of the saints usually end in martyrdom. And I care for you, Christa. And more."

"Yes," she said. "I know." Then, softly: "Also for me, more."

"And I think I should mention that hotel rooms, where journalists stay, are sometimes . . ." He cupped his hand around his ear. "Yes?"

By this, she was slightly ruffled. "I hadn't thought of that," she said.

"Nor did I, not immediately."

For a time, they were silent. Neither one of them looked at a watch, but Christa said, "Whatever else goes on with this room, it is also very warm." She stood and took off her jacket and skirt, then her shirt, stockings, and garter belt, and folded them over the top of the chaise longue. Usually, she wore expensive cotton underwear, white or ivory, and soft to the touch, but tonight she was in plum-colored silk, the bra with a lace trim, the panties low at the waist, high at the hip, and tight, a style called, Véronique had once told him, French-cut. They were new, he suspected, and bought for him, maybe bought that afternoon.

"Very appealing," he said, a certain look in his eyes.

"You like them?" She turned this way and that.

"Very much," he said.

She walked over to the desk, opened her purse, and took out a cigarette. Her walk was as always, like her, sensible and straight-forward, simply a way to get from here to there, but, even so, the plum-colored pant-ies made a difference, and maybe it took her a little longer, at that moment, to go from here to there. As she returned to the chaise longue, Weisz left his chair and, ashtray in hand, settled on the bed. "Come sit with me," he said.

"I like it over here," she said. "On this furniture, one can be languid." She lay back, crossed her ankles, cupped an elbow with one hand, while the other, with the cigarette, was held by her ear — a movie siren's pose. "But perhaps," she said, with a voice and smile that matched the pose, "you'll join me."

The following day, 13 March, the Czecho-slovakian situation deteriorated. Father Tiso had been summoned to Berlin, to meet personally with Hitler, and Slovakia, by noon, was on the way to declaring itself independent. Thus the nation, pasted to-gether at Versailles, then torn apart at Mu-nich, was in its final hours. At the Reuters bureau, Carlo Weisz was fully engaged — the telephones never stopped ringing, and the teleprinter bell chimed as it issued com-muniqués from the Reich ministries. Central Europe was, once again, about to explode.

In the middle of it, Gerda, with a certain knowing tenderness, called out, "Herr Weisz, it is Fräulein Schmidt." The conver-sation with Christa was difficult, darkened by approaching separation. Sunday, the seventeenth, would be his last day in Berlin, Eric Wolf was due back in the office on Monday, and Weisz was expected in Paris. This meant that Friday, the fifteenth, would be the last time they could be together.

"I can see you this afternoon," she said.

"Tomorrow I cannot, and Friday, I don't know, I don't want to think about it, maybe we can meet, but I don't want, I don't want to say goodby. Carlo? Hello? Are you there?"

"Yes, I'm here. The lines have been bad all day," he said. Then: "We'll meet at four, can you be there at four?"

She agreed.

Weisz left the office at three-thirty. Outside, the shadow of war lay over the city — people walked quickly, faces closed, eyes down, while *Wehrmacht* staff cars sped by, and Grosser Mercedes, flying pennants on their front bumpers, were lined up at the entry to the Adlon. Passing knots of guests in the lobby, he twice heard the word *again.* And, a few minutes later, the shadow was in his room. "Now it's coming," Christa said.

"I think so." They were sitting side by side on the edge of the bed. "Christa," he said.

"Yes?"

"When I leave, on Sunday, I want you to come with me. Take whatever you can, bring the dogs — they have dogs in Paris — and meet me at the ten-forty express, on the platform by the first-class *wagons-lits.*"

"I can't," she said. "Not now. I can't leave." She looked around the room, as though someone were hiding there, as though there might be something she could

157

see. "It isn't von Schirren," she said. "It's my friends, I cannot just, abandon them." Her eyes met his, making sure he understood her. "They need me."

Weisz hesitated, then said, "Forgive me, Christa, but, what you are doing, you and your friends, will it really change anything?"

"Who can say? But what I do know is that if I don't do something, it will change me."

He started to counter, then saw it wouldn't matter, she would not be persuaded. The more danger threatened, he realized, the less she would run from it. "Allright," he said, giving in, "we'll meet on Friday."

"Yes," she said, "but not to say goodby. To make plans. Because I will come to Paris, if you want me to. A few months, maybe, it's only a matter of time — it can't go on like this."

Weisz nodded. Of course. It couldn't. "I don't like saying this, but if, for some reason, I'm not here on Friday, stop at the desk. I'll leave a letter for you."

"You think you won't be here?"

"It's possible. If something important happens, they could send me anywhere."

There was no more to say. She leaned against him, took his hand, and held it.

■ ■ ■ ■

The morning of the fourteenth, the temperature dropped to ten degrees and it started to snow, a bad spring snow, thick and heavy. Perhaps that made a difference, perhaps it cooled tempers, in a city muffled and silent. The phones rang only now and then — tipsters calling in to report the same rumor: diplomats would defuse the crisis — and the teleprinter was quiet. Cables from the London office demanded news, but the only news was in London, where, late in the morning, Chamberlain issued a statement: when Britain and France had committed to protect Czechoslovakia from aggression, they'd meant *military* aggression, and this crisis was diplomatic. Weisz got back to the hotel after seven, tired, and alone.

At four-thirty in the morning, the telephone rang. Weisz rolled out of bed, staggered to the desk, and picked up the receiver. "Yes?"

The connection was terrible. Through crackling static, Delahanty's voice was just barely audible. "Hello, Carlo, it's me. How is it there?"

"It's snowing. Hard."

"Start packing, laddie. We've heard that

German troops are leaving their barracks in the Sudetenland. Which means that Hitler's done talking to the Czechs, and that puts you on the first train to Prague. Our man in the Prague office is down in Slovakia — independent Slovakia, this morning — where they've closed the border. Now, I'm looking at a timetable, and there's a train at five-twenty-five. We've cabled the Prague office, they're expecting you, and there's a room for you at the Zlata Husa. Anything else you need?"

"No, I'm on my way."

"Call or cable, when you get there."

Weisz went into the bathroom, turned on the cold water, and splashed his face. How did Delahanty, in Paris, know about German troop movements? Well, he had his sources. Very good sources. Dark sources, perhaps. Weisz packed quickly, lit a cigarette, then, from his overcoat pocket, he took the list he'd received from Christa's friend, thought for a moment, and hunted through his briefcase until he found a twelve-page press release — "Steel Production in the Saar Valley, 1936–1939." He carefully removed the staple, inserted the list of names between pages ten and eleven, refixed the staple, then slid the revised document into the middle of a sheaf of similar papers.

Short of calling on a clandestine tailor at four in the morning, that was the best he could do.

Then, on a sheet of Adlon stationery, he wrote: *My love, they've sent me to Prague, and I'll likely return to Paris when that's done. I'll write you from there, I'll wait for you there. I love you, Carlo.*

He put the letter in an envelope, addressed it *Frau von S.,* sealed it, and left it at the desk when he checked out.

On the 5:25 express, Berlin/Dresden/Prague, Weisz joined two other journalists in a first-class compartment: Simard, a sharply dressed little weasel from Havas, the French wire service, and Ian Hamilton, in a fur hat with flaps, from the *Times* of London. "I guess you've heard what I've heard," Weisz said, stowing his valise above the plush seat.

"No luck at all, the sorry bastards," Hamilton said. "Adolf will have them now."

Simard shrugged. "Yes, the poor Czechs, but they have Paris and London to thank for this."

They settled in for the four-hour trip — at least that, maybe more with the snow. Simard slept, Hamilton read the *Deutsche*

Allgemeine Zeitung. "Article on Italy today," he said to Weisz. "Have you seen it?"

"No. What's it about?"

"The state of Italian politics, struggle against the antifascist forces. Which are all Bolshevik-influenced, they'd have you believe."

Weisz shrugged, nothing new there.

Hamilton scanned the page, then read, " '. . . thwarted by the patriotic forces of the OVRA . . .' Tell me, Weisz, what does that stand for? You see it now and again, but mostly they just use the initials."

"It's said to mean *Organizzazione di Vigilanza e Repressione dell' Antifascismo,* which would be the Organization for the Vigilant Repression of Antifascism, but there's another version. I've heard that it comes from a memo Mussolini wrote, where he said he wanted a national police organization, with tentacles that would reach into Italian life like a *piovra,* which is a mythical giant octopus. But the word was mistyped as *ovra,* and Mussolini liked the sound of it, thought it was frightening, so OVRA became the official name."

"Really," Hamilton said. "That's worth knowing." He took out a pad and pen and wrote down the story. "Watch out, it's the *piovra!*"

Weisz's grin was tart. "Not so funny, in real life," he said.

"No, I suppose it isn't. Still, it's hard to take the man seriously."

"Yes, I know," Weisz said. Mussolini, the comic buffoon, a widely held view, but what he'd done wasn't comic at all.

Hamilton gave up on the German paper. "Care for a look?"

"No thanks."

Hamilton reached into his briefcase and opened to a dog-eared page in Raymond Chandler's *The Big Sleep*. "Better for train trips," he said.

Weisz looked out the window, hypnotized by the falling snow, thinking mostly about Christa, about her coming to Paris. Then he got out the Malraux novel and started reading, but, three or four pages later, he dozed off.

It was Hamilton's voice that woke him. "Well, well," he said, "look who's here." The railroad tracks, following the river Elbe, now ran by the road, where, dimly visible through the driving snow, a *Wehrmacht* column was headed south, toward Prague. Truckloads of infantry huddled under canvas tops, skidding motorcycles, ambulances, occasional staff cars. The three journalists watched in silence, then, after a

163

few minutes, went back to conversation, but the column never ended, and, an hour later, when the track crossed to the other side of the river, it was still moving slowly down the snow-covered road. At the next station, the express shifted over to a siding so a military train could go past. Pulled by two locomotives, endless flatcars rolled past, carrying artillery pieces and tanks, their long cannons poking out from beneath tied-down tarpaulins.

"Just like *la dernière*," Simard said — "the last one," as the French called it.

"And the next," Hamilton said. "And the one after that."

And the one in Spain, Weisz thought. And, again, he would write about it. He watched the train until it ended, with a caboose, which had a machine-gun emplacement on its roof; the protective rim of sandbags and the helmets of the gunners white with snow.

At the next scheduled stop, the Czech town of Kralupy, the train stood in the station for a long time, its locomotive emitting an occasional snort of steam. Eventually, as Hamilton rose "to see what's going on," the first-class conductor appeared at the door of their compartment. "Gentlemen, I beg your pardon, but the train cannot proceed."

"Why not?" Weisz said.

"We are not informed," the conductor said. "We regret the inconvenience, gentlemen, perhaps later in the day, we may continue."

"Is it the snow?" Hamilton said.

"Please," the conductor said. "We do regret the inconvenience."

"Well then," Hamilton said philosophically, "damn it all to bloody hell." He stood and yanked his valise off the luggage rack. "Where *is* beastly Prague?"

"About twenty miles from here," Weisz said.

They left the train and trudged across the platform, to the station café on the other side of the street. There, the proprietor made a telephone call, which produced, twenty minutes later, the Kralupy taxicab and its sullen giant of a driver. "Prague!" he said. "Prague?" How dare they call him away from hearth and home in such weather.

Weisz began to peel reichsmarks from the roll in his pocket.

"I'll take part of it," Hamilton said quietly, reading the driver's eyes.

"I can only help a little," Simard said. "At Havas, they . . . ."

Weisz and Hamilton waved him off, they

didn't care, were of a traveling class that mythically availed itself of oxcarts or elephants or sedan chairs with native bearers, so the overpriced Kralupy taxi barely deserved comment.

The taxi was a Tatra, with long, sloping rear end and bulbous body, and an extra headlight, like a cyclops's eye, between the usual two. Weisz and Simard sat in the spacious backseat, while Hamilton sat next to the driver. Who grumbled continually as he squinted into the snow, and pushed hard against the wheel as they churned through the higher drifts, internal combustion being, to him, only part of the locomotion process. The invading Germans had closed the road to Prague, as well as the railway, and, at one point, the taxi was flagged down by a *Wehrmacht* traffic-control unit — two motorcycles with sidecars that blocked the way. But a determined display of red press cards did the trick and they were waved through, with a casual stiff-armed salute and an amiable "*Heil* Hitler."

"So then, Prague, here we are," the driver said, stopping the taxi on some nameless road on the outskirts of the city. Weisz started to argue, in Slovenian, distant from Czech but in the same general family.

"But I don't know this place," the driver said.

"Go that way!" Hamilton said in German, waving generally south.

"Are you German?" the driver said.

"No, British."

From the look on the driver's face, that was worse. But he slammed the Tatra into gear and drove on. "We're going to Wenceslas Square," Weisz said, "in the old city." Hamilton was also staying at the Zlata Husa — the Golden Goose — while Simard was at the Ambassador. Once more, as they crossed a bridge over the Vltava, they were stopped by German traffic police, and got through by using their press cards. In the central districts, south of the river, there was hardly a soul to be seen — when your country is being invaded, better to stay home. As the taxi entered the old city, and began to work its way through the ancient winding streets, Simard called out, "We just passed Blkova, we're almost there." He had a *Guide Bleu,* open to a map, on his knees.

As the driver shifted down to first gear, trying to turn a corner never meant for automobiles, a boy ran in front of the taxi and waved his arms. Weisz's impression was *student* — maybe eighteen, with tousled fair hair and a battered wool jacket. The driver swore, and the car stalled as he slammed on the brakes. Then the back door flew open and another boy, similar to the first, dove headfirst onto the floor at Weisz's feet. He was breathing hard, and laughing, and bunched in his hand was a swastika flag.

The boy in front of the taxi ran around the car and joined his friend on the floor. His face was bright red. "Go ahead! Go, now. Hurry!" he shouted. The driver, muttering and cursing, started the taxi, but, as they began to move, they were hit from behind. Weisz, knocked halfway off the seat, turned around to see, through the snow-dappled rear window, a black Opel, which had been unable to stop on the slippery cobbles and rammed them, its front grille spewing steam.

The driver reached for the ignition key, but Weisz yelled, "Don't stop." He didn't. The back wheels slewed sideways, then the car gained traction and drove away. Behind them, two men in overcoats climbed out of the Opel and started to run, shouting in German, "Halt! Police!"

"What police?" Hamilton said, watching from the front seat. "Gestapo?"

Suddenly, a man in a black leather coat ran out of an alley, a Luger pistol in hand. Everybody ducked, a hole appeared in the windshield, and another round hit the back door panel. The boy in the wool jacket yelled, "Get out of here," and the driver stepped on the gas. The man with the gun had run in front of the taxi, now he tried to leap out of the way, slipped, and fell. There was a bump beneath the wheels, accompanied by a furious squawk, then the taxi sideswiped a wall — metal grinding on stone — and, with the driver hauling maniacally at the wheel, slid around a corner, wheels spinning, and swerved crazily down the street.

Just before they turned, Weisz had seen the man with the pistol, obviously in pain, trying to crawl away. "I think we ran over his foot," he said.

"Serves him right," Hamilton said. Then, to the boys on the floor, in German: "Who are you?" A reporter's question, Weisz heard it in his voice.

"Never mind that," the boy in the wool jacket said, now leaning against the door. "We took their fucking flag."

"You're students?"

The two looked at each other. Finally, the one in the wool jacket said, "Yes. We were."

Merde," Simard said, mildly irritated, as though he'd lost a button. Gingerly, he raised the cuff of his trouser leg, to reveal a red gash that pulsed blood down his shin and into his sock. "I am shot," he said, barely able to believe it. He took a handkerchief from the breast pocket of his jacket and dabbed the wound. "Don't dab at it," Hamilton said. "Press it."

"Don't tell me what to do," Simard said. "I've been shot before."

"So have I," Hamilton said.

"Use pressure," Weisz said. "To stop bleeding." He found his own handkerchief, held the ends, and twirled it around to make a tourniquet.

"I'll do it," Simard said, taking the handkerchief. His face was very pale, Weisz thought he might be in shock.

In the front seat, as the taxi hurtled down a broad, empty street, the driver turned around to see what was going on in back. He started to speak, then didn't, and held a hand to his forehead. Of course his head ached — his windshield had a bullet hole, his doors were scraped, trunk dented, and, now, blood on the upholstery. Behind them, in the distance, the high and low notes of a siren.

The student holding the flag got to his knees and peered out the window. "You had better hide your taxi," he said to the driver.

"*Hide* it? Under the bed?"

"Pavel, maybe," the other student said.

His friend said, "Yes, of course." Then, to the driver: "A friend of ours lives in a building with a stable in back, we can hide it there. You can't drive around like this."

The driver blew out his breath in a great sigh. "A stable? With horses?"

"Go two more streets, then slow down and turn right. It's a narrow alley, but a car goes through."

"What's going on?" Hamilton said.

"The car must be hidden," Weisz said. "Simard, do you want to go to a hospital?"

"This *morning?* No, a private doctor, the hotel will know."

Weisz took the *Guide Bleu* and looked at a street sign. "Can you walk?"

Simard made a face, then nodded — he could if he had to.

"Where we turn, we can get out. It's a short walk to the hotels."

From a window in a baroque parlor at the Zlata Husa, Carlo Weisz watched the *Wehrmacht* parade up the broad boulevard in front of the hotel, red-and-black swastika flags stark against the white snowfall. Later in the day, the journalists gathered in the bar and traded news. The president, Emil Hacha, aged and in ill health, had been

171

summoned to Berlin, where Hitler and Goering had screamed at him for hours, swearing they would bomb the city of Prague into ashes, until the old man fainted. Hitler feared they'd killed him, the story went, but he was revived, and forced to sign papers that made it all legitimate — *diplomatic crisis resolved!* The army stayed in its barracks, because the Czech defenses, up north in the Sudetenland, had been given away at Munich. Meanwhile, in newspapers across the Continent, the snowstorm had been named "God's Judgment."

In Berlin, late in the afternoon, Christa von Schirren telephoned the Reuters bureau. News on the radio foretold that Weisz would not be at the Adlon that day, but she wanted to make sure. The secretary was not unkind. No, Herr Weisz could not come to the telephone, he had left the city. Still, there was to have been a letter, and she fretted about that, finally going to the Adlon and asking if a message had been left for her. At the front desk, the assistant manager seemed troubled, and did not answer immediately, as though, despite the many ways, so native to his vocation, of saying things without saying them, there were, nowadays, things that could not be said at all. "I am sorry, madam, but there is no message."

No, she thought, *he would not do that.* It was, something else.

In Prague, Weisz wrote out his cable in block letters. TODAY, THE ANCIENT CITY OF PRAGUE CAME UNDER GERMAN OCCUPATION, AND RESISTANCE BEGAN. IN THE OLD TOWN DISTRICT, TWO STUDENTS. . . .

And the cable back said: GOOD WORK SEND MORE DELAHANTY END.

18 March, near the city of Tarbes, southwestern France.

Late in the morning, S. Kolb peered out at an arid countryside, rocks and brush, and wiped the beads of sweat from his brow. The man once said to have "the balls of a gorilla" sat, at that moment, straight as a stick, rigid with fear. Yes, he could live the subterranean life, hunted by police and secret agents, and yes, he could survive amid the tenements and back alleys of perilous cities, but now he was engaged in the one task that squeezed his heart with terror: he was driving an automobile.

Worse, a beautiful, valuable automobile, hired at a garage on the edge of Tarbes. "So very much money," the *garagiste* had said in a melancholy voice, one hand resting on the car's polished hood. "I must accept it. But, monsieur, I beg of you, you will be careful with it. Please."

Kolb tried. Hurtling along at twenty miles an hour, hands white on the steering wheel, one twitch of his tired foot producing a horrible roar and a breathtaking burst of speed. Suddenly, from behind, the thunderous blast of a Klaxon horn. Kolb glanced in the rearview mirror, where a monster of a car filled the frame; close, closer still, its giant chrome grille leering at him. Kolb jerked the wheel over hard and jammed his foot onto the brake pedal, stopping at a peculiar angle on the side of the road. As the tormentor sped past, it issued a second blast on its horn. *Learn to drive, you worm!*

An hour later, Kolb found the village south of Toulouse. From here, he needed directions. He'd been told that the elusive Colonel Ferrara had slipped across the Spanish border into France, where, like thousands of other refugees, he'd been interned. The French found the expression *concentration camp* distasteful so, to them, a guarded barbed-wire enclosure was an *assembly center.* And that was what Kolb called it, first at the village *boulangerie.* No, never heard of such a place. Oh? Well, anyhow, he would have one of those well-done *baguettes.* Mmm, better make it two — no, three. Next he stopped at the *crémerie.* A slab of that hard, yellow cheese, *s'il vous plaît.* And that round one, goat? No, ewe. He'd have that, as well. Oh, and by the way . . . But, in answer, only an eloquent shrug, nothing like that here. At the grocery, after the purchase of two bottles of red wine filled from a spout in a wood cask, the same story. Finally, at the *tabac,* the woman behind the counter looked away and shook her head, but when Kolb stepped outside, a young woman, likely the daughter, followed him and drew a map on a scrap of paper. As Kolb walked back toward the car he heard, from within the store, the beginning of a good family fight.

Under way once again, Kolb tried to follow the map. But these weren't roads, these were *paths,* sand bordered by brush. Was this the left? No, it ended suddenly, at a rock wall. So then, back up, the car whining, unhappy, the rocks hurt its handsome tires. In time, after a frightful hour, he found it. High barbed wire, Senegalese guards, dozens of men shuffling slowly to the wire to see who might be coming in the big automobile.

Kolb talked his way past the gate and

found an office with a commandant, a French colonial officer with a drunk's purplish nose and bloodshot eyes, glaring suspiciously from the other side of a plank desk. Who consulted a well-thumbed type-written list and, finally, said yes, we have this individual here, what do you want with him? *Credit the SIS,* Kolb thought. Someone had descended deep into the catacombs of the French bureaucracy and managed, miraculously, to find the single bone he needed.

A family tragedy, Kolb explained. His wife's brother, that foolish dreamer, had gone off to fight in Spain and now found himself interned. What was to be done? This poor fellow was needed back in Italy to run the family business, a successful business, a wine brokerage in Naples. And, worse yet, the wife was pregnant, and sickly. How she, how they all, needed him! Of course there were expenses, that was well understood, his lodging, and food, and care, so generously supplied by the camp administration, had to be paid for, and they would see to that. A fat envelope was produced and laid on the desk. The bloodshot eyes widened, and the envelope was opened, revealing a thick wad of hundred-franc notes — a *lot* of money. Kolb, at his most diffident, said he hoped it would be sufficient.

As the envelope disappeared into a pocket, the commandant said, "Shall I have him brought here?" Kolb said he'd prefer to go and look for him, and a sergeant was summoned. It took a long time to find Ferrara — the camp stretched out endlessly, a flat wasteland of sand and rock, open to a cutting wind. There were no women to be seen, evidently they were held elsewhere. The internees were of every age, hollow-cheeked — obviously underfed, unshaven, their clothes in tatters. Some wore blankets, against the cold, some stood in groups, others sat on the ground, playing cards, using torn strips of newspaper marked with pencil. Behind one of the barracks, a sagging net, tied to two poles, hung half on the ground. Maybe they'd had a volleyball, Kolb thought, months earlier, when they were first brought here.

Wandering past the groups of internees, Kolb heard mostly Spanish, but also German, Serbo-Croatian, and Hungarian. From time to time, one of the men would ask for a cigarette, and Kolb gave away what he'd bought at the *tabac,* then simply held his open hands out. *Sorry, no more.* The sergeant was persistent. "Have you seen the man called Ferrara? An Italian?" Thus, at last he was found, sitting with a friend, leaning against the wall of a barracks. Kolb thanked the sergeant, who saluted, then headed back toward the office.

Ferrara was dressed as a civilian — a soiled jacket and trousers with ragged cuffs — his hair and beard chopped off, as though he'd done the cutting himself. But, nonetheless, he was clearly *somebody,* stood out from the crowd — curving scar, sharp cheekbones, eyes hooded. Kolb had been told to expect black gloves, but Ferrara's hands were bare, the left one disfigured by the ridged skin, pink and shiny, of a badly healed burn. "Colonel Ferrara," Kolb said, and, in French, wished him good morning.

Both men stared at him, then Ferrara said, "And you are?" His French was very slow, but correct.

"I'm called Kolb."

Ferrara waited for more. *And so?*

"I wonder if we could talk for a moment. Just the two of us."

Ferarra said something to his friend in fast Italian, then stood up.

They walked together, past clusters of men, who glanced at Kolb, then looked away. When they were alone, Ferrara turned, faced Kolb, and said, "First of all, Monsieur *Kolb,* you can tell me who sent you here."

178

"Friends of yours, in Paris."

"I have no friends in Paris."

"Carlo Weisz, the Reuters journalist, considers himself your friend."

For a time, Ferrara thought about it. "Well, maybe," he said.

"I've arranged your release," Kolb said. "You can come back to Paris with me, if you like."

"You work for Reuters?"

"Sometimes. My job is to find people."

"A confidential agent."

"Something like that."

After a moment, Ferrara said, "Paris." Then: "Perhaps by way of Italy." His smile was ice cold.

"No, it isn't that," Kolb said. "There'd be three or four of us, if it was. There's just me. From here we go to Tarbes, then to Paris by train. I have a car, outside the gate, you can drive it if you want."

"You said 'arranged,' what did that mean?"

"Money, Colonel."

"Reuters paid for this?"

"No, Weisz and his friends. Emigrés."

"Why would they do that?"

"For politics. They want you to tell your story, they want you to be a hero against the fascists."

Ferrara didn't quite laugh, but he stopped walking and met Kolb's eyes. "You're serious, aren't you."

"I am. And so are they. They've found you a place to stay, in Paris. What kind of papers do you have?"

"An Italian passport," Ferrara said, the irony still in his voice.

"Good. So then, let's be going, these things work better if you move quickly."

Ferrara shook his head. Here was a sudden turn of fate, yes, but what sort of fate? So, stay? Go? Finally, he said, "Allright, yes, why not."

As they walked back toward the barracks, Ferrara turned and gestured to his friend, who'd been following them, and the two men spoke for a time, the friend staring at Kolb as though to memorize him. Ferrara, in the stream of Italian, mentioned Kolb's name, and his friend repeated it. Then Ferrara went into the barracks and emerged with a bundle of clothing, tied with a string. "It's long past being worn," he said, "but it does for a pillow." When they reached the car, Kolb offered him the food he'd bought. Ferrara gathered up almost all of it, except for half a bread, said, "I'll just be a minute," and walked back through the gate.

■ ■ ■ ■

As it happened, Ferrara did drive the automobile, after he got a taste of Kolb behind the wheel, thus it took only twenty minutes to reach the village, and then, an hour later, they left the car at the garage and took a taxi into Tarbes. Near the station, they found a haberdashery, where Ferrara selected a suit, shirt, underwear, everything but shoes — his army boots had survived well in the camp — and Kolb paid for it. As Ferrara changed, in the back of the store, the owner said, "He was in the camp, I imagine, they often come here, if they're lucky enough to get out." After a moment, he said, "A disgrace, for France."

By late afternoon, they were on the train to Paris. In the last light of day, the arid south gave way slowly to patches of snow on plowed fields, to the soft hill country of the Limousin — pollarded trees lining little roads that wound away into the distance. *Invitations,* Kolb thought. They spoke, now and again, about the times they lived in. Ferrara explained that he'd learned French in the camp, to pass the empty hours, and for his new life as an émigré — if the government let him stay. He'd been in Paris

181

once before, years earlier, but Kolb could tell from his voice that he remembered it and that now, for him, it meant refuge. He was, at times, still suspicious of Kolb, but then, this was not unusual. Somehow, Kolb's work lingered in his presence, the cast shadow of a secret life, and could, however faintly, be apprehended. "Have you really," Ferrara said, "been sent by the — how to say, what we call the *fuorusciti?*" Which meant — and it took both of them a few minutes to figure out the words — "those who have fled," the Italian émigrés' preferred description of themselves.

"Yes. They know all about you, of course." Surely they did, so at least that much was true, though everything else that Kolb had said was pure lies. "And that's what they want, your story." *Anyhow, that's what we want.*

But let's not concern ourselves with such things, Kolb thought, there would be plenty of time, later on, for the truth, better just then to watch the winter valleys, in their faded colors, as they drifted by to the rhythm of the wheels on the track.

It was just breaking dawn when they reached Paris, red streaks of light in the eastern sky, the street sweepers, old women, mostly, at work with twig brooms and water trucks. At the Gare de Lyon, Kolb found a taxi, which took them up to the Sixth Arrondissement and the Hotel Tournon, on the street of the same name.

The SIS had likely thought a long time, Kolb suspected, about where to put Ferrara. In superb accommodations? Overawe their newest pawn? Knock him senseless with luxury? With war coming, the treasury had perhaps opened its fist a little, but the Secret Intelligence Service had been starved all through the thirties, and they'd had to think hard about money — only Hitler could really open the bank, and, for the moment, though he'd snatched Czechoslovakia, it didn't really matter all *that* much. Therefore, the Hotel Tournon — *get him a decent room, Harry, nothing too grand.* And the neighborhood was also, for their purposes, rather convenient, because Pawn Two lived there, and would be able to walk to work. Make it easy, keep them both happy, life went better that way.

Still, SIS rich or poor, the night clerk had been well greased. She rose from her couch in the lobby when Kolb hammered on the door, then appeared, in frightful housedress, wild auburn hair, and magnificent breath, to let them in. *"Ah, mais oui! Le nouveau monsieur pour numéro huit!"* Yes, here's the new roomer in number eight, such generous friends, surely he would be, too.

Up a flight of creaky wooden stairs, the room was spacious, with a tall window. Ferrara walked around, sat on the bed, opened the shutters so he could look out on the sleeping courtyard. Not bad, not bad at all, certainly not a tiny room in the apartment of some *fuorusciti,* and not a dirt-cheap hotel packed with Italian refugees. "Emigrés?" Ferrara said, clearly skeptical. "They paid for this?"

From Kolb, a shrug, and the most angelic of smiles. *May all your abductions be so sweet, my little lamb.* "You like it?" Kolb said.

"Of course I *like* it." Ferrara left the rest unsaid.

"Well then," Kolb replied, himself no slouch at leaving things unsaid.

Ferrara hung his jacket up on the hanger in the armoire, and took from his pockets his passport, a few papers, and a sepia photograph of his wife and three children in a cardboard frame. It had, at some point, been bent, and straightened out, so the photograph was broken across the upper corner.

"Your family?"

"Yes," Ferrara said. "But their lives go on

184

a long way from mine — it's been more than two years since I last saw them." He put the passport in the bottom drawer of the armoire, closed the door, and rested the photograph on the windowsill. "And that's that," he said.

Kolb, who knew too well what he meant, nodded in sympathy.

"I left a lot behind, crossing the Pyrenees on foot, at night, then the people who arrested me took pretty much everything else." He shrugged and said, "So, I'm forty-seven years old, and that's what I have."

"The times we live in, Colonel," Kolb said. "Now, I think, we'll go to the café downstairs, for coffee with hot milk, and a *tartine.*" Which was a long, skinny bread. Cut in half. And amply buttered.

19 March.

The seers of weather predicted the rainiest spring of the century, and so it was when Carlo Weisz returned to Paris. It dripped off the brim of his hat, ran in the gutters, and did nothing to improve his state of mind. From train to Métro and then to the Hotel Dauphine, he thought up a dozen useless schemes to bring Christa von Schirren to Paris, not one of which was worth a sou. But he would, at least, write her a letter —

185

a disguised letter, as though it came from an aunt, or an old school friend, perhaps, traveling in Europe, pausing in Paris, and collecting mail at the American Express office.

Delahanty was happy to see him that afternoon, he'd scored a beat on the opposition with the *resistance in Prague* story, though the London *Times* had run a version of it the following day. From Delahanty, the old saw, "Nothing quite like being shot at, if they miss."

Salamone was also happy to see him, though not for long, when they met at the bar near his office. Raindrops, lit red by the neon sign, ran slowly down the window, and the bar dog shook off a great spray of water when she was let in the door. "Welcome back," Salamone said. "I assume you're glad to be out of there."

"A nightmare," Weisz said. "And no surprise. But, no matter how much you read the papers, you don't know about the little things, not unless you go there — what people say when they can't say what they want to, how they look at you, how they look away. And then, after two weeks of that, I went to Prague, where they've been occupied, and they know what it will mean for them."

"Suicides," Salamone said. "So it's reported in the newspapers here. Hundreds of them, Jews, others. The ones who didn't get out in time."

"It was very bad," Weisz said.

"Well, it's not much better back home. And I have to tell you that we've lost two runners."

He meant *distributors* — bus drivers, barmen, storekeepers, janitors, anybody who had contact with the public. Thus it was said that if you wanted to know what was really going on in the world, best to visit the second-floor lavatory at the National Gallery of Antique Art, in the Palazzo Barberini in Rome. Always something to read, there.

But distribution was mostly managed by teenaged girls from the fascist student organizations. They had to join, just as their fathers joined the *Partito Nazionale Fascista,* the PNF. *Per Necessità Familiare,* the joke went, for family necessity. But a lot of the girls hated what they had to do — march, sing, collect money — and signed up to distribute newspapers, getting away with it because people thought that girls would never do such a thing, would never dare. The *fascisti* had it a little wrong there, but still, now and again most often by betrayal, the police caught them.

"Two of them," Weisz said. "Arrested?"

"Yes, in Bologna. Fifteen-year-old girls, cousins."

"Do we know what happened?"

"We don't. They went out with papers, in their school satchels, to leave them at the railroad station, but they never came back. Then, the following day, the police notified the parents."

"And now they'll go before the Special Tribunals."

"Yes, as always. They'll get two or three years."

Weisz wondered, for a moment, whether the whole thing was worth it; girls in jail while the *giellisti* conspired in Paris, but he knew it for a question that couldn't be answered. "Perhaps," he said, "they can be pried loose."

"Not in this case," Salamone said. "The families are poor."

They were silent for a time, the bar was quiet, only the sound of the rain in the street. Weisz unbuckled his briefcase and put the lists of German agents on the table. "I've brought you a present," he said. "From Berlin."

Salamone worked away at it; leaned on his elbows, soon enough pressed his fingers against his temples, then moved his head slowly from side to side. When he looked up, he said, "What is it with you? First that fucking torpedo, now this. Are you, some kind of, *magnet?*"

"It would seem so," Weisz said.

"How'd you get it?"

"From a man in a park. It comes from the Foreign Ministry."

"A man in a park."

"Leave it at that, Arturo."

"Fine, but at least tell me what it means."

Weisz explained — German penetration throughout the Italian security system.

"Mannaggia," Salamone said quietly, still reading through the list. "What a gift, it's a death sentence. Next time, maybe a little stuffed bear, eh?"

"What do we do?"

Weisz watched Salamone as he tried to work it out. Yes, he was called a *giellisti,* but so what. The man on the other side of the table was in late middle age, a former shipping broker, his career destroyed by the government, and now a clerk. Nothing in life had prepared him for conspiracy, he had to figure it out as he went along.

"I'm not sure," Salamone said. "We can't just print it, that I do know, it would bring them down on us like — I don't know, like hellfire, or think up something worse. And

189

we'd have the Germans as well, the local Gestapo, with their pals in Berlin tearing the Foreign Ministry apart until they find out who went to the park."

"But we can't burn it, not this time."

"No, Carlo, this hurts them. Remember the rule, anything that forces Germany and Italy apart, we want. And this does, this will make some of the *fascisti* mad — our people are mad already, which doesn't mean shit to a snail, but, get *them,* the fearful *them,* mad, and we've done something worthwhile."

"It's *how* we do it."

"Yes, I think so. We can't be cowards and slip this to the Communists, though I admit it crossed my mind."

"That's where it comes from, I suspect. I was told as much."

Salamone shrugged. "I'm not surprised. To do such a thing as this, in Germany, under the Nazi regime, would take somebody very strong, very committed, somebody with real *ideology.*"

"Maybe," Weisz said, "maybe we can just say we know, that we've heard this is going on. The fascists will know how to find out the rest, since it's in the heart of their machine. It's disloyalty, to Italy, to allow another country to prepare for an occupa-

190

tion. Thus, even if you don't like us, when we print this, we're patriots."

"How would you put it?"

"Just as I've said. A concerned official in an Italian bureau has informed *Liberazione* . . . Or an anonymous letter, which we believe."

"Not bad," Salamone said.

"But then, we have the real thing to deal with."

"Give it to somebody who can use it."

"The French? The British? Both? Hand it to a diplomat?"

"Don't do that!"

"Why not?"

"Because they'll be back in a week, wanting more. And they won't say please."

"In the mail, then. Mail it to the Foreign Ministry and the British embassy. Let them deal with the OVRA."

"I'll take care of it," Salamone said, sliding the list toward his side of the table.

Weisz took it back. "No, I'm responsible for it, I'll do it. Should I, maybe, retype it?"

"Then it's from your typewriter," Salamone said. "They can figure these things out. In the crime novels, they can, and I think that's true."

"But it would be on the man in the park's

typewriter. What if somebody figured *that* out?"

"So, find another typewriter."

Weisz grinned. "I think this game is called *hot potato.* Where in hell will I find another typewriter?"

"Buy it, my friend. Out at Clignancourt, in the flea market. Then get rid of it. Pawn it, throw it out, or leave it in the street somewhere. And do it before the mail is delivered."

Weisz refolded the list and put it back in its envelope.

At eight that evening, Weisz went looking for dinner. *Mère* this? *Chez* that? He'd read that day's *Le Journal,* so he stopped at a newsstand and bought a *Petit Parisien* as a dinner companion. It was a terrible rag, but he secretly enjoyed it, all that lust and greed in high places somehow went well with dinner, especially dinner alone.

Walking through the rain, he took a side street, and came upon a little place called Henri. The window was well steamed, but he could see a black-and-white tile floor, diners at most of the tables, and a blackboard with that night's menu. When he entered, the proprietor, properly heavy and red-faced, came to greet him, wiping his hands on his apron. A *couvert* for one, monsieur? Yes, please. Weisz hung his raincoat and hat on the clothes tree by the door. In very crowded restaurants, in bad weather, the thing would in time become overladen, and could be depended on to tip over at least once during the evening, which always made Weisz laugh.

What Henri offered that night was a large plate of steamed leeks, followed by *rognons de veau,* morsels of veal kidney, sautéed with mushrooms in a brown sauce, and a mound of crisp *pommes frites.* Reading the paper, following the prodigious love affairs of a nightclub singer, Weisz finished most of his carafe of red wine, mopping up the veal sauce with a piece of bread, then decided to have the cheese, a *vacherin.*

Weisz was seated at a corner table, and, when the door opened, he glanced sideways to see who might be coming in for dinner. The man who entered took off his hat and coat and found an unused peg on the clothes tree. He was a fattish, benign sort of fellow, a pipe clenched in his teeth, a slip-over sweater worn beneath his jacket. The man looked around, searching for somebody, and, as Henri approached, eventually spotted Weisz. "Well, hello," he said. "Mr. Carlo Weisz, what luck."

"Mr. Brown. Good evening."

"Don't suppose I might join you. Are you waiting for somebody?"

"No, I'm just finishing up."

"Hate to eat alone."

Henri, wiping his hands on his apron, was not quite following this, but when Mr. Brown took a step toward Weisz's table, he smiled and pulled out a chair. "Much appreciated," Brown said, settling himself at the table and putting on his glasses to peer at the blackboard. "How's the food?"

"Very good."

"Kidneys," he said. "That will do nicely." He ordered, then said, "I've been meaning to get in touch with you, actually."

"Oh? Why is that?"

"A small project, something that might interest you."

"Really? Reuters pretty much takes up all my time."

"Yes, I imagine they would. Still, this is quite out of the ordinary, and it's a chance to, well, to make a difference."

"A difference?"

"That's it. In Europe these days, the way things are going, what with Hitler and Mussolini . . . I think you know what I mean. Anyhow, the world is too much with me, getting and spending, as the man said, but

194

one does want to do something more, and I'm associated with a few like-minded fellows, and, every now and again, we try to do a little something worthwhile. Very informal, you understand, this group, but we pitch in a few pounds, and use our business connections, and, you never know, it might just, as I said, make a difference."

A waiter brought a carafe of wine and a basket of bread. Mr. Brown said, "Mmm," by way of thanks, poured himself a glass of wine, took a sip, and said, "Good. Very good, whatever it is. They never tell you, do they." He had another sip, tore a piece of bread in half, and ate it. "Now," he said, "where was I? Oh yes, our small project. Actually, it began the night we had drinks at the Ritz bar, with Geoffrey Sparrow and his girl, you recall?"

"I do, of course," Weisz said cautiously, apprehensive about what might be coming next.

"Well, you know, it got me thinking. Here was an opportunity to do a little something for the sorry world out there. So I had a friend make inquiries, and, by a lucky chance, we actually found this Colonel Ferrara you wrote about. Poor bastard, his unit retreated to Barcelona, where they had to get rid of their uniforms and make a run for it, across the Pyrenees at night, which is very damn dangerous, I don't have to tell you. Once in France, he was arrested, naturally, and interned at one of those wretched camps down in Gascony. Where we actually found him, through a friend in one of the French ministries."

Worse and worse. "Not easy to do, something like that."

"No, not easy. But, damn it all, worth it, don't you think? I mean, *you're* the one who told his story, so you know who he is — *what* he is, I should say. He's a hero. Don't see that word too much these days, it ain't fashionable, but that's the truth of it. In the midst of all this whining and hand-wringing, here's a man who stands up for what he believes in, and —"

The waiter arrived with a generous wedge of *vacherin,* soft and smelly. Not that Weisz particularly wanted it, not anymore. Brown and his like-minded fellows had, with whatever else they were about, whipped his appetite away and replaced it with a cold knot in the stomach.

"Ah, the cheese. Nice and ripe, I'd say."

"It is," Weisz said, testing it lightly with his thumb. He cut a piece — a proper diagonal, not the nose — and stuck his fork in it, but that was as far as he got. "You were saying?"

"Uh, oh yes, Colonel Ferrara. A hero, Mr. Weisz, and one the world ought to know about. You certainly thought so, and, evidently, so did Reuters. Really, can you name another? Plenty of victims, out there, and plenty of nasty villains, but then, where are the heroes, tonight?"

Weisz wasn't meant to answer this, and he didn't. "And so?"

"So this, Mr. Weisz: we think that Colonel Ferrara should make his story known. In detail, in public."

"And how would he do that?"

"The usual way. Always the best way, the usual way, and in this case that would mean, a book. His book. *Soldier of Freedom,* something like that. *To Fight for Freedom?* Is that better?"

Weisz wouldn't bite. His expression said, *who knows?*

"But, whatever the title, it's a good story. We start in the camp — will he ever get out? Then we find out how he got there. He grows up in a poor family, he joins the army, becomes an officer, fights with an elite force at the Piave River, in the Great War, is ordered to Ethiopia, Mussolini's quest for empire, then resigns his commission, in protest, after Italian planes spray the tribal

197

villages with poison gas, goes to Spain, and fights the fascists, Spanish *and* Italian. Now, here he is, at the end, preparing to fight fascism again. That's a book I'd read, wouldn't you?"

"I guess I would."

"Of course you would!" Brown made a bracket of his thumb and index finger, then moved it across the title as he said, "*My Fight for Freedom,* by 'Colonel Ferrara.' In quotation marks, of course, and no first name, because it's a *nom de guerre,* which makes for a rather tasty dust jacket, don't you think? You get to buy a book by a fellow who must keep his real identity a secret, has to use an alias. Why? Because tomorrow, when he finishes writing, he goes back to war, against Mussolini, or Hitler, in Roumania, or Portugal, or little Estonia — who knows where it might break out next. So we feel, my friends and I, that here is a book which should see the light of day. Now, how does this sound to you. Can it be done?"

"I would think so," Weisz said, his voice as neutral as he could possibly make it.

"Only one problem, as far as we can see. This Colonel Ferrara, a gifted army officer, can do many things, but one thing he can't do is write books."

"*Les poireaux,*" the waiter said, sliding a

plate of leeks onto the table. It was no more than a momentary flicker of the eyes, as Mr. Brown regarded the plate, but it revealed to Weisz that Mr. Brown didn't actually like steamed leeks, probably didn't like veal kidneys, maybe didn't like French food, or the French, or France.

"So then," Brown said, "what we thought is that maybe the journalist Carlo Weisz could help us out in this area."

"I don't think that's possible."

"Oh yes it is."

"I have too much work, Mr. Brown. Really, I'm sorry, but I can't do it."

"I'd wager you can. A thousand pounds, I'd wager."

That was a great deal of money, but the cost of it! "Sorry," Weisz said.

"Are you sure? Because I can see that you haven't thought this over, you haven't seen all the possibilities, all the benefits. It would be a chance, certainly, to enhance your reputation. Your name won't be on the book, but your bureau chief, what's-his-name, Delahanty, would know about it. Likely he'd see it as patriotism, on your part, to take a hand in the fight against Britain's enemies. Wouldn't he? I know Sir Roderick would."

This thrust went home. *We'll tell your boss, if you don't do what we want.* Sir Roderick

Jones was the managing director of the Reuters bureau — a famous tyrant, a holy terror. Wore the school ties of schools he'd never attended, implied service in regiments he was too short to have joined. At night, when his chauffeured Rolls-Royce took him home from the office, an employee was sent out to jump on a rubber pad in the street, which, as the car approached, turned the traffic light to green. And he was said to have berated a servant for not ironing his shoelaces.

"How do you know he would?" Weisz said.

"Oh, he's a friend of a friend," Brown said. "Eccentric, sometimes, but his heart's in the right place. Especially when it's a matter of patriotism."

"I don't know," Weisz said, searching for some way out. "If Colonel Ferrara is all the way down in Gascony . . ."

"Good heavens no! He's not in Gascony, he's right here, in Paris, up on the rue de Tournon. So, now that that's out of our way, will you, at least, think it over?"

Weisz nodded.

"Good," Brown said. "Better to consider these sorts of things, take some time, see how the wind blows."

"I'll think it over," Weisz said.

"You do that, Mr. Weisz. Take your time.

I'll call you in the morning."

By nine-thirty, Carlo Weisz wasn't ready to jump into the Seine, but he did want to look at it. Brown had made a fast exit from the restaurant, tossing franc notes on the table, more than enough to pay for both dinners, sparing himself the veal kidney, and leaving Henri to gaze anxiously out the door as he went down the street. Weisz didn't dawdle, paid for his own dinner, and left a few minutes later. So, for the waiter, a gratuity to be remembered.

There was no going back to the Dauphine, not just then. Weisz walked and walked, down to the river and onto the Pont d'Arcole, the Notre Dame cathedral looming up behind him, a vast shadow in the rain. All his life he'd gazed at rivers, from London's Thames to Budapest's Danube, with the Arno, the Tiber, and the Grand Canal of Venice in between, but the Seine was queen of the poetic rivers, to Weisz it was. Restless and melancholy, or soft and slow, depending on the mood of the river, or his. That night it was black, dappled with rain, and running high in its banks, just beneath the lower quay. *What shall I do?* he wondered, leaning on a parapet made for leaning, staring at the river as though it would answer. *Why not try running down to the sea? Suits me.*

But that he couldn't do. He didn't like being trapped, but he was. Trapped in Paris, trapped in a good job — all the world should be so trapped! But add Mr. Brown's trap and the equation changed. What would he do if they booted him out of Reuters? He would not soon find another Delahanty, who liked him, who protected him, who had fashioned a job particularly for his abilities. In his mind, he went down the list of little jobs the *giellisti* had managed to acquire. Not a good list — a place to go in the morning, a little money, not much more. And, he feared, a life sentence. Hitler wasn't going to fall anytime soon, history was ripe with forty-year dictatorships, and that made him a free man at last, at the age of eighty-one. Time to begin anew!

Perhaps he could delay the project, he thought, say *yes* but mean *no,* then disentangle himself in some clever way. But if Brown had the power to get him fired, he might also have the power to have him expelled. Weisz had to face that possibility. *In the morning light, Zanzibar was not so grim as he'd feared.* Or worse, the letter to Christa — a change of plans, my love. No, no, impossible, he had to survive, to stay where he was. And then, despite the cold ironic twist in Brown's soul, such a project might in truth be good for the sorry world out there, might inspire other Colonel Ferraras to take arms against the devil. Was it, really, so different from the work he did with *Liberazione?*

This was enough to get him moving, to the end of the bridge, past the traditional embracing couple, and onto the upper quay of the right bank, walking east, away from the hotel. A whore blew him a kiss, a *clochard* got five francs, a woman with a stylish umbrella didn't exactly give him a look, and a few lonely souls, heads down in the rain, weren't going home, not yet. He walked for a long time, past the Hotel de Ville, past the garden shops across the street, and found himself eventually at the Canal Saint-Martin, where it met the place Bastille.

A few steps down a narrow street off Bastille was a restaurant called Le Brasserie Heininger. At the entry, stalls of crushed ice displayed lobsters and shellfish, while a waiter, dressed as a Breton fisherman, worked at opening oysters. Weisz had once written about the Heininger, in June of 1937. *The political intrigues of Bulgarian émigrés in Paris took a violent turn last night at the popular Brasserie Heininger, just off the*

203

place de la Bastille, near the dance halls and nightclubs of the notorious rue de Lappe. Just after 10:30 in the evening, the popular head-waiter of the brasserie, one Omaraeff, a refugee from Bulgaria, was gunned down while attempting to hide in a stall in the ladies' WC. Then, to show they meant business, two men wearing long coats and fedoras — gang-sters from Clichy, according to the police — sprayed the elegant dining room with submachine-gun fire, sparing the terrified patrons but smashing all the gold-framed mir-rors, save one, which survived, a single bullet hole in its lower corner. "I will not replace that one," said Maurice "Papa" Heininger, owner of the brasserie. "I will leave it as it is, a memo-rial to poor Omaraeff." The police are investi-gating.

There was no going further east, Weisz realized, in that direction lay dark, empty streets, and the furniture workshops of the Faubourg Saint-Antoine. So then, how to avoid going home? Maybe a drink, he thought. Or two. At the Brasserie Heininger, a refuge, bright lights and people, why not. He walked down the street, entered the brasserie, and climbed the white marble staircase to the dining room. What a crowd! Laughing and flirting and drinking, while waiters with mutton-chop whiskers hurried by, carrying silver platters of oysters or *chou-croute garni,* the room all red plush banquettes, painted cupids, and polished wood. The maître d' fingered his velvet rope and gave Weisz a long look, not very welcoming. Who was this lone wolf, dripping wet, trying to come down to the campfire? "I fear it will be quite a long wait, monsieur, we are very full tonight."

Weisz hesitated for a moment, hoping to see someone call for a check, then turned to leave.

"Weisz!"

He searched for the source of the voice.

"Carlo Weisz!"

Working his way through the crowded room was Count Janos Polanyi, the Hungarian diplomat, tall and bulky and white-haired, and, tonight, not perfectly steady on his feet. He shook Weisz's hand, took him by the arm, and led him toward a corner table. Pushed up against Polanyi in the narrow path between chair backs, Weisz caught a strong smell of wine, mixed with the scents of bay rum cologne and good cigars. "He'll be joining us," Polanyi called back to the maître d'. "At table fourteen. So bring a chair."

At table fourteen, just beneath the mirror with the bullet hole, a sea of upturned faces.

Polanyi introduced Weisz, adding, "a journalist at the Reuters bureau," and a chorus of greetings followed, all in French, apparently the language of the evening. "So then," Polanyi said to Weisz, "left to right, my nephew, Nicholas Morath, his friend Cara Dionello. André Szara, the *Pravda* correspondent." Szara nodded to Weisz, they'd met, now and again, at press conferences. "And Mademoiselle Allard." The latter was leaning against Szara, on the end of the banquette, not asleep, but fading fast. "Then Louis Fischfang, the screenwriter, and next the famous Voyschinkowsky, who you'll know as 'the Lion of the Bourse,' and, by his side, Lady Angela Hope."

"We've met," Lady Angela said, with a certain smile.

"Have you? Splendid."

The maître d' arrived with a chair and everybody moved closer together to make room. "We're drinking Echézeaux," Polanyi said to Weisz. Clearly they were, Weisz counted five empty bottles on the table, and half a sixth. To the maître d', Polanyi said, "We'll need a glass, and another Echézeaux. No, better make it two." The maître d' signaled to a waiter, then took Weisz's coat and hat and headed toward the cloakroom. Moments later, a waiter arrived with a glass and the new bottles. As he worked at opening them, Polanyi said to Weisz, "What brings you out in this vile weather? Not after a story, are you?"

"No, no," Weisz said. "Not tonight. I'm just out for a walk in the rain."

"Anyhow," Fischfang said.

"Oh yes, we were in the middle of a story," Polanyi said.

"A Hitler's parrot joke," Fischfang said. "Number whatever it is. Is anybody counting?" Fischfang was a tense little man with bent wire-framed glasses, which made him look like Leon Trotsky.

"Start over, Louis," Voyschinkowsky said.

"In this one, Hitler's parrot is asleep on his perch, Hitler's working at his desk. Suddenly, the parrot wakes up and cries, 'Here comes Hermann Goering, head of the *Luftwaffe*.' Hitler stops working. What goes on? Then the door opens and it's Goering. So Hitler and Goering start to talk, but the bird interrupts. 'Here comes Joseph Goebbels, minister of propaganda.' And, lo and behold, a minute later, it's true. Hitler tells what's going on, but Goering and Goebbels think he's kidding. 'Ah, go on, Adolf, it's a trick, you're giving the bird a signal.' 'No, no,' Hitler says. 'This bird somehow knows who's coming, and I'll prove it to you. We'll hide in the closet, where the bird can't see me, and wait for the next visitor.' So there they are, in the closet, and the bird starts up again. But this time it just trembles and hides its head under its wing and squawks." Fischfang hunched over, hid his head beneath his arm, and produced a series of frightened squawks. At nearby tables, a few heads turned. "After a minute, the door opens, and it's Heinrich Himmler, head of the Gestapo. He looks around, thinks the office is empty, and goes away. 'Allright, boys,' the parrot says, 'it's safe to come out now. The Gestapo's gone.' "

A few smiles, a tepid laugh from the courteous Voyschinkowsky. "Gestapo jokes," Szara said.

"Not so funny, is it," Fischfang said. "A friend of mine picked that up in Berlin. But, anyhow, they're still working at it."

"Why don't they work at shooting that bastard?" Cara said.

"I'll drink to that," Szara said, his French flavored with a strong Russian accent.

The Echézeaux was something that Weisz had never tasted — far too expensive. The first sip told him why.

"Patience, children," Polanyi said, setting his glass back on the tablecloth. "We'll get him."

"To us, then," Lady Angela said, raising her glass.

Morath was amused, and said to Weisz, "You've fallen among, well, not thieves, exactly, ah, citizens of the night."

Szara laughed, Polanyi grinned. "Not thieves, Nicky? But, let's all remember that Monsieur Weisz is a journalist."

Weisz didn't like being excluded. "Not tonight," he said. "I'm just one more émigré."

"From where did you emigrate?" Voyschinkowsky said.

"He's from *Trieste*," Lady Angela said, a nudge and a wink in her voice. Now everybody was amused.

"Well then, he has honorary membership," Fischfang said.

"As what?" Lady Angela said, all innocence.

"As, uh, what Nicky said. 'Citizen of the night.' "

"To Trieste, then," Szara said, ready to drink.

"Trieste, and the others," Polanyi said. "Geneva, say. And Lugano."

"Certainly Lugano. The so-called Spyopolis," Morath said.

"Have you heard that?" Voyschinkowsky asked Weisz.

Weisz smiled. "Yes, Spyopolis. Like any border city."

"Or any city," Polanyi said, "with Russian émigrés."

"Oh good," Lady Angela said. "Now we can include Paris."

"And Shanghai," Fischfang said. "And Harbin, especially Harbin, 'where the women dress on credit and disrobe for cash.' "

"To them," Cara said. "The White Russian women of Harbin."

They drank to that, and Polanyi refilled the glasses. "Of course, we should include the others. Hotel doormen, for example."

Szara liked that idea. "Then, embassy code clerks. Nightclub dancers."

"And tennis pros," Cara said. "With perfect manners."

"Yes," Weisz said. "And the journalists."

"Hear, hear," Lady Angela said in English.

"Long life," Polanyi said, raising his glass.

Now everyone laughed, drank the toast, and drank again. Except for Mlle. Allard, whose head lay against Szara's shoulder, eyes closed, mouth slightly open. Weisz lit a cigarette and looked around the table. Were they all spies? Polanyi was, and so was Lady Angela Hope. Morath, Polanyi's nephew, probably was, and Szara, a *Pravda* correspondent, had to be, given the voracious appetite of the NKVD. And Fischfang as well, from what he'd said. And all on the same side? Two Hungarians, an Englishwoman, a Russian. What was Fischfang? Likely a Polish Jew, resident in France. And Voyschinkowsky? French, of, maybe, Ukrainian ancestry. Cara Dionello, who was sometimes mentioned in the gossip columns, was Argentine, and very rich. What a crowd! But all, it would seem, working against the Nazis, one way or another. And don't forget, he thought, one Carlo Weisz, Italian. No, Triestine.

It was just after two in the morning when the Triestine climbed out of a taxi in front of the Hotel Dauphine, managed, on his eighth try, to get his key in the lock, opened the door, made his way past the deserted reception desk, and, eventually, after stumbling back a step at least three times, up the stairs to his refuge. Where he shed his clothes, down to shorts and undershirt, hunted through his jacket pockets until he found his glasses, and sat down at the Olivetti. The opening volley sounded loud to Weisz, but he ignored it — the other tenants never seemed to mind the late-night tapping of a typewriter. Or, if they did, they never said anything about it. Typing late at night had near saintly status in the city of Paris — who knew what wondrous flights of imagination might be in progress — and people liked the idea of an inspired soul, pounding away after a midnight visit from the muse.

An inspired clandestine journalist, anyhow, writing a short, simple article about German agents at the heart of the Italian security system. It was pretty much as he'd told Salamone in the bar, earlier that day. The *Liberazione* editors had heard, from friends in Italy, about these Germans, some official, some not, working inside the police and security organizations. Shameful, really, if it were true, and they believed it was, that Italy, so often invaded, would invite foreign agents inside its defensive walls, inside its castle. A Trojan horse? Preparation for another, a German, invasion? An invasion supported by the fascists themselves? *Liberazione* hoped not. But then, what did it mean? How would it end? Was this the proper course for those who called themselves *patriots? We giellisti,* he wrote, *have always shared one passion with our opponents: love of country. So please, our readers in the police and security services — we know you read our newspaper, even though it's forbidden — take some time to think about this, about what it means to you, about what it means to Italy.*

The following day, a telephone call at the Reuters bureau. Had Mr. Brown, at this point, been his cold, hard self, and leaned on his advantage, he might have been issued a brisk *va f'an culo* and sent on his way. But it was a mild, sensible Mr. Brown, trudging along through a vocational morning, on the other end of the line. Hoping Weisz had thought over his proposition, hoping that, in the politics of the moment, he saw the point of *Soldier for Freedom*. Their interests were, in this instance, mutual. A little time, a little hard work, a blow against the common enemy. And they would pay him only if he wanted to be paid. "That's up to you, Mr. Weisz."

They met that day after work, at the café — down three steps from the street — below the Hotel Tournon. Mr. Brown, Colonel Ferrara, and Weisz. Ferrara was glad to see him — Weisz had wondered about that, because he'd brought this down on Ferrara's head. But that head had recently been locked up in a camp, so Weisz was a savior, and Ferrara let him know it.

Mr. Brown spoke English at the meeting,

213

while Weisz translated for Ferrara. "Naturally, you'll write in Italian," Brown said. "And we have somebody who will do the English version, pretty much day by day. Because first publication, as soon as possible, will be in London, with Staunton and Weeks. We considered Chapman & Hall, or maybe Victor Gollancz, but we like Staunton. For the Italian publication, maybe a small French house, or we'll use one of the émigré journals — their name, anyhow — but we'll get copies into Italy, you can depend on that. And it must go to the United States, it could be influential there, and we want the Americans to think about going to war, but Staunton will make that sale. Allright so far?"

After Weisz told him what had been said, the colonel nodded. The reality of being an *author* was just beginning to reach him. "Please ask," he said to Weisz, "what if the publisher in London doesn't like it?"

"Oh, they'll like it well enough," Brown said.

"Don't worry," Weisz said to Ferrara. "This is the best kind of story, a story that tells itself."

Not quite. Weisz found, through the end of March and the early days of April, that

214

considerable embroidery was needed, but this came more easily to him than he would have suspected — he knew Italian life, and he knew the history. Still, he held tight to the narrative, and Ferrara, on prompting, had a good memory.

"My father worked for the railroad, in the town of Ferrara. As a brakeman in the railroad yards."

And your father — stern and distant? Warm and tender? A bad temper? Tall? Short? The house, what did it look like? Family? Holidays? A scene at Christmas? That could be appealing, snow, candles in the windows. Did he play at being a soldier?

"If I did, I don't remember."

"No? With a broomstick, maybe, for a rifle?"

"What I recall is football, every spare minute I had. But we didn't play all that much, I had chores to do, after school. Bringing water from the pump or coal for the little stove we had. It took a lot of work, just to live day to day."

"So, nothing military."

"No, I never thought about it. When I was eleven, I brought my father his dinner, at the yards, and I would meet his friends. It was understood that I would do the same work he did."

"You liked that idea?"

"It wasn't up to me to like it." He thought for a time. "Actually, now that I think about it, my mother's brother had been a soldier, and he let me wear a sort of canvas belt he had, with a canteen on it. I did like that. I wore it, and I filled the canteen and drank the water. Which tasted, different."

"Like what?"

"I don't know. Water from a canteen has a certain taste. Musty, but not bad, canteen water is not like other water."

Ahh.

By 10 April, the new issue of *Liberazione* was, against all odds, ready for publication. Weisz's evenings were taken up with the book, and his days belonged to Reuters, which left Salamone, and eventually Elena, to do much of the editorial work. Weisz had to tell Salamone what he was doing, but Elena knew only that he was "involved in work on another project." This she accepted, saying, "I don't have to know the details."

For the 10 April *Liberazione,* there was plenty to write about, and both the Roman lawyer and the art historian from Siena contributed articles. Mussolini had issued an ultimatum to King Zog of Albania, demanding, essentially, that he give his country to Italy. Britain was asked to intercede, but declined and, on 7 April, the Italian navy bombarded the Albanian coast, and the army invaded. This invasion violated the Anglo-Italian agreement signed a year earlier, but the Chamberlain government was silent.

Not so *Liberazione.*

A New Imperial Adventure, they said. More dead and wounded, more money, all for Mussolini's frantic competition with Adolf Hitler, who, on 22 March, had taken the port of Memel by sending a registered letter to the Lithuanian government, then sailing into the port, to grinding newsreel cameras and popping flashbulbs, on a German warship. *Very saucy,* as Hitler liked to say, with the sort of panache guaranteed to infuriate Mussolini.

But, just in case it didn't, the April *Liberazione* surely did — if the palace stooges allowed him to see it. For there was not only the editorial about German agents but also a cartoon. Talk about *saucy.* It's nighttime, and here's Mussolini, as usual, on a balcony. This balcony, however, is off a bedroom, the outline of a bed barely visible in the darkness. It's the familiar *Il Duce;* big jaw thrust out, arms folded, but he's wearing only a pajama top — with medals, of course

217

— revealing hairy, knobby cartoon legs, while, from behind the French door, a pair of woman's eyes, very alarmed, are peering out of the gloom, suggesting that all has not gone well in the bedroom. A suggestion confirmed by the old Sicilian proverb used as the caption: *"Potere è meglio di fottere."* Nice rhyme, there, the sort of thing that made it fun to say, and easy to remember. "Power is better than fucking."

It had been three weeks since Weisz's return from Berlin, and he had to call Véronique — casual as the love affair had been, he couldn't just vanish. So, on a Thursday afternoon, he telephoned and asked her to meet him after work at a café near the gallery. She knew. Somehow she knew. And, Parisian warrior that she was, had never looked so lovely. So soft — her hair soft and simple, eyes barely made up, blouse falling softly over her breasts, with a new perfume, sweet, not sophisticated, clouds of it. Three weeks' absence and a meeting at a café made words practically pointless, but decency demanded an explanation. "I have met, somebody," he said. "It is, I think, serious."

There were no tears, only that she would miss him, and he realized, just at that moment, how much he'd liked her, what good times they'd had together, in bed and out.

"Someone you met in Berlin, Carlo?"

"Someone I met a long time ago."

"A second chance?" she said.

"Yes."

"Very rare, the second chance." *You won't get one here.*

"I will miss you," he said.

"You're sweet, to say that."

"It's true, I'm not just saying it."

A melancholy smile, a lift of the eyebrows.

"May I call you, sometime, to see how you're doing?"

She put a hand, also soft, and warm, on his, by way of telling him what a jackass he'd just been, then stood up and said, "My coat?"

He helped her on with her coat, she turned, shook out her hair so that it fell properly over her collar, rose to give him a dry kiss on the lips, and, hands in pockets, walked out the door. When, later, he left the café, from the woman behind the cash register, another melancholy smile, another lift of the eyebrows.

The following day, he forced himself to deal with the list he'd brought out of Berlin. Leaving the office at lunchtime, he took an endless Métro ride out to the Porte de Clignancourt, wandered through the flea market, and bought a valise. It had been born cheap — cardboard covered with pebbled fabric — then lived a long, hard life; a tag on the handle evidence of a stay at a railway baggage room in Odessa.

That done, he walked and walked, past stalls of prodigious furniture and racks of old clothes, until, at last, he found an old gent with a goatee and a dozen typewriters. He tried them all, even the red Mignon portable, and finally chose a Remington with a French, AZERTY, keyboard, haggled a little, put it in the valise, dropped it off at the hotel, and returned to the office.

Long hours, the spy business. After an evening with Ferrara — the troop transport to Ethiopia, the misgivings of a fellow officer — Weisz walked back to the Dauphine, took the list from its hiding place, beneath the bottom drawer of his armoire, and went to work. The thing was a bear to retype, the old ribbon had barely any ink, and he had to do it twice. Finally, he typed two envelopes, one to the French Foreign Ministry, the other to the British embassy, added stamps, and went to bed. They would know what had been done — French keyboard, umlauts put in by hand, local mailing —

but Weisz didn't so much care, by that point, what anybody did with it. What he did care about was keeping his word to the man in the park, if he was still alive, and especially if he wasn't.

It was very late by the time he finished, but he wanted badly to be done with the whole business, so he burned the list, flushed the ashes down the toilet, and set out to dispose of the typewriter. Valise in hand, he walked down the stairs and out into the street. Harder than he thought, to lose a valise — people everywhere, and the last thing he wanted was some Frenchman running after him, waving his arms and crying, *"Monsieur!"* At last he found a deserted alley, set the valise by a wall, and walked away.

14 April, 3:30 A.M. Weisz stood at the corner where the rue Dauphine met the quay above the Seine and waited for Salamone. And waited. *Now what?* It was the fault of that accursed Renault, old and mean. Why did nobody in his world ever have anything new? Everything in their lives was worn-out, used up, hadn't really worked right for a long time. *Fuck this,* he thought, *I'll go to America.* Where he would be poor again, in the midst of wealth. That was the

221

old story, for Italian immigrants — the famous postcard back to Italy saying, "Not only are the streets not paved with gold, they are not paved, and we are expected to pave them."

The line of thought was interrupted by the coughing engine of Salamone's car, and darkness pierced by one headlight. Butting the door open with his shoulder, Salamone said, by way of greeting, *"Ché palle!"* What balls! Meaning, *what balls life has to do this to me!* Then, "You have it?"

Yes, he had it, the 10 April *Liberazione,* a sheaf of paper in his briefcase. They drove along the Seine, then turned and took the bridge across the river, working through small streets until they came to the all-night café near the Gare de Lyon. The conductor was waiting for them, drinking an *apéritif* and reading a newspaper. Weisz brought him to the car, where he sat in the backseat and spent a few minutes with them. "Now that *cazzo*" — that prick — "has us in *Albania,*" he said, sliding the *Liberazione* into a trainman's leather case he wore over his shoulder. "And he's got my poor nephew there, with the army. A kid, seventeen years old, a very good kid, sweet-natured, and they'll surely kill him, those fucking goat thieves. Is that in here?" He tapped the leather case.

"Very much in there," Weisz said.

"I'll read it on my way down."

"Tell Matteo we're thinking about him." Salamone meant their Linotype operator in Genoa.

"Poor Matteo."

"What's gone wrong?" Salamone's voice was tight.

"It's his shoulder. He can barely raise his arm."

"He hurt it?"

"No, he's getting old, and you know what Genoa's like. Cold and damp, and the coal is hard to find these days, and it costs an arm and a leg."

14 April, 10:40 A.M. On the 7:15 to Genoa, the conductor made his way to the baggage car and sat on a trunk. Finding himself alone, with no stop until Lyons, he lit a panatella and settled in to read *Liberazione.* Some of it he knew already, and the editorial was puzzling. What were the Germans doing? Working for the security? So what? They were no different than the Italians, and they should all burn in hell. But the cartoon made him laugh out loud, and he liked the piece about the Albanian invasion. *Yes,* he thought, *give it to them good.*

15 April, 1:20 A.M. The printing plant of *Il Secolo,* Genoa's daily newspaper, was not far from the giant refineries, on the road to the port, and tank cars were shunted back and forth all night long on the railway track behind the building. *Il Secolo,* in better days, had been the oldest democratic newspaper in Italy, then, in 1923, a forced sale had brought it under fascist management, and the editorial policy had changed. But Matteo, and many of the people he worked with, had not changed. As he finished up a run of leaflets for the Genoa association of fascist pharmacists, the production foreman stopped by to say good night. "You almost done?"

"Almost."

"Well, see you tomorrow."

"Good night."

Matteo waited a few minutes, then started the setup for a run of *Liberazione.* What was it this time? Albania, yes, everybody agreed about that. "Why? To grab four rocks?" So the latest line in the *piazza* — in the public square, thus everywhere. You heard it on the bus, you heard it in the cafés. Matteo took great satisfaction in his night printing, even though it was dangerous, because he was one of those people who really *didn't* like being pushed around, and that was the fascist specialty: making you do what they wanted, then smiling at you. *Well,* he thought, setting the controls, then pulling a lever to print a sample copy, *sit on this. And spin.*

16 April, 2:15 P.M. Antonio, who drove his coal-delivery truck from Genoa down to Rapallo, didn't read *Liberazione,* because he couldn't read. Well, not exactly, but anything written took him a long time to figure out, and there were a lot of words in this newspaper that he didn't know. The delivery of these bundles was his wife's idea — her sister lived in Rapallo and was married to a Jewish man who used to own a small hotel — and it had, without question, increased his stature in her eyes. Maybe she'd had some doubts when she'd faced the fact, two months pregnant, that it was definitely time to get married, but not so much these days. Nothing was said, in the house, but he could feel the change. Women had ways of letting you know something without actually saying it.

The road to Rapallo ran straight, past the town of Santa Margherita, but Antonio slowed down and hauled the wheel around to turn onto a dirt road that ran up into the hills, to the village of Torriglia. Just outside the village was a big, fancy house, the country villa of a Genoese lawyer, whose daughter, Gabriella, went to school in Genoa. One of these bundles was hers to distribute. All of sixteen years old, she was, and something to look at. Not that he, a married man and the mere owner of a coal truck, had any notion of trying anything, but he liked her just the same, and she had a very appealing way about her when she looked at him. *You are a hero,* something like that. For a man like Antonio, pretty rare, very nice. He hoped she was careful, fooling around with this smuggling business, because the police in Genoa were pretty tough customers. Well, maybe not all of them, but many.

17 April, 3:30 P.M. At the Sacred Heart Academy for Girls, in the best neighborhood of Genoa, field hockey was compulsory. So Gabriella spent the late afternoon running about in bloomers, waving at a ball with a stick, and calling out instructions to her teammates, which they rarely followed. After twenty minutes, the girls were redfaced and damp, and Sister Perpetua told them to sit down and cool off. Gabriella sat on the grass, next to her friend Lucia, and informed her that the new *Liberazione* had

226

arrived, hidden at her country house, but she had, in her locker, ten copies for Lucia and her secret boyfriend, a young policeman.

"I'll get them later," Lucia said.

"Give them out quickly," Gabriella said. Lucia could be lazy, and required an occasional prod.

"Yes, yes. I know, I will." Nothing to be done with Gabriella, a force of nature, best not to resist.

Gabriella was the saint-in-training of the Sacred Heart Academy. She knew what was right, and, when you knew what was right, you had to do it. This was the most important thing in life, and always would be. The fascists, as she'd seen, were brutal men, and wicked. And wickedness had always to be overcome, otherwise the lovely things in the world, beauty, truth, and romance, would all be ruined, and nobody would want to live in it. After school, she rode her bicycle the long way home, newspapers folded beneath her schoolbooks in the basket, stopping at a *trattoria,* a grocery, and a telephone booth at the post office.

19 April, 7:10 A.M. Lieutenant DeFranco, a detective in the rough waterfront district of Genoa, visited the WC at the precinct house

at this time every morning, the high wooden stall an island in the general bustle that accompanied the arrival of the day shift. The station had been renovated two years earlier — the fascist government cared for the comforts of its policemen — and new, sitdown toilets had been installed, to replace the old porcelain squares. Lieutenant De-Franco lit a cigarette and reached behind the bowl to see if there was anything to read today and, luck was with him, there was, a copy of *Liberazione.*

As always, he wondered idly who'd put it there, but that was hard to figure out. Some of the policemen were Communists, so maybe one of them, or it might be anybody, against the regime for whatever reason, idealism or revenge, because these days, people were quiet about such feelings. On the first page, Albania, cartoon, editorial. They weren't so wrong, he thought, not that there was much to be done about it. In time, Mussolini would falter, and the other wolves would be on him. That was, had always been, the way in this part of the world. One simply had to wait, but, while you waited, something to read with your morning ritual.

At ten-thirty that morning, he visited a dockside bar that catered to the stevedores of the port, to have a chat with a petty thief, who now and again passed along a few bits of local gossip. No longer young, the thief believed that when he was eventually caught, climbing in a window somewhere, the law might go a little easier on him, maybe a year instead of two, and that was well worth the occasional chat with the neighborhood cop.

"I was over at the vegetable market yesterday," he said, leaning across the table. "The Cuozzo brothers' place, you know?"

"Yes," DeFranco said. "I know it."

"I notice they're still around."

"I believe they are."

"Because, well, you remember what I told you, right?"

"That you sold them a rifle, a carbine, that you stole."

"I did, too. I wasn't lying."

"And so?"

"Well, they're still there. Selling vegetables."

"We're investigating. You wouldn't be telling me how to do my job, would you?"

"Lieutenant! Never! I just, you know, wondered."

"Don't wonder, my friend, it isn't good for you."

DeFranco himself wasn't sure why he'd put the information aside. He could, if he applied himself, probably find the rifle and arrest the Cuozzo brothers — glum, pugnacious little men who worked from dawn to dusk. But he hadn't done this. Why not? Because he wasn't sure what they had in mind. He doubted they meant to use it for some simmering feud, he doubted they intended to resell it. Something else. They were forever, he'd heard, grumbling about the government. Could they be so foolish as to contemplate an armed uprising? Could such a thing actually happen?

Maybe. There was, certainly, a fierce opposition. Only words, for the moment, but that could change. Look at this *Liberazione* crowd, what were they saying? *Resist. Don't give up.* And they were not angry little vegetable merchants, they'd been important, respectable people, before Mussolini. Lawyers, professors, journalists — one didn't rise to such professions by wishing on a star. In time, they might just prevail — they surely thought they would. With guns? Perhaps, depending how the world went. If Mussolini changed sides, and the Germans came down here, the best thing to have would be a rifle. So, for the moment, let the Cuozzo brothers keep it. Wait and see, he thought. Wait and see.

THE PACT OF STEEL

20 April, 1939.

Il faut en finir.

"There must be an end to this." So said the customer in the chair next to Weisz, at Perini's barbershop in the rue Mabillon. Not the rain, the politics — a popular sentiment that spring. Weisz had heard it at *Mère* this or *Chez* that, from Mme. Rigaud, proprietor of the Hotel Dauphine, from a dignified woman, to her companion, at Weisz's café. The Parisians were in a sour mood: the news was never good, Hitler wouldn't stop. *Il faut en finir,* true, though the nature of the ending was, in a particularly Gallic fashion, obscure — *somebody* must do *something,* and they were fed up with waiting for it.

"It cannot continue," the man in the next chair said. Perini held up a mirror so the man, turning left and right, could see the

233

back of his head. "Yes," he said, "looks good to me." Perini nodded to the shoe-shine boy, who brought the man his cane, then helped him maneuver himself out of the chair. "They got me the last time," he said to the men in the barbershop, "but we'll have to do it all over again." With a sympathetic murmur, Perini undid the protective sheet fastened at the customer's neck, whipped it away, handed it to the shoe-shine boy, then took a whisk broom and gave the man's suit a good brushing.

Weisz was next. Perini tilted the chair back, nimbly drew a steaming towel from the metal heater and wrapped it around Weisz's face. "As usual, Signor Weisz?"

"Just a trim, please, not too much," Weisz said, his voice muffled by the towel.

"And a nice shave, for you?"

"Yes, please."

Weisz hoped the man with the cane was wrong, but feared he wasn't. The last war had been pure hell for the French, slaughter followed slaughter, until the troops could stand it no longer — there had been sixty-eight mutinies in the hundred-and-twelve French divisions. He tried to relax, the wet heat working its way into his skin. Somewhere behind him, Perini was humming opera, content with the world of his shop, believing that nothing could change that.

On the twenty-first, a phone call at Reuters. "Carlo, it's me, Véronique."

"I know your voice, love," Weisz said gently. He was startled by the call. It had been ten days or so since they'd parted, and he'd expected that he'd never hear from her again.

"I must see you," she said. "Immediately."

What was this? She loved him? She couldn't bear for him to leave her? *Véronique?* No, this was not the voice of lost love, something had frightened her. "What is it?" he said cautiously.

"Not on the telephone. Please. Don't make me tell you."

"Are you at the gallery?"

"Yes. Forgive me for . . ."

"It's allright, don't apologize, I'll be there in a few minutes."

As he passed Delahanty's office, the bureau chief looked up from his work, but said nothing.

When Weisz opened the door to the gallery, he heard heels clicking on the polished floor. "Carlo," she said. She hesitated — an embrace? No, a brush kiss on each cheek, then a step back. This was a Véronique he'd never seen; tense, agitated, and vaguely hesitant — not entirely sure she was glad to see him.

Standing to one side, a spectre of old, bygone Montmartre, with graying beard, and suit and cravat from the 1920s. "This is Valkenda," she said, her voice implying great fame and stature. On the walls, swirling portraits of a dissolute waif, almost nude, covered here and there by a shawl.

"Of course," Weisz said. "Pleased to meet you."

As Valkenda bowed, his eyes closed.

"We'll go back to the office," Véronique said.

They sat on a pair of spindly gold chairs. "Valkenda?" Weisz said, with half a smile.

Véronique shrugged. "They jump off the walls," she said. "They pay the rent."

"Véronique, what's happened?"

"Ouf, I'm glad you're here." The words were followed by a mock shudder. "I had, this morning, the *Sûreté.*" She emphasized the word, *of all things.* "A dreadful little man, who showed up and, and, *interrogated* me."

"About what?"

"About you."

"What did he ask?"

"Where did you live, who did you know.

236

The details of your life."

"Why?"

"I have no idea, you tell me."

"I meant, did he say why?"

"No. Just that you were a 'subject of interest' in an investigation."

Pompon, Weisz thought. But why now? "A young man?" Weisz said. "Very neat and correct? Called Inspector Pompon?"

"Oh no, not at all. He wasn't young, and anything but neat — he had greasy hair, and dirt under his fingernails. And his name was something else."

"May I see his card?"

"He didn't leave a card — is that what they do?"

"Generally, they do. What about the other one?"

"What other one?"

"He was alone? Usually, there are two of them."

"No, not this time. Just Inspector . . . something. It started with a *D,* I think. Or a *B.*"

Weisz thought it over. "Are you sure he was from the *Sûreté?*"

"He said he was. I believed him." After a moment, she said, "More or less."

"Why do you say that?"

"Oh, it's just, *snobisme,* you know how

that goes. I thought, is this the sort of man they employ, this, I don't know, something crude, about him, about the way he looked at me."

"Crude?"

"The way he spoke. He was not, overly educated. And not a Parisian — we can hear it."

"Was he French?"

"Oh yes, certainly he was. From down south somewhere." She paused, her face changed, and she said, "A fraud, you think? What then? Do you owe somebody money? And I don't mean a bank."

"A gangster."

"Not the movie sort, but his eyes were never still. Up and down, you know? Maybe he thought it was seductive, or charming." From the expression on her face, the man had not been anything like "charming." "Who was he, Carlo?"

"I don't know."

"Please, we're not, strangers, you and I. You think you know who he was."

What to tell her? How much? "It may have something to do with Italian politics, émigré politics. There are people who don't like us."

Her eyes widened. "But wouldn't he be afraid you'd figure it out? That he'd said he was from the *Sûreté* when he was, an imposter?"

"Well," Weisz said, "to these people, it wouldn't matter. It might be better. Did he say you had to keep it to yourself?"

"Yes."

"But you didn't."

"Of course not, I had to tell you."

"Not everybody would, you know," Weisz said. He was silent for a moment. She had been courageous, on his behalf, and the way he met her eyes let her know he appreciated that. "You see, it works either way — I'm suspected of something criminal, so your feelings about me are changed, or you tell me, and I have to worry about the fact that I'm being investigated."

She thought about what he'd said, puzzled for a moment, then understanding. "That is, Carlo, a very ugly thing to do."

His smile was grim. "Yes, isn't it," he said.

Heading back to the office, Weisz stood swaying in a crowded Métro car, the faces around him pale and blank, and private. There was a poem about that, by some American who loved Mussolini. What was it — faces like, like "petals on a wet, black bough." He tried to remember the rest of it, but the man who'd questioned Véronique wouldn't leave him alone. Maybe he was exactly who he'd said he was. Weisz's experience of the *Sûreté* went no further than the two inspectors who'd interrogated him, but there were others, likely all sorts. Still, he'd come alone, and left no card, no telephone number. Never mind the *Sûreté,* this was not the way police anywhere operated. Information was often best recollected in private, later on, and *flics* all the world over knew it.

He didn't want to face what came next. That this was the OVRA, operating from a clandestine station in Paris, using French agents, and launching a new attack against the *giellisti.* Getting rid of Bottini hadn't worked, so they'd try something else. The timing was right, they'd seen the new *Liberazione* a week earlier, and here was their response. It worked. From the time he'd left the gallery he'd been apprehensive, literally and figuratively looking over his shoulder. *So,* he told himself, *they got what they came for.* And he knew it wouldn't stop there.

He left work at six, saw Salamone at the bar and told him what had happened, and was at the Tournon, with Ferrara, by seven-forty-five. All he'd had to do was forget about dinner, but, the way he felt by nightfall, he wasn't all that hungry.

Being with Ferrara made him feel better. Weisz had begun to see Mr. Brown's point about the colonel — the antifascist forces weren't all fumbling intellectuals with eyeglasses and too many books, they had warriors, real warriors, on their side. And *Soldier for Freedom* was moving along swiftly, had now reached Ferrara's flight to Marseilles.

Weisz sat on one chair, with the new Remington they'd bought him on the other, between his knees, while Ferrara paced about the room, sitting sometimes on the edge of the bed, then pacing again. "It was strange to be on my own," he said. "The military life keeps you occupied, tells you what to do next. Everybody complains about it, makes fun of it, but it has its comforts. When I left Ethiopia . . . we talked about the ship, the Greek tanker, right?"

"Yes. Big, fat Captain Karazenis, the great smuggler."

Ferrara grinned at the memory. "You mustn't make him out too much of a scoundrel. I mean, he was, but it was a pleasure to be around him, his answer to the cruel world was to steal it blind."

"That's how he'll be, in the book. Called

only 'the Greek captain.' "

Ferrara nodded. "Anyhow, we had engine trouble off the Ligurian coast. Somewhere around Livorno. That was a bad day — what if we had to put into an Italian port? Would one of the crew give me away? And Karazenis liked to play games with me, said he had a girlfriend in Livorno. But, in the end, we made it, just made it, into Marseilles, and I went to a hotel in the port."

"What hotel was that?"

"I'm not sure it had a name, the sign said 'Hotel.' "

"I'll leave it out."

"I never knew you could stay anywhere for so little money. Bed bugs, yes, and lice. But you know the old saying: 'Filth, like hunger, only matters for eight days.' And I was there for months, and then–"

"Wait, wait, not so fast."

They worked away at it, Weisz hammering on the keys, churning out pages. At eleven-thirty, they decided to call it quits. The air in the room was smoky and still, Ferrara opened the shutters, then the window, letting in a rush of cold night air. He leaned out, looking up and down the street.

"What's so interesting?" Weisz said, putting on his jacket.

"Oh, there's been some guy lurking about in doorways, the last few nights."

"Really?"

"We're being watched, I guess. Or maybe the word is *guarded.*"

"Did you mention it?"

"No. I don't know that it has anything to do with me."

"You should tell them about it."

"Mm. Maybe I will. You don't think it's some kind of, problem, do you?"

"I have no idea."

"Well, maybe I'll ask about it." He went back to the window and looked up and down the street. "Not there now," he said. "Not where I can see him."

The streets were deserted as Weisz walked back to the Dauphine, but he had an imagined Christa for company. Told her about his day, a version made entertaining for her amusement. Then, back in his room, he fell asleep and found her in his dreams — the first time they'd made love, on a yacht in Trieste harbor. She had worn, that late afternoon, a pair of oyster-colored pajamas, sheer and cool for a summer week at sea. He'd sensed that she had some kind of sensual affinity for the pajamas, so he did not take them off, the first time. Unbuttoned the top, slid the bottoms down her thighs. This inspired both of them, and, when the dream woke him, he found himself again inspired, and then, in the darkness, lived those moments once more.

The editorial meeting for the new *Liberazione* was at midday on the twenty-ninth of April. Weisz hurried to get to the Europa, but he was the last one there. Salamone had waited for him, and began the meeting as he was sitting down. "Before we discuss the next issue," he said, "we have to talk a little about our situation."

"Our situation?" the lawyer said, alert to a note in Salamone's voice.

"Some things are going on that have to be discussed." He paused, then said, "For one thing, a friend of Carlo's was questioned by a man who represented himself as an inspector of the *Sûreté*. There's reason to believe that he wasn't who he said he was. That he came from the opposition."

A long silence. Then the pharmacist said, "Do you mean the OVRA?"

"It's a possibility we have to face. So take a minute, and think about how things are going in your own lives. Your daily lives, anything not normal."

From the lawyer, a forced laugh. "Normal?

My life at the language school?" But nobody else thought it was funny.

The art historian from Siena said, "It all goes on as usual, with me."

Salamone, a sigh in his voice, said, "Well, what's happened to me is that I've lost my job. I've been discharged."

For a moment, dead silence, broken only by the muted sounds of café life on the other side of the door. Finally, Elena said, "Did they tell you why?"

"My supervisor wouldn't quite say. Something about not enough work, but that was a lie. He had some other reason."

"You think that he, too, had a visit from the *Sûreté*," the lawyer said. "And not the real one."

From Salamone, spread hands and raised eyebrows. *What else can I think?*

This was immediately personal. Every one of them worked at whatever they could find — the lawyer at Berlitz, the Sienese professor as a meter reader for the gas company, Elena selling hosiery at the Galeries Lafayette — but that was common émigré Paris, where Russian cavalry officers drove taxis. Around the table, the same reaction: at least they *had* jobs, but what if they lost them? And as Weisz, perhaps the luckiest of them all, thought about Delahanty, the rest thought about their own employers.

"We survived Bottini's murder," Elena said. "But this . . ." She could not say, out loud, that it was worse, but, in its way, it was.

Sergio, the businessman from Milan, who'd come to Paris with the passage of the anti-Semitic laws, said, "For the moment, Arturo, you won't have to worry about money."

Salamone nodded. "I appreciate that," he said. He left it there, but what didn't need to be said was that their benefactor couldn't support them all. "This may be the time," he went on, "for all of us to consider what we want to do now. Some of us may not want to continue with this work. Think it over, carefully. Leaving for a few months won't mean you can't return, and leaving for a few months might be what you should do. Don't say anything here, telephone me at home, or stop by. It may be for the best. For you, for the people who depend on you. This isn't a question of honor, it's practical."

"Is *Liberazione* finished?" Elena said.

"Not yet," Salamone said.

"We can be replaced," the pharmacist said, more to himself than anybody else.

"We can," Salamone said. "And that goes

for me, too. The *Giustizia e Libertà* in Turin was destroyed in 1937, all of them arrested. Yet here we are today."

"Arturo," the Sienese professor said, "I work with a Roumanian man, at one time a ballet master in Bucharest. The point is, is that I think he's leaving, in a few weeks, to go to America. Anyhow, that's one possibility, the gas company. You have to go down into the cellars, sometimes you see a rat, but it's not so bad."

"America," the lawyer said. "Lucky man."

"We can't all go to America," the Venetian professor said.

Why not? But no one said it.

Report of Agent 207, delivered by hand on 30 April, to a clandestine OVRA station in the Tenth Arrondissement:

The *Liberazione* group met at midday on 29 April at the CafÈ Europa, the same subjects attending as in previous reports. Subject SALAMONE reported his discharge from the Assurance du Nord company and discussed the possibility that a clandestine operative had defamed him to his employer. SALAMONE suggested that a friend of subject WEISZ had been similarly approached, and warned the group

247

that they may have to reconsider their participation in the *Liberazione* publication. An editorial meeting followed, with discussion of the occupation of Albania and the state of Italo-German relations as possible subjects for the next issue.

The following morning, with a hesitant spring day, the real *Sûreté* was back in Weisz's life. The message came this time, thank heaven, to the Dauphine, and not to Reuters, said simply, "Please contact me immediately," had a telephone number, and was signed "Monsieur," not "Inspector," Pompon. Looking up from the slip of paper, he said to Madame Rigaud, on the other side of the reception desk, "A friend," as though he needed to explain the message. She shrugged. One has friends, they telephone. For your room rent, as long as you pay it, we take your messages.

He'd worried about her, lately. It wasn't that she'd stopped being nice to him, just, lately, not quite so warm. Was this simply another Gallic shift of mood, common enough in this moody city, or something more? There had always been, in her demeanor, a night visit on the horizon. She was playful, but she'd let him know that her black dress could, at some point, be removed, and that beneath it lay a lovely treat for a good boy like him. This bothered Weisz, the first few weeks of his tenancy — what if something went wrong? Was love-making a covert condition of room rental?

But that wasn't true, she simply liked to flirt with him, to tease him into the bawdy landlady fantasy, and, in time, he began to relax and enjoy it. She was hatchet-faced, hatchet-minded, and henna-dyed, but the accidental brush or bump — *"Oh pardon, Monsieur Weisz!"* — revealed the real Madame Rigaud, curved and firm, and all for him. Eventually.

That was, the last week or so, gone. Where did it go?

On the way to the Métro, he stopped at a post office and telephoned Pompon, who suggested a meeting at nine the following morning, at a café across from the Opéra — the lobby floor of the Grand Hotel — and conveniently close to the Reuters office. These arrangements were, *oh no,* considerate, and, *uh-oh,* thoughtful, and led to one more day of trying to work while fighting off the urge to speculate. *Britain and France Offer Guarantees to Greece:* calls to Devoisin at the Quai d'Orsay, then to other sources, swimming deeper in the tidal pools of French diplomacy, as well as contact with the Greek embassy, and the editor of an émigré Greek newspaper — the Paris side of the news.

Weisz worked hard. Worked for Delahanty, to show how truly crucial he was to the Reuters effort, worked for Christa, so he wouldn't be driving a delivery van when she came to Paris, worked for the *giellisti* — the paper was on the edge of mortality and losing his job might very well be the last straw. And for his own pride — not money, pride.

A long night. And then, the café meeting, and a topic he should have, he realized, foreseen. "We have come into possession of a document," Pompon said, "originally mailed to the Foreign Ministry. A document that should be made public. Not directly, but in a covert manner, in, perhaps, a clandestine newspaper."

Oh?

"It contains information that the newspaper *Liberazione* mentioned, as rumor, in its last issue, but that was rumor, and what we've got our hands on now is specific. Very specific. Of course we know you have contact with these émigrés, and someone like you, in your position, would be a realistic source for such information."

Maybe.

"The document reveals German penetration of the Italian security system, a massive penetration, in the hundreds, and revealing it could create antagonism toward Germany, toward these sorts of tactics, which are dangerous to any state. The rumor, as published in *Liberazione,* was provocative, but the actual *list,* now that could really cause problems." Did Weisz see what he was getting at?

Well — what the French called *un petit oui,* a little *yes* — yes.

"I have a copy of the document with me, Monsieur Weisz, would you care to see it?"

Ah, naturally.

Pompon unbuckled his briefcase and withdrew the pages, folded so that they would fit into an envelope, and handed them to Weisz. It wasn't the list he'd typed, but a precise copy. He unfolded the pages and pretended to study them; at first puzzled, then interested, finally fascinated.

Pompon smiled — the pantomime had evidently worked. "Quite a coup for *Liberazione,* no? To publish the real evidence?"

He certainly thought so. But . . .

But?

The present condition of that journal was uncertain. Some members of the editorial board had come under pressure — he'd heard that the paper might not survive.

Pressure?

Lost jobs, harassment by fascist agents.

A silent Pompon stared at him. Amid tables of chattering Parisians, who'd been shopping at the nearby Galeries Lafayette, hotel guests with guidebooks, a pair of newlyweds from the provinces, arguing about money. All in clouds of smoke and perfume. Waiters flew past — who on earth was ordering éclairs at this time of the morning?

Weisz waited, but the inspector did not bite. Or maybe bit in some way that Weisz could not observe. "Fascist agents" pestering émigrés was not the subject for today, the subject for today was inducing a resistance organization to do a little job for him. Or for the Foreign Ministry, or God only knew who. That other business, a different department handled that, down the hall, one flight up, and who'd want their inquisitive snouts poking into his carefully tended émigré garden? Not Pompon.

Finally, Weisz said, "I will talk to them, at *Liberazione.*"

"Do you wish to keep that copy? We have others, though you must be very careful with it."

No, he knew what it was, he would prefer

to leave the document with Pompon.

As he'd earlier said to Salamone: *hot potato.*

The taxi sped through the Paris night. A soft May evening, the air warm and seductive, half the city out on the boulevards. Weisz had been happy enough in his room, but the night manager at Reuters had sent him off, pad and pencil in hand, to the Hotel Crillon. "It's King Zog," he'd said on the Dauphine telephone. "The local Albanians have discovered him, and they're gathering on the place Concorde. Go and have a look, will you?"

Weisz's driver took the Pont Royal bridge, turned on Saint-Honoré, drove ten feet down the rue Royale, and stopped behind a line of cars that disappeared into a crowd. There they were stuck, and were now honking their horns, making sure that nobody got out of their way. The driver threw his taxi into reverse, waving at the car behind him to back up. "Not me," he said to Weisz, "not tonight." Weisz paid, jotted down the fare, and got out.

What was Zog, Ahmed Zogu, former king of Albania, doing there? Thrown out by Mussolini, he'd wandered through various capitals, the press keeping track of him, and had apparently landed at the Crillon. But, local Albanians? Albania was the lost mountain kingdom of the Balkans — and that was very lost indeed — independent in 1920, then snatched at, north and south, by Italy and Yugoslavia, until Mussolini grabbed the whole thing a month earlier. But, as far as Weisz knew, there was not much of a political émigré community in Paris.

There was certainly a crowd on the rue Royale, mostly curious passersby, and, when Weisz finally pushed his way through, on Concorde, where he realized that however many Albanians had made their way to Paris, they'd showed up that night. Six or seven hundred, he thought, with a few hundred French supporters. Not the Communists — no red flags — because what you had in Albania was a little dictator eaten up by a big dictator, but those who thought it was never a good idea for one nation to occupy another, and, on a lovely May night, why not take a stroll over to the Crillon?

Weisz worked toward the front of the hotel, where a bedsheet nailed to a pair of poles, swaying with the motion of the crowd, said something in Albanian. Up here they were also chanting — Weisz caught the words *Zog* and *Mussolini,* but that was about it. At the Crillon entry, a score of porters and bellmen were ranged protectively in front of the door and, as Weisz watched, the *flics* began to show up, truncheons tapping their legs, ready for action. All across the face of the hotel, guests were looking out, pointing here and there, enjoying the show. Then a window on the top floor opened, a light went on in the room, and a matinee idol, with dashing mustache, leaned out and gave the Zogist salute: hand flattened, palm forward, over the heart. King Zog! From behind the drape, someone reached out, and now the king wore a general's hat, heavy with gold braid, above his Sulka bathrobe. The crowd cheered, Queen Geraldine appeared at the king's side, and both waved.

Now some idiot — *anti-Zogist elements in the crowd,* Weisz wrote — threw a bottle, which shattered in front of a bellboy, who lost his little cap as he leapt away. Then the king and queen stepped back from the window, and the light went off. Next to Weisz, a bearded giant put his hands beside his mouth and shouted, in French, "That's right, run away, you little pussy." This drew a snicker from his tiny girlfriend, and an angry Albanian shout from somewhere in the crowd. On the top floor, another window opened, and a uniformed army officer looked out.

The police began to advance, barring their truncheons and forcing the crowd back from the front of the hotel. The fighting started almost immediately — surging knots of people in the crowd, others pushing and shoving, trying to get out of the way. "Ah," said the giant with some satisfaction, *"les chevaux."* The horses. The cavalry had arrived, mounted police with long truncheons, advancing down the avenue Gabriel.

"You don't like the king?" Weisz said to the giant — he had to get some kind of quote from somebody, jot down a few lines, find a telephone, file the story, and go out for dinner.

"He doesn't like anybody," said the giant's girlfriend.

What was he, Weisz wondered. A Communist? Fascist? Anarchist?

But this he was not to learn.

Because the next thing he knew, he was on the ground. Someone behind him had hit him in the side of the head, with something, he had no idea what, hit him hard enough to knock him over. Not a good place to be, down here. His vision blurred, a forest of shoes moved away, and a few indignant oaths followed somebody, whoever'd hit him, as the man sliced his way through the crowd.

"You are bleeding," said the giant.

Weisz felt his face, and his hand came away red — maybe he'd cut himself on the sharp edge of a cobblestone — then he started groping around for his glasses. "Here they are." A hand offered them, one lens cracked, the temple piece gone.

Somebody put his hands beneath Weisz's armpits and hauled him to his feet. It was the giant, who said, "We better get out of here."

Weisz heard the horses, in a swift walk, advancing toward him. He got a handkerchief from his back pocket and held it to the side of his head, took a step, almost toppled over. Only one eye, he realized, saw properly, the other had everything out of focus. He went down on one knee. *Maybe,* he thought, *I'm hurt.*

The crowd broke around him as it ran away, pursued by the mounted police, swinging their truncheons. Then a tough old Parisian *flic* appeared at his side — he was now alone on a vast stretch of the place Concorde. "Can you stand up?" the *flic* said.

"I think so."

"Because, if you can't, I have to put you in an ambulance."

"No, it's allright. I'm a journalist."

"Try and stand."

He was very wobbly, but he managed. "Maybe a taxi," he said.

"They don't stick around, when these things happen. How about a café?"

"Yes, that's a good idea."

"See who hit you?"

"No."

"Any idea why?"

"No idea."

The *flic* shook his head — saw too much of human nature and didn't like it. "Maybe just for fun. Anyhow, let's try for the café."

He held Weisz up on one side and walked him slowly over to the rue de Rivoli, where a tourist café had emptied out as soon as the fighting started. Weisz sat down hard, a waiter brought him a glass of water and a bar towel. "You can't go home like that," he said.

Weisz invited Salamone out for dinner the following night — by way of encouraging a friend in difficulties. They met at a little Italian place out in the Thirteenth, the second-best Italian restaurant in Paris — the best owned by a well-known supporter of Mussolini, so there they could not go. "What happened to you?" Salamone said, as Weisz arrived.

Weisz had gone to his doctor that morning, and now wore a white gauze bandage on the left side of his face, badly scraped by the rough surface of a cobblestone, and a puffy red mark below his temple on the other side. His new glasses would be ready in a day or two. "A street demonstration last night," he told Salamone. "Somebody hit me."

"I'll say they did. Who was it?"

"I have no idea."

"No confrontation?"

"He was behind me, ran away, and I never saw him."

"What, somebody followed you? Somebody, ah, we know?"

"I thought about it all night. With a handkerchief tied around my head."

"And?"

"Nothing else makes sense. People don't just do that."

Salamone's oath was more in sorrow than in anger. He poured red wine from a large carafe into two straight-sided glasses, then handed Weisz a bread stick. "It can't go on like this," he said, an Italian echo of *il faut en finir*. "And it could have been worse."

"Yes," Weisz said. "I thought about that, too."

"What do we do, Carlo?"

"I don't know." He gave Salamone a menu, and opened his own. Cured ham, spring lamb with baby artichokes and potatoes, early greens — from the south of France, he supposed — then figs preserved in syrup.

"A feast," Salamone said.

"That's what I intended," Weisz said. "For morale." He raised his glass, *"Salute."*

Salamone took a second sip. "This isn't Chianti," he said. "It's, maybe, Barolo."

"Something very good," Weisz said.

They looked over at the proprietor, by the cash register, whose nod and smile acknowledged what he'd done: *Enjoy it, boys, I know who you are.* Saying *thank-you,* Weisz and Salamone raised their glasses to him.

Weisz signaled the waiter and ordered the grand dinners. "Are you managing?" he said to Salamone.

"More or less. My wife is angry with me — this politics, enough is enough. And she hates the idea of taking charity."

"And the girls?"

"They don't say much — they're grown, and they have their own lives. They were in their twenties when we came here in 'thirty-

260

two, and they're getting to be more French than Italian." Salamone paused, then said, "Our pharmacist is gone, by the way. He's going to take a few months off, as he put it, until things cool down. Also the engineer, a note. He regrets, but goodby."

"Anyone else?"

"Not yet, but we'll lose a few more, before this is over. In time, it could be just Elena, who's a fighter, and our benefactor, you and me, maybe the lawyer — he's thinking it over — and our friend from Siena."

"Always smiling."

"Yes, not much bothers him. He takes it all in stride, Signor Zerba."

"Anything about the job, at the gas company?"

"No, but I may have something else, from another friend, at a warehouse out in Levallois."

"Levallois! A long way — does the Métro go out there?"

"Close enough. You take a bus, or walk, after the last stop."

"Can you use the car?"

"The poor thing, no, I don't think so. The gasoline is expensive, and the tires, well, you know."

"Arturo, you can't work in a warehouse, you're fifty . . . what? Three?"

"Six. But it's just a checker's job, crates in and out. A friend of ours pretty much runs the union, so it's a real offer."

The waiter approached with plates bearing slices of brick-colored ham. *"Basta,"* Salamone said, enough. "Here's our dinner, so we'll talk about life and love. *Salute,* Carlo."

They kept work out of it for the duration of the dinner, which was very good, the leg of young lamb roasted with garlic, the early greens fresh and carefully picked over. When they'd finished the figs in syrup, and lit cigarettes to go with their espressos, Salamone said, "I guess the real question is, if we can't protect ourselves, who is there to protect us? The police — the people at the *Préfecture?*"

"Not likely," Weisz said. "Oh officer, we're engaged in illegal operations against a neighbor country, and, as they're attacking us, we'd like you to help us out."

"I guess that's right. It is, technically, illegal."

"Technically nothing, it's illegal, period. The French have laws against everything, then they pick and choose. For the moment we're tolerated, for political expediency, but I don't think we qualify for protection. My inspector at the *Sûreté* won't even admit

262

I'm the editor of *Liberazione,* though he surely knows I am. I'm a friend of the editor, the way he puts it. Very French, that approach."

"So, we're on our own."

"We are."

"Then how do we fight back? What do we use for weapons?"

"You don't mean guns, do you?"

Salamone shrugged, and his "No" was tentative. "Maybe influence, favors. That too is French."

"And what do we do for them in return? They don't do favors here."

"They don't do favors anywhere."

"The inspector at the *Sûreté,* as I told you, asked us to publish the real list, from Berlin. Should we do that?"

"*Mannaggia* no!"

"So then," Weisz said, "what?"

"How do the English feel about you, lately?"

"Christ, I'd rather publish the list."

"Could be we're fucked, Carlo."

"Could be. What about the next edition? Farewell?"

"That hurts my heart. But we have to think about it."

"Fine," Weisz said. "We'll think."

■ ■ ■ ■

After dinner, walking from the Luxembourg Métro to the Hotel Tournon for his evening session with Ferrara, Weisz passed a car, parked facing him, on the rue de Médicis. It was an unusual car for this quarter — it would not have been remarkable over in the Eighth, on the grand boulevards, or up in snooty Passy, but maybe he would have noticed it anyhow. Because it was an Italian car, a champagne-colored Lancia sedan, the aristocrat of the line, with a chauffeur, in proper cap and uniform, sitting stiff and straight behind the wheel.

In back, a man with carefully brushed silver hair, gleaming with brilliantine, and a thin silver mustache. On the lapels of his gray silk suit, an Order of the Crown of Italy, and a silver Fascist party pin. This was a type of man that Weisz easily recognized: fine manners, scented powder, and a certain supercilious contempt for anyone beneath him in the social order — most of the world. Weisz slowed for a moment, didn't quite stop, then continued on. This momentary hesitation appeared to interest the silvery man, whose eyes acknowledged his presence, then pointedly looked away, as though

Weisz's existence was of little concern.

It was almost nine by the time Weisz arrived at Ferrara's room. They were still working on the colonel's time in Marseilles, where he'd found a job at a stall in the fish market, where he'd been discovered by a French journalist, then defamed in the Italian fascist press, and where, in time, he'd made contact with a man recruiting for the International Brigades, a month or so after Franco's military insurrection against the elected government.

Then, beginning to worry about page count, Weisz took Ferrara back to his 1917 service with the *arditi,* the elite trench raiders, and the fateful Italian defeat at Caporetto, where the army broke and ran. A national humiliation, which, five years later, was more than a little responsible for the birth of fascism. In the face of poisoned-gas attacks by German and Austro-Hungarian regiments, many Italian soldiers had thrown away their rifles and headed south, shouting, *"Andiamo a casa!"* We're going home.

"But not us," Ferrara said, his expression dark. "We took the losses, and retreated because we had to, but we never stopped killing them."

As Weisz typed, a timid knock at the door.

"Yes?" Ferrara said.

The door opened, to admit a seedy little man, who said, in French, "So, how goes the book tonight?"

Ferrara introduced him as Monsieur Kolb, one of his minders, and the operative who had extracted him from the internment camp. Kolb said he was pleased to meet Weisz, then looked at his watch. "It's eleven-thirty," he said, "time for all good authors to be in bed, or out raising hell. It's the latter we have in mind for you, if you like."

"Raising what?" Ferrara said.

"An English expression. Means to have a good time. We thought you might like to go up to Pigalle, to some disreputable place. Drink, dance, who knows what. You've earned it, Mr. Brown says, and you can't just sit in this hotel."

"I'll go if you will," Ferrara said to Weisz.

Weisz was exhausted. He was working at three jobs, and the steady grind was beginning to get to him. Worse, the espresso he'd drunk earlier in the evening had had absolutely no effect on the Barolo he'd shared with Salamone. But their conversation was still on his mind, and an informal chat with one of Mr. Brown's people might not be a bad idea, better than approaching Mr. Brown himself. "Let's go," Weisz said. "He's right, you can't just sit here."

Kolb had evidently sensed they would agree, and had a taxi idling in front of the hotel.

Place Pigalle was the heart of it, but the strip of nightclubs, neon-lit, marched up and down the boulevard Clichy, suggesting bountiful sin for every taste. There was plenty of real sin to be had in Paris, in well-known bordellos thoughout the city, whipping rooms, harems with veiled girls in balloon pants, high erotic — instructive Japanese prints on the walls — or low and beastly, but up here it was more the promise of sin, offered to wandering crowds of tourists sprinkled with sailors, thugs, and pimps. Gay Paree. The famous Moulin Rouge and the flipped skirts of its cancan dancers, the La Bohème at Impasse Blanche, Eros, Enfants de la Chance, El Monico, the Romance Bar, and Chez les Nudistes — Kolb's, and likely Mr. Brown's, choice for the evening.

The nudist colony. Which described the women, dressed only in high heels and powdery blue light, but not the men dancing with them, to the slow strains of Momo Tsipler and his Wienerwald Companions — according to a sign at the corner of a raised platform. Five of them, including the oldest cellist in captivity, a tiny violinist, cigarette stuck in the corner of his mouth, wings of white hair fluffed out above his ears, Rex the drummer, Hoffy on the clarinet, and Momo himself, in a metallic green dinner jacket, astride the piano stool. A weary orchestra, drifting far from their hometown Vienna on the nightclub sea, playing a schmaltz version of "Let's Fall in Love" as the couples shuffled about in circles, doing whatever dance steps the male patrons could manage.

Weisz felt like an idiot, Ferrara caught his eye and looked to heaven, *what have we done?* They were led to a table, and Kolb ordered champagne, the only available beverage, delivered by a waitress dressed in a money pouch on a red sash. "You don't want no change, do you?" she said.

"No," Kolb said, accepting the inevitable. "I suppose not."

"Very good," she answered, her blue behind wobbling as she plodded away.

"What is she, Greek, you think?" Kolb said.

"Somewhere down there," Weisz said. "Maybe Turkish."

"Want to try another place?"

"Do you?" Weisz said to Ferrara.

"Oh, let's have this bottle, then we'll like it better."

They had to work at it, the champagne was dreadful, and barely cool, but did in time elevate their spirits, and kept Weisz from falling dead asleep with his head on the table. Momo Tsipler sang a Viennese love song, and that got Kolb talking about Vienna, in the old days, before the *Anschluss* — the tiny Dollfuss, not five feet tall, the chancellor of Austria until the Nazis killed him in 1934 — and the infinitely bizarre personality — high culture, low lovelife — of that city. "All those high-breasted fraus in the pastry shops, noses in the air, proper as the day is long, well, I knew a fellow called Wolfi, a salesman of ladies' undergarments, and he once told me . . ."

Ferrara excused himself and disappeared into the crowd. Kolb went on with his story, for a time, then wound down to silence when the colonel emerged with a dancing partner. Kolb watched them for a moment, then said, "Say this for him, he certainly picked the best."

She was. Brassy blond hair in a French roll, a sulky face accented by a heavy lower lip, and a body both lithe and fulsome, which she clearly liked to show off, all of it alive and animated as she danced. The two of them made, in fact, an attractive couple. Momo Tsipler, his fingers walking up and down the keyboard, swiveled around on his piano stool for a better view, then gave them a grand Viennese wink, somewhere well beyond lewd.

"There is something I want to ask you," Weisz said.

Kolb wasn't entirely sure he wanted to be asked — he'd perfectly heard a certain note in Weisz's voice, he'd heard it before, and always it preceded inquiries that touched on his vocation. "Oh? And what is that?"

Weisz laid out a condensed version of the OVRA attack on the *Liberazione* committee. Bottini's murder, the interrogation of Véronique, Salamone's lost job, his own experience on the place Concorde.

Kolb knew exactly what he was talking about. "What is it you want?" he said.

"Can you help us?"

"Not me," Kolb said. "I don't make decisions like that, you'd have to ask Mr. Brown, and he'd have to ask someone else, and the final answer would be, I expect, no."

"Are you sure of that?"

"Pretty much, I am. Our business is always quiet, to do what has to be done, then fade into the night. We aren't in Paris to pick a fight with another service. That's bad form, Weisz, that's not the way this work is done."

"But you oppose Mussolini. Certainly the British government does."

"What gave you that idea?"

"You're having an antifascist book written, creating an opposition hero, and that's not fading into the night."

Kolb was amused. "Written, yes. Published, we'll see. I have no special information, but I would bet you ten francs that the diplomats are hard at it to bring Mussolini over to our side, just like last time, just like 1915. If that doesn't work, then, maybe, we'll attack him, and it will be time for the book to appear."

"Still, no matter what happens politically, you'll want the support of the émigrés."

"It's always nice to have friends, but they're not the crucial element, by far, not. We're a traditional service, and we operate on the classic assumptions. Which means we concentrate on the three *C*'s: Crown, Capital, and Clergy. That's where the influence is, that's how a state changes sides, when the leader, king, premier, whatever he calls himself, and the big money — captains of industry — and the religious leaders, whatever God they pray to, when these people want a new policy, then things change. So, émigrés can help, but they're famously a pain in the ass, every day some new problem. Forgive me, Weisz, for being frank with you, but it's the same with journalists — journalists work for other people, for Capital, and that's who gets to tell them what to write. Nations are run by oligarchies, by whoever's powerful, and that's where any service will commit its resources, and that's what we're doing in Italy."

Weisz wasn't so very good at hiding his reactions, Kolb could see what he felt. "I'm telling you something you don't know?"

"No, you aren't, it all makes sense. But we don't know where to turn, and we're going to lose the newspaper."

The music stopped, it was time for the Wienerwald Companions to take a break — the drummer wiped his face with a handkerchief, the violinist lit a fresh cigarette. Ferrara and his partner walked over to the bar and waited to be served.

"Look," Kolb said. "You're working hard for us, never mind the money, and Brown appreciates what you're doing, that's why you're being treated to a big night. Of course, this doesn't mean he'll get us into a war with the Italians, but — by the way, we never had this conversation — but, maybe, if you come up with something in return, we might talk to somebody in one of the French services."

Ferrara and his new friend came over to the table, champagne cocktails in hand. Weisz stood up to offer her his chair, but she waved him off and settled on Ferrara's lap. "Hello everybody," she said. "I am Irina." She had a heavy Russian accent.

After that, she ignored them, moving around on Ferrara's lap, toying with his hair, giggling and carrying on, whispering answers to whatever he was saying in her ear. Finally, he said to Kolb, "Don't bother looking for me when you go back to the hotel." Then, to Weisz: "And I'll see you tomorrow night."

"We can take you wherever you're going, in the taxi," Kolb said.

Ferrara smiled. "Don't worry about it. I'll find my way home."

A few minutes later, they left, Irina clinging to his arm. Kolb said good night, then gave them a few minutes, enough for her to get dressed. He looked at his watch as he stood up to leave. "Some nights . . ." he said with a sigh, and left it at that. Weisz could see he wasn't pleased — now he would have to spend hours, likely till dawn, sitting in the back of the taxi and watching some doorway, God only knew where.

11 May. Salamone called an editorial committee meeting for midday. As Weisz arrived, hurrying up the street, he saw Salamone and a few other *giellisti* standing silent in front of the Café Europa. Why? Was it locked? When Weisz joined them, he saw why. The entry to the café was blocked by a few scrap boards nailed across the door. Inside, shelves of broken bottles rose above the bar, in front of a charred wall. The ceiling was black, as were the tables and chairs, tumbled this way and that on the tile floor, amid puddles of black water. The bitter smell of dead fire, of burnt plaster and paint, hung in the air on the street.

Salamone didn't comment, his face said it all. From the others, hands in pockets, a subdued greeting. Finally, Salamone said, "I guess we'll have to meet somewhere else," but his voice was low and defeated.

"Maybe the station buffet, at the Gare du Nord," the benefactor said.

"Good idea," Weisz said. "It's just a few minutes' walk."

They headed for the railway station, and entered the crowded buffet. The waiter was helpful, found them a table for five, but

274

there were people all around them, who glanced over as the forlorn little group settled themselves and ordered coffees. "Not an easy place to talk," Salamone said. "But then, I don't think we have much to say."

"Are you sure, Arturo?" the professor from Siena said. "I mean, it's a shock, to see something like that. No accident, I think."

"No, not an accident," Elena said.

"It's maybe not the moment to make decisions," the benefactor said. "Why not wait a day or two, then we'll see how we feel."

"I'd like to agree," Salamone said. "But this has gone on long enough."

"Where is everybody?" Elena said.

"That's the problem, Elena," Salamone said. "I spoke to the lawyer yesterday. He didn't resign, officially, but when I telephoned, he told me his apartment had been robbed. A terrible mess, he said. They'd spent all night trying to clean it up, everything thrown on the floor, broken glasses and dishes."

"Did he call the police?" the Sienese professor said.

"Yes, he did. They said such things happened all the time. Asked for a list of stolen items."

"And our friend from Venice?"

"Don't know," Salamone said. "He said he would be here, but he hasn't shown up, so now it's just the five of us."

"That's enough," Elena said.

"I think we have to postpone the next issue," Weisz said, to spare Salamone from saying it.

"And give them what they want," Elena said.

"Well," Salamone said, "we can't go on until we can find a way to fight back, and nobody's come up with a way to do that. Suppose some detective from the *Préfecture* agreed to take the case, what then? Assign twenty men to watch all of us? Day and night? Until they caught somebody? This is never going to happen, and the OVRA perfectly well know it won't."

"So," the Sienese professor said, "it's finished?"

"Postponed," Salamone said. "Which is perhaps a nice word for *finished*. I suggest we skip a month, wait until June, then we'll meet once more. Elena, do you agree?"

She shrugged, unwilling to say the words.

"Sergio?"

"Agreed," the benefactor said.

"Zerba?"

"I'll go along with the committee," the

Sienese professor said.

"And Carlo."

"Wait until June," Weisz said.

"Very well. It's unanimous."

Agent 207 was precise, in a report to the OVRA delivered in Paris the following day, on the decision and the vote of the committee. Which meant, once the report reached the *Pubblica Sicurezza* committee in Rome, that their operation was not yet complete. Their objective was to finish *Liberazione* — not postpone its publication — and make an example, to let the others, Communist, socialist, Catholic, see what happened to those who dared to oppose fascism. Then, too, they were great believers in the seventeenth-century English adage, coined in civil war, which said, "He that draws his sword against his prince must throw away the scabbard." Thus inspired, they determined that the Paris operation, as planned, with dates and targets and various actions, would continue.

The conductor on the 7:15 Paris/Genoa Express was approached on the fourteenth of May. After the train left the station at Lyons, the passengers slept, or read, or watched the springtime fields passing by the windows, and the conductor headed for the baggage car. There he found two friends: a dining-car waiter, and a sleeping-car porter, playing two-handed *scopa,* using a steamer trunk turned on its side for a card table. "Care to join us?" the waiter said. The conductor agreed, and was dealt a hand.

They played for a time, gossiping and joking, then the sound of the train, the beat of the engine and the wheels on the track, rose sharply as the door at the end of the car was opened. They looked up, to see a uniformed inspector of the *Milizia Ferroviaria,* the railway police, called Gennaro, who they'd known for years.

The railway police were Mussolini's way of enforcing his most noted achievement, making the trains run on time. This was the result of a determined effort in the early 1920s, after a train headed for Turin arrived four hundred hours behind schedule, much too late. But that was long ago, when Italy seemed to be following Russia into Bolshevism, and the trains often stopped, for long periods, so the trainworkers could participate in political meetings. Those days were over, but the *Milizia Ferroviaria* still rode the trains, now investigating crimes against the regime.

"Gennaro, come and play *scopa,*" the

waiter said, and the inspector pulled a suitcase up to the steamer trunk.

Fresh cards were dealt and they started a new game. "Tell me," Gennaro said to the conductor, "you ever see anybody on this train with one of those secret newspapers?"

"Secret newspapers?"

"Oh come on, you know what I mean."

"On this train? You mean a passenger, reading it?"

"No. Somebody taking them down to Genoa. Bundled up, maybe."

"Not me. Did you ever see that?" he asked the waiter.

"No. I never did."

"What about you?" he asked the porter.

"No, not me either. Of course, if it's the Communists, you'd never know about it, they'd have some secret way of doing it."

"That's true," the conductor said. "Maybe you should look for the Communists."

"Are they on this train?"

"This train? Oh no, we wouldn't have that. I mean, you can't talk to those guys."

"So, you think it's the Communists," Gennaro said.

The waiter played a three of cups, from the forty-card Italian deck, the conductor answered with a six of coins, and the porter said, "Hah!"

Gennaro stared at his cards for a moment, then said, "But it's not a Communist paper. That's what they tell me."

"Who then?"

"The GL, they say, it's their paper." Cautiously, he laid down a six of cups.

"Sure you want to do that?" the waiter said.

Gennaro nodded. The waiter took the trick with a ten of swords.

"Who knows," the conductor said, "they're all the same to me, those political types. All they do is argue, they don't like this, they don't like that. *Va Napoli,* is what I say to them." Go to Naples, which meant *fuck you.*

The waiter dealt the cards for the next hand. "Maybe it's in the baggage," the waiter said. "We could be playing on it right now."

Gennaro looked around, at trunks and suitcases piled everywhere. "They search that at the border," he said.

"True," the conductor said. "That's not your job. They can't expect you to do everything."

"Bundle of newspapers," the porter said. "Tied up with a string, you mean. We'd be sure to see something like that."

"And you never did, right, you're sure?"

"Seen a lot of things on this train, but never that."

"What about you?" Gennaro said to the conductor.

"I don't remember seeing it. A pig in a crate, once. Remember that?"

The waiter laughed, pinched his nose with his thumb and forefinger, and said, "Phew."

"And we get a body, sometimes, in a coffin," the conductor said. "Maybe you should look in there."

"Maybe he'd be reading the paper, Gennaro," the waiter said. "Then you'd get a medal."

They all laughed, and went back to playing cards.

On the nineteenth of May, a tipster in Berlin, a telephone operator at the Hotel Kaiserhof, told Eric Wolf of the Reuters bureau that arrangements were under way for Count Ciano, the Italian foreign minister, to visit Berlin. Rooms had been booked for visiting officials, and feature writers from the Stefani agency, the Italian wire service. A travel agent in Rome, waiting to talk to a reservations clerk, had told the operator what was going on.

At eleven in the morning, Delahanty called Weisz into his office. "What are you working on?" he said.

"Bobo, the talking dog up in Saint-Denis. I just got back."

"Does it talk?"

"It says" — Weisz deepened his voice to a low growl and barked — " '*bonjour,*' and '*ça va.*' "

"Really?"

"Sort of, if you listen hard. The owner used to be in the circus. It's a cute dog, a little mongrel, scruffy, it'll make a good photo."

Delahanty shook his head in mock despair. "There may well be more important news. Eric Wolf has cabled London, and they telephoned us — Ciano is going to Berlin, with a grand entourage, and the Stefani agency will be there in force. An official visit, not just consultations, and, according to what we hear, a major event, a treaty, called 'the Pact of Steel.' "

After a moment, Weisz said, "So that's that."

"Yes, it looks like the talking's done. Mussolini is going to sign up with Hitler." The war on the horizon, as Weisz sat in the grimy office, had moved a step closer. "You'll have to go home and pack, then get out to Le Bourget, we're flying you over. The ticket's on the way to your hotel, by messenger. A one-thirty flight."

"Forget Bobo?"

Delahanty looked harassed. "No, leave the bloody dog to Woodley, he can use your notes. What London wants from you is the Italian view, the opposition view. In other words, give 'em hell, if it's what we think it is, both barrels and the cat's breakfast. This is *bad* news, for Britain, and for every subscriber we have, and that's the way you'll write it."

On his way to the Métro, Weisz stopped at the American Express office and wired a message to Christa at her office in Berlin. *must leave paris today forward mail aunt magda expect to see her tonight hans.* Magda was one of the whippets, Christa would know what he meant.

Weisz reached the Dauphine twenty minutes later, and checked at the desk, but his ticket had not yet arrived. He was very excited as he ran up the stairs, and his mind, caught in crosscurrents, sped from one thing to the next. He realized that Kolb had indulged, at the nightclub, in the sin of optimism — the British diplomats had failed, and had lost Mussolini as an ally. This was, to Weisz, pure heartache, his country was in real trouble now and it would suffer, would, if events played out as he believed, be made to fight a war, a war that would end badly. Yet, strange how life went, the coming political explosion meant that *Liberazione, his* war, might possibly be salvaged. A visit to Pompon and the *Sûreté* machine would be put in gear, because an Italian operation, soon an *enemy* operation, would be seen in a very different light, and what happened next would be far beyond the efforts of some yawning detective at the *Préfecture.*

But it also meant, to Weisz, a great deal more than that. As he climbed, affairs of state drifted away like smoke, replaced by visions of what would happen when Christa came to his room. His imagination was on fire, first this, then that. No, the other way. It was cruel to be happy that morning, but he had no choice. For if the world insisted on going to hell, no matter what he, what anyone, tried to do, he and Christa would, by evening light, steal a few hours of life in a private world. Last chance, perhaps, because that other world would soon enough come looking for them, and Weisz knew it.

Breathless from the four flights, Weisz paused at the door when he heard footsteps ascending the stairs. Was this the hotel porter, with his airplane ticket? No, the tread was strong and certain. Weisz waited, and saw he'd been right, it wasn't the porter, it was the new tenant, down the hall and across the corridor.

Weisz had seen him before, two days earlier, and, as it happened, didn't much care for him, he couldn't exactly say why. He was a large man, tall and thick, who wore a rubber raincoat and a black felt hat. His face, dark, heavy, closed, reminded Weisz of southern Italy, it was the kind of face you saw down there. Was he, in fact, Italian? Weisz didn't know. He'd greeted the man, the first time they met in the hall, but received only a curt nod in reply — the man did not speak. And now, curiously, the same thing happened.

Oh well, some people. In the room, Weisz took his valise from the armoire and, with the ease of the experienced traveler, folded and packed. Underwear and socks, a spare shirt — *two*-day trip? Maybe three, he thought. Sweater? No. Gray flannel trousers, which made his suit jacket into a sport coat — he liked to think it did, anyhow. In a leather case, toothbrush, toothpaste — enough? Yes. Old-fashioned straight razor, the throat-slitter, so-called, his father's, once upon a time, kept all these years. Shaving soap. The cologne called Chypre, which

Christa had said she liked. Put some on for the trip? No, she won't be at the airport, and why smell good for the border *Kontrolle?*

Ah, the ticket. He went to answer the knock, but it wasn't the porter. It was the new tenant, still wearing his hat, one hand in the pocket of his raincoat, who stared at Weisz, then looked over his shoulder into the room. Weisz's heart skipped a beat. He took a half step back, and started to speak. Then, on the stairs, a slow tread accompanied by wheezing. "Excuse me," Weisz said. He slid past the man and walked toward the staircase, calling out, "Bertrand?"

"Coming, monsieur," the porter answered. "As fast as I can." Weisz waited as a panting Bertrand — these errands would kill him yet — struggled up the last few steps, a white envelope in his trembling hand. Down the corridor, a door was slammed shut, hard, and Weisz turned and saw that the new tenant had disappeared. The hell with him, discourteous fellow. Or worse. Weisz told himself to calm down, but something about the man's eyes had scared him, had made him remember what happened to Bottini.

"This just arrived," Bertrand said, handing Weisz the envelope.

Weisz reached into his pocket for a franc piece, but his money was on the desk, with his glasses and wallet. "Come in for a moment," he said.

Bertrand entered the room and sat heavily in the chair, fanning his face with his hand. Weisz thanked him and gave him his tip. "Who's the new tenant?" he said.

"I couldn't say, Monsieur Weisz. I believe he is from Italy, a commercial gentleman, perhaps."

Weisz took a last look around, closed his valise, buckled his briefcase, and put his hat on. Looking at his watch, he said, "I have to get out to Le Bourget."

The franc piece in Bertrand's pocket had evidently hastened his recovery. He rose nimbly and, as the two of them chatted about the weather, accompanied Weisz down the stairs.

In the spring twilight, as the Dewoitine airplane began its descent to Berlin, the change of pitch in the engines woke Carlo Weisz, who looked out the window and watched the drifting cloud as it broke over the wing. On his lap, an open copy of Dekobra's *La Madone des Sleepings — the Madonna of the Sleeping Cars* — a 1920s French spy thriller, wildly popular in its day, which Weisz had brought along for the trip. The dark adventures of Lady Diana Wynham, siren of the Orient Express, bed-hopping from Vienna to Budapest, with stops at "every European watering-place."

Weisz dog-eared the page and stowed the book in his briefcase. As the plane lost altitude, it broke through the cloud, revealing the streets, the parks and church steeples, of small towns, then a squared patchwork of farm fields, still faintly green in the gathering dusk. It was very peaceful, and, Weisz thought, very vulnerable, because this was the bomber pilot's view, just before he set it all on fire. Weisz had been in the Spanish towns, when the German bombers were done with them, but who down there hadn't seen them, set to heroic music, in the Reich's newsreels. Did the people at supper, below him, realize it could happen to them?

At Tempelhof airport, the passport *Kontrolle* was all smiles and courtesy — the dignitaries and foreign correspondents, streaming in for the Ciano visit, must see the amiable face of Germany. Weisz took a taxi into the city, and asked for messages at the Adlon desk, but there was nothing for him. By nine-thirty, he had eaten dinner and, up in his room, spent a few minutes standing over the telephone. But it was late, Christa was home. Perhaps she would come tomorrow.

By nine the next morning he was at the Reuters office, greeted warmly by Gerda and the other secretaries. Eric Wolf peered out of his office and beckoned Weisz inside. Something about him — perpetual bow tie, puzzled expression, myopic eyes behind round-framed eyeglasses, made him look like a friendly owl. Wolf said hello, then, his demeanor conspiratorial, closed his office door. Anxious to tell a story, he leaned forward, his voice low and private. "I've been given a message for you, Weisz."

Weisz tried to seem unconcerned. "Oh?"

"I don't know what it means, and you don't have to tell me, of course. And maybe I don't want to know."

Weisz looked mystified.

"Last night, I left the office at seven-thirty, as usual, and I was walking back to my apartment when this very elegant lady, all in black, falls in beside me and says, 'Herr Wolf, if Carlo Weisz should come to Berlin, would you give him a message for me? A personal message, from Christa.' I was a bit startled, but I said yes, of course, and she said, 'Please tell him that Alma Bruck is a trusted friend of mine.' "

Weisz didn't answer immediately, then shook his head and smiled: *don't worry, it isn't what you think.* "I know what this is about, Eric. She's, like that, sometimes."

"Oh, well, naturally I wondered. It was, you know, rather sinister. And I hope I got the name right, because I wanted to repeat it, but we'd reached the corner and she took a sharp turn down the street and disappeared. The whole thing took only seconds. It was, how to say, perfect spy technique."

"The lady is a friend of mine, Eric. A very good friend. But a married friend."

"Ahh." Wolf was relieved. "You're a lucky chap, I'd say, she *is* stunning."

"I'll tell her you said so."

"You can understand how I felt. I mean, I thought, maybe it's a story he's working on, and, in this city, you have to be careful. But then, it could have been something else. Lady in black, Mata Hari, that sort of thing."

"No." Weisz smiled at Wolf's suspicions. "Not me, it's just a love affair, nothing more. And I appreciate your help. And your discretion."

"Happy to do it!" Wolf relaxed. "Not often one gets to play Cupid." With an owlish smile, he pulled back a pretend bowstring, then opened his fingers to let the arrow fly.

The invitation arrived while Weisz and Wolf were out for the morning press conference at the Propaganda Ministry. Inside the envelope of a messenger service, an envelope with his name in script, and a folded note: "Dearest Carlo, I'm giving a cocktail party, at my apartment, at six this evening, I'd be so pleased if you could come." Signed "Alma," with an address in the Charlottenstrasse, not far from the Adlon. Curious, Weisz went to the clipping file and, German efficiency at work, there she was. Small, slim, and dark, in a fur coat, smiling for the photographer at a benefit given for war widows on 16 March, the German Memorial Day.

On the Charlottenstrasse, a block of elaborate limestone apartment buildings, upper windows with miniature balconies. Time and soot turned the Parisian versions black, but the Prussians of Berlin kept theirs white. The street itself was immaculate, with well-scrubbed paving stones bordered by linden trees behind ornamental iron railings. The buildings, to Weisz's intuitive geometry, much larger inside than they looked from without. Across a white brick courtyard, and up two floors in a curlicue-caged elevator, Alma Bruck's apartment.

Had the invitation said six? Weisz swore to himself that it had, but, listening at the door, he heard no evidence of a cocktail party. Tentatively, he knocked. The unlocked door opened an inch. Weisz gave it a gentle push, and it opened further, revealing a dark foyer. "Hello?" Weisz said.

No answer.

Weisz took a cautious step inside and closed the door, but not all the way. What was going on? A dark, empty apartment. A trap. Then, from somewhere down the long hallway, he heard music, a swing band, which meant either a phonograph or a radio tuned to some station outside Germany, where such music was *verboten.* Again, he said, "Hello?" No answer, only the music. *Christa, are you in here?* Was this romantic, playful theatre? Or something very different? For a moment, he froze, the two possibilities at war inside him.

Finally, he took a deep breath. She was in here somewhere, and, if she wasn't, well, too bad. Slowly, he walked down the hallway, the old parquet flooring creaked with every step. He passed an open door, a parlor, its heavy drapes drawn, then stopped and said, "Christa?" No answer. The music was coming from the room at the end of the hall, its door wide open.

He stopped at the threshold. Inside a dark bedroom, a white shape was stretched full length on the bed. "Christa?"

"Oh my God," she said, sitting bolt upright. "I fell asleep." Slowly, she lay back down. "I meant to answer the door," she said. "Like this."

"I would have liked that," he said. He went and sat beside her, bent over and kissed her briefly, then stood and began to undress. "Next time, my love, leave a note on the door, or a garter, or something."

She laughed. "Forgive me." She propped her head on her hand and watched as he took off his clothes. Then she put a hand out, he took it in his, and she said, "I am so happy you're here, Carlo." He kissed her hand, then went back to unbuttoning his shirt.

"I did wonder," he said. "I thought I was going to a party."

"But my dear, you are."

Done with his clothes, he lay down on the bed and stroked her side. "I thought you might call, last night."

"Better for me now not to go to a hotel," she said. "That's why all of this, your friend

Wolf, and dear Alma. But, no matter." She put her arm around his shoulders and embraced him, her breasts against his chest. "I have what I want," she said, her voice softening.

"The front door is ajar," he said.

"Don't worry, you can close it later. Nobody comes here, it's a building of ghosts."

The skin of her legs was cool, and smooth to the touch. His hand moved slowly, up and back, he was in no hurry, took such pleasure in anticipation that what came next seemed somewhere in a distant future.

Finally, she said, "Perhaps you'd better close the door, after all."

"Allright." Reluctantly, he stood and headed for the door.

"Ghosts might hear things," she said as he left the room. "We wouldn't want that."

He was back in a moment. "Poor Carlo," she said. "Now we'll have to begin all over again."

"I guess I must," he said, his voice elated. After a time, she moved her legs apart, and guided his hand. "God," she said, "how I love this."

He could tell that she did.

Sliding down the bed, so that her head was level with his waist, she said, "Just stay where you are, there is something I have wanted to do for a long time."

"May I have one of those?" she said.

He took a cigarette from his pack of Gitanes, handed it to her, then lit it with his steel lighter. "I don't recall you smoking."

"I've taken it up. I used to, in my twenties, then I stopped."

She found an ashtray on the night table and put it between them on the bed. "Everybody smokes now, in Berlin. It helps."

"Christa?"

"Yes?"

"Why can't you go to the Adlon?"

"Too public. Somebody would tell the police."

"Are they after you?"

"They're interested, in me. They suspect I might be a bad girl, I have a few of the wrong friends. So, I asked Alma for a favor. She was very enthusiastic." After a moment, she said, "I wanted to make it exciting. Answer the door, all bare-assed and perfumed."

"You can do it tomorrow. Can we come here tomorrow?"

"Oh yes, we shall. How long can you stay?"

"Two days more, I'll find a reason."

"Yes, find some Nazi bastard and inter-view him."

"That's what I do."

"I know, you're strong."

"I never thought of it like that."

She inhaled her cigarette, letting the smoke come out with her words. "You are, though. One reason I like you."

He put his cigarette out and said, "There are more?"

"I love to fuck you, that's another." In her husky, aristocratic voice, the vulgarity was no more than casual.

He leaned over and put his lips on her breast. Surprised, she drew in her breath. Then she stubbed her cigarette out in the ashtray, reached down, and held him in her hand. Which was slightly cold, at first, but, not long after, warmed. "I have one nice thing to tell you," she said.

"What's that?" His voice wavered.

"We can stay here tonight. The official ver-sion is 'at Alma's.' So we can go to a char-ity breakfast, before work."

"Mm," he said. "Probably I'll wake you up, at some point."

"You better," she said.

It was nearly dawn, when that happened. He'd almost forgotten how much he liked to sleep beside her, spoon fashion, her legs drawn up. After they made love, they heard clinking bottles out in the corridor. The milkman.

"Apparently, the ghosts drink milk," Weisz said. "Why do you call them ghosts?"

"The rich used to live here. According to Alma, some of them were Jews, and some of the others find it opportune, lately, to be in Switzerland."

"Where is Alma?"

"She lives in a big house in Charlottenburg. She used to live here, now it's her place in town."

"What do we do about the sheets?"

"Her maid will change the bed."

"Is she dependable, the maid?"

"God knows," Christa said. "You can't think of everything, you have to trust in fate, sometimes."

22 May. The signing of the Pact of Steel took place at eleven in the morning, at the sumptuous Ambassadors Hall of the Reich Chancellery. In the press gallery, Weisz sat next to Eric Wolf. On his other side, Mary McGrath of the *Chicago Tribune*, who he'd last seen in Spain. As they waited for the ceremonies to begin, Weisz made notes. The scene had to be set, because here was the

power of the state, its wealth and strength, expressed in splendor: immense chandeliers of glittering crystal, marble walls, vast red drapes, miles of heavy carpet, brown and rose. Stationed by the doors, prepared to admit the cream of fascist Europe, were footmen dressed in black with gold braid, white stockings, and slipperlike black pumps. To one side of the room, the newsreel cameras and a crowd of photographers.

The journalists had been given handouts, with highlights of the treaty. "Look at the last paragraph," Mary McGrath said. " 'Finally, in case of war involving one partner, no matter how started, full mutual support with all military forces, by land, sea, and air.' "

"That's the deadly phrase," Wolf said, " 'no matter how started.' It means if Hitler attacks, Italy has to follow. Four little words, but enough."

The footmen walked the doors open, and the parade began. In the most splendid uniforms, set off by ranks of medals, a steady stream of generals and foreign ministers entered the hall, walking slowly, stately and dignified. Only one stood out, in the simplicity of his plain brown uniform, Adolf Hitler. There followed an endless procession of speeches, and, ultimately, the signing itself. Two groups, of four officials from the foreign department, carried large books, bound in red leather, to the table, where Count Ciano and von Ribbentrop awaited them. The officials set the books down and, with great ceremony, opened them, to reveal the treaties, then handed each man a gold pen. When the treaties were signed, they picked up the books and set them down for countersignature. Two powerful states were now joined together, and an elated Hitler, with a huge grin, took Count Ciano's hand in both of his and shook it so violently that he nearly lifted him off the floor. Then, Hitler presented Ciano with the Grand Cross of the German Eagle, the Reich's highest honor. In the handout, the press was informed that, later in the day, Ciano would bestow on von Ribbentrop the Collar of the Annunciata, Italy's supreme decoration.

Amid the applause, Mary McGrath said, "Is it over?"

"I think that's it," Weisz said. "The banquets are tonight."

"Think I'll skip those," McGrath said. "Let's get the hell out of this."

They did, but it wasn't so easy. Outside the hall, thousands of Hitler Youth filled the streets, waving flags and singing. As the three journalists worked their way across the boulevard, Weisz could feel the fearful energy of the crowd, intense eyes, rapturous faces. *Now,* he thought, *there will surely be war.* The people in the street would demand it, would kill relentlessly, and, in time, would have to be killed. These children would not surrender.

Christa was true to her word. When Weisz arrived at the apartment that evening, she made him wait — he had to knock a second time — then answered the door wearing only a modestly depraved smile and clouds of Balenciaga perfume. His eyes swept over her, then he ran his hands up and down before pulling her to him, for, even though it was no surprise, it had the effect she wanted. As she led the way down the hall to the bedroom, she swung her hips for him — his very own merry trollop. And so she was. Inventive, hungry, flushed with excitment, starting over again and again.

Eventually, they fell asleep. When Weisz woke up, he had, for a moment, no idea where he was. On a table by the bedroom door, the radio was tuned to a live broadcast of dance music from a ballroom in London, the orchestra faint and distant amid the crackling static. Christa was sleeping on her stomach, mouth open, one hand on his arm. He moved slightly, but she didn't wake up, so he touched her. "Yes?" Her eyes were still closed.

"Should I look at the time?"

"Oh, I thought you wanted something."

"I might."

She made a kind of sigh. "You could."

"Can we stay here tonight?"

She moved her head sufficiently for him to understand she meant they could not. "Is it late?"

He reached over her to the night table, retrieved his watch, and, by the light of a small lamp in the corner, left on so they could see, told her that it was eight-twenty.

"There is time," she said. Then, a moment later: "And, it seems, interest."

"It's you," he said.

"Now, if I could move."

"You are very tired, aren't you?"

"All the time, yes, but I don't sleep."

"What will happen, Christa?"

"So I ask myself. And there's never an answer."

He didn't have one either. Idly, he trailed a finger from the back of her neck down to where her legs parted, and she parted them a little more.

■ ■ ■ ■

At ten, they collected their clothes, from a chair, from the floor, and began to get dressed. "I'll take you home in a taxi," he said.

"I would like that. Let me off a block away."

"I wanted to ask you . . ."

"Yes?"

"What's become of your friend? The man we met at the carnival."

"You've been waiting to ask me that, haven't you."

"Yes, as long as I could."

Her smile was bittersweet. "You are considerate. What's the French? *C'est gentil de votre part?* They put it so nicely, a kindness of you. And also, I think, and not so nice, you sensed what I would have to say, and left it for our last night."

He had, and showed it.

"That he's gone. That he left for work one morning, a month ago, and was never seen again. Even though some of us, the ones who could, made telephone calls, talked to people, former friends, who might be able to find out, for the sake of old friendship, but even they were unsuccessful. Too deep,

302

even for them, in the *Nacht und Nebel,* night and fog, Hitler's very own invention — that people should simply vanish from the face of the earth, a practice dear to him for its effect on friends and family."

"When are you leaving, Christa? What date, what day?"

"And, worse, much worse, in its way, is that when he disappeared, nothing happened to the rest of us. You wait for a knock on the door, for weeks, but it doesn't come. And then you know that, whatever happened to him, he didn't tell them anything."

The taxi stopped a block from her house, in a neighborhood at the edge of the city, a curving street of grand homes with lawns and gardens. "Come with me for a moment," she said. Then, to the driver: "You'll wait, please."

Weisz got out of the taxi and followed her to an ivy-covered brick wall. In the house, a dog knew they were there and began to bark. "There's one last thing I must tell you," she said.

"Yes?"

"I didn't want to say it in the apartment."

He waited.

"Two weeks ago, we went to a dinner party at the house of von Schirren's uncle.

He's a general in the army, a gruff old Prussian, but a good soul, at heart. At one point in the evening, I remembered I had to call home, to remind the maid that Magda, one of my dogs, was to be given her medicine, for her heart. So I went into the general's study, to use the telephone, and on his desk, I couldn't help seeing it, was an open book, with a sheet of paper he'd used to make notes. The book was called *Sprachführer Polnisch für Geschäftsreisende,* a guide to Polish for the business traveler. And he'd copied out phrases to memorize, 'How far is it to,' put in the name, 'Where is the railway station?' You know the sort of thing I mean, questions for the local population."

Weisz glanced back at the idling taxi and the driver, who'd been watching them, turned away. "It seems he's going to Poland," Weisz said. "And so?"

"So the *Wehrmacht* is going with him."

"Maybe, it's possible," Weisz said. "Or maybe not, he could be going as a military attaché, or for some kind of negotiation. Who knows?"

"Not him. He's not the attaché type. A general of infantry, pure and simple."

Weisz thought about it. "Then it will be before winter, in the early summer, after spring planting, because half the army

304

works on farms."

"That's what I think."

"You know what this means, Christa, for you. In two months, at the latest. And, once it starts, it will spread, and it will go on for a long time — the Poles have a big army, and they'll fight."

"I will leave before that happens, before they close the borders."

"Why not tomorrow? On the plane? You don't know the future — tonight you can still go, but, the day after tomorrow . . ."

"No, not yet, I can't. But soon. We have one more thing we must do here, it's in progress, please don't ask me to tell you more than that."

"They'll arrest you, Christa. You've done enough."

"Kiss me, and say goodby. Please. The driver is watching us."

He embraced her, and they kissed. Then he watched her walk away until, at the corner, she waved to him, and disappeared.

Forever.

On the twelve-thirty flight to Paris, as the plane taxied down the runway, Weisz stared out the window at the fields bordering the tarmac. His spirits were very low. He'd worked his way around to the belief that

Christa's passionate lovemaking had been her way of saying farewell. *Remember me as I am tonight.* She was certainly capable of that. Just as she was capable of pursuing whatever clandestine business had hold of her until the operation collapsed and she, like her friend at the carnival, vanished into the *Nacht und Nebel.* He would never know what happened. Could he have said something that would have persuaded her to leave? No, he knew better than that, there were no words in the world that would change her mind. It was her life to live, her life to lose, she would stay in Berlin, she would fight her enemies, and she would not run away. The more Weisz thought about it, the worse he felt.

What helped, in the end, was that Alfred Millman, a *New York Times* correspondent, was seated next to him. He and Weisz had met before, and had exchanged nods and mumbled greetings when they'd taken their seats. Tall and stocky, with thinning gray hair, Millman had the presence of a man swimming always upstream, who, accepting that as his natural element, had early in life become a strong swimmer. Not a star of his newspaper, he was, like Weisz, a tireless worker, assigned to this or that crisis, filing his stories, then going on to the next war, or fallen government, wherever the fires broke out. Now, done with his *Deutsche All-gemeine Zeitung,* he flipped it closed and said to Weisz, "Okay, that's enough horse manure for today. Care to have a look?"

"No thanks."

"I saw you at the signing ceremony. Must've been hard for you, as an Italian, to watch that."

"Yes, it was. They think they're going to rule the world."

Millman shook his head. "They're living in a dream. Pact of Steel my foot, they don't *have* any steel — they have to import. And they don't have much coal, not a drop of oil, and their chief of military procurement is eighty-seven years old. How the hell are they going to fight a war?"

"They're going to get what they need from Germany, that's what they've always done. Now they'll trade soldiers' lives for coal."

"Yeah sure, until Hitler gets pissed off at 'em. And he always does, you know, sooner or later."

"They won't win," Weisz said, "because the people don't want to fight. What war will do is ruin the country, but the government believes in conquest, and so they signed."

"Yes, I saw it happen, yesterday. Pomp and

circumstance." Millman's sudden smile was ironic. "Do you know the old Karl Kraus line? 'How is the world ruled and how do wars start? Diplomats tell lies to journalists and then believe what they read.' "

"I know the line," Weisz said. "Actually, Kraus was a friend of my father."

"You don't say."

"They were colleagues, for a time, at the university in Vienna."

"He's supposed to be the smartest guy in the world, you ever meet him?"

"When I was young, a few times. My father took me up to Vienna, and we went to Kraus's personal coffeehouse."

"Ah yes, the coffeehouses of Vienna, feuilletons and feuds. Kraus surely had his share — the only man ever beaten up by Felix Salten, though I forget why. Not so good for one's public image, getting knocked around by the author of *Bambi*."

They both laughed. Salten had become rich and famous with his fawn, and Kraus had famously hated him.

"Still," Millman said, "it's troublesome, this Pact of Steel. Between Germany and Italy, a population of a hundred and fifty million, which makes, by the rule of ten percent, a fighting force of fifteen million. Somebody's going to have to deal with that, because Hitler's looking for a brawl."

"He'll have his brawl with Russia," Weisz said. "Once he's done with the Poles. Britain and France are counting on that."

"I hope they're right," Millman said. " 'Let's you and him fight,' as they say, but I have my doubts. Hitler is the worst bastard in the world, but one thing he isn't is dumb. And he isn't crazy either, never mind all that screaming. What he is, if you watch him carefully, is a very shrewd man."

"So is Mussolini. Former journalist, former novelist. *The Cardinal's Mistress,* ever read it?"

"No, I haven't had the pleasure. Actually a pretty good title, I'd say, makes you want to find out what happens." He thought for a moment, then said, "It's a damn shame, really, this whole business. I liked Italy. My wife and I were there, a few years ago. In Tuscany, her sister took a villa for the summer. It was old, falling apart, nothing worked, but it had a courtyard with a fountain, and I'd sit out there in the afternoon, the cicadas going a mile a minute, and read. Then we'd have drinks, and it would cool down as night came on, there was always a little breeze, about seven in the evening. Always."

■ ■ ■ ■

The Dewoitine's wings tilted as the airplane turned toward Le Bourget, and Paris lay suddenly below them, a gray city in its twilit sky, strangely isolated, an island amid the wheat fields of the Ile-de-France. Alfred Millman leaned over so he could see the view. "Glad to be home?" he said.

Weisz nodded. It was his home, now, but not so welcoming. As they'd neared Paris, he'd begun to wonder if he shouldn't maybe find some other hotel — for that night, anyhow. Because his thoughts were occupied by the new tenant, with his hat and raincoat, up on the fourth floor. Who, perhaps, was waiting for him. Was this simply foolish anxiety? He tried to tell himself it was, but his intuition would not be stilled.

When they rolled to a stop — "Let's have a drink, next time I'm in town," Millman said as they walked down the aisle — Weisz had still not come to a decision. That was left for the moment when he was seated in the back of a taxi and the driver turned around, one eyebrow aloft. "Monsieur?" *You have to go somewhere.*

Finally, Weisz said, "The Hotel Dauphine,

please. It's in the rue Dauphine, in the Sixth." The driver jammed his taxi into gear and sped away from the airfield, driving nobly, with swerving panache, in expectation of a juicy tip from a customer so grand as to descend from the heavens. And, in the event, he wasn't wrong.

Madame Rigaud was behind the hotel desk, writing tiny numbers on a pad as she scanned the reservation book. Counting her money? She looked up when Weisz came through the door. No secret smile for him now, only lingering curiosity — what goes on with you, my friend? Weisz countered with an extremely polite greeting. This tactic never failed, jarred the preoccupied French soul from its reverie and forced it into equal, if not greater, courtesy.

"I was wondering," Weisz said. "About the new tenant, up on my floor. Is he still there?"

Such questions were *not* polite, and Madame's face let him know it, but she was in a good mood at that moment, perhaps inspired by the numbers on her pad. "He's moved out." *If you must know.* "And his friend as well," she said, waiting for an explanation.

Two of them. "I was curious about him, Madame Rigaud, that's all. He knocked on

311

my door, and I never did find out why, because Bertrand arrived with my ticket."

She shrugged. Who could say, about guests in hotels, what they did, or why, twenty years of it.

He thanked her, politely, and climbed the stairs, valise bumping against his leg, heart flooded with relief.

30 May. It was Elena who telephoned and told Weisz that Salamone was in the hospital. "They've got him in the Broussais," she said. "The charity hospital up in the Fourteenth. It's his heart, maybe not a heart attack, technically, but he couldn't catch his breath, at the warehouse, so they sent him home, and his wife took him up there."

Weisz left work early, for the five o'clock visitors' hour, stopping on the way for a box of candy. Could Salamone have candy? He wasn't sure. Flowers? No, that didn't seem right, so, candy. At the Broussais, he joined a crowd of visitors led by a nursing nun to Men's Ward G, a long white room with rows of iron beds, inches apart, and the strong smell of disinfectant. Midway down the row, he found G58, a metal sign, much of the paint flecked off, hanging on the rail at the foot of the bed. Salamone was dozing, one finger keeping his place in a book.

"Arturo?"

Salamone opened his eyes, then struggled to sit upright. "Ah, Carlo, you came to see me," he said. "What a fucking nightmare, eh?"

"I thought I better come before they kicked you out." Weisz handed him the candy.

"*Grazie.* I'll give it to Sister Angelique. Or maybe you want some."

Weisz shook his head. "Arturo, what happened to you?"

"Not much. I was at work, all of a sudden I couldn't catch my breath. A warning, the doctor calls it. I'm fine, I should be out in a few days. Still, like my mother used to say, 'Don't ever get sick.' "

"My mother too," Weisz said. He paused for a moment, amid the ceaseless coughing, and the low murmur of visitors' hour.

"Elena told me you were away, on assignment."

"I was. In Berlin."

"For the pact?"

"Yes, the formalities. In the grand hall of the Reich Chancellery. Strutting generals, starched shirts, and little Hitler, grinning like a wolf. The whole filthy business."

Salamone looked glum. "We would have

313

had a thing or two to say about that. In the paper."

Weisz spread his hands; some things were lost, life went on. "Bad as it is, this pact, it's hard to take them seriously, when you see who they are. You keep waiting for Groucho to show up."

"Do you think the French will stand up to them, now that it's official?"

"They might. But, the way I feel lately, they can *all* go to hell. What we have to do now is take care of ourselves, you and me, Arturo. Which means we have to find you another job. At a desk, this time."

"I'll find something. I'll have to, they tell me I can't go back to what I was doing."

"Making check marks on a tally sheet?"

"Well, maybe I had to push a few boxes around."

"Just a few," Weisz said. "Now and then."

"But, you know, Carlo, I'm not so sure it was that. I think it was everything else; what happened to me at the insurance company, what happened to the café, what happened to all of us."

And it continues. But Weisz wasn't going to tell the story of the new tenant to a friend in a hospital bed. Instead, he turned the conversation to émigré talk — politics, gossip, how life would get better. Then a nun appeared and told them that Madame Sala-mone was in the waiting room, since the patient could have only one visitor. As Weisz turned to go, he said, "Forget all that other business, Arturo, just think about getting better. We did a good job, with *Liberazione,* but now it's in the past. And those people know it. So, they got what they wanted, and now it's done with, over."

31 May. At the Galeries Lafayette, a big spring sale. What a mob! They'd descended on the department store from every Ar-rondissement in Paris — *bargains galore, buy it today, every price reduced.* In the of-fice at the back of the ground floor, an as-sistant manager, "the Dragon," nicknamed for her fire-breathing temper, tried to cope with the onslaught. Poor little Mimi, from the millinery counter, had fainted. Now she was sitting in the reception area, white as a sheet, as a floorwalker fanned her with a magazine. Nearby, two children, both in tears, had lost their mothers. The toilet in the ladies' WC on the second floor had overflowed, the plumber had been called, where was he? Lilliane, from cosmetics, had called in sick, and an old woman had tried to leave the store wearing three dresses. In her office, the Dragon closed her door, the

tumult in the reception area was more than she could bear. So she would take a minute, sit quietly, by the telephone that would not stop ringing, and regain her composure. All sales ended, eventually. And everything that could possibly go wrong, had.

But not quite. What foolish soul was knocking on her door? The Dragon rose from her desk and wrenched the door open. To reveal a terrified secretary, old Madame Gros, her brow damp with perspiration. "Yes?" the Dragon said. "What now?"

"Pardon, madame, but the police are here. A man from the *Sûreté Nationale.*"

"Here?"

"Yes, madame. In the *réception.*"

"Why?"

"He's here about Elena, in ladies' hosiery."

The Dragon shut her eyes, took yet one more deep breath. "Very well, one must respect the *Sûreté Nationale.* So go to the hosiery counter and bring Elena here."

"But madame . . ."

"Now."

"Yes, madame."

She fled. The Dragon looked out into the reception area, a vision of hell. Now, which one was — over there? The man in the hat with a little green feather in the band? Nasty mustache, restless eyes, hands in pockets?

316

Well, who knew what they looked like, she certainly didn't. She walked over to him and said, *"Monsieur l'inspecteur?"*

"Yes. Are you the manager, madame?"

"An assistant manager. The manager is up on the top floor."

"Oh, I see, then . . ."

"You're here to see Elena Casale?"

"No, I don't wish to see her. But to speak with you about her, she is the subject of an investigation."

"Will this take long? I don't mean to be rude, monsieur, but you can see what's going on here today. And now I've sent for Elena, she's on her way to the office. Shall I send her back?"

This news did not please the inspector. "Perhaps I should return, say, tomorrow?"

"It would be much better, tomorrow, for our discussion."

The inspector tipped his hat, said goodby, and hurried off. *Strange sort of man,* the Dragon thought. And, even stranger, Elena the subject of an investigation. Something of an aristocrat, this Italian woman, with her sharp face, long, graying hair worn back in a clip, ironic smile — not a criminal type, not at all. What could she have done? But, who had time to wonder about such things, for here, at last, was the plumber.

Elena and Madame Gros forced their way down the center aisle. "Did he say what he wanted?" Elena asked.

"Only that he wished to speak with the manager. About you."

"And he said he was from the *Sûreté Nationale?*"

"Yes, that's what he said."

Elena was growing angrier by the minute. She remembered Weisz's story about the interrogation of his girlfriend, who owned an art gallery, she remembered how Salamone had been defamed, and discharged from his job. Was it now her turn? Oh, this was infuriating. It had not been easy, as a woman in Italy, to take a degree in chemistry; finding work, even in industrial Milan, had not been any easier, having to give up her position and emigrate had been harder still, and working as a sales clerk in a department store hardest of all. But she was staunch, she did what had to be done, and now these fascist bastards were going to try and take even that meager prize away from her. What would she do for money? How would she live?

"There he is," Madame Gros said. "Say, I

think you're in luck, he appears to be leaving."

"That's him? In the hat with the green feather?" They watched it, bobbing up and down as he tried to make his way through the mass of determined shoppers.

"Yes, just by the cosmetics counter."

Elena's mind worked quickly. "Madame Gros, would you please tell Yvette, at the hosiery counter, that I have to go away for an hour? Would you do this for me?"

Madame Gros agreed. After all, this was Elena, who always worked on Saturday, Elena, who never failed to come in on her day off when somebody was home with the grippe. How could you, the first time she'd ever asked for a favor, say no?

Keeping well behind him, Elena followed the man as he left the store. She was wearing a gray smock, like all the clerks at the Galeries. Her purse and coat were in a locker, but she'd learned, early on, to keep her wallet, with identification and money, in the pocket of her smock. The man in the hat with the green feather strolled along, not especially in a hurry. An inspector? He could be, but Weisz and Salamone thought otherwise. So, she would see for herself. Did he know what she looked like? Would he be

319

able to identify her, as she followed him? That was surely a possibility, but if he were a real inspector, she was already in trouble, and walking down the same street — well, was that even a crime?

The man wound his way through the crowds at the store display windows, then entered the Chaussée-d'Antin Métro station and put a *jeton* in the turnstile. Hah, he paid! A real inspector would simply show his badge at the change window, no? Had she not seen such things in the movies? She thought she had. Hands in pockets, he stood idly on the platform, waiting for the Line Seven train, *Direction La Courneuve.* That would, she knew, take him out of the Ninth Arrondissement and into the Tenth. Where was the *Sûreté* office? At the Interior Ministry, over on rue des Saussaies — you couldn't get there on this line. Still, he might be headed off to investigate some other poor creature. Hiding behind a pillar, Elena waited for the train, sometimes taking a small step forward to keep an eye on the green feather. Who was he? A confidential agent? An OVRA operative? Did he enjoy spending his days doing such miserable business? Or was it simply to earn a living?

The train rolled in, Elena positioned

herself at the other end of the car, while the man took a seat, crossed his legs, and folded his hands on his lap. The stations rolled by: Le Peletier, Cadet, Poissonière, deeper and deeper into the Tenth Arrondissement. Then, at the station for the Gare de l'Est, he stood and left the car. Here he could transfer to Line Four or take a train. Elena waited as long as she dared, then, at the last minute, stepped onto the platform. Damn, where was he? Just barely in time, she spotted him climbing the stairs. She followed as he went through the grilled turnstile and headed for the exit. Elena paused, pretending to study a Métro map on the wall, until he disappeared, then left the station.

Vanished! No, there he was, heading south, away from the railway station, on the boulevard Strasbourg. Elena had never been in this part of the city, and she was grateful that it was mid-morning — she would not have wanted to come here at night. A dangerous quarter, the Tenth; grim tenements for the poor. Dark men, perhaps Portuguese, or Arabs from the Maghreb, gathered in the cafés, the boulevards lined with small, cluttered stores, the side streets narrow, silent, and shadowed. Amid the crowds at the Galeries, and in the Métro, she'd felt invisible, anonymous, but not now.

Walking alone on the boulevard, she stood out, a middle-aged woman in a gray smock. She did not belong here, who was she?

Suddenly, the man stopped, at a shop window displaying piles of used pots and pans, and, as she slowed down, he glanced at her. More than glanced — his eyes acknowledged her as a woman, attractive, perhaps available. Elena looked through him and kept walking, passing within three feet of his back. *Find a way to stop!* Here was a *pâtisserie,* a bell above the door jingled as she entered. From the back, a girl, wiping her hands on a flour-dusted apron, walked to the other side of the counter, then waited patiently while Elena stood before a case of soggy pastries, looking sideways, every few seconds, out into the street.

The girl asked what madame might desire. Elena peered into the case. A *Napoleon?* A *religieuse?* No, there he was! She mumbled an apology and left the shop. Now he was thirty feet away. Dear God, let him not turn around, he'd noticed her earlier, and if he saw her again, he would, she feared, approach her. But he did not turn around — he looked at his watch and walked faster, for half a block, then turned sharply and entered a building. Elena dawdled a moment at the entry to a *pharmacie,* giving him time to leave the ground floor of the building.

Then she followed. To 62, boulevard de Strasbourg. Now what? For a few seconds, she hesitated, standing in front of the door, then opened it. Facing her was a stairway, to her right, on the wall, a row of open wooden letter boxes. From the floor above, she could hear footsteps moving down the old boards of a hallway, then a door opened, and clicked shut. Turning to the letter boxes, she found 1 A — *Mlle. Krasic* printed in pencil across the base, and 1 B — with a business card tacked below it.

A cheaply printed card, for the Agence Photo-Mondiale, worldwide photo agency, with address and telephone number. What was this? Perhaps a stock house, selling photographs to magazines and advertising agencies, or a photojournalism organization, available for assignment. Could he have gone into the Krasic apartment? Not likely, she was sure he'd gone down the hall to Photo-Mondiale. Not an uncommon sort of business, where just about anybody might turn up, perhaps a false business, from which one could run a secret operation.

She had a pencil in the pocket of her smock, but no paper, so she took a ten-franc note from her wallet and wrote the number on it. Was she making the right assumption? She thought so — why would he go to the apartment of Mlle. Krasic? No, she was almost certain. Of course, the way to be absolutely sure was to go to the top of the stairway and turn left, in the direction of the footsteps, cross back over the entryway, and take a fast look at the door. Elena folded the note and tucked it away in her pocket. In the vestibule, it was very still, the building seemed deserted. Up the stairs? Or out the door?

The staircase was uncarpeted, made of wood covered with worn-out varnish, the steps hollowed by years of traffic. She would take, anyhow, one step. No creak, the thing was solid. So, another. Then, another. When she was halfway up, the door above opened, and she heard a voice — two or three muffled words, then footsteps headed along the corridor, a man whistling a tune. Elena stopped breathing. Then, light on her feet, she turned and scampered down the stairs. The footsteps came closer. Did she have time to get out of the building? Maybe, but the heavy door would be heard as it shut. Looking down the hallway, she saw open shadow beneath the staircase and ran for it. There was room enough to stand beneath the stairs. Inches away, the undersides of the steps gave as weight fell on them. But the door did not open. Instead, the man who'd come down the stairs, still whistling, was waiting in the vestibule. Why? *He knew she was there.* She froze, forced herself against the wall. Then, above her head, someone else, walking down the staircase. A voice spoke — a mean, sarcastic voice, the way she heard it — and another voice, deeper, heavier, laughed and, briefly, answered. *Hey, that was a good one!* Or, she thought, something like that — she couldn't understand a single word. Because it was a language she had never in her life heard spoken.

He'd be late for Ferrara, Weisz realized, because Elena was waiting for him on the street outside the Reuters bureau. It was chilly, the first night in June, with a damp mist that made him shiver as he stepped out the door. *A new Elena,* Weisz thought as they said hello; her eyes alive, voice charged with excitement. "We'll walk down to Opéra and take a taxi," he told her. Her nod was enthusiastic: thrift be damned, this night is important. On the way, she told him the story she'd promised on the telephone, her pursuit of the false inspector.

It was slow going, in the evening traffic, as

the taxi made its way toward an art gallery in the Seventh Arrondissement. Every driver beeped his horn at the idiot in front of him, and swarms of bicyclists rang their bells, as the idiots in their cars came too close. "You no longer see her?" Elena said. "I didn't know."

"We're good friends," Weisz said. "Now."

From Elena, in the darkened back of the taxi, one of her half smiles, a particularly sharp one.

"It's possible," Weisz said.

"I'm sure it is."

Véronique came hurrying to the door of the gallery as they entered. She kissed Weisz on each cheek, one hand on his arm. Then Weisz introduced her to Elena. "Just a minute while I lock the door," Véronique said. "I've had Americans all day long, and not one sale. They think it's a museum." On the walls, Valkenda's dissolute waifs were still staring at the cruel world. "So," she said, closing the bolt, "no art tonight."

They sat in the office, gathered around the desk. "Carlo tells me we have something in common," Véronique said to Elena. "He was at his most mysterious, on the phone."

"Apparently we do," Elena said. "A very unpleasant man. He showed up at the Galeries Lafayette, where I work, and tried

326

to see the manager. But I was lucky, and, in the confusion, he tried to leave, and I followed him."

"Where did he go?"

"Out into the Tenth. To a photo agency."

"So, not from the *Sûreté*, you think." Véronique glanced at Weisz.

"No. He's a fraud. He had friends, in that office."

"That's a relief," Véronique said. Then, thoughtfully, she added, "Or maybe not. You're sure it was the same man?"

"Of medium height. With a slim mustache, face pitted on one side, and something about his eyes, the way he looked at me, I didn't like. He wore a gray hat, with a green feather in the band."

"The man who came here had dirty fingernails," Véronique said. "And his French was not Parisian."

"I never heard him speak, although I can't be sure of that. He went up to the office, then one man came out, followed by two others, who spoke, not French, I'm not sure what it was."

Véronique thought it over. "The mustache is right. Like Errol Flynn?"

"A long way from Errol Flynn, the rest of him, but, yes, he tries for the same effect. What to call it, 'dashing.' "

Véronique grinned, *men*. "The mustache just makes it worse — whatever it is, about him." She scowled with distaste at the image in her memory. "Smug, and sly," she said. "What a vile little man."

"Yes, exactly," Elena said.

Weisz looked dubious. "So what shall I tell the police? Look for 'a vile little man'?"

"Is that what we're going to do?" Elena said.

"I suppose we will," Weisz said. "What else? Tell me, Elena, was the language you heard Russian?"

"I don't think so. But perhaps something like it. Why?"

"If I said that to the police, it would stir their interest."

"Better not," Elena said.

"Let's go to the café," Véronique said. "I need a brandy, after this."

"Yes, me too," Elena said. "Carlo?"

Weisz stood, smiled, and waved a gallant hand toward the door.

2 June, 10:15 A.M.

Weisz dialed the number on the ten-franc note. After one ring, a voice said, "Yes?"

"Good morning, is this the Agence Photo-Mondiale?"

A pause, then: "Yes. What do you want?"

328

"This is Pierre Monet, from the Havas wire service."

"Yes?"

"I'm calling to see if you have a photograph of Stefan Kovacs, the Hungarian ambassador to Belgium."

"Who gave you this number?" The accent was heavy, but Weisz's ear for French wasn't sharp enough to go beyond that.

"I think somebody here wrote it on a piece of paper, I don't know, maybe from a list of photo agencies in Paris. Could you take a look? We used to have one, but it's not in the files. We need it today."

"We don't have it. Sorry."

Weisz spoke quickly, because he sensed the man was about to hang up. "Maybe you could send somebody out — Kovacs is in Paris today, at the embassy, and we're very pressed, over here. We'll pay well, if you can help us out."

"No, I don't think we can help you, sir."

"You're a photo agency, aren't you? Do you have some specialty?"

"No. We're very busy. Goodby."

"Oh, I just thought . . . Hello? Hello?"

10:45.

"Carlo Weisz."

"Hello, it's Elena."

"Where are you?"

"I'm at a café. They don't let us make personal calls at the store."

"Well, I called them, and whatever they do, they don't sell photographs, and I don't believe they take assignments."

"Good. Then that's done. Next we have to meet with Salamone."

"Elena, he's only home a few days from the hospital."

"True, but imagine what he'll think when he finds out what we're doing."

"Yes, I suppose you're right."

"You know I am. He's still our leader, Carlo, you can't shame him."

"Allright. Can we meet late tonight? At eleven? I can't take another night off from, from the other work I'm doing."

"Where should we meet?"

"I don't know. I'll call Arturo, see how he wants to do it. Can you call me back? Can I call you?"

"No, you can't. I'll call after work, I get off at six."

Weisz said goodby, hung up the phone, and dialed Salamone's number.

At the Hotel Tournon, Colonel Ferrara was a new man. Smiling, relaxed, living in a better world and enjoying his life there. The book had moved to Spain, and Weisz pressed the colonel for details of the fighting. What was commonplace to Ferrara — night ambushes, sniping from the cover of stone walls, machine-gun duels — would be exciting for the reader. Liberal sympathies could be invoked, but when it came to bullets and bombs, to putting one's life on the line, here was the ultimate reality of idealism.

"And so," Weisz said, "you took the school?"

"We took the first two floors, but the Nationalists held the top floor and the roof, and they wouldn't surrender. We climbed the stairs and threw hand grenades up on the landing, and the plaster, and a dead soldier, came down on our heads. There was a lot of yelling, commands, and a lot of ricochet. . . ."

"Bullets whining . . ."

"Yes, of course. It is very awkward fighting, nobody likes it."

Weisz worked away on his typewriter.

A productive session, most of what Ferrara described could go directly into print. When they were almost done, Ferrara, still telling battle stories, changed his shirt, then combed his hair, carefully, in the mirror.

"You're going out?" Weisz said.

"Yes, as usual. We'll drink somewhere,

then go back to her room."

"Is she still at the nightclub?"

"Oh no. She's found something else, at a restaurant, a Russian place, Gypsy music and a cossack doorman. Why not come along? Irina may have a friend."

"No, not tonight," Weisz said.

Kolb arrived as they were finishing up. When Ferrara hurried off, he asked Weisz to stay for a few minutes. "How's it going?" he said.

"As you'll see," Weisz said, nodding toward that night's pages. "We're doing war scenes, from Spain."

"Good," Kolb said. "Mr. Brown and his associates have been reading right along, and they're pleased with your progress, but they've asked me to suggest that you empha-size — and you can go back in the manu-script, of course — the German role in Spain. The Condor Legion — pilots bomb-ing Guernica in the morning, then playing golf in the afternoon. I think you know what they're after."

So, Weisz thought, the Pact of Steel has had its effect. "Yes, I know. And I'd imagine they'd want more about the Italians."

"You're reading their minds," Kolb said. "More about the alliance, what happens when you get into bed with the Nazis. Poor

Italian boys slaughtered, Blackshirts strutting in the bars. As much as Ferrara remembers, and make up what he doesn't."

"I know the stories," Weisz said. "From when I was there."

"Good. Don't spare the details. The worse the better, yes?"

Weisz stood and put on his jacket — he had his own, far less appealing, night meeting ahead of him.

"One more thing, before you go," Kolb said. "They're concerned about this affair Ferrara's having, with the Russian girl."

"And?"

"They're not really sure who she is. You know what goes on here, *femmes galantes*" — the French expression for female spies — "behind every curtain. Mr. Brown and his friends are very concerned, they don't want him in contact with the Soviet spy services. You know how it is with these girls" — Kolb used a squeaky voice to imitate a woman — " 'Oh here's my friend Igor, he's lots of fun!' "

Weisz gave Kolb a who's-kidding-who look. "He's not going to break it off because he might meet the wrong Russian. He could well be in love, or damn close to it."

"In love? Sure, why not, we all need somebody. But maybe she's the wrong somebody, and you're the one who can talk to him about that."

"You'll just make him mad, Kolb. And he won't let her go."

"Of course he won't. He may be in love, who can say, but he's definitely in love with getting laid. Still, all they're asking is that you raise the issue, so, why not. Make me look good, let me do my job."

"If it makes you happy . . ."

"It'll make them happy — at least, if something goes wrong, they tried. And making them happy, right now, wouldn't be the worst thing for you, for both of you. They're thinking about the future, Ferrara's future, and yours, and it's better if they think good thoughts. Believe me, Weisz, I know."

The eleven P.M. meeting with Salamone and Elena was held in Salamone's Renault. He picked Weisz up in front of his hotel, and stopped for Elena at the building, not far from the Galeries, where she rented a room in an apartment. Then Salamone drove, aimlessly, winding through the back streets of the Ninth, but, Weisz noted, heading always east.

Weisz, in the backseat, leaned over and said, "Let me give you some money for gas."

"Kind of you, but no thanks. Sergio is more the benefactor than ever, he sent a messenger to the house with an envelope."

"Your wife didn't mind? Coming out this time of night?" Weisz knew Signora Salamone.

"Of course she minded. But she knows what happens to people like me — if you go to bed, if you leave the world, you die. So she gave me her worst glare, told me I better be careful, and made me wear this hat."

"She's just as much an émigrée as we are," Elena said.

"True, she is, but . . . Anyhow, I wanted to tell you that I've telephoned the entire committee. All but the lawyer, who I couldn't reach. I was, however, rather careful. I said only that we had some new information, about the attacks, and we may need help, over the next few days. No mention of you, Elena, or what happened. Because who knows, with the telephone, who's listening."

"Probably better," Weisz said.

"Just being careful, that's all."

Salamone took the rue La Fayette, to the boulevard Magenta, then turned right onto the boulevard de Strasbourg. Dark, and almost deserted; metal shutters over the storefronts, a group of men loitering on one corner, and a crowded, smoky café, lit only by a blue light above the bar.

"Say where, Elena."

"Sixty-two. It's a little way yet. There's the *pâtisserie,* a little further, further, there."

The car rolled to a stop. Salamone turned off the one working headlight. "First floor?"

"Yes."

"No lights on."

"Let's go and have a look," Elena said.

"Oh wonderful," Salamone said. "Breaking and entering."

"What then?"

"We'll watch it, for a day or two. Maybe you could come at lunchtime, Carlo. For you, Elena, after work, just for an hour. I'll come back tomorrow morning, in the car. Then Sergio, in the afternoon. There's a shoemaker across the street, he can get new heels, wait while they're put on. We can't be here every minute, but we might get a look at who goes in and out. Carlo, what do you think?"

"I'll try. But I don't believe I'll see anything. Will this help, Arturo? What would we see, that could be reported to the police? We can describe the man who came to the gallery, we can say we don't believe it's a real photo agency, we can tell them about the Café Europa, maybe arson, and the burglary. Isn't that enough?"

"We have to try, is what I think," Salamone said. "Try anything. Because we can go to the *Sûreté* only once, and we have to give them as much as we can, enough so they can't ignore it. If they see us as whining, nervous émigrés, maybe bullied by other émigrés, political enemies, they'll just fill out a form and put it in a file."

"Would you go in there, Carlo?" Elena said. "On some pretext?"

"I could." The idea scared Weisz — if they were any good at their job, they would know who he was, and there was a fairly good chance he might never come out.

"Very dangerous," Salamone said. "Don't do that."

Salamone shifted the car into gear. "I'll make up a schedule. For a day or two. If we don't see anything, then we'll just use what we have."

"I'll be here tomorrow," Weisz said. The light of day would make a difference, he thought. And then, he'd see how he felt. *What pretext?*

3 June.

For Weisz, a bad morning at the office. Wandering attention, a knot in the stomach, a look at his watch every few minutes. At last, lunchtime, one o'clock. "I'll be back at three," he told the secretary. "Maybe a little

337

later." Or never. The Métro took forever to come, the car was empty, and he emerged from the Gare de l'Est station into a light, steady rain.

It didn't help the neighborhood, grim and desolate, and not much improved by daylight. He strolled along the side of the boulevard opposite to number 62, just to get his bearings, then crossed over, visited the *pâtisserie,* bought a pastry, and, back out on the street, got rid of it — there was no way in the world he could eat the thing. He paused at 62, as though searching for an address, walked by, crossed back over the boulevard, stood at a bus stop until the bus came, then left. All of which absorbed twenty minutes of his assigned surveillance time. And not a soul had entered or left the building.

For ten minutes, he paced back and forth on the corner where the boulevard met the rue Jarry, looking at his watch, a man waiting for a friend. Who never arrived. *Arturo, this is a ridiculous idea.* He was getting soaked out here, why on earth had he not brought his umbrella? The sky had been cloudy and threatening when he left for work. What if he said he was looking for a job? He was, after all, a journalist, and Photo-Mondiale would be a logical place for such employment. Or, maybe better, he could say he was looking for a friend. Old Duval? Who'd once said he worked there? But then, what would he see? A few men in an office? So what? Damn, why did it have to rain. A woman who'd passed him a few minutes earlier now came back with a string bag full of potatoes, and gave him a suspicious glance as she walked by.

Well then, the hell with it — go up there, or go back to the office. Do *something.* Slowly, he approached the building, then stopped short. Because here came the postman, limping along, the heavy leather bag at his side hung by a strap from his opposite shoulder. He stopped in front of 62, looked inside his bag, and entered the building. Less than a minute later, he reappeared, and headed off to number 60.

Weisz waited until he'd worked his way to the end of the street, then took a deep breath and walked up to the door of 62, pushed it open, and went inside. For a moment, he stood there, heart racing, but the vestibule was hushed and still. *Go find old Duval,* he told himself, *and don't be furtive.* He walked quickly up the stairs, then, at the landing, listened again, and, recalling Elena's description, turned left down the corridor. The door at the end of the hallway

339

had a business card tacked below the stenciled *1 B. Agence Photo-Mondiale.* Weisz counted to ten, and raised his hand to knock, then held back. Inside, a telephone, a soft double ring. He waited to hear it answered, but heard only a second ring, a third, and a fourth, followed by silence. *They're not in!* Weisz knocked twice on the door, the sound loud in the empty hallway, and waited for footsteps. *No, there's nobody in there.* Cautiously, he tried the doorknob. But the door was locked. Salvation. He turned away and walked quickly toward the other end of the corridor.

He hurried down the staircase, anxious for the safety of the street, but, just as he reached for the door, the envelopes in a wooden mailbox caught his attention. The box labelled *1 B* held four. Watching the door, prepared to put them back in an instant if it so much as moved, he took a fast look. The first was a bill from the electric company. The second came from the Marseilles office of the Banque des Pays de l'Europe Centrale. The third had a typed address on a brown manila envelope. With, to Weisz's eyes, an exotic stamp: *Jugoslavija, 4 Dinars,* a blue-toned image of a peasant woman in a scarf, hands on hips, staring solemnly at a river. The cancellation, first in

Cyrillic, then Roman letters, said *Zagreb.*
The fourth letter was personal, penciled
script on a small, cheap envelope, and addressed to *J. Hravka,* with a return address,
I. Hravka, also in Zagreb. With one eye on
the door, Weisz dug into his pocket, came
up with pen and pad, and copied the two
Zagreb addresses — the French bank, for
the countries of Central Europe, he would
remember.

As Weisz hurried toward the Métro, he
was excited, and elated. It *had* worked, Salamone had been right. *Zagreb,* he thought,
Croatia.

Of course.

SOLDIERS FOR
FREEDOM

5 June, 1939.

Carlo Weisz stared out the office window at the Parisian spring — the chestnut and lime trees in bright new leaf, the women in cotton frocks, the sky deep blue, with cloud castles towering over the city. Meanwhile, according to the melancholy papers stacked in his in box, it was also spring for the diplomats — French and British swains sang to the Soviet maiden in the enchanted forest, but she only giggled and ran away. Toward Germany.

So life went — forever, it seemed to Weisz — until the tedious drumbeat of conference and treaty was broken, suddenly, by real tragedy. Today, it was the story of the SS *St. Louis,* which had sailed from Hamburg with 936 German Jews in flight from the Reich, but could find no harbor. Barred from landing in Cuba, the refugees appealed to President

Roosevelt, who first said yes, then said sorry. Political forces in America were violently set against Jewish immigration. So, the previous day, a final statement: the *St. Louis,* waiting at sea between Cuba and Florida, would not be allowed to dock. Now she would have to return to Germany.

In the Paris office, they'd elicited a French reaction, but the Quai d'Orsay, in six paragraphs, had no comment. Which left Weisz staring out the window, unwilling to work, his mind in Berlin, his heart untouched by the June day.

Two days earlier, when he'd returned from the boulevard de Strasbourg to the Reuters office, he'd immediately telephoned Salamone and told him what he'd done. "Someone in that office has connections with Croatia," he'd said, and described the envelopes. "Which suggests that OVRA may be using *Ustasha* operatives." They both knew what that meant: Italy and Croatia had a long, complicated, and often secret relationship, the Croatians seeking Catholic kinship in their endless conflict with the Orthodox Serbs. The *Ustasha* was a terrorist group — or nationalist, or insurgent; in the Balkans, it depended on who was speaking — sometimes used by the Italian secret services. Dedicated to an independent

346

Croatia, the *Ustasha* had possibly been involved in the 1934 assassination of King Alexander, in Marseilles, and other terrorist actions, notably the bombing of passenger trains.

"This is not good news," Salamone had said, his voice grim.

"No, but it is *news*. News for the *Sûreté*. And there is reason to suspect that funds may be moving through a French bank in Marseilles, a bank that also operates in Croatia. On that, they'll bite."

Salamone had volunteered to approach the *Sûreté,* but Weisz told him not to bother — he was already involved with them, he was the logical informant. "But," he'd said, "we'll keep this between the two of us." He'd then asked Salamone if the surveillance had produced anything further. Only a sighting, Salamone said, by Sergio, of the man in the hat with the green feather. Weisz advised Salamone to call it off; they had enough. "And the next time we call a meeting," he'd said, "it will be an editorial conference, for the next *Liberazione.*"

That was more than optimistic, he thought, staring out the window, but first he would have to telephone Pompon. He considered doing it, almost reaching for the number, then, once again, put it off. He'd do it later, now he had to work. Taking the first paper off the stack, he found a release from the Soviet embassy in Paris, regarding continuing negotiations with the British and French for alliance in case of a German attack. A long list of potential victims was named, with Poland first and foremost. A visit to the Quai d'Orsay? Maybe. He'd have to ask Delahanty.

He put the release aside. Next up, a cable from Eric Wolf that had come in an hour earlier. *Propaganda Ministry Reports Spy Network Broken in Berlin.* It was a lean story: an unspecified number of arrests, some at government ministries, of German citizens who'd passed information to foreign operatives. The names had been withheld, investigation continued.

Weisz went cold. Could he telephone? Cable? No, that might only make it worse. Could he telephone Alma Bruck? No, she might be involved. Christa had only said she was a friend. Eric Wolf, then. Maybe. He could, he felt, ask for one favor, but no more than that. Wolf already had his hands full, and he hadn't been all that pleased to be involved with a colleague's clandestine love affairs. And, Weisz forced himself to admit, Wolf had likely done all he could — surely he'd asked for names, but they had been "withheld." No, he had to keep Wolf in reserve. Because, if by some miracle she survived this, if by some miracle this was a *different* spy network, he was going to get her out of Germany, and for that he would require at least one communication.

Yet he couldn't make himself give up. As his hands pressed against the cable, flat on his desk, his mind flew from one possibility to the next, around and around, until the secretary came in with another cable. *Germany Proposes Alliance Negotiations with the USSR.*

She's gone. There's nothing you can do. Sick at heart, he tried to work.

By evening, it was worse. The images of Christa, in the hands of the Gestapo, would not leave him. Unable to eat, he was early for his eight o'clock work at the Tournon. But Ferrara wasn't there, the room was locked. Weisz went back downstairs and asked the clerk if Monsieur Kolb was in his room, but was told there was no such person at the hotel. That was, Weisz thought, typical — Kolb appeared from nowhere and returned to the same place. He was likely staying at the Tournon, but evidently using a different name. Weisz went out onto the rue de Tournon, crossed the street to the

Jardin du Luxembourg, sat on a bench, and smoked cigarette after cigarette, mocked by the soft spring evening and, it seemed to him, every pair of lovers in the city. At eight-twenty, he returned to the hotel, and found Ferrara waiting for him.

This town, that river, the heroic corporal who picked up a hand grenade from the bottom of a ditch and threw it back. What helped Weisz, that night, was the automatic process of the work, typing Ferrara's words, editing as he went along. Then, a few minutes after ten, Kolb appeared. "We'll finish early tonight," he said. "All going well?"

"We're getting close to the end," Ferrara said. "There's the time at the internment camp, then it's finished. I'd guess you won't want us to write about my time in Paris."

From Kolb, a wolfish grin. "No, we'll just leave that to the reader's imagination." Then, to Weisz: "You and I will be going up to the Sixteenth. There's someone in town who wants to meet you."

From the way Kolb said it, Weisz didn't really have a choice.

The apartment was in Passy, the aristocratic heart of the *très snob* Sixteenth Arrondisse-ment. Red and gold, in the best Parisian tradition, it was all heavy drapes and fabrics, paneled with *boiserie,* one wall a bookcase. A darkened room, lit only by a single Oriental lamp. The concierge had telephoned their arrival from her loge, so, when Kolb opened the elevator gate, Mr. Brown was waiting by the door. "Ah, hello, glad you could come!" A cheery call and a rather different Mr. Brown — no more the amiably rumpled gent with pipe and slipover sweater. Instead, a new suit, expensive and dark blue. As Weisz shook hands and entered the apartment, he saw why. "This is Mr. Lane," Brown said.

A tall, spindly man unfolded himself from a low sofa, gripped Weisz's hand, and said, "Mr. Weisz, a pleasure to meet you." Crisp white shirt, solemn tie, perfectly tailored suit, the British upper class resplendent, with steel-colored hair and thin, professionally hesitant smile. But the eyes, deep-set, webbed with deep lines, were worried eyes, almost apprehensive, that came close to contradicting all the signals of his status. "Come sit with me," he said to Weisz, indicating the other end of the sofa. Then: "Brown? Can you get us a scotch? As it comes?"

This turned out to mean neat, two inches of amber liquid in a crystal glass. Lane said,

"We'll see you later." Kolb had already evaporated, now Mr. Brown went off to another room in the apartment. "So," he said to Weisz, his voice low and mellow and pleased, "you're our writer."

"I am," Weisz said.

"Damn fine work, Mr. Weisz. *Soldier for Freedom* should do rather well, we think. I'd surmise you have your heart in it."

"That's true," Weisz said.

"Shame about your country. I don't believe she'll be happy with her new friends, but that can't be helped, can it. Not that you haven't tried."

"Do you mean *Liberazione?*"

"I do. Seen the back issues, and it's easily at the top of its class. Leaves the politics alone, thank God, and leans hard on the facts of life. And your cartoonist is a delightfully nasty man. Who is he?"

"An émigré, he works for *Le Journal.*" Weisz didn't say a name, and Lane let it go.

"Well, we hope to see lots more of that."

"Oh?"

"Indeed. We see a bright future for *Liberazione.*" Lane's voice caressed the word, as though it were the name of an opera.

"The way life goes at the moment, it doesn't really exist, not anymore."

If Lane's face did anything well, it was *disappointment.* "No, no, don't say such things, it must go on." The *must* worked both ways, *simply must,* and *really must* — or else.

"We've been under siege," Weisz said. "By the OVRA, we believe, and we've had to suspend publication."

Lane took a sip of his scotch. "Then you'll just have to unsuspend it, won't you, now that Mussolini's gone and joined the wrong side. What do you mean, under siege?"

"An assassination, attacks on the committee members — trouble at work, possibly arson, a burglary."

"Have you gone to the police?"

"Not yet. But we may try, it's under consideration."

From Lane, an emphatic nod: *That's a good fellow.* "Can't just let it die, Mr. Weisz, it's simply too good. And, we have reason to believe, effective. People in Italy talk about it — we know that. Now, we may be able to help you out, with the police, but you ought to give it a try on your own. Experience says that's the best way. And, fact is, your *Liberazione* ought to be bigger, and more widely read, and there we really can do something. Tell me, what are your distribution arrangements?"

Weisz paused, how to describe it. "They've always run themselves, since 1933, when the editorial committee of the *Giustizia e Libertà* committee worked in Italy. It is, well, it grew by itself. First there was a single truck driver, in Genoa, then another, a friend of his, who went up to Milan. It isn't a pyramid, with a Parisian émigré at the top, it's just people who know one another, and who want to participate, to do something, whatever they can, to oppose the fascist regime. We're not the Communists, we're not in cells, with discipline. We have a printer in Genoa, he hands bundled papers off to three or four friends, and they spread it out among their friends. One takes ten, another takes twenty. And from there it goes everywhere."

Lane was delighted, and showed it. "Blessed chaos!" he said. "Cheerful Italian anarchy. I hope you don't mind, my saying that."

Weisz shrugged. "I don't mind, it's true. In my country, we don't like bosses, it's the way we're made."

"And your print run?"

"Around two thousand."

"The Communists run twenty thousand."

"I didn't know the number, I assumed it was larger. But they get themselves arrested more than we do."

"I take your point — we can't have too much of *that*. And readers?"

"Who knows. Sometimes one to a paper, sometimes twenty. We couldn't begin to guess, but it is shared, and not thrown away — we ask for that, right on the masthead."

"Could one say, twenty thousand?"

"Why not? It's possible. The paper's left on benches in railway waiting rooms, and on the trains. Anywhere public you can imagine."

"And your information — if you don't mind my asking?"

"By mail, by new émigrés, by gossip and rumor."

"Naturally. Information has a life of its own, which is something we know very well, to our joy, and, sometimes, to our sorrow."

From Weisz, a sympathetic nod.

"How's your drink?"

Weisz looked down and saw he'd almost finished the scotch.

"Let me top that up for you." Lane stood, walked over to a cabinet by the doorway, and poured them both a second drink. When he returned, he said, "I'm glad we had a chance to talk. We've made some plans for you, in London, but I wanted to see who we'd be working with."

"What plans have you made, Mr. Lane."

"Oh, as I said. Bigger, better distribution, more readers, many more. And I think we might be able to help out, now and then, with information. We're good at that. Oh, by the way, what about paper?"

"We print at the Genoa daily newspaper, and our printer, well, it's like everything else — he finds a way, a friend upstairs, in the office, or maybe the records aren't kept all that well."

Once again, Lane was delighted, and laughed. "Fascist Italy," he said, shaking his head at the absurdity of such an idea. "How in God's name . . ."

Like the rest of the world, Weisz had had his bad nights — lost love, world gone wrong, money — but this was by far the worst; slow hours, spent staring at the ceiling of a hotel room. Yesterday, he would have been excited by his meeting with Mr. Lane — a change of fortune in the war he fought. Good news! An investor! Their little company approached by a big corporation. Which might turn out to be not such good news, and Weisz was aware of that. But, where were they now? It was, certainly, an event, a sudden turn of fate, and Weisz typically rose to such challenges, but now all he could think about was Christa. In Berlin. In a cell. Interrogated.

Fear and rage rose within him, first one, then the other. He hated her captors, he would pay them back. But, how to reach her, how to find out, what could he do to save her? Could she still be saved? No, it was too late. Could he go to Berlin? Could Delahanty help him? The Reuters board of directors? Desperately, he reached for power. But found only one source. *Mr. Lane.* Would Lane help him? Not as a favor. Lane was an executive, and shared with others of his breed a sublime talent for deflection — Weisz had *felt* it. His purpose, in the sea he swam in, was to acquire, to succeed. He could not be pleaded with, he could only be forced, forced to bargain, in order to get what he wanted. Would he bargain?

Weisz had thought about asking, during the meeting in Passy, but had held back. He needed time to think, to work out how to do what needed to be done. He knew very well who he was dealing with; a man whose job it was, that week, to spread clandestine newspapers through an enemy country. Would he ask only Weisz? Only *Liberazione?* Who else had he seen that night? What other émigré journals had he approached? No, Weisz thought, let him win, let him bring this game home in his bag. Then, attack. He could launch only one, he knew, so it had to work. And, executive that he was, Lane had never actually asked the crucial question: will you do this? Thus avoided the awkwardness of an answer he didn't want to hear. No, that job would be left to Brown. *So, Mr. Brown.*

Weisz never did sleep that night, never took his clothes off, but dozed now and then, toward dawn, finally exhausted. Then, on another heaven-sent June morning, he went early to work, and telephoned Pompon. Who wasn't in, but called back an hour later. A meeting was arranged, after work, at the Interior Ministry.

It was still dusk when Weisz arrived at the rue des Saussaies; the vast building filled the sky, the men with briefcases streaming in and out through its shadow. As before, he was directed to Room 10; a long table, a few chairs, high window behind a grille, dead air heavy with the smell of cooked paint and stale cigarette smoke. Inspector Pompon awaited him, accompanied by his older colleague, his superior, *the cop,* as Weisz thought of him, grizzled and slumped, who now introduced himself as Inspector

Guerin. They were informal that evening, jackets off, ties loosened. So, *friendly* inspectors, for this meeting. Still, Weisz sensed both tension and expectation. *We've got him. Do we?* On the table before them, the green dossiers, and, once again, it was Pompon who took notes.

Weisz wasted no time getting down to business. "We've obtained information," he said, "that may interest you."

Pompon led the questioning. "We?" he said.

"The editorial committee of the émigré newspaper, *Liberazione.*"

"What do you have, Monsieur Weisz, and how did you get it?"

"What we have is evidence of an Italian secret service operation, in this city. It's at work now, today." Weisz went on to describe, without using names, Elena's pursuit of the man who'd approached her supervisor, the interrogation of Véronique and the subsequent meeting with Elena, his telephone call to the Photo-Mondiale agency and his doubts about its legitimacy, the committee's attempt at surveillance of 62, boulevard de Strasbourg, and the letters he'd found in the agency's mailbox. Then, from the notes he'd brought with him, he read out the names of the French bank, and the addresses in Zagreb.

"Playing detective?" Guerin said, more amused than annoyed.

"Yes, I suppose so. But we had to do something. I mentioned, earlier, the attacks on the committee."

Pompon slid the dossier over to his colleague, who read, using his index finger, the notes of a meeting with Weisz at the Opéra café. "Not much, for us. But the investigation of the murder of Madame LaCroix is still open, and that's why we're talking to you."

Pompon said, "And you believe this is related material. This spy business."

"Yes, that's what we think."

"And the language your associate heard, beneath the staircase, was Serbo-Croatian?"

"She didn't know what it was."

For a moment, silence, then the inspectors exchanged a glance.

"We may look into it," Guerin said. "And the newspaper?"

"We've suspended publication," Weisz said.

"But, if your, ah, *problems* are eliminated, what then?"

"We'll continue. More than ever, now that Italy has allied herself with Germany, we feel it's important."

Guerin sighed. "Politics, politics," he said. "Back and forth."

"And then you get war," Weisz said.

Guerin nodded. "It's coming."

"If we investigate," Pompon said, "we may be back in touch with you. Has anything changed? Employment? Domicile?"

"No, it's all as before."

"Very well, if you should find out anything else, you'll let us know."

"I will," Weisz said.

"But," Guerin said, "don't go trying to help, not anymore, right? Leave that to us."

Pompon went back over his notes, making sure of the names and addresses in Zagreb, then told Weisz he could go.

As Weisz left, Guerin smiled and said, "*A bientôt,* Monsieur Weisz." See you soon.

Back on the rue des Saussaies, Weisz found a café, likely the Interior Ministry café, he thought, from the look of the men eating dinner and drinking at the bar, and a certain muted quality to the conversation. Pressed for time, he gobbled down the *plat du jour,* a veal stew, drank two glasses of wine, then called Salamone from a pay telephone at the back of the café. "It's done," he said. "They're going to investigate. But I need to see you, and maybe Elena."

"What did they say?"

"Oh, maybe they'll look into it. You know how they are."

"When do you want to meet?"

"Tonight. Is eleven too late?"

After a moment, Salamone said, "No, I'll pick you up."

"At the rue de Tournon, the corner of the rue de Médicis."

"I'll call Elena," Salamone said.

Weisz found a taxi outside the café, and by eight he was at Ferrara's hotel.

They worked hard that evening, doing more pages than usual. They were up to Ferrara's entry into France and his internment at a camp near the southwestern city of Tarbes. Ferrara was still angry, and didn't spare the details, well focused on the bureaucratic sin of *indifference.* But Weisz toned it down. A flood of refugees from Spain, the sad remnants of a lost cause, the French did what they could. Because the Pact of Steel had changed the political chemistry, and this book was, after all, propaganda, British propaganda, and France was now, more than ever, Britain's ally in a divided Europe. At eleven Weisz rose to leave — where was Kolb? Out in the corridor, as it happened, headed for the room.

"I have to see Mr. Brown," Weisz said. "As soon as possible."

"Anything wrong?"

"It isn't the book," Weisz said. "Something else. About the meeting last night."

"I'll talk to him," Kolb said. "And we'll arrange it."

"Tomorrow morning," Weisz said. "There's a café, called Le Repos, just down the rue Dauphine from the Hotel Dauphine. At eight."

Kolb raised an eyebrow. "That's not how we do things," he said.

"I know, but this is a favor. Please, Kolb, time is important."

Kolb didn't like it. "I'll try. But, if he doesn't show up, don't be surprised. You know the routine — Brown picks the time, and the place. We have to be careful."

Weisz was an inch away from pleading. "Just try, that's all I ask."

Out on the street, Weisz walked quickly to the corner. The Renault was there, its engine missing as it idled. Elena was sitting next to Salamone, and Weisz climbed into the backseat, then apologized for being late.

"Don't worry about it," Salamone said, ramming the shift lever until it clunked into first gear. "You're our hero, tonight."

Weisz described the meeting at the Interior

Ministry, then said, "What we have to discuss now is something else — something I found out about last night."

"Now what?" Salamone said.

Weisz told Elena, briefly but accurately, about the Ferrara book, an operation of the British SIS. "Now they've approached me on the subject of *Liberazione*," he said. "Not only are they eager to see us back in business, they want us to grow. Bigger printing, more readers, wider distribution. They say they'll help us to do that, and they'll provide information. And, I have to add that I want to use the opportunity to save a friend's life, a woman's life, in Berlin."

For a moment, nobody said anything. Finally, from Salamone: "Carlo, you're making it hard for us to say no."

"If it's no, it's no," Weisz said. "For my friend, I'll find another way."

" 'Provide information'? What is that? They'll tell us what to print?"

"It's the alliance," Elena said. "They wanted Italy to stay neutral, but, whatever they were doing, it didn't work. So, now, they have to turn up the heat."

"Jesus, Carlo," Salamone said, hauling at the wheel and turning into a side street. "You of all people — it sounds like you want to let them do it. But you know what happens. A foot in the door, then a little more, and soon enough they own us. We're spies, us." He laughed at the idea. "Sergio? The lawyer? Zerba, the art historian? *Me?* The OVRA will take us apart, we can't survive in that world."

Weisz's voice was tense. "We have to try, Arturo. What we always wanted was to make a difference, in Italy, to fight back. Well, this is our chance."

The dark interior of the Renault was suddenly lit by the headlights of a car that had turned into the street behind them. Salamone glanced in the mirror as Elena said, "How would we even do that? Find another printer? More couriers? More people to hand out copies? In more cities?"

"*They* know how, Elena," Weisz said. "We're amateurs, they're professionals."

Again, Salamone looked in the mirror. The car had come up close to them. "Carlo, really I don't understand you. When we took over from the *giellisti* in Italy, we faced intrusion of this kind, and fought it off. We're a resistance organization, and that has its perils, but we must remain independent."

"There will be a war here," Elena said. "Like 1914, but worse, if you can imagine that. And every resistance organization, every nose-in-the-air idealist, will be pulled into it. And not for their saintly opinions."

"Are you with Carlo?"

"I don't like it, but yes, I am."

Salamone turned the corner and sped up. "Who is that? Behind us?" The Renault was back on the street that ran adjacent to the Jardin du Luxembourg, and going faster, but the headlights stayed fixed in the mirror. Weisz turned and looked out the back window, saw two dark shapes in the front seat of a big Citroën.

"Maybe we should let them help us," Salamone said. "But I think we'll regret it. Just tell me, Carlo, is it this personal reason, this friend, that's changed your mind? Or would you do it anyhow?"

"The war isn't coming, it's here. And if it isn't the British today, it will be the French tomorrow, the pressure's just beginning. Elena's right — this is just a matter of time. We're all going to fight, some with guns, some with typewriters. And, as for my friend, it's a life worth saving, no matter who she is to me."

"I don't care why," Elena said. "We can't go on by ourselves, the OVRA proved that. I think we should accept this offer, and, if the British can help Carlo, can save his friend, so be it, and why not. What if it were you or me, Arturo? In trouble in Berlin, or

Rome? What would you want Carlo to do?"

Salamone slowed down, then, staring at the rearview mirror, rolled to a stop. The Citroën also stopped. Then, slowly, swung around the Renault and pulled up beside it. A man in the passenger seat turned and looked at them for a moment, then said something to the driver, and the car drove away.

"What was that all about?" Elena said.

7 June, 8:20 A.M.

The Café le Repos was busy in the morning, customers two deep at the bar, saving a few sous on their coffee. In search of privacy, Weisz had taken a table in the far corner, backed up to the pebbled-glass partition. And there he waited, *Le Journal* unread before him, his coffee a dark stain at the bottom of the tiny cup, but no sign of Mr. Brown. Well, Kolb had warned him, these people had their own ways of doing business. Then, a man in a peaked cap left the bar, walked over to his table, and said, "Weisz?"

"Yes?"

"Come with me."

Weisz left money on the table and followed the man outside. In the street a taxi was idling in front of the café. The man in the cap got behind the wheel and Weisz climbed into the back, where Mr. Brown was waiting for him. The usual Mr. Brown today, the smell of pipe smoke sweet in the air. "Good morning," he said tartly. The taxi drove away and merged with the slow traffic on the rue Dauphine. "Pleasant morning, we have today."

"Thank you for doing this," Weisz said. "I had to talk to you, about your plans for *Liberazione*."

"You're referring to your little chat with Mr. Lane."

"That's right. We think it's a good idea, but I need your help. To save a life."

Brown's eyebrows rose, and the pipe sent up an exclamatory puff of smoke. "What life is that?"

"The life of a friend. She's been involved with a resistance group, in Berlin, and now she may be in trouble. Because, two days ago, I saw a cable at Reuters that could mean she's been arrested."

For a moment, Brown looked like a physician who's been told something awful — bad as it was to you, he'd heard it all before. "You require a miracle, then everything will be hunky-dory. Is that the idea, Mr. Weisz?"

"Maybe a miracle, for me, but not for you."

Brown took the pipe from his mouth and gave Weisz a long look. "Girlfriend, is it?"

"More than that."

"And, truly, doing things in Berlin, against the Nazis? Not just being vocal at dinner parties?"

"The former," Weisz said. "A circle of friends, some of them working in the ministries, stealing papers."

"And passing 'em to who? If you don't mind my asking. Not to us, surely, you couldn't be that lucky."

"I don't know. It could be the Soviets, or even the Americans. She made a point of not telling me."

"Even in bed."

"Yes, even there."

"Then good for her," Brown said. "Bolsheviks, these people?"

"I don't believe they are. Not the Stalinist kind, anyhow. It's more acts of conscience, against an evil regime. And whoever they've found, to receive what they take, that's likely by chance — somebody, some diplomat, maybe, they happened to know."

"Or who contrived to know them, I daresay."

"Probably. Somebody guessed right."

"I'll be frank with you, Weisz. If the Gestapo's got her, there isn't much we can do. She couldn't possibly be a British citizen, could she."

"No, she's German. Hungarian on her father's side."

"Mm." Brown turned away from Weisz and looked out his window. After a moment, he said, "We assume that it's a committee of some sort, that runs your journal. Have you spoken with them?"

"I have. They're prepared to do what you ask."

"And you?"

"I'm in favor."

"You'll go?"

"Go along with the idea, yes."

"Go along with the idea, he says. No, Weisz, go to *Italy*. Or did Lane not quite get around to telling you that part of it?"

You're mad. But he was caught. "Actually, he didn't. Is that part of the plan?"

"That *is* the bloody plan, boyo. It's your hide, we're after."

Weisz took a breath. "If you'll help me, I'll do whatever you say."

"Conditions?" Brown, his eyes cold, left the word hanging in the air.

Give the right answer. Weisz felt a muscle tick at the corner of his eye. "It isn't a condition, but . . ."

"Do you know what you're asking? What

you're after is an *operation,* do you have any idea what that entails? It ain't 'Good old Weisz, let's just hop over to Berlin and snatch his chickadee from the Nazis.' There will have to be *meetings* about this, in *London,* and if, for some absurd reason, we choose to even *try,* you'll be ours. Henceforth. Like that word? I quite like it, myself. It tells a story."

"Done," Weisz said.

Under his breath, Brown mumbled, "Bloody nuisance." Then, to Weisz: "Very well, write this down." He waited while Weisz retrieved pen and pad. "What I'll want from you, today, in your handwriting, is everything you know about her. Her name, maiden name, if she's been married. A very precise physical description — height, weight, what she wears, how she does her hair. And every photograph you have, and I mean *every* photograph. Her addresses, all of 'em, where she lives, where she works, and the telephone numbers. Where she shops, if you know, and when she shops. Where she goes to dinner, or lunch, the names of servants, and the names of any friends she's mentioned, and their addresses. Her parents, who they are, where they live. And some phrase that's private between the two of you, 'my apple dumpling,' that sort of thing."

"I don't have any photographs."

"No, of course you wouldn't."

"Should I give it to Kolb, tonight?"

"No, write 'Mrs. Day' on the outside of an envelope and leave it at the desk of the Bristol. Before noon, is that clear?"

"It will be there."

Brown, much persecuted by life's sudden surprises, shook his head. Then, resignation in his voice, said, "Andrew."

The driver knew what that meant, slid the taxi through traffic to the curb, then stopped. Brown leaned across Weisz and opened his door. "We'll let you know," he said. "And, meanwhile, best finish up your work with Ferrara."

Weisz headed for the office, anxious to write what Brown had requested, and equally anxious to have a look at the previous night's dispatches, but there was nothing further on the Berlin spy ring. For a moment, he had himself persuaded that this was a reasonable pretext for a call to Eric Wolf, then acknowledged it wasn't, unless Delahanty asked. Delahanty did not ask, though Weisz mentioned it. Instead, Delahanty told him he had to be on the one o'clock train to Orléans, where the president

372

of a bank had left town with his seventeen-year-old girlfriend and a substantial portion of his depositors' money. Off to Tahiti, it was rumored, and not, as he'd announced at the bank, to a meeting in Brussels. Weisz worked hard for an hour, writing down everything he knew about Christa's life, then, on his way back to the Dauphine to pack his valise, he stopped at the Bristol.

When Weisz returned to Paris, at midday on the ninth, there was trouble at the office. "Please go immediately to see Monsieur Delahanty," the secretary said, a malicious gleam in her eye. She'd long suspected that Weisz was involved in some sort of monkey business, now it looked like she'd been right and he was going to get his comeuppance.

But she was wrong. Weisz sat in the visitor's chair, across from Delahanty, who stood and closed his office door, then winked at him. "I did have some doubts about you, laddie," he said, returning to his desk, "but now it's all cleared up."

Weisz was mystified.

"No, no, don't say a word, you don't have to. You can't blame me, can you? All this running off, here and there. I asked myself, what the hell's going on with him? Emigrés always up to something, the way the world sees it, but work has to come first. And I'm not saying it hasn't, almost always, since you started here. You've been faithful and true, on time, on the story, and no nonsense with the expense reports. But then, well, I didn't know what was going on."

"And now you do?"

"From on high, laddie, as high as it gets. Sir Roderick and his crowd, well, if they value anything, they value patriotism, the old roar of the old British lion. Now I know you won't take advantage of this, because I do need you, got to have the stories, every day, or there's no bureau, but, if you have to, well, *disappear,* now and then, just let me know. For God's sake don't just vanish on me, but a word will suffice. We're proud of you, Carlo. Now get out of here and write me a follow-up on your filing from Orléans, that naughty banker and his naughty girl-friend. We've got her photo, from the local rag, it's on your desk. Smoldering little thing she is, in a confirmation gown, no less, with a fooking bouquet in her hot little hand. Go to it, laddie. Tahiti. Gauguin! *Sarongs!*"

Weisz stood up to leave, then, as he opened the door, Delahanty said, "And, as for this other business, I won't mention it again. Except to say good luck, and be careful."

Somewhere, Weisz thought, in the backstage apparatus of his life, someone had turned a wheel.

10 June, 9:50 P.M., Hotel Tournon.

Itís something I never want to go through again, but it made me the brother of every soul in Europe who looks out at the world through barbed wire, and there are thousands of them, no matter how much their governments try to deny it. It was my good fortune that I had friends, who secured my release, then helped me to start life anew in the city where Iím writing this. Itís a good city, a free city, where people value their freedom, and all I would wish for you, for people everywhere in Europe, everywhere in the world, is that they can, some day, share this precious freedom.

It wonít be easy. The tyrants are strong, and grow stronger every day. But it will happen, believe me it will. And, whatever you have to do, whatever you may turn to, I will be there beside you. Or someone like me ó there are more of us than you might think, we are just down the street, or in the next town, prepared to ght for what we believe in. We fought for Spain, and you know what happened there, we lost the war. But we haven't lost hope, and, when the next fight comes, we will be there. And, as for me personally, I won't give up. I will remain, as I have been these many years, a soldier for freedom.

Weisz lit a cigarette and leaned back in the chair. Ferrara came around behind him and read the text over his shoulder. "I like it," he said. "So, we're finished?"

"They'll want changes," Weisz said. "But they've been reading the pages every night, so I'd say it's pretty much what they're after."

Ferrara patted him on the shoulder. "Never thought I'd write a book."

"Well, now you have."

"We should have a drink, to celebrate."

"Maybe we will, when Kolb shows up."

Ferrara looked at his watch, it was new, and gold, and very fancy. "He usually comes at eleven."

They went downstairs to the café, below street level, at one time the cellar of the Tournon. Inside, it was dark and almost deserted, with only one customer, half a glass of wine at his elbow, writing on sheets of yellow paper. "He's always here," Ferrara said. They ordered brandies at the bar and sat at one of the battered tables, the wood stained, and scarred by cigarette burns.

"What will you do, now that the book's finished?" Weisz said.

"Hard to say. They want me to go on a speaking tour, after the book comes out. To England, maybe America."

"That's not unusual, for a book like this."

"Can I tell you the truth, Carlo? Will you keep a secret?"

"Go ahead. I don't tell them everything."

"I'm not going to do it."

"No?"

"I don't want to be their toy soldier. I'm not like that."

"No, but it's a good cause."

"Sure it is, but not for me. Trying to read a speech, for some church group . . ."

"What then?"

"Irina and I are going away. Her parents are émigrés, in Belgrade, we can go there, she says."

"Brown doesn't care for her, I guess you know that."

"She's my life. We make love all night."

"Well, they won't like it."

"We're just going to slip away. I'm not going to England. If there's a war, I'll go to

Italy, and do my fighting there, in the mountains."

Weisz promised not to tell Kolb, or Brown, and when he wished Ferrara well, meant it. They drank for a time, then, just before eleven, returned to the smoky room. That night, Kolb was prompt. When he'd read over the ending, he said, "Fine words. Very inspiring."

"You'll let me know," Weisz said, "about any changes."

"They're really in a hurry now, I don't know what's gotten into them, but I doubt they'll take much more of your time." Then his voice turned confidential and he said, "Would you step outside for a moment?"

In the hallway, Kolb said, "Mr. Brown asked me to tell you that we have news about your friend, from our people in Berlin. She's not in custody, yet. For the moment, they're watching her. Closely. Sounds to me like our people kept their distance, but the surveillance is in place — they know what it looks like. So, keep away from her, and *don't* try to use the telephone." He paused, then said, concern in his voice, "I hope she knows what she's doing."

For a moment, Weisz couldn't speak. Finally, he managed to say, "Thank you."

"She's in danger, Weisz, you'd better be aware of that. And she won't be safe until she can find a way to get out of there."

For the next few days, silence. He went up to Le Havre for a Reuters assignment, did what he had to do, then returned. Every time the office telephone rang, every evening when he stopped at the desk of the Dauphine, hope rose inside him, then evaporated. All he could do was wait, and he'd never realized how poorly he did that. He spent his days, and particularly his nights, preoccupied with Christa, with Brown, with going to Italy — back and forth, and nothing he could do about any of it.

Then, late on the morning of the fourteenth, Pompon telephoned. Weisz was to come to the *Sûreté* at three-thirty that afternoon. So, once again Room 10. This time, however, no Pompon, only Guerin. "Inspector Pompon is gathering the dossiers," he explained. "But, while we're waiting, there is one thing we have to clear up. You've withheld the names of your editorial committee, and we respect that, it's an honorable instinct, but now, in order to go forward with the investigation, we'll need to interview them, to help us with identification. It is in their interest, Monsieur Weisz, for their safety as well as yours." He slid a tablet and pencil over to Weisz. "Please," he said.

Weisz wrote down the names of Véronique and Elena, and added the address of the gallery, and Elena's room. "They're the ones who've been in contact," Weisz said, then explained that Véronique had nothing to do with *Liberazione.*

Pompon showed up a few minutes later, with dossiers and a heavy manila envelope. "We won't keep you too long today, we simply want you to look at some photographs. Take your time, study the faces, and let us know if you recognize any of them."

He took an eight-by-ten print from the envelope and handed it to Weisz. Nobody he'd ever seen. A pale man, about forty, sturdily built, with close-cropped hair, photographed in profile as he walked down a street, the shot taken from some distance away. As Weisz studied the photograph, he saw, at the extreme left of the image, the doorway of 62, boulevard de Strasbourg.

"Recognize him?" Pompon said.

"No, I've never seen him."

"Maybe in passing," Guerin said. "On a street somewhere. In the Métro?"

Weisz tried, but he couldn't remember ever seeing the man. Was he the one they especially wanted? "I don't think I've ever seen him," Weisz said.

"And her?" Pompon said.

An attractive woman, walking past a stall at a street market. She wore a stylish suit and a hat with a brim that shadowed one side of her face. She'd been caught in full stride, likely walking quickly, her expression absorbed and determined. On her left hand, a wedding ring. *The face of the enemy.* But she seemed so commonplace, in the midstream of whatever life she lived, which simply happened to include employment by the Italian secret police, whose job it was to destroy certain people.

"Don't recognize her," Weisz said.

"And this fellow?"

Not a clandestine photograph this time, but a mug shot; front face, and profile, with an identification number across the chest, below the name Jozef Vadic. Young and brutal, Weisz thought. A killer. Defiance glowed in his eyes — the *flics* could take his picture all they wanted, he would do as he liked, because it was the right thing to do.

"Never saw him," Weisz said. "Better that I haven't, I'd say."

"True," Guerin said.

Waiting for the next photograph, Weisz thought, *where is the man who tried to enter my room at the Dauphine?*

"And him?" Pompon said.

Weisz knew who this was. Pitted face, Errol Flynn mustache, though, from this angle, he could see no feather in the hatband. He'd been photographed sitting on a chair in a park, legs crossed, very much at ease, hands folded in his lap. Waiting, Weisz thought, for someone to come out of a building or a restaurant. And good at waiting, daydreaming, maybe, about something he liked. And — he recalled Véronique's words — there was a certain set to his face that could well be described as "smug, and sly."

"I believe he's the man who interrogated my friend, who owns the art gallery," Weisz said.

"She'll have her chance to identify him," Guerin said.

Weisz knew the next one, as well. Once again, the photograph had been taken with the entry of 62, boulevard de Strasbourg in the frame. It was Zerba, the art historian from Siena. Fair hair, rather handsome, self-assured, not too troubled by the world. Weisz made sure. No, he wasn't wrong. "This man's name is Michele Zerba," Weisz said. "He is a former professor of art history, at the University of Siena, who emigrated to Paris a few years ago. He is a member of the editorial committee of *Liberazione*." Weisz pushed the photograph back across the table.

Guerin was amused. "You should see your face," he said.

Weisz lit a cigarette and moved an ashtray toward him — a café ashtray, likely from the nearby *Sûreté* café.

"And therefore," Pompon said, his voice rich with victory, "a spy for the OVRA. How do you call it? A *confidente?*"

"That's the word."

"Never would have suspected . . ." Guerin said, as though he were Weisz.

"No."

"Thus life." Guerin shrugged. "He's not the type, you think."

"Is there a type?"

"If it were me, I'd say yes — one gets a feel for it, over time. But, in your experience, I would say no."

"What will happen to him?"

Guerin thought it over. "If all he's done is report on the committee, not much. The law he's broken — don't betray your friends — isn't on the books. He did no more than try to help the government of his country. Maybe doing it in France isn't technically legal, but you can't tie that to the assassination of Madame LaCroix, unless someone talks. And, believe me, this crowd won't. Probably, at the worst, we'll send him back to Italy. Back to his friends, and they'll give him a medal."

Pompon said, "Is it *Zed, e, r, b, a?*"

"That's correct."

"Does Siena have two *n*'s? I can never remember."

"One," Weisz said.

There were three more photographs: a heavyset woman with blond braids, wound into "Gretchen plaits" on the sides of her head, and two men, one of them Slavic in appearance, the other older, with a drooping white mustache. Weis had never seen any of them. As Pompon slid the photographs back in their envelope, Weisz said, "What will you do with them?"

"Watch them," Guerin said. "Have a look through the office, at night. If we can catch them with documents, if they're spying on France, they'll go to prison. But new ones will be sent, in some new fake business, in some other arrondissement. The man who impersonated a *Sûreté* inspector *will* go to prison, for a year or two. Eventually."

"And Zerba? What do we do about him?"

"Nothing!" Guerin said. "Don't say a word. He comes to your meetings, he files his reports. Until we're done with our investigation. And, Weisz, do me a favor, and please don't shoot him, allright?"

"We won't shoot him."

"Really?" Guerin said. "I would."

Later that day, he met Salamone at the gardens of the Palais Royal. It was a warm, cloudy afternoon, rain coming, and they were alone, walking the paths lined by low parterre and floral beds. To Weisz, Salamone looked old and worn-out. The collar of his shirt was too large for his neck, there were shadows beneath his eyes, and, as he walked, he pressed the point of his furled umbrella into the gravel path.

Weisz told him that he'd been summoned, earlier that day, to the *Sûreté*. "They had taken photographs," he said. "Secretly. Of the people connected to the Agence Photo-Mondiale. Some of them here and there in the city, others of people entering or leaving the building."

"Any that you could identify?"

"Yes, one. It was Zerba."

Salamone stopped walking and turned to face Weisz, his expression a mixture of disgust and disbelief. "Are you certain of that?"

"Yes. Sad to say."

Salamone ran a hand over his face, Weisz thought he was going to cry. Then he took a deep breath and said, "I knew."

Weisz didn't believe it.

"I knew but I didn't know. When we started to meet with Elena, and nobody else, it was because I'd begun to be suspicious, that one of us was working for the OVRA. It happens, to all the émigré groups here."

"We can't do anything," Weisz said. "That's what they said — we can't let on that we know. Maybe they'll send him back to Italy."

They returned to walking, Salamone punching his umbrella into the path. "He should be floating in the Seine."

"Are you prepared to do that, Arturo?"

"Maybe. I don't know. Probably not."

"If this ever ends, and the fascists go away, we'll deal with him then, in Italy. Anyhow, we should celebrate, because this means that *Liberazione* comes back to life. In a week, a month, the *Sûreté* will have done their work and these people won't bother us anymore, not *these* people."

"Others, perhaps."

"It's likely. They won't give up. But we won't either, and now our print runs will be larger, and the distribution wider. Maybe it doesn't feel like it, but this is a victory."

"Bought by British money, and subject to their so-called help."

Weisz nodded. "Inevitable. We are stateless people, Arturo, and that's what happens." For a time, they walked in silence, then Weisz said, "And they've asked me to go to Italy, to organize the expansion."

"When was this?"

"A few days ago."

"And you said yes."

"I did. You can't go, so it will have to be me, and I'll need whatever you have — names, addresses."

"What I have is a few people in Genoa, people I knew when I lived there, two or three shipping agents — we were in the same business — a telephone number for Matteo, in the printing department of *Il Secolo,* some contacts in Rome, and Milan, who survived the *giellisti* arrests a few years ago. But, all in all, not much — you know how it works; friends, and friends of friends."

"Yes, I know. I'll just have to do the best I can. And the British have their own resources."

"Do you trust them, Carlo?"

"Not at all."

"And yet you'll do this, this very dangerous thing."

"I will."

"The *confidenti* are everywhere, Carlo. Everywhere."

"Clearly they are."

"In your heart, do you believe you will return?"

"I'll try. But, if I don't, then I don't."

Salamone started to answer, then didn't. As always, his face showed everything he felt — it was the saddest thing there was, to lose a friend. After a moment, with a sigh in his voice, he said, "So, when do you leave?"

"They won't tell me when, or how, but I'll need your information as soon as possible. At the hotel. Today, if you can manage it."

They walked on, as far as the arcade that bordered the garden, then turned onto another path. For a time, they didn't speak, the silence broken only by the local sparrows and the sound of footsteps on gravel. Salamone seemed lost in his thoughts, but finally, he could only shake his head very slowly and mutter, more to himself and the world than to Weisz, "Ahh, fuck this."

"Yes," Weisz said. "And that will do for an epitaph."

They shook hands and said goodby, and

Salamone wished him luck, then went off toward the Métro. Weisz watched him until he disappeared beneath the arch that led out to the street. He might not, he thought, see Salamone again. He stayed at the garden for a time, walking on the paths, hands deep in the pockets of his raincoat. When a few drops of rain pattered down, he thought *here it comes,* and stepped into the covered arcade, in front of a milliner's shop window, dozens of madly eccentric creations climbing the hat trees — peacock feathers and red spangles, satin bows, gold medallions. The clouds rolled and shifted above the garden, but there was no more rain. And he was, as he often was, surprised at how much he loved this city.

17 June, 10:40 A.M.

A final meeting with Mr. Brown, in some bar down a lost alley in the Marais. "The time draws near," Brown said, "so we'll need some passport photos — drop 'em off at the Bristol tomorrow." Then he read off a list of names, numbers, and addresses, which Weisz wrote down on a pad. When he was done, he said, "You'll commit all this to memory, of course. And destroy your notes."

Weisz said he would.

"Nothing personal goes with you, and if

you have clothing that was bought in Italy, wear it. Otherwise, cut the French labels off."

Weisz agreed.

"What matters is that they see you, down there, you will be onstage every minute. Because it will mean a great deal, to the people who have to do the work, and put themselves in harm's way, that you were brave enough to return. Right under old Mussolini's nose — all that sort of thing. Any questions?"

"Have you heard anything more, about my friend in Berlin?"

This was not the sort of question Brown had in mind, and he showed it. "Don't worry about that, it's being taken care of, just concentrate on what you have to do now."

"I will."

"It's important, concentration. If you are not aware, every minute, of where you are, and who you're with, something could go wrong. And we wouldn't want that, would we?"

20 June, Hotel Dauphine.

At dawn, a knock on the door. Weisz called out, "One minute," and put on a pair of undershorts. When he opened the door,

S. Kolb was grinning at him. Kolb tipped his hat and said, "Fine morning. A perfect day to travel." *How the hell did he get up here?*

"Come in," Weisz said, rubbing his eyes.

Kolb stood a briefcase on the bed, undid the buckles, and flipped the top open. Then he peered inside and said, "What have we here? A whole new person! Why, who could he be? Here's his passport, an Italian passport. By the way, one should try to remember one's name. Quite awkward, at border stations, not to know one's name. Liable to provoke suspicion, though, I have to say, it's been survived. Oh, and look here, *papers.* All sorts, even a" — Kolb held the document away from him, the typical gesture of the farsighted — "a *libretto di lavoro,* a work permit. And where does our person work? He is an officer of the *Istituto per la Ricostruzione Industriale,* the IRI. Now, what in God's name does *that* do? It interviews bankers, it buys stock, it moves government money into private industry, an agency central to fascist economic planning. But, more important, it employs our newly born gentleman as a lordly bureaucrat, of unknown, ergo frightening, power. Not a policeman in Italia that won't go pale in the presence of such dizzying status, and our gent will fly through street controls at a speed causing flames to leap from his behind. Now, not only does our boy have papers, they're all properly stamped, and *aged.* Folded and refolded. Weisz, I have to tell you I've spent time thinking about that job. I mean, they never tell you who does that, folding and refolding, but somebody must. What else? Oh look, money! And lots of it, thousands and thousands of lire, our gentleman is rich, loaded. Anything more in here? Mmm, I guess that does it. No, wait, one more item, I almost missed it. A first-class ticket to Marseilles! For today! At ten-thirty! Now it happens to be a one-way ticket, but don't let that make you nervous. I mean, our man wouldn't want a French railway ticket in his pocket — you never know, you reach for your handkerchief and, whoops! So, when you return to Marseilles, you'll just buy a ticket for Paris, and then, we'll celebrate a job well done. Any comments? Questions? Curses?"

"No questions." Weisz smoothed his hair back and went looking for his glasses. "You've done this before, haven't you?"

From Kolb, a melancholy smile. "Many times. Many, many times."

"I appreciate the light touch."

Kolb made a certain face: *might as well.*

■ ■ ■

22 June, Porto Vecchio, Genoa.

The Greek freighter *Hydraios,* flying the Panamanian flag, docked at the port of Genoa just before midnight. Sailing in ballast from Marseilles, due to take on cargo of flax, wine, and marble, the ship carried one extra crew member. As the crew hurried down the gangplank, laughing and joking, Weisz was in the middle of the crowd, next to the second engineer, who'd retrieved him from the dock in Marseilles. Most of the crew was Greek, but some of them knew a few words of Italian, and one called out to the sleepy passport officer at the doorway of a cargo shed. "Hey! Nunzio! *Hai cuccato?*" Getting laid?

Nunzio made a certain gesture, in the area of his crotch, which constituted an affirmative answer. *"Tutti avanti!"* he sang out, waving them along, stamping each passport without so much as looking at the owner. The second engineer could have been born anywhere, but he spoke merchant seaman's English, enough to say, "We take care of Nunzio. So we don't have no trouble in the port."

■ ■ ■ ■

For a time, Weisz just stood there, alone on the wharf, as the crew disappeared up a flight of stone steps. When they'd gone, it was very quiet, only a buzzing dock light, a cloud of moths fluttering in its metal hood, and the lapping of the sea against the quay. The night air was warm, a familiar warmth, soft on the skin, and fragrant with the scents of decay — damp stone and drains, mud flats at low tide.

Weisz had never been here before, but he was home.

He'd thought himself alone, except for a few wandering cats, but, he saw now, he wasn't. There was a Fiat parked in front of a shuttered storefront, and a young woman in the passenger seat was watching him. When he met her eyes, she gave him a nod of recognition. Then the car drove off, slowly, bumping over the cobbled quay. A moment later, the church bells began to ring, some near, some far away. It was midnight, and Weisz set off to find the via Corvino.

The *vicoli,* the Genoese called the quarter behind the wharf, "the alleys." All of them ancient — the merchant adventurers had been sailing out of here since the thirteenth century — narrow, and steep. They climbed up the hill, became lanes, bordered by high walls hung with ivy, turned into bridges, then to streets made of steps, with, now and then, a small statue of a saint in a hollow niche, so the lost could pray for guidance. And Carlo Weisz was good and lost. At one point, thoroughly discouraged, he simply sat down on a doorstep and lit a Nazionale — thanks to Kolb, who'd tossed a few packets of the Italian cigarettes into his valise as he was packing. Leaning back against the door, he looked up: below a starless heaven, an apartment building leaned out over the street, windows open on a June night, and, from one of them, came a steady rhythm of long, mournful snores. When he finished the cigarette and rose to his feet, he slung his jacket over his shoulder and returned to the search. He would keep at it until dawn, he decided, then he would give up and go back to France, a footnote in the history of espionage.

Trudging up an alley, sweating in the warm night air, he heard approaching footsteps as someone rounded a corner ahead of him. Two policemen. There was nowhere to hide, so he told himself to remember that his name was now Carlo *Marino,* while his fingers involuntarily made sure of the passport in his back pocket.

"Good evening," one of them said. "You lost?"

Weisz admitted he was.

"Where are you going?"

"The via Corvino."

"Ah, that's difficult. But go back down this alley, then turn left, uphill, cross the bridge, then left again. Follow the curve, don't give up, you will be on Corvino, you must look for the sign, raised letters carved into the stone on the corner of the building."

"Grazie."

"Prego."

Just then, as the policeman started to go, something flickered in his attention — Weisz saw it in his eyes. *Who are you?* He hesitated, then touched the bill of his cap, the courtesy salute, and, followed by his partner, walked off down the alley.

Following his directions — much better than the ones he'd memorized, or thought he had — Weisz found the street, and the apartment house. And the big key was, as promised, on a ledge above the entry. Then he climbed, his footsteps echoing in the darkness, three flights of marble stairs, and, above the third door on the right, found the key to the apartment. He got it to work, entered, and waited. Deep silence. He flicked his cigarette lighter, saw a lamp on the table in the foyer, and turned it on. The lamp had an old-fashioned shade, satin, with long tassels, and so it was everywhere in the apartment — bulbous furniture covered in faded velvet, cream-colored draperies yellowed with age, painted-over cracks in the walls. Who lived here? Who *had* lived here? Brown had described the apartment as "empty," but it was more than that. There was, in the dead air of the place, an uncomfortable stillness, an absence. In a tall bookcase, three spaces. So, they'd taken these books with them. And pale squares, on the walls, had once been home to paintings. Sold? These people, were they *fuorusciti* — the ones who'd fled? To France? Brazil? America? Or to prison? Or the graveyard?

Now he was thirsty. On a wall in the kitchen, an ancient telephone. He lifted the receiver but heard only silence. He took a cup from a cabinet crammed with the good china and turned on the water tap. Nothing. He waited then went to turn it off, but heard a distant hiss, then a rattle, and then, a few seconds later, a thin stream of rusty water splashed into the sink. He filled the cup, let a few particles float to the bottom, and took a sip. The water tasted like metal, but he drank it anyhow. Carrying the cup, he went to the back of the apartment, to the largest bedroom, where a chenille spread had been carefully pulled over a feather mattress. He took off his clothes, crawled under the spread, and, exhausted by tension, by journey, by return from exile, fell dead asleep.

In the morning, he went out to find a telephone. The sun worked its way into the alleys, caged canaries were set on window-sills, radios played, and in the small piazzas, people were as he remembered them — the shadow that lay over Berlin had not fallen here. *Not yet.* There were, perhaps, a few more posters plastered on the walls, mocking the French and the British. On one of them, a bloated John Bull and a haughty Marianne rode together in a chariot, with wheels that crushed the poor people of Italy. And when he paused to look in the window of a bookstore, he found himself staring at the disconcerting fascist calendar, revised by Mussolini to begin with his ascension to power in 1922, so giving the date as *23 Giugno, Anno XVII.* But then, the bookstore owner had chosen to display this nonsense in the window, next to Mussolini's autobiography, and that said something, to Weisz, about the persistence of the national character. He recalled Mr. Lane, the night of the meeting in Passy, amused and perplexed, in his upper-class way, by the idea that there could be fascism in Italy.

Weisz found a busy café, drank coffee, read the paper — mostly sports, actresses, an opening ceremony at a new waterworks — then used the public telephone by the WC. The number for Matteo, at *Il Secolo*, rang for a long time. When at last it was answered, he could hear machinery, printing presses running in the background, and the man on the other end of the phone had to shout. *"Pronto?"*

"Is Matteo around?"

"What?"

Weisz tried again, louder. Out in the café, a waiter glanced at him.

"It'll take a minute. Don't hang up."

Finally, a voice said, "Yes? Who is it?"

"A friend, from Paris. From the newspaper."

"What? From where?"

"I'm a friend of Arturo Salamone."

"Oh. You shouldn't call me here, you know. Where are you?"

"In Genoa. Where can we meet?"

"Not until tonight."

"*Where,* I said."

Matteo thought it over. "On the via Caffaro there's a wine shop, the Enoteca Carenna, it's called. It's, it's crowded."

"At seven?"

"Maybe later. Just wait for me. Read a magazine, the *Illustrazione,* so I'll recognize you." He meant the *Illustrazione Italiana,* Italy's version of *Life* magazine.

"I'll see you then."

Weisz hung up, but did not return to his table. From Paris, he could not telephone his family — the international lines were known to be tapped, and the rule for émigrés was: don't try it, you'll get your family in trouble. But now he could. For a call outside of Genoa, he had to use the operator, and when she answered, he gave her the number in Trieste. The phone rang, again and again. Finally, she said, "I am sorry, Signor, but they do not answer."

23 June, 6:50 P.M.

The wine shop on the via Caffaro was very popular — customers at the table and the bar, the rest filling in every available space, a few out in the street. But in time, a watchful Weisz saw his chance, took a vacated table, ordered a bottle of Chianti and two glasses, and settled in with his magazine. He'd read it twice, and was on his third time through, when Matteo appeared, saying, "You're the one who called?" In his forties, he was a tall, bony man with fair hair, and ears that stuck out.

Weisz said he was, Matteo nodded, took a look around the room, and sat down. As Weisz poured a Chianti, he said, "I'm called Carlo, I've been the editor of *Liberazione* since Bottini was murdered."

Matteo watched him.

"And I write under the name Palestrina."

"You're Palestrina?"

"I am."

"I like what you write." Matteo lit a cigarette and shook out the match. "Some of the others . . ."

"Salute."

"Salute."

"What you're doing for the paper," Weisz said. "We appreciate that. The committee wanted me to thank you for it."

Matteo shrugged, but he didn't mind the gratitude. "Have to do *something*," he said. Then: "What goes on, with you? I mean, if you are who you say you are, what the hell are you doing here?"

"I'm here secretly, and I'm not here long. But I had to talk to you, in person, and some other people as well."

Matteo was dubious, and showed it.

"We're changing. We want to print more copies. Now that Mussolini's in bed with his Nazi pals . . ."

"That didn't happen yesterday, you know. There's a place we eat lunch, near the *Secolo,* just up the street from here. A few months ago, these three Germans show up, all of a sudden. In SS uniform, the skull and all that. Brazen bastards, it's like they own the place."

"That could be the future, Matteo."

"I suppose it could. The local *cazzi* are bad enough, but this . . ."

Weisz, following Matteo's eyes, saw two men in black, standing nearby, who had fascist pins on their lapels, and were laughing with each other. There was something subtly aggressive in the way they occupied space, in the way they moved, and in their voices. This was pretty much a workingman's bar, but they didn't care, they'd drink anywhere they liked.

"You think it's possible?" Weisz said. "A bigger print run?"

"Bigger. How many?"

"Maybe twenty thousand."

"Porca miseria!" Pigs of misery, meaning too many copies. "Not at *Il Secolo*. I have a friend upstairs, who doesn't keep such good track of the newsprint, but, a number like that . . ."

"What if we took care of the newsprint?"

Matteo shook his head. "Too much time, too much ink — can't do it."

"What about friends? Other pressmen?"

"Of course I know a few guys. From the union. From what *used* to be, the union." Mussolini had destroyed the unions, and Weisz could see that Matteo hated him for it. Printers were considered, by themselves and most of the world, to be the aristocrats of the trades, and they didn't like being pushed around. "But, I don't know, twenty thousand."

"Could it be done at other printing plants?"

"Maybe in Rome, or Milan, but not here. I have a pal at the *Giornale di Genova* — that's the Fascist party daily — and he could manage another two thousand, and, believe me, he would, too. But that's about what we could do in Genoa."

"We'll have to find another way," Weisz said.

"There's always a way." Matteo stopped talking as one of the men with lapel pins brushed past them to get refills at the bar. "Always a way to do anything. Look at the reds, down at the docks and in the shipyards. The *questura,* the local police, don't mess with them — somebody would get his head broken. They have their paper everywhere, hand out leaflets, put up posters. And everybody knows who they are. Of course, once the secret police show up, the OVRA, it's finished. But, a month later, they've got it going again."

"Could we run our own shop?"

Matteo was impressed. "You mean presses, paper, everything?"

Why not?

"Not out in the open."

"No."

"You'd have to be pretty smart about it. You couldn't just have trucks pull up to the door."

"Maybe one truck, at night, now and then. The paper comes out every two weeks or so, a truck pulls up, takes two thousand copies, drives them down to Rome. Then, two nights later, to Milan, or Venice, or anywhere. We print at night, you could do some of it, your friends, guys from the union, could do the rest."

"That's how they did it in '35. But then, they're all in prison now, or sent off to the camps on the islands."

"Think it over," Weisz said. "How to do it, how not to get caught. And I'll call you in a day or two. Can we meet here, again?"

Matteo said they could.

24 June, 10:15 P.M.

You had to meet with Grassone during his office hours — at night. And the dark streets off the piazza Caricamento made the Tenth Arrondissement look like convent school. Passing the jackals in these doorways, Weisz wished, really wished, he had a gun in his pocket. From the piazza, he'd been able to see the ships in the harbor, including the *Hydraios,* lit by floodlights as her cargo was loaded, and due to sail for Marseilles in four nights, with Weisz aboard. That is, if he made it as far as Grassone's office. And, then, made it back out.

Grassone's office was a room, ten by ten. *Spedzionare Genovese* — Genoa Transport — on the door, naughty calendar on the wall, barred window that looked out on an air shaft, two telephones on a desk, and Grassone in a rolling office chair. Grassone was a nickname, it meant "fat boy," and he easily lived up to that — when he barred the door and returned to his desk, Weisz was reminded of the old line, *walked like two pigs fucking under a blanket.* Younger than Weisz expected, he had the face of a malign cherub, with bright, clever eyes staring out at a world that had never liked him. On closer inspection, he was broad as well as fat, broad across the shoulders, and thick in the upper arms. A fighter, Weisz thought. And if anybody had doubts about that, they would soon enough notice, beneath his double chin, a white band of scar tissue, from one side of the neck to the other. Apparently, somebody had cut his throat, but, equally apparent, here he was. In the words of Mr. Brown, "our black market chap in Genoa."

"So, what will it be?" he said, pink hands folded on the desk.

"Can you get paper? Newsprint, in big rolls?"

This amused him. "I can get, oh, you'd be surprised." Then: "Newsprint? Sure, why not." *Is that all?*

"We'll want a steady supply."

"Shouldn't be a problem. As long as you pay. You're starting a newspaper?"

"We can pay. What would it cost?"

"That I couldn't tell you, but by tomorrow night, I'll know." He leaned back in his chair, which didn't like it and squeaked. "Ever try this?" He reached into a drawer and rolled a black ball across the desk. "Opium. Fresh from China."

Weisz turned the sticky little ball over in his fingers, then handed it back, though he'd always been curious. "No, thank you, not today."

"Don't like sweet dreams?" Grassone said, returning the ball to his drawer. "Then what?"

"Newsprint, a dependable supply."

"Oh, I am dependable, Mr. X. Ask around, they'll tell you, you can count on Grassone. The rule down here, on the docks, is what goes on a truck, comes off. I was just thinking, since you made the trip, you might want a little something more. Parma hams? Lucky Strikes? No? Then what about, a gun. These are difficult times, everybody is nervous. You're a little nervous, Mr. X, if you don't mind my saying so. Maybe what you need is an automatic, a Beretta, it'll fit right in your pocket, and the price is good, best in Genoa."

"You said tomorrow night, a price for the paper?"

Grassone nodded. "Stop by. You want the big rolls, maybe you need a truck."

"Maybe," Weisz said, standing up to leave. "See you tomorrow night."

"I'll be here," Grassone said.

Back at the via Corvino, Weisz had too much time to think — haunted by the ghosts of the apartment, troubled by visions of Christa in Berlin. And troubled, as well, by a telephone call he would have to make in the morning. But if *Liberazione* was to have its own printing plant, there was one contact he had to make before he left, a contact he'd been warned about. "Not unless absolutely necessary," Brown had said. This was a man known as Emil, who, according to Brown, could handle "anything that needs to be done *very* quietly." Well, after his conversation with Matteo, it *was* necessary, and he would have to use the number he'd memorized. Not an Italian name, Emil, it might be from anywhere. Or perhaps it was an alias, or a codename.

Restless, Weisz wandered from room to room; closets filled with clothing, empty drawers in the desk. No photographs, nothing personal anywhere. He couldn't read, he couldn't sleep, and what he wanted to do was go out, get away from the apartment, even though it was after midnight. At least, out in the street, there was life. Which seemed, to Weisz, to be going on much as it always had. Fascism was powerful, and it was everywhere, but the people abided, bent with the wind, improvised, got by, and waited for better times. *Ahh, one more rotten government, so what.* They weren't all like that; Matteo wasn't, the girls who distributed the newspapers weren't, and neither was Weisz. But, the way the city felt to Weisz, nothing had really changed — the national motto was still *do what you have to do, keep your mouth shut, keep your secrets.* That was the way life went on here, no matter who ruled. People spoke with their eyes, with small gestures. Two friends meet a third, and one of them signals to the other — eyes closed, a fast, subtle shake of the head. *Don't trust him.*

Weisz went into the kitchen, the study, finally the bedroom. He turned out the light, lay down on the spread, and waited for the night to pass.

At noon, he called home again, and this time his mother answered. "It's me," he said, and she gasped. But she did not ask where he was, and she did not use his name. A brief, tense conversation: his father had retired, quietly, unwilling to sign the teacher's loyalty oath, but not making a point of it. They lived now on his pension, and her family money, thank God for that. "We don't talk on the phone, these days," she said to him, a warning. And, a minute later, she said she missed him terribly, and then said goodby.

In the café, he had a Strega, then another. Maybe he shouldn't have called, he thought, but he'd probably gotten away with it. He believed he had, he hoped he had. Done with the second Strega, he summoned the number for Emil from his memory and returned to the telephone. A young woman, foreign, but fluent in Genoese Italian, answered immediately, and asked him who he was. "A friend of Cesare," he said, as Mr. Brown had directed. "Hold the line," she said. By Weisz's watch, it took more than three minutes to return to the phone. He was to meet Signor Emil at the Brignole railway station, on the platform for track twelve, at five-ten that afternoon. "Carry a book," she said. "What tie will you wear?"

Weisz looked down. "Blue with a silver stripe," he said. Then she hung up.

At five, the Stazione Brignole swarmed with travelers — everyone in Rome had come to Genoa, where they pushed and shoved the population of Genoa, which was trying to get on the 5:10 for Rome. Weisz, holding a copy of *L'Imbroglio,* Moravia's short stories, was swept along in the crowd until an approaching traveler waved at him, then grinned, so happy to see him, and took his elbow. "How is Cesare?" Emil said. "Seen him lately?"

"Never saw him in my life."

"So," Emil said, "we'll walk a little."

He was very smooth, and ageless, with the ruddy face of the freshly shaved — he was always, Weisz thought, freshly shaved — a face without expression beneath light brown hair combed back from a high forehead. Was he Czech? Serb? Russian? He'd spoken Italian for a long time and it came naturally to him, but it wasn't native, a slight foreign accent touched his words, from somewhere east of the Oder, but, beyond that, Weisz couldn't guess. And there was something about him — the smooth, blank exterior with its permanent smile — that reminded Weisz of S. Kolb. They were, he suspected, members of the same profession.

"How can I help you?" Emil said. They'd paused before a large signboard where a uniformed railway employee, standing on a ladder, wrote times and destinations in chalk.

"I need a place, a quiet place. To set up some machinery."

"I see. For a night? A week?"

"For as long as possible."

A telephone on a table by the ladder rang, and the railway employee wrote the departure time for the train to Pavia, which drew a low murmur of approval, almost an ovation, from the waiting crowd.

"In the country, perhaps," Emil said. "A farmhouse — isolated, private. Or maybe a shed somewhere, in one of the outlying districts, not the city, but not quite the countryside. We are talking about Genoa, aren't we?"

"Yes, we are."

"What do you mean, machinery?"

"Printing presses."

"Ahh." Emil's voice warmed, his tone affectionate, and nostalgic. He had fond memories of printing presses. "Pretty good-sized, and not silent."

"No, it's a noisy process," Weisz said.

Emil pressed his lips together, trying to think. Around them, dozens of conversations, a public-address system producing announcements that made everyone turn to his neighbor: "What did he say?" And the trains themselves, the drumming of locomotive engines echoing in the domed station.

"This kind of operation," Emil said, "should be in a city. Unless you're contemplating armed insurrection, and that hasn't

412

come here yet. *Then* you move everything out to the countryside."

"It would be better in the city. The people who are going to run the machines are in the city — they can't be going up into the mountains."

"No, they can't. Up there, you have to deal with the peasants." To Emil, the word was simply descriptive.

"In Genoa, then."

"Yes. I know of one very good possibility, likely a few more will occur to me. Can you give me a day to work on it?"

"Not much more."

"It will do." He wasn't quite ready to leave. "Printing presses," he said, as though he were saying *romance* or *summer mornings.* He was, evidently, in the normal course of life, more of a guns and bombs man. "Call the number you have. Tomorrow, around this time of day. There will be instructions for you." He turned and faced Weisz. "A pleasure to meet you," he said. "And please be careful. The state security in Rome is becoming concerned with Genoa. Like all dogs, they have fleas, but, lately, the Genoese flea is beginning to annoy them." He made sure Weisz understood what he meant, then turned and, after a few steps, vanished into the crowd.

25 June.

Weisz worked his way through the alleys of the waterfront district, and was at Grassone's room by nine-thirty.

"Signor X!" Grassone said, opening the door, and happy to see him. "Have you had a good day?"

"Not too bad," Weisz said.

"It continues," Grassone said, settling himself in the rolling chair. "I've found your newsprint. It comes down in freight cars, from Germany. Which is where the trees are."

"And a price?"

"I took you at your word, about the big rolls. They price the stuff in metric tons, and for you that would be something in the neighborhood of fourteen hundred lire a metric ton. How many rolls I don't know, but that should keep you in paper, no? And we beat the local price — or the local price wherever you're printing."

Weisz thought it over. A man's suit cost about four hundred lire, a cheap apartment rented for three hundred a month. He assumed they would be buying at a thieves' price, and, even with fat commissions for Grassone and his associates, would still be getting the newsprint below the market rate. "That's acceptable," he said. On his fingers, he went from lire to dollars, twenty to one, then British pounds at five dollars a pound. Surely, he thought, Mr. Brown would pay that.

Grassone was watching him work. "Comes out good?"

"Yes. Very good. And, of course, it stays a secret."

Grassone wagged a heavy finger. "Don't you worry about that, Signor X. Of course, I'll need a deposit."

Weisz reached into his pocket and counted out seven hundred lire. Grassone held one of the bills up to the desk lamp. "Such a world we live in, these days. People printing money in the cellar."

"It's real," Weisz said.

"So it is," Grassone said, putting the money in his drawer.

"Now, I don't know when and where — it could be a few weeks — but the next thing we'll want is a printing press, and a Linotype machine."

"Do you have a list? Size? Make and model?"

"No."

"You know where to find me."

"In a day or so, I'll have it."

"You're in a hurry, Signor X, aren't you." Grassone leaned forward and flattened his hands on the desk. He wore, Weisz saw, a gold ring with a ruby gemstone on his pinkie. "I see half of Genoa in here, and the other half sees my competitors, and not much goes wrong, because we take care of the local police, and it's just business. Now here you are, starting up a newspaper. Fine. I wasn't born yesterday, and I don't care what you do, but, whatever that is, it's liable to make some of the wrong people mad, and I don't want it coming down on my head. That's not going to happen, is it?"

"Nobody wants that."

"You give me your word?"

"You have it," Weisz said.

It was a long walk back to the via Corvino, thunder rumbling in the distance, and flashes of heat lightning on the horizon, out over the Ligurian Sea. A girl in a leather coat fell into step with him as he crossed a piazza. In a warm, husky voice, she wondered if he liked this? Or maybe that? Did he want to be alone tonight? Then, at the apartment house, an old couple passed him, going downstairs as Weisz climbed. The man said good evening, the woman looked him over — who was he? They knew everybody here, they didn't know him. Back in the apartment, he dozed, then woke suddenly, his heart racing, from a bad dream.

In the morning, the sun was out, and, in the streets, life went on at full throb. The waiter in the café knew him now, and greeted him like a steady customer. In his newspaper, La Spezia had beaten Genoa, 2–1, on a goal in the final minute. The waiter, looking over Weisz's shoulder as he served coffee, said that it shouldn't have been allowed — hand ball — but the referee had been bought, everybody in town knew that.

Weisz telephoned Matteo at *Il Secolo,* and met him an hour later in a bar across the street from the newspaper, where they were joined by Matteo's friend from the *Giornale* and another pressman. Weisz bought coffee and rolls and brandies; the munificent visitor from out of town, confident, and amusing. "Three monkeys go into a brothel, the first one says . . ." It was all very relaxed, and amiable — Weisz used their names, asked about their work. "We'll have our own print shop," he said. "And good equipment. And, if sometimes you need a few lire at the end of the month, you only have to ask." Was it safe, they wanted to know. These days, Weisz said, nothing was safe. But he and his friends were very careful — they didn't want anybody to get in trouble. "Ask Matteo," he said. "We keep things quiet. But the people of Italy have to know what's going on." Otherwise, the *fascisti* would get away with every lie they told, and they didn't want that, did they? No, they didn't. And, Weisz thought, they truly didn't.

After Matteo's friends left the bar, Weisz wrote down a list of what would have to be bought from Grassone, then said he would like to meet the truck driver, Antonio.

"He hauls coal in the winter, produce in the summer," Matteo said. "He does an early run up the coast, then he's back in town about noon. We could see him tomorrow."

Weisz said that noon was a good time, decide where, he'd be in touch later in the day. Then, after Matteo had gone back to work, Weisz called the number for Emil.

The young woman answered immediately. "We've been waiting for your call," she said. "You are to meet him tomorrow morning. At a bar, called La Lanterna in one of the little streets, the vico San Giraldo, off the piazza dello Scalo, down by the docks. The time is five-thirty. You can be there?"

Weisz said he could. "Why so early?" he said.

She didn't answer immediately. "This is not Emil's habit, it's the man you will meet at La Lanterna, he owns the bar, he owns many things in Genoa, but he's careful about where he goes. And when. Understood?"

"Yes. Five-thirty, then."

Weisz called Matteo after three — to learn that they would meet the truck driver at noon the following day, in a garage on the northern edge of the city. Matteo gave him the address, then said, "You made a good impression on my friends. They're ready to sign on."

"I'm glad," Weisz said. "If we all work together, we can get rid of these bastards."

Maybe, some day, he thought, as he hung up the phone. But more likely, they would, all of them, Grassone, Matteo, his friends, and everyone else, be going to prison. And it would be Weisz's fault. The alternative was to sit quiet and hope for better times, but, since 1922, better times hadn't shown up. And, Weisz thought, if the OVRA didn't like *Liberazione* in the past, they'd like it even less now. So, at the end of the day, when the operation was betrayed, or however it fell apart, Weisz would be, one way or another, in the next cell.

That night, he took Matteo's list of equipment to Grassone's office, then wound his way uphill toward the via Corvino. *Two more days,* he thought. Then he would return to Paris, having played the part Mr. Brown had written for him: a daring appearance, and a few early steps toward the expansion of *Liberazione.* There was more to be done — someone would have to come back here. Did this mean that Brown had other people he could deploy? Or would it be him? He didn't know, and he didn't care. Because what mattered to him now was the hope — and it was well beyond hope — that once he'd done what Mr. Brown wanted, Mr. Brown would do, in Berlin, what he wanted.

27 June, 5:20 A.M.

In the piazza dello Scalo, a gray, drizzling dawn, ocean cloud heavy over the square. And a morning street market. As Weisz walked across the piazza, the merchants, unloading an exotic assortment of ancient cars and trucks, were setting up their stalls; the fishmonger kidding with his neighbors — two women stacking artichokes, kids carrying crates, porters with open barrows shouting for people to get out of the way, flocks of pigeons and sparrows in the trees, waiting for their share of the market's bounty.

Weisz turned down the vico San Giraldo and, after missing it the first time, found La Lanterna. There was no name outside, but a board, hanging from a rusty chain, bore a weathered painting of a lantern. Beneath the sign, a low doorway led to a tunnel, then a long, narrow room, its floor black with centuries of dirt, its walls brown with cigarette smoke. Weisz moved among the early patrons — market vendors, and stevedores in leather aprons — until he sighted Emil. Who waved him over, the permanent smile widening a little on his freshly shaven face. The man by his side did not smile. He was tall and somber, and very dark, with a thick mustache and sharp eyes. He wore a silk suit but no tie, his chocolate-colored shirt buttoned at the throat.

"Good, you're on time," Emil said. "And here is your new landlord."

The tall man looked him over, gave him a brief nod, then checked a fancy watch and said, "Let's get busy." From his pocket he brought out a large ring of keys, thumbing through them to find the one he wanted. "This way," he said, heading to the far end of the tavern.

"It's a good place, for you," Emil said to

421

Weisz. "People in and out, all day and all night. It's been here since . . . when?"

The landlord shrugged. "There's been a tavern on this site since 1490, so they say."

At the back of the room, a low door made of thick planks. The landlord unlocked it, then ducked down beneath the frame and waited for Emil and Weisz. When they were through the door, he locked it behind them. Right away Weisz found it difficult to breathe, the air was an acid fog of spoiled wine. "It used to be a warehouse," Emil said. The landlord took a kerosene lamp from a peg on the wall, lit it, then led them down a long flight of stone steps. The walls glistened with moisture, and Weisz could hear the rats as they scampered away. At the foot of the stairway, a corridor — it took them over a minute to walk to the end — opened to a massive vault, its ceiling a series of arches, with wooden casks lining the walls. The wine-laden air was so strong that Weisz had to wipe tears from his eyes. From the central arch, a lightbulb hung on a cord. The landlord reached up and turned on the light, which threw shadows on the wet stone block. "See? No torches for you," Emil said, winking at Weisz.

"Must have electricity," Weisz said.

"They put it in here in the twenties," the

landlord said.

From somewhere behind the walls, Weisz could hear the rhythmic sloshing of water. "Is this still in use?" he said. "Do people come down here?"

From the landlord, a dry rattle that passed for a laugh. "Whatever's in there" — he nodded toward the casks — "you couldn't drink it."

"There's another exit," Emil said. "Down the corridor."

The landlord looked at Weisz and said, "So?"

"How much do you want for it?"

"Six hundred lire a month. You pay me in advance, two months at a time. Then you can do whatever you want."

Weisz thought it over, then reached in his pocket and began counting out hundred-lira notes. The landlord licked his thumb and made sure of the count while Emil stood by, smiling, hands in pockets. Then the landlord opened his key ring and handed Weisz two keys. "The tavern, and the other entrance," he said. "If you need to find me, see your friend here, he'll take care of it." He turned off the light, lifted the kerosene lamp, and said, "We can leave from the other end."

Outside the vault, the corridor made a

sharp turn and became a tunnel, which led to a stairway that climbed back to street level. The landlord blew out the lamp, hung it on the wall, and unlocked a pair of heavy iron doors. He put his shoulder against one of them, which squeaked as it opened, to reveal the courtyard of a workshop, littered with old newspapers and machine parts. At the far end of the courtyard, a door in a brick wall led out to the piazza dello Scalo, where the market's first customers, women carrying net bags, were busy at the stalls.

The landlord looked up at the sky and scowled at the drizzle. "See you next week," he said to Emil, then nodded to Weisz. As he turned to go, a man stepped from a doorway and took him by the arm. For an instant, Weisz froze. *Run.* But a hand closed on the collars of his shirt and jacket and a voice said, "Just come along with me." Weisz spun around and, with his forearm, knocked the man's hand off him. From the corner of his eye, he saw Emil, running full speed down an aisle between the stalls, and the landlord, struggling with a man half his size, who was trying to bar his arm up behind his back.

The man facing Weisz was built thick, hard-faced and hard-eyed, a cop of some kind, with the belt of a shoulder holster, run beneath a flowered tie, across his chest. He produced a small case and flipped it open to reveal a badge, saying, "Understand?" He grabbed for Weisz's arm, Weisz eluded him, then was slapped on the side of the face, and slapped again on the backswing. The second slap was so hard that his feet came off the ground, and he stumbled backward and sat down. "So, let's make my life difficult," the cop said. Weisz rolled over twice, then scrambled to his feet. But the cop was too fast, swung his leg, and kicked Weisz's feet out from beneath him. He landed hard, realized there was a lot more of this to come, and tried to crawl under a market stall. From people nearby, a rising murmur, muted sounds of anger or sympathy, at the sight of a man being beaten.

The cop's face turned bright red. He shoved an old woman out of his way, then reached down, caught Weisz by the ankle, and started to pull. "Come out of there," he said under his breath. As Weisz was dragged from beneath the stall, an artichoke bounced off the cop's forehead. Startled, he let go of Weisz and stepped backward. A carrot sailed past his ear, and he raised his hand to ward off a strawberry, while another artichoke hit him in the shoulder. From somewhere behind Weisz, a woman's voice. "Leave him alone, Pazzo, you sonofabitch."

Evidently, they knew this cop, and they didn't like him. He drew a revolver, aimed it left, then swung it right, provoking a shouted "Yes, go ahead and shoot us, you miserable prick." The fusillade increased: three or four eggs, a handful of sardines, more artichokes — in season and cheap that day — a lettuce, then a few onions. The cop pointed his gun at the sky and fired two shots.

The market people were not intimidated. Weisz saw a woman in a bloody apron, at the stall of the pork butcher, plunge a long-handled fork into a bucket and spear a pig ear, which, using the fork like a catapult, she fired off at the cop. Who now trotted backward until he stood at the edge of the piazza, beneath a crooked old tenement. He put two fingers in his mouth and produced a shrill whistle. But his partner was busy with the landlord, nobody appeared, and, when the first basin of water flew out of a window and splashed at his feet, he turned, and with one savage glare over his shoulder, *I won't forget this,* left the piazza.

Weisz, his face burning, was still beneath the stall. As he started to crawl out, an immense woman, wearing a hair net and an apron, came rushing toward him, her eyeglasses, on a chain around her neck, bouncing with every step. She held out a hand, Weisz took it, and she hauled him effortlessly to his feet. "You better get out of here," she said, voice almost a whisper. "They'll be back. Do you have a place to go?"

Weisz said he didn't — he sensed danger in the idea of returning to the via Corvino.

"Then come with me."

They hurried down a row of stalls, then out of the piazza into the *vicoli.* "That bastard would arrest his mother," the woman said.

"Where are we going?"

"You'll see." She came to a sudden stop, took him by the shoulders, and turned him so that she could see his face. "What did you do? You don't look like a criminal. Are you a criminal?"

"No, I'm not a criminal."

"Ah, I didn't think so." Then she took him by the elbow and said, *"Avanti!"* Walking as fast as she could, breathing hard as they climbed the hill.

The church of Santa Brigida was not splendid or ancient, it had been built of stucco, in a poor neighborhood, a century earlier. Inside, the market woman went down on one knee, crossed herself, then walked down the aisle and disappeared through a door opposite the altar. Weisz sat in the back. It had been a long time since he'd been in church, but he felt safe, for the moment, in the pleasant gloom touched with incense. When the woman reappeared, a young priest followed her up the aisle. She bent over Weisz and said, "Father Marco will take care of you," then gripped his hand — *be strong* — and went on her way.

When she'd gone, the priest led Weisz back to the vestry, then to a small office. "She's a good soul, Angelina," he said. "Are you in trouble?"

Weisz wasn't quite sure how to answer this. Father Marco was patient, and waited for him. "Yes, in some trouble, Father." Weisz took a chance. "Political trouble."

The priest nodded, this was not new. "Do you need a place to stay?"

"Until tomorrow night. Then I'll be leaving the city."

"Until tomorrow night we can manage." He was relieved. "You can sleep on that couch."

"Thank you," Weisz said.

"What sort of politics?"

From the way he spoke, and listened, Weisz sensed that this was not a typical parish priest. He was an intellectual, destined to rise in the church or be banished to a remote district — it could go either way. "Liberal politics," he said. "Antifascist politics."

In the priest's eyes, both approval and a hint of envy. *If life had been different . . .* "I'll help you any way I can," he said. "And you can keep me company at supper."

"I'd like that, Father."

"You're not the first one they've brought to me. It's an old custom, sanctuary." He stood, looked at a clock on the desk, and said, "I have to serve Mass. You are welcome to take part, if it's your custom."

"Not for a long time," Weisz said.

The priest smiled. "I do hear that, quite often, but it's as you wish."

Weisz went out once, that afternoon, walking over to a post office, where he used the telephone to call the contact number for Emil. It rang for a long time, but the woman never answered. He had no idea what that meant, and no idea what had happened at the piazza. He suspected it might have been, in his case, an accident — with the wrong person at the wrong time, the landlord spotted and denounced when he entered the neighborhood. For what? Weisz had no idea.

But this was not the OVRA, they would have been there in force. Of course, it was just barely possible that he'd been betrayed — by Emil, by Grassone, or someone in the via Corvino. But it didn't matter, he would sail on the *Hydraios* the next day, at midnight, and, in time, it would be for Mr. Brown to sort things out.

28 June, 10:30 P.M.

Sitting on the rim of a dry fountain, at the top of the staircase that led down to the wharf, Weisz could see the *Hydraios*. She was still tied to the pier, but a thin column of smoke drifted from her stack as she got up steam, prepared to sail at midnight. He could see, as well, the shed opposite the pier, and Nunzio, the customs officer for the crews of merchant ships, his chair tilted back against the table where he processed documents. Very relaxed, Nunzio, his night duty a soft job, idly passing the time, this evening, with two uniformed policemen, one lounging against the door of the shed, the other sitting on a crate.

Weisz could also see the crew of the *Hydraios*, drifting back from their liberty in Genoa. They'd left together, the night the ship docked, but now they returned, rather the worse for wear, in twos and threes. Weisz watched as three of the sailors approached the shed; two of them holding up a third, his arms around their shoulders, sometimes venturing a few steps, sometimes losing consciousness, the tips of his shoes bumping over the cobbles as he was towed along.

At the table, the two sailors produced their passports, then, a bad moment, hunted for their friend's papers, finally discovering them tucked in the back of his pants. Nunzio laughed, and the cops joined in. What a head he'd have tomorrow morning!

Nunzio took the first sailor's passport, laid it flat on the table, and looked up and down, twice, the action of a man checking a photograph against a face. Yes, it was him allright. Nunzio gave his port-and-date stamp an officious wiggle on an ink pad, then brought it down emphatically on the passport. As he worked, one of the policemen strolled up to the table and, peering over Nunzio's shoulder, had a look. Just making sure, might as well.

11:00. The church bells rang. 11:20. A rush of sailors headed for the *Hydraios,* hurrying to get on board, two or three officers in their midst. Ten minutes later, the second engineer showed up, dawdling, strolling along the wharf, waiting for Weisz, so he could walk him through the passport control. Eventually, he gave up, joined the crowd at the table, and, with a final glance back toward the quay, climbed up the gangway.

Weisz never moved. He was not a merchant seaman, he was, according to his *libretto di lavoro,* a senior official. Why would he be traveling to Marseilles on a Greek freighter? At 11:55, a deep blast on the ship's foghorn echoed over the waterfront, and two seamen cranked the gangway up to the deck, while others, assisted by a stevedore, hauled in the lines that had secured the ship to the pier.

Then, at midnight, with one more wail of its horn, the *Hydraios* steamed slowly out to sea.

7 July.

A warm summer night in Portofino.

Paradise. Below the terrace of the Hotel Splendido, lights twinkled in the port, and, when the breeze was right, music from parties on the yachts came drifting up the hillside. In the card room, British tourists played bridge. At the pool, three American girls were sprawled in steamer chairs, drinking Negronis, and seriously considering the possibility of *never* going back to Wellesley.

In the pool, their friend floated languidly on her back, swished her hands now and then to keep from sinking, gazed up at the stars and dreamed of being in love. Well, dreamed of doing what people did when they were in love. A kiss, a caress, another kiss. *Another caress.* Twice, he'd danced with her, the night before: gentle, courtly, his eyes, his hands, his Italian accent with a British lilt. "May I have this dance?" Oh yes. And, on her last night in Portofino, he could have had a little more, could Carlo, *Car-lo,* if he wanted.

They'd talked, for a time, after they'd danced, strolling along the candlelit terrace by the bar. Talked idly, of this or that. But when she'd told him she'd be going off to Genoa, where she and her friends would sail for New York on an Italian liner, he seemed to lose interest, and the intimate question had never been asked. And now, she would be going back to Cos Cob, going back — *intact.* Still, nothing could stop her from dreaming about him; his hands, his eyes, *his lips.*

True, he had lost interest, when he'd learned that she had not come to Portofino on a yacht. Not that she wasn't appealing. He could see her down there as he looked out his window, a white star on blue water, and, if it had been a few years earlier . . . But it wasn't.

After the *Hydraios* had sailed off without him, he'd spent the night at the Brignole railway station, then taken the first train down the coast to the resort town of Santa Margherita. There he'd bought a valise, and the best resort clothes — blazer, white slacks, short-sleeved tennis shirts — he could find. Oh he spent money like water, and what an S. Kolbish lesson this had turned out to be! Then, after the purchase of razor and shaving soap and toothbrush and the rest of it, he'd packed the valise and taken a taxi — there was no train — off to Portofino, and the Hotel Splendido.

Plenty of rooms, that summer, some of their regular guests weren't traveling to Italy, that summer. For Weisz, good fortune, and the morning he arrived, he changed clothes and embarked on his campaign: a presence at the pool, in the bar, at afternoon tea in the salon; talkative, charming, the most amiable fellow imaginable. He'd tried with the British, joining this party and that, people off the yachts, but they wanted nothing to do with him — the discouragement of ingratiating foreigners a skill learned early, in the public schools, by the sort of people who came to Portofino.

And he was beginning to despair, was beginning to consider a journey to a nearby fishing village — good-size boats, poor fishermen — when he discovered the party of Danes, and their effusive leader. "Just call me Sven!" What a dinner! Table for twelve — six Danes and their new hotel friends — bottles of champagne, laughter, winks and sly references on the subject of nighttime merriment aboard the *Ambrosia,* Sven's yacht. It was Sven's wife, white-haired and breathtaking, who'd finally, in her slow Scandinavian English, said the magic words: "But we must find our way to see you more, dear man, for the Thursday we sail to the Saint-Tropez."

"Maybe I should just come along with you."

"Oh Carlo, could you?"

A last look out the window, then Weisz stood at the mirror and combed his hair. This was the Danes' last night in Portofino, and the dinner was sure to be elaborate and noisy. One final glance at the mirror, lapels brushed, and off to war.

It was as he'd thought — champagne, grilled sole, cognac, and great affection all 'round the table. But Weisz caught the host looking at him, more than once, some question lurking in the back of his mind. Sven was jovial, and good fun, but that was on the surface. He'd made his money owning lead mines in South Africa, was no fool, and was, Weisz sensed, on to him. So, after the cognac, Sven suggested that the company gather at the bar, while he and his friend Carlo had themselves a promised game of billiards.

And so they did — the angles of Sven's face sharpened by the light above the table in the shadowy billiard room. Weisz did his best, but Sven could really play, and whisked the beads across the brass wire with the tip of his cue as the score mounted. "So, my friend, are you coming with us to Saint-Tropez?"

"Certainly I would like to."

"So I see. But, can you leave Italy so easily? Do you not require, ah, some form of permission?"

"True. But I could never get it."

"No? That is annoying — why not?"

"Sven, I must leave this country. My wife and children went to France two months ago, and now I have to join them."

"Leave, without permission."

"Yes. Secretly."

Sven bent over the table, ran the cue

across his open bridge, and sent his ball rolling easily over the felt until it bumped against a cushion and clicked against the red ball and the other white. Then he reached up and recorded the point. "It will be a rotten war, when it comes. Do you think you will avoid it in France?"

"I might," Weisz said, chalking the tip of his cue. "Or I might not. But either way, I cannot fight on the wrong side."

"Good," Sven said. "I admire that. So perhaps we shall be allies."

"Perhaps we will, though I hope it doesn't come to that."

"Keep hoping, Carlo, it's good for the spirit. We sail at nine."

5 July. Berlin.

How he hated these horrible fucking Nazis! Look at that one, standing on the corner as though he didn't have a care in the world. Short and stocky, the color of meat, with rubbery lips, and the face of a vicious baby. Now and then he strolled up the street, then back, keeping his eyes always on the entry to the office of the *Bund Deutscher Maedchen,* the teenaged girls division of the Hitler Youth. And keeping watch, and making no secret of it, on Christa von Schirren.

S. Kolb, in the backseat of a taxi, was close to giving up. He'd been in Berlin for days, and he couldn't get near her. The Gestapo watchers were everywhere — in cars, doorways, delivery vans. Were surely listening to her phone and reading her mail, and they would take her when it suited them. Meanwhile, they waited, since maybe, just maybe, one of the other conspirators would grow desperate, break from cover, and try to make contact. And, Kolb could see it, she knew exactly what was going on. She'd been all confidence, once upon a time, a self-assured aristocrat, but no more. Now there were deep shadows beneath her eyes, and her face was pale and drawn.

Well, he wasn't in much better shape himself. Scared, bored, and tired — the spy's classic condition. He'd been on the move since the twenty-ninth of June, when he'd spent the night in Marseilles, waiting for Weisz, but, when the crew of the *Hydraios* left the freighter, he was nowhere to be seen. And, according to the second engineer, the ship had left Genoa without him. "Gone," Mr. Brown said when Kolb telephoned. "Maybe the OVRA got him, we'll never know."

Too bad, but so life went. Then Brown told him he had to go up to Berlin and exfiltrate the girlfriend. Was this necessary? "Our end of the bargain," Brown said, from the comfort of his Paris hotel. "And she may come in handy, you never know." He'd have some help in Berlin, Brown told him, the SIS was thin there, thin everywhere, but the naval attaché at the embassy had a taxi driver he could use.

That was Klemens, former Communist and streetfighter, back in the twenties, with the scars to prove it, now resting his weight on the steering wheel of the taxi and lighting his tenth cigarette of the morning. "We're sitting here too long, you know," he said, catching Kolb's eyes in the rearview mirror.

Shut up, you ape. "We can wait a little longer, I think."

They waited, ten minutes, another five. Then a bus pulled up in front of the office, its engine idling, black smoke puffing from its exhaust pipe. And, a minute later, here came the girls, in brown uniforms, knee-high stockings, and knotted scarves, a flock of them, some with picnic baskets, marching in pairs, followed by von Schirren. When they boarded the bus, the thug on the corner looked over at a car parked across the street, which, when the bus drove away, swung out into traffic, directly behind it.

"Go ahead," Kolb said. "But stay well back."

They drove to the edge of the city, headed east, toward the Oder, and soon enough out in the countryside. Then, a stroke of fortune. In the town of Müncheberg, the Gestapo car pulled into a gas station, and two bulky men got out to stretch their legs. "What shall I do?" Klemens said.

"Follow the bus."

"That car will soon catch up with us."

"Just drive," Kolb said. A hot day, and humid. Irritating weather, for Kolb — if he had to walk, his underpants would chafe. So, at the moment, he didn't care what the other car did.

A few minutes later, a second stroke of fortune: the bus turned off onto a tiny dirt road. Kolb's heart lifted. *Here's my chance.* "Follow!" he said. Klemens kept well behind the bus, a trail of dust showing its progress as it climbed up into the hills near the Oder. Then it stopped. Klemens backed up and parked the car just off the road, at a point where the people on the bus wouldn't be able to see them.

Kolb gave the group a few minutes to get wherever they were going, then climbed out. "Open the hood," he said. "You've had engine problems — this may take some time."

Kolb walked up the road, then circled well away from the bus, into a pine woods. *Nature,* he thought. He didn't like nature. In a city, he was a clever rat, at home in the maze, out here he felt naked and vulnerable, and, yes, he'd been right about his underpants. From a vantage point up the hill, he could see the *Deutscher Maedchen,* swarming at the edge of a small lake. Some of the girls unpacked the picnic, while others — Kolb's eyes widened — undressed to go swimming, and not a bathing suit to be seen. They shrieked as they ran into the cold water, splashing each other, wrestling, a frolic of naked girls. All this lovely, pale, Aryan flesh, bouncing and jiggling, free and unfettered. Kolb couldn't get enough, and, quite soon, found himself more than a little unfettered.

Von Schirren took off her shoes and stockings. Would there be more? No, her mood was beyond swimming, she paced about, staring at the ground, at the lake, at the hills, with sometimes a pallid smile when one of the *Maedchen* shouted at her to join them.

Kolb, moving from tree to tree for cover, worked his way down the hill. Eventually, he came to the edge of the woods, and hid behind a bush. Von Schirren wandered toward the lake, stood for a time, then moved back toward him. When she was ten feet away, Kolb looked out from behind the bush.

"Pssst."

Von Schirren, startled, glared at him, fury in her eyes. "You vile little thing. Go away! At once. Or I'll set the girls on you."

By all means. "Listen to me carefully, Frau von Schirren. Your friend Weisz arranged this, and you'll do what I say, or I'll walk off and you'll never see me, or him, again."

She was, for a moment, speechless. "Carlo? Sent you here?"

"Yes. You're leaving Germany. It starts now."

"I must get my shoes," she said.

"Tell your chief girl that you are unwell and you're going to lie down in the bus."

And then, at last, in her eyes, gratitude.

They climbed the wooded hillside, only birds broke the silence, and shafts of sunlight lit the forest floor. "Who are you?" she said.

"Your friend Weisz, in his profession, has a broad acquaintance. I happen to be one of the people he knows."

After a time, she said, "I am followed, you know, everywhere."

"Yes, I've seen them."

"I suppose I cannot go to my house, even for a moment."

"No. They'll be waiting for you."

"Then where?"

"Back to Berlin, to an attic. Hot as hell. Where we'll change your appearance — I have purchased the most dreadful gray wig — then I will take your photograph, develop the film, and put the photo in your new passport, in your new name. After that, a change of cars, and a few hours' drive to Luxembourg, the border crossing at Echternach. After *that,* it will be up to you."

They circled the bus and descended to the road. Klemens was lying on his back beside the taxi, his hands clasped beneath his head. When he saw them, he rose, banged the hood shut, slid into the driver's seat, and started the engine.

"Where shall I sit?" she said, approaching the car.

Kolb walked around the taxi and opened the trunk. "It's not so bad," he said. "I've done it a few times."

She climbed in, and curled up on her side.

"Nice and snug?" Kolb said.

"You're good at this, aren't you," she said.

"Very good," Kolb said. "Ready?"

"The reason I asked, about going to my house, is that my dogs are there. They are dear to me, I wanted to say goodby."

"We can't go anywhere near your house, Frau von Schirren."

"Forgive me," she said. "I should not have asked."

No, you shouldn't have, I mean, really, dogs. But the look in her eyes reached him, and he said, "Perhaps you can have a friend bring them to Paris."

"Yes, it might be possible."

"Ready now?"

"Now I am."

Kolb lowered the lid of the trunk, then pressed it down until it locked.

11 July.

It was after ten at night by the time Weisz climbed out of a taxi in front of the Hotel Dauphine. The night was warm, and the front door was propped open. Inside, it was quiet, Madame Rigaud sitting in a chair behind the desk, reading the newspaper. "So," she said, taking off her spectacles, "you have returned."

"Did you think I wouldn't?"

"One never knows," she said, quoting the French adage.

"Is there, perhaps, a message for me?"

"Not a one, monsieur."

"I see. Well then, good evening, madame. I'm off to bed."

"Mmm," she said, putting on her spectacles and rattling the newspaper.

He was on the fourth step when she said, "Oh, Monsieur Weisz?"

"Madame?"

"There has been one inquiry. A friend of yours has come to stay with us. And she did ask, when she arrived, if you were here. I've given her Room Forty-seven, just down the hall from you. It looks out on the courtyard."

After a moment, Weisz said, "That was kind of you, Madame Rigaud, it's a pleasant room."

"A very cultured sort of woman. German, I believe. And she is, one suspects, anxious to see you, so perhaps you should be on your way upstairs, if you don't mind my saying so."

"In that case, I will wish you a good night."

"For all of us, monsieur. For all of us."

ABOUT THE AUTHOR

Alan Furst is widely recognized as the master of the historical spy novel. He is the author of *Night Soldiers, Dark Star, The Polish Officer, The World at Night, Red Gold, Kingdom of Shadows, Blood of Victory*, and *Dark Voyage*. Born in New York, he has lived for long periods in France, especially Paris. He now lives on Long Island, New York.

Visit the author's website at www .alanfurst.net